# Good
# Girl

# Good
# Girl

A NOVEL

## Aria
## Aber

HOGARTH
*London / New York*

Published in the United States by Hogarth, an imprint of Random House, a division of Penguin Random House LLC, New York.

HOGARTH is a trademark of the Random House Group Limited, and the H colophon is a trademark of Penguin Random House LLC.

Library of Congress Cataloging-in-Publication Data

Names: Aber, Aria, author.
Title: Good girl: a novel / by Aria Aber.
Description: First edition. | New York, NY: Hogarth, 2025.
Identifiers: LCCN 2024016238 (print) | LCCN 2024016239 (ebook) |
ISBN 9780593731116 (hardback) | ISBN 9780593731123 (ebook)
Subjects: LCGFT: Novels.
Classification: LCC PS3601.B49 G66 2025 (print) | LCC PS3601.B49 (ebook) |
DDC 811/.6—dc23/eng/20240412
LC record available at lccn.loc.gov/2024016238
LC ebook record available at lccn.loc.gov/2024016239

International ISBN 9780593978474

Printed in the United States of America on acid-free paper

randomhousebooks.com

9  8  7  6  5  4  3  2  1

First Edition

*Book design by Debbie Glasserman*

For Visar

*Was he an animal if music could move him so? He felt as if the path to the unknowable sustenance for which he yearned was coming to light.*

Franz Kafka, *The Metamorphosis*

# Part
# One

# One

THE TRAIN BACK to Berlin took seven hours, and the towel in my suitcase was still wet from my last swim in the lake, dampening the pages of my favorite books. I took the S-Bahn and then the U-Bahn home to Lipschitzallee and walked past the discount supermarket, the old pharmacy, and the Qurbani Bakery with the orange shop cat lounging outside its door. In our building's elevator, an intimate odor assaulted my nostrils: urine mixed with ash. *Hello, spider*, I said, looking at the cobweb in the corner. The ceiling lamp twitched, turning alien the swastika graffiti. My key, fastened by a pink ribbon, turned in the old lock. Nobody was home. I kicked off my shoes. The cat meowed for food, its dander floating in the air. My room was merely all it had been for so many years: a suffocating box with a tiny window, pink sheets, and that Goethe quote I'd painted in golden letters above my desk. The popcorn ceiling seemed lower than before. I wiped the kitchen counters, walked into my parents' bedroom, opened their closet, and pulled out my mother's cashmere frock. Maybe I cried, maybe

I didn't. What I did was lie in bed and sleep until dark, covering my face with her dress.

IT'S BEEN OVER a decade now, but the colors of that summer day are as precise as yesterday: I was eighteen when I returned from boarding school, and my sense of melancholy was even more overwhelming than I anticipated. My cousins called me pretentious. The Arab boys who loitered outside the shisha bar sneered at me. *You changed*, they said, meaning my relative lack of vernacular and my newfound obsession with eyeliner.

Back then, I still wanted to be a photographer, a small Olympus point-and-shoot knocking around in my backpack. In my first days back, Berlin bloomed at the seams with rotten garbage. Ants crawled out of the sockets in my father's living room, a small street of them always leading up the wall and out the window; no matter how much poison we sprayed into the electrical outlets or taped them shut—they just returned. And though prophesied to soon be extinct, the bees were also everywhere. They covered the overflowing trash cans in the city, or you'd see them lazily dozing on outdoor café tables, where they fattened themselves on crumbs of sugar or lay unconscious next to jars of cherry jam. I brushed the dirt out of my hair and rinsed it from my face and all I could hear, even in the early morning, was the howling of sirens over the frenzied songs of birds, which chirped and chirped and chirped.

In August, I enrolled at Humboldt Universität for philosophy and art history, not because I wanted to study but because I wanted the free U-Bahn pass. And so I let the glittery, destructive underworld of Berlin sink its fangs into me, my solitude alleviated only when I went out at night and got lost in some apartment with tattooed men and women who did poppers underneath a framed picture of Ulrike Meinhof. Then I went home, my nose bleeding, my hair smelling of cigarette smoke, and was confronted by that disappointed look on my father's face, my grandmother's suspended in a perpetual frown. I had been lifted out of the low-income district of hopelessness and sent to one of the best schools in the country, and yet here I was, my mother was dead, soon the city would be covered in snow again, and I was ravaged by the hunger to ruin my life.

AUTUMN WAS SHORT and humid, and then, overnight, it was winter. On the news, I saw middle-aged men with pearlescent smiles and young blond TV anchors in starched suits reporting about the financial crisis, the lack of jobs, the jammed Eurotunnel, snow collecting on the spires of basilicas in Northern Italy, and somewhere, everywhere, a missing girl, or an Arab man detained for terrorism, or a building with asylum seekers set on fire. In Berlin, the cathedrals' stained glass was covered with frost, and most days, I put on my red hat and my black coat and walked out into the crunchy snow to my job at the jazz café in Kreuzberg, the kind of place with red-painted walls and old leather seats, which tried to present a facsimile of a gone century. I served old German couples, and sometimes they were so close to me I could smell their shampoo, the salt on their skin, and despite myself, the hairs on the back of my neck stood up in desire. To pass the time, I imagined the men touching me while their wives watched. Instead, they ignored me or, when I bowed down to serve their burgers, asked which God I believed in. How old I was. Where I was from. And occasionally one of them would trace my earring or touch my butt when I passed, and my body surged with repulsion.

I FINISHED MY shift and walked to the most famous club in the city. Staggering past the tree-starved DDR-style council blocks on the Straße der Pariser Kommune, the wind slapping my face. The ghosts of the East were still present between the buildings, shadows filtering through every snow-covered crack. Now only foreigners lived in the high-rises, people who looked like me and who congregated in sweatpants in their courtyards, smoking cigarettes and chatting about casinos. The high-rises and council blocks were the same everywhere. I hated them. I hated everyone who had the same fate as I did. So when I walked past a group of Moroccan men on the corner of Rüdersdorfer Straße, I avoided making eye contact. Of course, once they computed I was no one's little sister, they whistled. They whistled and called me degrading names, because the philosophers were wrong and the meaning of life is not that it ends but that your one job on earth is to make everyone as miserable as your own sad self.

IT WAS HARD to keep my eyes open in such severe cold, and the line for the club was long. In front of me were two Spaniards in expensive clothing: black leather, dark platform shoes. They were of a different world than I was, and still, because of naïveté or boredom, I inserted myself into their conversation about Kate Moss's cellulite, and we bantered until they offered me one of their blue Nike ecstasy pills for six euros. The blue Nikes had started appearing that summer and, according to safe-consuming websites, consisted of 183 milligrams of MDMA, probably laced with 2C-B— guaranteed to roll for ten hours, fifteen if you were lucky. I took only a quarter, washed it down with a gulp from their flask, and kept the rest for later. The Spaniards were turned away at the door, and I shouted a thank-you after them; then it was my turn.

THE GATEKEEPERS OF techno were unpredictable despots. Large and legendary as Cyclopes, they had fully tattooed faces, other lives in which they made art and literature, and, despite their intellectual curiosity, they liked to stand here in the snow exerting power based on prestige and exclusivity. Although I had been coming here since my sixteenth birthday, I had been turned away a handful of times. It always presented a gamble. Tonight I wore a cheap, oversized faux-fur coat and smelled like pizza grease and popcorn, but I was a girl, and so I smiled the dumbest smile I could come up with.

"Are you alone?" they asked, and exchanged a suggestive glance.

"What do you think?"

"Be careful out there, doll." They waved me in. A girl can get in almost anywhere, even if she can't get out.

THE BUNKER WAS a shock of steel and concrete, glass and chains, with sixty-foot ceilings. A wall of warm air and muffled techno battered me, and within a minute my dress was lined with sweat, but the club was dark, and darkness was an authority to which I submitted. The music seemed to come from somewhere deep inside the earth, as if pulsating through the magmatic core—there was a logic to abrasive bass and insistent drum machines, but 138 beats per minute never cohered unless you were grinding your neural pathways to a prehistoric pulp, so I hoped for a swift high. I threw my jacket into the corner and climbed the stairs to the dance floor, every step under me vibrating to that familiar bass line. My legs still functioned, even if they were shaking: soft, soft lows, like seasickness. I pushed my way past a group of wannabe goth models, babes in chunky white sneakers, and emaciated, androgynous trendsetters in mesh and leather. Their bodies were warm next to mine; they smelled of patchouli. Photographs and mirrors were not permitted in these establishments, rendering my desire for representation obsolete. And yet, images reigned: The first time I came here, I saw a man in a safari hat with a toothbrush.

"Toothbrush?" I asked.

"Yes," he said, "I've been here for three days." I saw him every time.

"What a high ponytail," a young Black man in a dog collar whispered to me in American English. He wore contact lenses that turned his irises red, and when he smiled, there was the flash of golden braces.


THE CLUB WASN'T really called the Bunker, but that's what I will call it, because that's how we experienced it: a shelter from the war of our daily lives, a building in which the history of this city, this country, was being corroded under our feet, where the machines of our bodies could roam free and dream. A place like the Bunker attracted an eclectic mixture of gestalts, and I liked them all. But mostly I liked the strange bald men whose political affiliations, checking-account balances, and sexual preferences you couldn't categorize. They were from Detroit or Freiburg or Dublin; they spoke of Rilke and shared the last dregs of amphetamines with you at sunrise. Their eyes were large and full of secrets and a bit watery by the end of the night. They were the first to come and the last to leave. They were always here, the ones who actually used the dark rooms. You could tell by their leathery faces that they were professionals at this business of techno, of living a double life in the city's underbelly, because they truly didn't care what anyone thought. No audience for them, no performance: No, this was their life. Yet there was a tenderness to their carelessness. They had been partying since before my birth, since before the wall even fell. And, most important, they never judged you, no matter what kind of fool you made of yourself.

NONE OF MY friends were there. Not that I had many—I dumped Felix, my first boyfriend, the second I moved back from school, because technically I wasn't allowed to have a boyfriend, and he was bad in bed. And Melanie had moved to London to study textile design. The only people left were Anna and Romy, with whom I'd also gone to school and who moved to Berlin for university. Lately they'd been telling me to slow down, but they didn't understand the accelerating feeling in my chest, this race car of a heart that I couldn't stop. Anna had promised to come to the Bunker, but her text message predicted an arrival time of an hour from now. So I did a line in the bathroom with this peroxide-blond girl whom I would never see again, then went upstairs to the other dance floor, where the house beat was slick with synth and soulful samples. I stood at the bar, hoping that my aloneness was not betraying my insecurity. I played with my hair, trying to look arrogant and un-approachable.

I noticed his smell before I saw him: pink pepper and smoke. There he stood, Marlowe Woods, all six feet three inches of him, wearing a battered leather jacket. I usually liked my men blond and severe or dark as tar, but Marlowe was neither, somewhere smack in the middle, with a square jaw and dimpled chin, the nose of an emperor. Greasy hair that fell in almost girlish waves down to his chin. I kept my composure when he put his hand on my shoul-der, even though I was almost nauseous with attraction. He was chewing gum, and I noticed a small spider tattoo pulsing on the side of his neck. He stood with his back to the bartender, his el-bows leaning on the counter. Looked at me from the side with a sly smile.

"Hey. I'm Marlowe." Everybody knew who he was: the Amer-ican writer who always carried speed. He had published a book in his early twenties, which was translated into a few languages. I had seen a picture of him in a magazine feature on Berlin artists. Though I couldn't remember the details, I'd never forgotten his face in that glamorous photograph. Windswept and serious, a cig-arette between his lips. The picture alone had exercised a strange pull on me; his blue eyes pierced the page with intelligence. I had seen him before, in some club by the water, where the sun turned the dance floor into a laceration of light and the sound was happier than here. Of course, he hadn't noticed me. He was a prince who moved through rooms as if they belonged to him, surrounded by a large group of friends, among them his blond girlfriend, who in my memory always wore a Sonic Youth shirt.

"I'm Nila." I shook his clammy hand, a surprisingly formal gesture.

"By the way, you lost this." He stretched out his palm and, in the strobing lights, I saw a small gray lighter.

"Not mine."

"Yes, it probably fell out of your pocket." I shook my head, and he laughed, his smile all gap-toothed and dimpled.

"Well, I think you should keep it." His breath warm against my neck, he slid the lighter into my tote bag, and there was this feeling of a pinprick in my heart.

"Okay," I said, unable to meet his gaze. "Do you have speed?"

"Can I buy you a drink first?"

TWENTY MINUTES LATER he pushed hard against me in the bathroom stall, everything sticky with grime and sweat. He stubbed out his cigarette on the wall right next to my face, and I believed I could smell the faint sulfur of scorched hair.

"I'm sorry, it's just so tight in here," he said. Against the visual noise of stickers and tags, I studied the rest of him: V-neck of his green shirt, golden necklace with a coin that refracted the light. So this was him, the glamorous man from the magazine. Grinning, he blew on my face, and I calculated how far I was ready to go in exchange for a line, but after he got out the little folded-up flyer of speed from his pants pocket, he only asked me where I was from.

"Berlin," I said, which was the truth. But he did the dreadful thing I always feared people would do—he asked again, he asked where I was really from, and because my head was a structureless melting pot of serotonin and my jaw was behaving like a carousel horse, or because even here I was afraid, I said, "My parents are from Greece," which was a lie but seemed like an approximate explanation for my dark and aquiline face, my unruly curls. Sometimes I lied that I was Colombian; sometimes I was from Spain or Israel. I didn't want to speak about what had brought my parents over from Kabul or tell him that he had probably met my uncle driving a taxi in which he sat in the back seat feeling sorry for that dark man in front of him broken by all the things he had to leave behind. Or say that I was not even allowed to be here, that my being here was a big, ugly secret. Here, truth had no place. And anyway, nine times out of ten, it was easier to tell a lie than to watch pity distort someone's face. I didn't want to be pitied. He seemed intrigued.

"Greece," he repeated. "Interesting." The speed was wet and potent, and when I snorted the line, the burning sensation unblocked my sinuses, and I forgot the low yank of the lie.

"I do this only for research," I sniffled, and he laughed. It was so easy to make men laugh. It was the easiest thing in the world. "I'm writing a paper on it for class."

"I'm American. I would believe anything," he said with that gentle lull in his voice.

"I know."

"Well, then, I need to come up with other facts about myself to surprise you."

"Why is your German so good?" I countered.

"Because I am . . . I had a girlfriend. And I studied it in high school."

"Really? You retained your high school German?" I willfully ignored the part about the girlfriend.

"And my mother was German, technically speaking."

"Technically." I tried to compute that this man had a German mother—where was her family from, what flavor of German was she?

"My turn. Why is your English so good?"

"Bilingual school," I said, and let him believe what he wanted to believe. I knew what it made me sound like—someone who came from money. When I returned his flyer, my hand lingered on his for a moment too long. We stared at each other, charged by the disorderly pulse of the air. I took the square red-tinted sunglasses from his head and put them on; the lenses were smudged. He touched the hollow between my collarbones, and I closed my eyes to the warmth and subdued techno drifting from the dance floor, snippets of Spanish and German in adjacent booths.

"You're very beautiful," he said. I started laughing and threw my head back, because I had never been beautiful. I had a strong, regal look to my face due to my high cheekbones and my almond-shaped eyes, and maybe I was young, but I knew what beauty was. I had a different quality, what my mother had wanted to slap out of me and my father spat at. What men love. Beauty was a tragic virtue often abused because we are fooled by it, but I emanated something darker, something uglier. Like a fraught hunger for life, like a voice that said I would do anything.

"In America we say thank you to compliments," he said, and grabbed the sunglasses from my face.

I grinned. "Thank you, sir."

———

SMALL TALK, SHOUTING across the bar, distorted faces in the corridor. Laughter. We couldn't hear each other because the music
was too loud. Marlowe's hand on the small of my back or on my
shoulder, speaking loudly in my ear about the importance of places
such as these. I smiled and nodded, because illusions were frail and
had to be kept intact. I drifted behind him, and we sat down on one
of those dingy leather couches, his fingers drumming on my knee.
Slurped the melted ice of my mojito, the sugar filming my teeth. I
did not see his kind-of girlfriend, and I did not have to think anymore. Slowly, the real world faded away, like the color of a memory I successfully repressed. Or ink when it got into contact with
water—it was still there but smeared. I could barely recall below-
freezing temperatures or the fact that I owned a phone. Finally,
Anna: Her face hovered above me.

"It's snow," she giggled. "I have snow in my hair."

"Where were you?" I kissed her cheek. I introduced her to
Marlowe, and she pointed at the group of people she came with, no
one I recognized. She had a doll's face, and the entire time she
spoke, her breath was perceptible as a cloud, and I wanted to
cradle her in my arms. Was it very cold? I loved her. I was home,
finally. . . . Marlowe's face appeared again, telling me to open my
mouth, and he planted a crumbling pill on the center of my tongue.
Uncritically, I swallowed.

"Oh my God," Anna said. "Your pupils. They look like dinner
plates." Then there was this loud noise, incredibly loud, like a
thousand fire alarms ringing in my ears.

"Come, come, we need to go now." Marlowe took not my hand
but my wrist—I remember this unusual gesture—and led me
through the murky, dancing mass, through people whose expres-

sions glowed then wilted in the strobe lights, face after face like a photograph. He guided me down the next stairway, through groups of leather-clad men and women in rhinestone-studded mesh, through the door, past the Cyclopes, past the walk of shame of those who did not get in, into the icy morning air, into a car, and it took one minute or ten, I don't remember, but what I remember is that none of my uncles was driving the taxi.

# TWO

I DON'T RECALL IF there was an actual fire alarm or if it was a sound effect of the music, because we didn't talk about that. In the cab, we were laughing, as I had forgotten my coat and my shoulders were nude and freezing, but we were too high to carp about the cold, and he cracked open a window and let the snowflakes enter the car, and one could see the holiday lights on some of the solemn trees blur into the dark-blue light of dawn. It was the first weekend of November, and the city was still very much asleep. Germany has a habit of respecting the departed sanctity of Sundays, and I was grateful for that as we rolled into Warschauer Straße. He paid and slipped his leather jacket over my shoulders when we climbed out of the cab. I stood there in front of his building for a second, hesitating to go in. *My life will change.* Suddenly I was sure of it, and the anticipatory recognition made me freeze.

"Are you coming?" He held open the blue door.

"Yes." I breathed in and followed him. We walked through the courtyard, then into the back building, five stories up, and I touched the walls that hundreds of people before me had touched, before the first war even began. His apartment, I realized immediately, was a statement of contradictions—it wasn't the loft that people said it was. It wasn't even really the apartment of a grown-up, and yet it exuded the kind of rugged sophistication of a place that I imagined Edie Sedgwick would live in. There was no hallway; the door opened immediately into the living room. High ceilings, gold light fixtures, and a coffee table that I now know to be cherrywood but then only suspected to be expensive and rare. Clothes were scattered everywhere; the scent of cold ash and incense filled the air. Records were stacked on the floor, and, as in every bachelor apartment within a fifty-mile radius of Berlin, there stood a high table with two Audio-Technicas. Pioneer mixer. Bottles and cans cluttered the surfaces, and a giant canvas with off-white paint leaned against the wall. Long linen sheets hung from his windows, in a powdery blue that tinted the light. I remembered, in some ancient part of my heart, that I was supposed to be with Anna at the Bunker right now. But it didn't matter. It was hours like these when even my name seemed to be a completely arbitrary measure, and nothing could contain or define my essence. I could have been anyone and wanted anything, and I wanted to be with him. My neighborhood was vacuumed away. Friedrichshain, the Oberbaumbrücke, Kreuzberg behind the water. I lay down on a rug pockmarked with cigarette burns, still wearing his jacket. Heard the trains rumble on the bridge close by, and the apartment floors started moving.

"I didn't realize you could hear the floors move, even here, so high up."

"The building breathes. It's alive," he said as he walked into the kitchen.

"Put on some music," I shouted from the shag carpet.

"What do you want to listen to?" His voice was tinny in the other room.

"Anything." My ears were full of the techno from the club, and everything sounded fuzzy and distant. "Anything, really. I can hear my thoughts."

"Oh, we don't want that," he said, and though I expected a house track, it was Bowie's "Rebel Rebel" that bloomed in the air. I smiled to myself: It was one of my favorite songs. He returned with two White Russians mixed with soy milk, a popular drink at the time. "They don't even taste like booze. Which I love." He was still wearing those red-tinted sunglasses. From where I lay on the carpet, he looked ridiculous.

"Come down here," I said.

"Not yet." He made an awkward gesture with his hands and disappeared back into the kitchen. "We need to refresh our nasal passages with some amphetamines first." I got up to take a sip of the creamy, bitter drink and walked over to his bookshelf. American and Russian novels, books on architecture, photography, obscure philosophy, and fantasy novels with whimsical covers. Three copies of his own book, *Ceremony,* two in the original English and one in the German translation. I traced his name, embossed on the spine of the green hardcover. I had never read it. On the top row of his bookshelf there stood an old SLR camera—a Canon—and a small animal skull I couldn't identify.

"You take pictures?" I asked when he returned carrying a blue tile with little white maids painted on it. He had put on a brown sweater, and his shoulders looked broader and bulkier than before. My desire, though nascent, already felt so profound that it seemed close to hatred.

"Not really," he said, then snorted a line from the tile. "Not anymore. I'd rather play music these days. But jobs are not that important, are they?"

"So you've stopped writing?"

"Why do you care so much? I like you party girls because, usually, you do not care."

"I guess I'm curious."

"Work is for the weak. I don't believe in it."

"But isn't what we do outside of parties the most intimate thing? That's why we're there, anyway. To forget about what bothers us."

"I disagree. You have it all wrong—the party is what I live for." He smiled a sheepish smile and pulled the necklace out from under his turtleneck. "In a capitalist society, being unemployed is the most radical thing you can do. And the party—the underground of the world—is where we unleash the id and present our truest desires. What is more authentic than your base desire? Fucking strangers in the dark—now, that's interesting."

"So you're unemployed."

"Very witty," he said. "I'm working on a book about architecture."

"That sounds cool."

"Does it?"

"Well, I love buildings," I said stupidly. I sat down next to him, on the worn spot of the sofa. When I lowered my head over the table to snort a line, I noticed he was wearing dark-gray slippers. As always when I was unnerved by the vulnerability of another person, I made a joke, but he ignored me.

Drawing a circle on my forehead, he asked, "And what is the darkness in there?"

"Oh, I don't speak about that."

"You're trying to be mysterious."

"No." I smirked. "I'm just a student. Philosophy and art history."

"Hmm. And you're a real Berliner, then?"

I nodded.

"How was it growing up here?" I recalled the broken elevator lamp with the cobweb. Insects, incredibly, alive in that lightbulb's orifice. And days of waiting in line at offices and job centers, where I had to translate documents for my parents. The flurry of silverfish alive in our bathroom; waiting in the blue light of the bus stop in the snow; the sound of my mother's voice, like a star irradiating the country of childhood.

"Good," I said. "It was good." It was a disease. The lies bubbled out of me: I told him we lived in a house in Rudow, that my father was happy and healthy, that we had a garden. The fabrications were interspersed with true facts like boarding school, the girls' matte Longchamp bags, the Latin teacher who was obsessed with *deus ex machina*, weeping willows, canals, and the ancient, dying priest who always called me *Nina*. The sprawling meadows around Rosenwald, the cobblestoned streets leading from one gothic structure to another—our medieval school building, once a cloister to Catholic nuns. He laughed, comparing it to his own public high school with linoleum floors and metal lockers, and then we talked about European architecture.

"I love the idea, but architecturally, socialist housing was a huge mistake." His fingers glided over my black dress, the cheap satin of it. "I mean, where is the beauty? Who would want to live in a brutalist square?"

"No one." I omitted the fact that I came from exactly those

brutalist squares. He slipped off part of the jacket, revealing my shoulder. I tried out the sentence in my mind before it even happened: *I slept with Marlowe Woods.* Marlowe Woods, the infamous writer. Touched his jawline and moved closer so that I could smell the chewing gum on his breath, the pink pepper of his perfume. That putrid sweetness of alcohol.

He put a hand on my leg, stroked my inner thigh with his fingers.

"Oh," I said, and sank deeper into the couch. His hand wandered up my waist and he started circling my nipple through my dress.

"How old are you?" He was mumbling, pulling my ponytail down with his other hand.

"Turning nineteen in a week."

"Is that the truth?"

"Do I need to show you my ID?"

And, as he drew me closer by my hair, he said, "I just need you to know that I'm thirty-six."

"It's okay." I was surprised by how small and hoarse my voice sounded. I had never slept with an older man, but everyone I knew had—and I felt it was the rite of passage into adulthood. "It's attractive."


THE LIGHT WAS blue, and he touched my face, and I let him. We made out, in that gooey, haphazard way that you do when you're high, and I slipped out of the jacket and my dress. I was wearing mismatched underwear—a red lace bra I had stolen at H&M, and black cotton panties under my tights—and he took a minute just to study me. It was the look from the photograph in the magazine again, and his eyes were charged with something hungry and un-ashamed. I was waiting for him to undress, but the only thing he took off were the slippers.

"You shouldn't be at a party like that," he said. "It's not good for you." His long fingers were everywhere—on my face and waist, my thighs. He breathed on my neck and pushed the length of his hand along my throat. I let out a low moan.

"Shut up." I wanted to die. Marlowe wasn't the first person who had touched me—there was Felix, of course, who made me read Adorno and only rarely wanted to have sex, and men in the back seats of cars and in dingy, sticky club toilets, and the girl with incredible breasts who shared her humid sheets and orange sham-poo with me for one summer—but this was unlike anything else; the substances enhanced every sensation. That slow, deliberate pace of his movements. Feverish, I slithered from his touch, but when I reached for his belt buckle, he pushed my hand away.

"No," he said. "I decide when I want to fuck you." I felt ex-cited and reckless all at once.

"Okay," I said, surmising that my role was to yield. He wasn't like Felix with the low libido, who thought my incessant hunger for touch was disgusting. But he wasn't like the guys with whom I cheated on Felix either—the young men who ripped off their pants and treated sex like a drive-through. No, Marlowe's withholding was suggestive. Refined, almost, were it not for that grin. Unsure whether I was a participant in his fantasy or he in mine, I smiled.

"You're such a good girl," he said. The humiliation burned in my cheeks. "Just wait."

A few minutes later he got up, and his face darkened, as if noth-ing transgressive had happened between us, and I understood that he expected me not to talk about it to anyone. That this was our secret now. Then, slowly, my thoughts came back to me, and with them an awareness of my body. I was embarrassed and went into the bathroom to get dressed. I had always felt that getting dressed was more intimate than getting undressed—I wasn't ready for him to see me put on my armor. Back in the living room, he was dancing in slow motion to a song he said was by Cream. "One of the best records ever made." I had never heard the album and just nodded. He was awkward, his movements too sluggish, resembling a modern dancer on sedatives, and the silence between us swelled, viscous with guitar strings.

"I think I should go," I said, as I was beginning to feel useless.

"Don't you dare. I'm not done with you yet." It was what I had hoped to hear. I thought maybe we would have sex now, so I sat down on the couch and waited. He walked out of the room and I heard his cough, the shuttering of doors. There was a second level in this apartment, connected not by stairs but by a white-painted ladder. It was the kind of architecture I loved—crown molding, old hallways that smelled of musk and dust, a front building, and a back building. It was still true that the front in most prewar buildings was more expensive. In the middle was the courtyard, just big enough for a horse-drawn fire engine. Sometimes I thought I could smell it, the perfume of those who lived here over a hundred years ago, when carriages were still a part of the city. The phantom hooves, the triste trash cans and playgrounds, so much like the drawings by Heinrich Zille: *You can kill a person with an apartment as with an ax.* . . . When I startled out of my daydream, I felt warm and soft. He placed a glass of wine on the table. The window blinds were open to a light snowfall.

"Let me tell you something," he said. "I had never seen snow anywhere except on a mountain until I was fifteen years old." He told me he grew up in Northern California. He'd always wanted to be a writer, but then his mother died, and he had trouble forming a sentence. He had periods of bohemian bliss, insecurity. But here he was, in his own apartment. "I bought it with my savings," he said. He told me he was sixteen when his mother died, and when he was twenty-one, his father died. A few years later, in a haze, the writing impulse of childhood returned: He wrote *Ceremony*, his only book, about their troubled marriage, his father's alcoholism, his mother's cancer, the horses, the fables he grew up reading. German was the only other language he spoke, except for snippets of Spanish. The camera was hers: She was a hobby photographer, always documenting their lives. His inheritance from her was what had allowed him to come here. The success, he said, was unexpected. For three years he didn't have to work, lived off royalties and interviews. He moved from California to London, then to Spain, then Berlin.

"And now what?"

"You have to be creative . . . and I have an advance for the next book." A dim memory floated through my mind, of having read in an Internet forum that Americans thought it coarse to speak about money.

When I told him that my mother was dead too, that she died when I was sixteen, his face opened with a kind of bruised sympathy I had detected in other orphans and half orphans too, as if we had been ushered through different exits into a shared reformatory of grief. Perhaps it was true—maybe we really did all share the same kind of ordinary sorrow.

"It unyokes something from you. But you have already understood that. I can see it." He didn't say much after that, and I was grateful for it.

"You know," I said, trying to change the topic, "I've never seen the ocean. Or the sea. I went to Italy with my school once, to Rome. But I've never seen the sea. Not even the North Sea. It sounds childish, I am aware."

"We can rectify that." He winked. "And it doesn't sound childish at all. Only provincial."

"Great."

"And what are you going to be when you grow up? A philosopher, yes?"

"Funny you should ask. I actually want to be an artist." Nothing in my life I said with as much earnestness as this; for nothing was I so ridiculed. Everybody wanted to be an artist, especially the boys my age that the cool Berlin girls dated. Boys who had gained some fame in Germany over the last few years—the kind who listened to the Smiths and wore skinny jeans and kept battered copies of *Steppenwolf* in their tote bags and cheated on all their girlfriends. But I had the idiocy of the very inexperienced, which made me believe in my own greatness. And perhaps I wanted to prove myself to him. "I am going to be a photographer."

"I believe you," he said, and I laughed loudly again, because I was not used to people taking me seriously.

"You should come up with me," he said after a while. "I'd like to take your picture. Time to be a muse." I climbed the white ladder, which led to a large bedroom with slanted ceilings. The floorboards were painted white. There was a mattress on the floor, next to a stool that functioned as a nightstand, on which I noticed a Proust book, earplugs, a glass water bottle, and a beer can. On one side of the room there were dressers, a small desk. He retrieved another SLR camera and told me to sit down on the mattress.

"Nice Minolta."

"Who taught you about cameras?" He removed the lens cap and played around with the settings.

"Oh, no one." At the foot of the mattress, I crossed my legs and thought of my father, who also used an old Minolta, which was still under his bed, collecting a film of dust. He came over, pushed up my skirt all the way, and told me to turn my head to the side.

"I hate my nose."

"I don't care." He took three or four shots. No flash. The quiet click of the camera shutter. Motionless, I shuddered and closed my eyes for the last one. Then we switched positions, and I took pictures of him standing in front of the bed. He looked away, didn't smile. He cocked his chin to the right. He was still and controlled, as if he too were composing the image. Then, through the crosshairs of the viewfinder, I saw him walk toward me; just before the shutter clicked for the last picture, he snapped the camera out of my hands.

"Enough." He sighed and walked over to the window. Opened it a crack, cold air entering the room. Side by side we looked at the city from his apartment, high up above everything else. The view was spartan—other roofs, the courtyard, some bicycles, the balconies shining blue and gray—but he said it was the idea that counted, that the absence of the city implied and amplified its power, that a part was representative of its whole. Eight hours: Eight hours had passed since I'd come here, the amount of time it took for the first known photograph to be completed, and I thought of it, Niépce's *View from the Window at Le Gras*, light etched on a heavy pewter plate coated in bitumen of Judea.

"I wish I could write about this," he said. "Nothing is as perfect as snow."

"You could still write about it."

"Oh, bunny." He touched my hair. "You say this because the world hasn't broken you yet. But it will, trust me."

"Sure thing," I laughed.

"But look at this whiteness," he said with a strange urgency in his voice. "One could do anything to it, it's so defenseless." Of course, I didn't know what he meant back then.

# Three

WE DIDN'T SLEEP together that first Sunday, but when I left, he lent me a woolen coat, and in return I gave him my number. He said we would see each other again, and on the train home, I trawled loose cigarette filters and a receipt for tomatoes out of his coat pocket. An expired monthly train pass, which I kept as souvenir. The buildings passed, one after the other, their shadows occupied by snow. Sirens. Cafés filled with stern faces, kebab shops, Spätis, people drinking wine and eating dinner, and between them, everywhere, there was a Mohammed or an Ali or an Aisha trying to get by. I was on so much speed that I was very paranoid on the train, so I hid under my sunglasses, but underneath the anxiety burned an ancient coal of anger, kindled by the cruelty of fate. I was returning to the life I did not think should be mine.

When I arrived in our concrete neighborhood, I stood in the doorway of another building and lined my tongue with three pumps of mouth spray and coated my hair with perfume. Then I took the elevator seven stories up, and with the precision of a surgeon, I turned the key in apartment number 7C. I needed to make it to my room, which was on the far left side of the narrow hallway, and then back to the bathroom. There was no way to avoid my father, who sat in the living room, which opened to the hallway, so I didn't even try.

"Oh, there she is, the celebrity," he said with raised eyebrows. "Look at her deigning to come home. What an honor." He wore a knitted large pullover and the green slippers I had bought him when I was eleven. A Persian music video played on TV.

I didn't say anything and just untied my boots.

"Where were you? Why didn't you call me back? You are going to give me a stroke, just like your mother."

"Sorry. But I am here now, am I not?" I had been ignoring my phone all weekend.

"And whose coat is that?"

"Romy's."

"Quite big for her, isn't it." In his green eyes, which were sunken into his prematurely aged face, there was a flicker of meanness. I could feel the anxious tremble in his voice—the tremble that made me think of a knife, the tremble that signaled to me that he did not know what was happening to me.

"Did you run into anyone?" Ever since my father had figured out that I went to parties, he was concerned with my being detected by the neighborhood uncles and aunts, not the fact that I actually went out. You could do anything in an Afghan household, as long as it was kept secret.

"No," I said. "I am still an honorable girl."

———

AFTER I LOCKED myself in the bathroom, I installed three fingers into the cavern of my throat and immediately vomited the contents of the last wine into the ceramic bowl. It was an attempt to sober myself, and usually it worked. I stripped off all my clothes and sat on the rim of the bathtub as it filled with water. Sitting there like that, a small and dark-haired figurine in the steam, I stared at myself in the vintage full-length mirror I'd bought at a flea market several years ago, when I still believed we could make this place beautiful. Two glossy carpet beetles crawled up the gold rim. My father had stopped cleaning the apartment after my mother's death two years before. But what I dreaded about these moments was not the tongue of hair in the sink or all these mismatched bottles and napkins and surgical gloves scattered everywhere; it was that everyone was gone, and this throbbing noise in my head returned, and it wasn't the techno from before or the voices of my friends, it was a noise so ancient it had always been there, since before my birth, and at some point I must've tuned into it and now couldn't, for the better part of my life, tune out. And then there was this inevitable sense of loneliness, that there was no one to talk to about this, not Romy or Anna in their clean apartment with their linen napkins, not my father behind that wall, not Marlowe. I thought in those moments of the bald men at the party, and I wondered what it was they felt, because sometimes I thought I could feel it too.

# Four

GOOD, I SAID to Marlowe. But I could've said this: Berlin is onerous. The city is particular and historical and shattering. And I was born inside its ghetto-heart, as a small, wide-eyed rat, in the months after reunification. My birth was the consequence of a long chain of geopolitical events, which began with the U.S. national security advisor, Brzezinski, considering Afghanistan a chessboard to save Poland, his home, and ended a decade later with the Russians rolling their tanks back north, ready to accede to the collapse of the USSR. GRAVEYARD OF EMPIRES, the news headlines said. *Graveyard of empires,* we parroted, not entirely without pride. My parents hailed from Kabul, the capital, as did their parents and their parents before that. Our gene pool contained the amalgam of every nation committing that mountainous error: Iran and Northern India, the DNA of homesick soldiers from Kazakhstan, Mongolia, and even Britannia.

In Germany, a baby was needed as an anchor to postpone deportation, and so I began as a clump of cells multiplying with fury in my mother's uterus. I took my first steps exactly three months after the Rostock riots, where neo-Nazis threw Molotov cocktails at asylum blocks, and was raised in Gropiusstadt in Neukölln, a district you might know from that memoir on the heroin babies of Bahnhof Zoo. And all the ugly is true. We were thrust into a nightmare of brutalist concrete and unemployment rates, wedged into a fourteen-story building that even now, a decade after I left, lingers under my skin like a cauterizing substance, so that everyone who touches me can feel it: long, deserted summers and the gleam of sun on needles buried in playground sand; elevators in which I too pissed my pants as a child, waiting to reach our impossible floor; the skinheads in biker boots who tagged swastikas on walls; Arab boys who sold weed and Turkish girls who got kicked out for having secret boyfriends.

MY PARENTS, YOU understand, were doing okay in the other country. Karim fell in love with Anahita's long black hair in a college chemistry class, and a year later they were married behind the barbed wire of a hotel in the hills, dancing while the buildings fell in the city. And then, as med students at the end of their residency, they were forced to forfeit the security of the petite bourgeoisie, with walls of books and a white-tiled kitchen my mother liked to make coffee in. My father pocketed one key, then left the yellow-roofed house in Karte Char to the live-in help, who came from generations of indentured servitude, which was sad, my parents said, but "that's the way it was." And my mother, the story goes, picked a dozen orange tulips from the garden. Her fist curled tight around the wet bouquet, my father's hand on her wrist. They boarded a plane to Prague with false papers—my father pretended to be a neighbor needing surgery in the West, my mother masquerading as his uneducated wife. They brought with them a thin pile of photos, hidden in my mother's sweater, but otherwise they abandoned the archive that makes up a person's life. They didn't flee by boat. They didn't carry an infant wrapped in a blanket over a perilous mountain pass or walk through shrubbery by foot. They weren't illiterate. They didn't even live in a refugee camp. They were educated, middle-class people with idealist cores who liked dinner parties and walks in the park, and one day they boarded a plane and never returned.

But exile makes you do the strangest things: When they arrived in Prague, border control forbade my mother from bringing in "foreign seeds." Wordlessly, she ripped the dying petals off the stems and ate them one by one. And my father, once we moved into our own apartment, looped the key to the Kabul house onto his key chain. Just in case. Even now, long after that brick structure was destroyed in the war, and more than thirty years since he last saw the white pigeons pass over the flecked rooftops of his hometown, the key sits in his pocket.

After two weeks in a dim hotel in Prague, where my mother lay cramping in bed, they took the train to Berlin and set up camp in my grandmother's apartment in Gropiusstadt, where my father's family had been living for seven years. We were asylum seekers until I was eleven, and then, one morning, a man in a pinstripe suit handed us three wine-dark passports embossed with the golden lettering of citizenship. And still my parents could not work as doctors, the road to a new medical license too labyrinthine for someone with limited linguistic skills. The Afghan government refused to release their degrees, since they had boarded that plane under deceptive circumstances, to flee. I was tasked with sitting at the family computer and writing CV after CV.

MY MOTHER STARTED working at the local retirement home under the euphemized title of "nurse," though really she was just a maid for old people. My father applied for one job after the other, yet the rejections piled up, arriving in envelopes with company letterheads. He neatly stapled and collected them in a red plastic binder. When I came home from school, my father would be asleep on the sofa, his mouth slightly ajar, the creases on his forehead relaxed, adrift in a dream that didn't contain any of us.

My parents coasted in and out of unemployment and took out loans to fund my schooling, keen to return to the social class from which they had been ripped. If they couldn't do it, then perhaps I could—and lend them a hand, pull them up. Other Afghans called them *Dr. Karim, Dr. Anahita*. At family gatherings, relatives reminisced about the big houses that were lost to bombs and the hopeful, sunny years when everyone was an activist—even my shy, dogged parents, when even they were detained as political prisoners. When their faces were indistinct with baby fat, and they were students at university. It was the early eighties. Russians occupied their city, the Pakistanis inculcated a militia of orphans, but my parents and their friends huddled in clandestine back rooms, drinking wine out of plastic bottles, and read Marx and Engels and Mao, dreaming of a better world. In which Afghanistan was not cursed by geographical misfortune but would regain dignity and sovereignty. My mother became entangled with the Revolutionary Association of the Women of Afghanistan, handing out flyers about gender equality, communism, and a secular, independent country. Pictures of the founder, Meena Keshwar Kamal, were pasted in our photo book. *She died for you,* my mother said of this assassinated woman. This is what I came from: mountains alive with a mysterious intelligence, ultramarine and amber minerals that glint and whisper from their caves, boys hiding lapis in the assholes of donkeys, moonlight rusting the sky.

MY FATHER HAD a good heart, the disposition of an artist. Too sensitive to face the cruelties of earth, his face lined with Nietzschean *Urschmerz*. And still he was a tyrant. *I hate that everything is tied to money,* he said. He started working as a taxi driver for my uncle Rashid's business. Lurched home at dawn, snored on the couch. Barely ate. His mouth, the stink of ash.

MY GRANDMOTHER HAD the face of a fox, or that of a Soviet actress: thin, tattooed eyebrows over gray-green eyes, hair always bleached blond. She loved complaining and gave birth to seven children, including my father. She was the only one who wore chador, and God was a guideline more than a law.

MY MOTHER WAS very pretty and very neurotic, always brushing her long waves in front of the mirror. She controlled the house: checked my toothbrush for moisture to see if I had really brushed my teeth. Woke me up, even in elementary school, with ice packs on my feet. She wanted to love life, this ambitious woman, to be a doctor again, to have a house. After shifts, she read books on medical engineering, desperate for a career. The Afghan government changed power soon after she died; because irony lingers ever close to tragedy, a random bureaucrat in Kabul saw her death certificate and finally released the papers that documented her life, all sent to the embassy in Germany in a manila envelope: birth certificate, high school degree, and, at last, that medical license.

THE LEBANESE PEOPLE from apartment 12 bought a semi-detached. The Iranian girls snubbed me, called me *Gypsy Child* and *Jew Nose*, made fun of my parents' barbarian dialect and stern belief in tradition. In turn, I pitied their unschooled parents, their cheerfulness and lack of dignity. But in truth, we were the wanting ones who missed the quick, red-hot train to upward mobility. We didn't make it. Dregs of families: Afghans, Belarusians, Eastern Germans with names such as Chantal and Kevin, clusters of skinheads, and Kurds. New families moved in, families sculpted by tragedy. Lives financed by food stamps, coupons, the ink of unemployment benefits. The ones who managed to move out ended up driving Mercedeses and Audis. Shopped at better supermarkets, paid taxes. Lived in apartments that weren't riddled with spores, houses that included soil and rosebushes and open kitchen plans with stainless steel. Inheritance and acquisition. Mortgage. Ownership, a concept that would remain alien to us.

When I'd walk out of the district, farther into Rudow, I sauntered by their new houses, my hands buried in my coat pockets. Stole glances at windows. Christmas trees. New couch sets. Envy, that dusky, ancient tree, releasing its resin. Burrowing its roots into the mud of my heart.

When my cousins came over, we locked our hands. Sang old songs. Made it a point to tell one another over and over again that we were born in Germany. As though telling it endowed us with some privilege. As if it weren't a fact that meant nothing in the grand scheme of things—because we were still poor, we were still from Neukölln, and the Nazis were alive and well.

*You can't trust anyone in this country,* my father said, always sur-veilling the door. *Look what they did to the Jews.* "But they aren't Nazis," my schoolmates said. "They aren't Nazis," my teacher said, "the word means something specific, it is dangerous to gener-alize." They said it too when a bomb was detonated in a pre-dominantly Turkish neighborhood of Bremen, wounding twenty, killing a kiosk owner in his shop. "It was probably insurance fraud," the police said, "an inside job." The kiosk owner's widow was all blue eyes and hooked nose, squinting into the camera as she said, "He was a normal man; he liked to be home and cook bean soup. He wasn't a criminal."

"She isn't even crying," my mother said. "Look at what they've done to her." My father turned off the news, put his fork down, and walked out of the apartment, forgetting his jacket. He loved leaving, my father; he loved opening a door and shutting it behind him, leaving us trapped as if in a painting.

Stretches of his life were invisible to us, like when I was born. He was in Kabul, in Hamburg, in Montreal. He despised system-atically planted Scots pine and subzero winds. Yearned instead for mandarin trees and violent sunshine, a landscape so defiant and cruel it could tan even the scars of war. Months in the gritty footage of Southern California. He brought back the Minolta, developed rolls of film to show me unknown relatives in a certain kind of light I believed existed only in movies set by the Pacific. I fell asleep dreaming of a life behind a camera lens, a life that would allow me to finally get out of here.

"Your father is in prison," teased the neighbors' girls. Dilara's father really was imprisoned, serving three years for the rape of a white girl. Sasha's father was an alcoholic who massaged his adipose calves under casino lamps. I knew my father was different, even if the shapes were unclear. We never knew what he worked for, and he didn't tell us when he returned from America or Thailand with the newest Britney and Wu-Tang albums wrapped in cellophane. Gucci perfumes and susurrant silk for my mother, a bejeweled watch, gold vermeil, but no money to buy food at the end of the month. Eventually I realized he'd been working for a dubious friend, moonlighting as a "translator" to evade taxes, being paid under the table and saving the cash—when and if it came—under the bed in a locked metal suitcase. When my father was away, my aunt Sabrina offered to pay for groceries. Left us envelopes of money. My mother, too vain to accept, instead turned pennies in her hand.

LINDEN TREES SWEPT up the streets; maples eclipsed shopping malls. Flea markets were assaulted with the cacophony of disorder: Russian men with fat black moles on their cheeks selling bootleg DVDs; my mother haggling for a faux YSL bag, or a real vintage one—it was hard to say. She smelled the leather, inspected signs of wear. She wanted socialism but loved shiny objects—it didn't square, my father often reprimanded her.

"Am I not allowed to love style?" she said. "Does a good heart mean no style?"

Ash from barbecues in the park blackened our lungs. Poverty seeped and screeched from every corner, poverty and need—and I felt misunderstood, as if something terrible had gone wrong in my life. Like cockroaches and ants, we scurried through our district. And already I didn't feel at home in the world: untethered. My parents' gauche gestures, their inability to communicate in German, embarrassed me. Even at ten years old I was an adult, marching on, translating, correcting their grammar.

At elementary school, we all made fun of one another. My cross to bear was that I had the cheapest water possible. "Who buys water at Aldi?" they teased. "Who wears shoes like these?" Our furniture was made of particle grain and cardboard, and our wallpaper shone in a garish silver fleur-de-lis imitation. When I slept, I dreamed of untreated wood and high ceilings, of *style*. When I woke up and looked down at my outlandish, dark-haired body, I screamed for twenty minutes straight.

*We had a normal life once* was the refrain of my childhood. My parents were ashamed of their fate in this country with vandalized mosques and women with headscarves stabbed on the streets. My father's brief stint at McDonald's constituted a big secret: He insisted on night shifts, flipped burgers in the back, afraid to be seen. His collar reeked of fried grease in the mornings when he collapsed on the couch. And that's how I was raised: in the shadow of a fairer, better life. My father loved pictures of Athens and the ruins of Rome; my mother loved Elvis Presley and listening to radio stations where old women traced their lives' hardships and triumphs. When I was a child, before the towers fell and we learned to lie, my family dressed in suits to go to the bakery; my mother wore perfume to pick up yogurt at the discount supermarket. Comical, to see these formal Afghans walk through the elevator doors of a government-subsidized building, to see them enter the job center. My mother, wearing a thrifted fur coat, standing in queue for the food bank. They were kings and queens exiled from a myth, stranded at the shore of this German tristesse.

# Five

THE WEEK THAT followed was devoid of communication. Marlowe didn't text me, and mostly I was embarrassed by the crush I was developing. In vain, I tried to google the photograph from that magazine article but instead found some older interviews with him. The reviews of his book were favorable in a predictable way. They considered him an enfant terrible, breaking *the conventions of genre . . . veering between the poetic and the documentary.* They insisted he portrayed *searing scenes of a lonely childhood.* I rolled my eyes, not entirely without envy, and yet I was drawn to him, the way everyone is to the gifted. In one interview, he mentioned the poetry of T. S. Eliot and the plays of Christopher Marlowe, after whom he'd been named. His own website was defunct, which surprised me. After hours of searching on Myspace, Blogspot, and Facebook—there was an Italian café in Mitte named Marlowe and a female musician with a stern bob—I found the Facebook profile of his girlfriend: Doreen Hübner. A scan of an analog photograph showed her grinning on a street, fingers resting on the handle of a purple bike. Her profile was public; the last update had been a few months ago. And just as I was about to commit the humiliating act of "accidentally" sending Doreen a friendship request, an email popped up.

Melanie, who was enrolled at the London College of Fashion, had emailed me a list of universities to apply to: four in London, one in Bristol, and two in Paris. We'd always dreamed of leaving Germany and moving to London to become artists: she a designer, me a photographer. To Melanie, London was the goal; to me, it seemed like the only realistic option, the stepping stone before the mythical city of New York, where I secretly imagined my real life unfolding, far away from the fangs of my family. But I didn't qualify for a student visa, because I couldn't afford education in that city, where a semester of tuition cost as much as my father's yearly unemployment benefits. So London it was. But when application season came up, I missed the deadlines. Now I tried again to imagine my life there—wearing a black jacket, on the way to meet a professor or a friend, an apple in my hand, a Rolleiflex in my bag.

I clicked through the scans of my photographs, the Portra 160 film texturing the faces of my friends from summer days. My mother holding an orange. I had started shooting at fourteen, already obsessed with documenting my life. To take a picture was a way to control the narrative, to frame only what you wanted to see. I despised the austere flatness of early point-and-shoot digital photography, yearning instead for the texture and rigor of 35mm film. Because of aesthetics and because of need—I couldn't afford a digital SLR—I only knew how to work in analog. It titillated me that the images rarely turned out the way they looked in my mind: Family and friends, when asked to pose, were too elusive, the light unpredictable. My favorite shots had happened spontaneously after hours, sometimes days, of sitting with my subject, watching the sun in the room change; my sense of composition, consequently, was iconoclastic. Viewpoints and angles bored me. I liked Nan Goldin best—photos that looked as if torn right out of life. I was trying to do the impossible: to be transposed into ecstasy, into a kind of unconsciousness, and become one with the camera to chronicle strangers on the street or the faces of my friends when they were lost in thought at a party, a sadness in their eyes. I collected Polaroids of men with face piercings in ramshackle bars, Anna crying at after-hours, or Romy in a bathtub, hiding her breasts with her red hair like fire.

Staging was easier with self-portraits, where I had unlimited attempts and full control. In one of my favorite pictures, I'm wearing all black, sitting on a stool in an empty classroom at boarding school, looking blankly at the camera, which I'd positioned on the teacher's desk. My father's blazer hangs from my shoulders like a uniform, though I never wore one. The film's blur smooths the harsh angles of my face and makes me look both younger and sterner than I was. Sunlight enters from the left side, washing out the blackboard. Flowers are scattered on every table—I do not recall now why the students received them, but the atmosphere is one of displacement, of erroneous celebration. My other favorite picture is of my mother: She sits on a rounded chair, looking at herself in the gold-rimmed mirror in my grandmother's bedroom. The large black eyes are full of shock, her hair long and curled, lips a vermilion red. She looks like she is the only person on earth, even though I am standing right behind her, holding my father's heavy Minolta, in an imitation of Edouard Boubat's 1950 *Self-Portrait with Lella.* What chills me even now is not the aura of sickness, knowing that she would unexpectedly die a few weeks later, nor the scalloped, outdated curtains in the background, but that neither of us looks at the other: The photograph is two self-portraits melded into one.

But you couldn't comprise a portfolio of just two photos. I knew I wasn't good enough, not yet, to leave Berlin.


FOR A WEEK, the only fresh air I breathed was the cold wind on the balcony, where I smoked when my father wasn't home, watching the bus stop and boys loitering outside the shisha bar. Otherwise, I stayed in bed with the blinds closed. Didn't want to see daylight or eat or consume anything, except for the cookies and off-brand Diet Coke my father kept in the fridge for me. I fantasized about Marlowe's voice, the way he had spoken about writing. The flash of his belt buckle. The phone never lit up with a message, but then it was my birthday and the only person who remembered besides my dad and Romy was Setareh, a girl I had once been in love with. I considered her profile picture: her dark hair, the thin nose and pouty mouth. The formality of her Facebook message infuriated me. I blocked her, unblocked her, zoomed in to her photos, and put the laptop away. Went to work at the café and wiped the tables halfheartedly. I dropped two plastic pints, the Guinness sticking to my tights.

After my seminar on French cathedrals the next day, I walked to the Alte Bibliothek. Colonial maple stain shone on wooden floors and spiny staircases, all from the pompous nineteenth century. In the dimmed light of the stacks, my skin had a green hue. I remembered girls in boarding school calling me *alien blood*. Asking me if I wanted to eat the pig heart we dissected in biology class. One day, someone in the neighboring town to my school burned down a restaurant because they assumed the man who owned it was a Muslim. The owner's wife found her husband inside, shot, his mouth a repository of blood, and teeth had to be scraped from his throat during the autopsy. When it turned out that the man was Greek, the mayor apologized profusely. *We didn't know.* . . . And I barely realized what his words were really saying, the old, old narrative: It would have been only half as bad if he had been a Muslim.

"He's olive-skinned, isn't he?" One of my teachers had pointed at his face in the newspaper, grainy and washed out. "He does look southern. It's always easy to confuse those people." *Those* people. My whole existence, neatly packed into one demonstrative adjective.

At last, in the stacks of American literature, I found Marlowe's book. The glossy jacket, the corners rough with use. The dedication: *For Adrienne.* And then I started reading.

His mother had been a hippie—she tramped through America, bored with Illinois and her family on the outskirts of Champaign. Wore leather boots and emerald earrings, smoked cloves, and ended up in California. She adored horses. He was an only child, but foster kids sifted through the doors. Girls with names like Blueberry Jean and Amerada, whose mothers had abandoned them at road stops, boys whose parents were in cults. And his first love was in the book too—their innocent romance, almost unbelievable, having begun sometime in school. He sat behind her in class, enticed by the grace of her neck under the high ponytail, by the way the sun caught in her hair. Her name, in the book, was Ade.

Like Adrienne, in the dedication. The description of her hands, as if painted with bone-colored gouache—I reread the sentence twice. The glassy beads of her bracelets. How she had fallen in love with a musician, and so Marlowe started learning music too. Drums, then the guitar, his fingers callused from the strings. She always pointed out birds, found money on the street.

The ranch his father lived on was close to Mendocino, in eucalyptus-scented woods. Dark-wood panels on the ceiling; a lizard flitting through his bedroom. Loneliness and wilderness, a sky clotted with stars at night. It was the same landscape my father described on his trips back from California, when I was a child and touched his earlobe as I fell asleep, a vastness diametrically opposed to the boxed claustrophobia of my own life.

From the first page, from the words *And then there was almost nothing left in my childhood bedroom, except for the blue tile my mother had given me for the stones I collected at the beach*, I wanted to throw the book away. My stomach turned, and I remembered the moment in front of his blue door, the recognition of upheaval on the other side. *I could love this person*, I thought—and the thought pierced the bitter pit of my stomach like a germ, ferocious with possibility.

His father, he described, was of Irish descent, prone to bouts of melancholy and laughter. He was thirteen years older than his mother, obese, a connoisseur of exotic cuisines. A chipper man who sang folk songs in the mornings, drank whiskey in his coffee, and shouted at night, kicking in doors. Kicking the family dog, a border collie with a sweet howl. Hitting his wife.

Marlowe's mother left when he was a teenager, but she was attached to her only son: He visited her carpeted apartment in San

Jose. She bought ice cream sandwiches, read his horoscope for him. The swimming pool in the apartment complex; the browned leaves and bugs they trawled out of it. She spoke in her sleep, telling him stories of her parents, whom he never met. Their road trip to Southern California, the car spinning through canyons, a sapphire coast, all those ramshackle shops. Then weeks on end with his choleric father on the horse ranch. Wildfires raged; foresters wrapped redwoods in tinfoil. Blond hills at which he squinted; an ant crawling on his fingertip. And earthquakes that shook books from shelves. I imagined the young Marlowe, misunderstood, ambling through vivid streets, skipping under the shade of palm trees.

When I walked out of the library, I was febrile, as if carrying a wet and helpless animal in my hands. My breath quickened, and I walked into a café with a stupid grin on my face, ordered the cheapest thing on the menu. The ginger tea tasted awful, but I did not care. How important it seemed suddenly, that blue ceramic tile with the Dutch maids painted on it, his mother biting her nails on the linen sofa. As if it had happened in my own life, as if those details belonged to me. I stared out the window, where a girl in a red coat ran laughing through the snow.

# Six

BECAUSE HE NEVER texted me, I tried to engineer artificial run-ins with Marlowe: I went to every party, eyeliner caked on my lids, wearing my old, oversized suede jacket with black cowboy boots, tying my hair up in a strict ponytail. I was shivering and dreamy at bus stops, but I felt pretty and electrified by a new-found, startling determination. I emailed Melanie in London absentmindedly, telling her of the snowstorm or sending pictures of my breakfast, oatmeal steaming in a green bowl. I cleaned the apartment with a superficial sweep. With my feet on the coffee table, I shoveled salty crackers into my mouth and watched reruns of *Richterin Barbara Salesch*. The Nazis next door screamed, *Alles ist Scheiße*, and I saw a rat in the elevator. Then night came, and I went out. A small club by the water, constructed of wood and overlooking the glinting Spree. Everyone paraded single items of costume: bunny ears, tutus, glittering makeup. I leaned against a wall, sweat lining my trousers, a vegan hot dog cooling in my hands. I peeled the silver label off a beer. I didn't see him there.

———

I TRIED TO bring Anna and Romy with me, but Romy refused to come after the first two times. "All this partying is bad for my skin," she said. She sent me pictures of Japanese skin-care products in pink and lacquered tubes. "You should try it," she said, prompting me to wipe the foggy mirror with my fist and inspect my pores and skin after my showers. Two dark eyes stared back at me, freckles covering the bridge of my nose. If I had looked less Oriental, I would've even liked my face.

Anna, on the other hand, was down to party. In school we had always been together, our companionship fastened by our mutual exclusion—she was a weirdo, with piercings and an appetite for punk music, conspicuous among those girls with Ralph Lauren sweaters and leather pencil pouches and family trees that went back centuries. But without the confines of boarding school, our configuration was too loose. We didn't fit together anymore, here in the real world. When we entered a group of acquaintances who we knew could supply us with drugs, she immediately shoehorned herself into the middle of conversations and started ignoring me, all shiny in her white dress and Prada heels. As if I were the coat she needed to take off at the doors of the real event. I wasn't invited to whatever she created with her words then. She sat on people's laps and danced in the middle or made obvious jokes to the group, cackling through the room, her voice a desperate and pathetic tremor. When she looked at me, a coldness moved her face. And I was hurt—by her nonchalant will to ignore me. By how she rearranged the social order whenever she wanted. I was too proud to seek her attention during these outings, to even try to talk to her. I talked to other people, went dancing, but from the corner of my eye I was observing her with bitterness. She would land a very good joke and, high from her audience's attention, follow it immediately with weaker, more pat remarks; when people laughed less or ignored her, I was triumphant, relishing the rimy jab of humiliation I imagined shooting through her. I wondered if she noticed my refusal to laugh at her jokes, if she was hurt by a word I said, or if—and this would be the worst possibility—she was merely bored by my existence. Afterward, when we left the group and took the train back home, she was warm as ever to me. Rested her head on my shoulder, took my hand in hers.

"Are you mad at me?" I asked on the train.

"No, oh my God, is this about your birthday? I'm sorry I forgot it! I'm not mad at you." I was appalled by how happy it made me, her affection. But generally, I stood on the fringes, clutching my bottle of beer or listening to a random man with a wrinkly forehead tell me about how he missed his girlfriend while he put a hand on the nude part of my shoulder where the strap had slipped off.

I DIDN'T SEE him at the second party, which was at a pool hall with a heavy fog machine, where everyone was on PCP and a woman in a pink wig stripped onstage to the *Kill Bill* soundtrack; and I didn't see him at the third party or the fourth or the fifth; and after the seventh I had become so ravenous I wondered if I had imagined him, sniffing his coat in the back of my closet, touching the soft wool. I went to class and then to work, polished cutlery in the corner, and scrolled through the sanitized modern websites of those

British and American schools during my break. The silly logos, the vast and sprawling college greens, and South Asian students laughing into the camera. I thought of Sanjay and Sita Gupta, the siblings in our English textbooks, and how absurd their inclusion had seemed—hundreds of years of colonialism, and now this, a little face in a textbook.

THEN I DRAGGED Anna to the Bunker again, but she disappeared into the inky dark, dancing with a man with curly hair. It was the same old power dynamic. I wasn't worth her attention. I had no real friends here except for her, and to her I was a chore: I went dancing, uneasy in my body and agitated, ready to cry. I scanned the crowd for him or for Anna. I let a man with pronounced muscles swelling out of a camouflage shirt buy me two tequila shots and lead me to a part of the Bunker I hadn't seen before. A rectangular area between the dance floor and hallway, with only a few errant people passing through. Fitted with a table clad in leather and a frosty window that let in milky light. The stark stench of beer and something sweeter I couldn't identify. No one else was in the room; I heard only the chatter of people walking up and down the stairs. His voice was rough, and he had the kind of slimy aura my uncles had.

"Are you lost?" His face had the crackle of age, of an experience I had no understanding of.

"Yes." I smiled. He was in his forties or fifties. "I need help."

Deep bass reverberated through the walls, the floor: an ancient, evil pulse. I was about to cry, muddied by a kind of sadness over Anna. Yet driven by a perplexing determination to play it cool, to play along. Like I was a marionette in someone else's hands. My soul was elsewhere, in a different room, trying to find Anna.

"Come sit down," he said, and led me to the armchairs against the chalky window. I could feel the plastic leather through the nylon of my tights, cold against my thighs. He put a hand on my knee and asked me if I had been abandoned.

"Yes," I said. "My friend. Not abandoned, but she went dancing."

"Now, why would she leave a lovely girl like you alone?"

My nipples hardened despite myself. It was a script, we were adhering to an ancient script, like when I was working in the café and imagining the men touching me. Like the porn websites smoldering through cathode-ray tubes on the screen, the pixelated pink mouths of girls letting out a scream. The glow of the family computer against my retinas, a hard fact of youth. His hand wandered up my knee and between my thighs.

"Oh, you're wet already. Honey." I bit my lower lip. He rubbed hard against the nylon of my tights, my underwear. I realized that I was afraid of his sheer experience and age and his probable link to criminality, but not enough to ask him to stop. He kept rubbing and whispering into my ear, his other hand massaging my neck. The smell of smoke, the pop of his chewing gum. I could hear laughter in the hallway next to us, loud and tinny like in a public pool. I came and shivered against his hand, then got up and pulled my dress down.

"My turn." He grinned, and I saw the silver incisors in his smile, the tattoo of a diamond under his right eye, like a teardrop. I smiled and walked the other way, and it was only when I was out the door that he realized I was leaving. "Man," he shouted. "You have to be kidding! You pathetic little thing!" But he did not get up to come get me. I was elated and freaked out by this experience; I ran up the stairs into a different lounge, desperate to find Anna and tell her, *You won't believe what I just did.* I laughed loudly to no one, asked one of the bald men in a leather vest for a cigarette, too unsteady to light it myself. I was asking for a lighter when I found Elias, my friend from a long time ago, standing in the same area, rolling a cigarette.

"Nila?" His voice, though intimate, startled me. "Nila," Eli said again, this time more certain.

"Your voice is as annoying as ever," I said.

He came and hugged me. Said he missed me. He was high, but his affection rang genuine and warm, his arms around me a familiar weight. An augury to find him here, as if remembering profound and true things about myself. As if I were coming up for air. It had always been like this when I saw him. I met him during my boarding school years. Eli had gone to school with Felix and moved to Berlin for college about a year ago. Back then we often played chess in corners or begged the group to stretch the night a little further, propelled by the desperate and tacky need to blow our brains out. When we were lost, we were lost together. What connected us, I realized early, was that we didn't like to speak about our families and that we did not want to go home, our feet dirty on the asphalt, killing hours by the canal, waiting for sun to break, for even us to get tired. He was a few years older than me and had dark, glossy hair, an Albanian face. A handsome grin.

Next to him was Doreen: Marlowe's girlfriend. A flicker of recognition passed between us. I knew she had seen me around. She stared at me with a loopy smile, her facial muscles overactive due to the amphetamines, I assumed. Smeared mascara on her cheek. I resisted the urge to dab it off. Both excitement and jealousy moved around in me, like twin catalysts: If she was here, was Marlowe? She wore a long black blouse as a dress, gathered at the waist with a leather belt, and a white plastic camellia decorated her hair. An ode to old Chanel looks, though her breasts vulgarized any elegance.

"I'm Doreen," she said, and I suddenly felt overwhelmed by her physical presence: her clammy hand resting on my shoulder, the salt and sweat of her body odor mixed with a heavy perfume. I forgot my plan to look for Anna. Instead, I followed Eli into one of the bathrooms, where one of their friends was handing out ketamine.

He wore black swathes of cotton as clothes, ripped and decorated with oversized safety pins. I could see his brown nipples, the relief of his rib cage pressing against his skin when he breathed. He had a pleasant Roman face, like the busts you saw in museums or profiles on ancient coins. His name was Rico, and he stood with both feet on the toilet, tall and erect. The rest of us draped around him like petals on a flower, looking up. There were too many people crammed into the booth: Rico, Eli, Doreen, and two gaunt, long-haired girls named Laura and Tamara in matching electric-black lamé leggings. And me. Limbs hugged other limbs. Snippets of two French girls shouting to each other in an exaggerated fake English over the sound of their peeing, crisscrossed between the booths. The music from the dance floor traveled to us in slow motion, like sounds underwater. I felt someone's cold sweat against my arm, and I could tell, from a metallic and putrid odor lingering in the air, that one of the girls had their period. Doreen kept touching my hair and telling me how pretty I looked.

"She's Eli's old friend," Doreen said of me. "She's one of us." She began humming the chant from *Freaks*, and although I desperately wanted to hate her at that moment, a cold thrill possessed me. Embarrassingly, I wanted to be one of them. When I was thirteen or fourteen, I would close my eyes at night and imagine exactly this: not necessarily a bacterial bathroom stall in a dingy club, where it smelled like sex and fecal matter, but a group of artists who accepted me. It was different with Romy and Anna. I couldn't let them get too close, or they'd smell the rot of my childhood on me. And I'm sure it embarrassed them, the whiff of my poverty and family history.

After taking turns scraping the key into the baggie of yellowish powder, we went dancing and drinking, shouting at one another over the music. The party growing a repetitive life of its own. Then, sitting down in the lounge, Eli and I caught up on the gaps in our friendship: He had broken up with his mean girlfriend with the watery face; he was working as a coat-check guy at the Bunker, and yes, he could get guest-list passes; he'd dropped out of university; he never saw Felix anymore.

"He kind of bored me."

"So that means you can be my friend again?" Eli laughed and smoked a hand-rolled cigarette and crossed his legs.

I remembered Felix's family's sprawling house outside Münster, his seven siblings, the father's starched suit when he went to work in the morning, the mother's long dark hair and crowded teeth.

"An exotic face," his grandmother had said to me, perched at the head of the large dining table. "Very sixties sense of fashion." She loved speaking of me as if I were a foreign wine begging to be described. Everyone had their own room, and Felix's was in the attic, with massive windows overlooking the elm trees, and on summer nights, when you felt the cold stones of their yard under your feet, you could see bats zip through the sky, mice disheveling the grasses. The extended howl of a wolf in the distance, tearing at a smaller, squeaking thing. Their fridge was resplendent with glossy bell peppers and mandarins, and when something went bad, the Kurdish maid was quick to throw it out. Her eyes darted at me suspiciously when I lazed through the house in tennis socks and a sweater, as if she were about to find me out. The way I snuck out of boarding school to get to his place, the sleepy mouths of my classmates in summers. Eli kept on talking and I remembered it all—Felix's rough elbow skin, the scent of his detergent, hours I spent waiting on the saggy, striped sofa in a garage while the boys practiced their instruments for the local band.

THE REST OF the night was tinged with the blurry density of nostalgia. I observed Doreen, who spoke with ease about some book by Brecht during smoke breaks, charmingly playing with her hair, or danced with a great sense of rhythm, throwing her hands in the air and rotating her hips in a way too sensual for the techno music, her eyes closed, a faint smile on her lips. "I love everyone," she said, her voice slurred and sluggish. Rico hugged her from behind and kissed her on the cheek, and for an instant I wondered if Marlowe had broken up with her, if he was sullen and sad right now, nursing a broken heart over cans of beer in the dark mouth of his apartment. I wondered too what she and I would have been like as classmates, a few years ago: Would we have been friends?

I WAS SUBMERGED in the sea of people in the strobing lights. Flash of white teeth, sickly sweet odor of marijuana ballooning from all directions. The floor underneath my feet began to feel soft and giving, like cotton, or like the discounted waterbed my aunt had in the nineties. I stared at my hand, and a sea of information, though distant and cold, passed through my brain. Felix and Eli playing guitar and bass, my parents in their Soviet-style apartment, my father's murky eyes shining in the sun. Those were blips, swirling at the bottom of a sink. I was drained of a sense of self. The trip was unlike psychedelics like acid or mushrooms, whose revelations bloomed personal and acute. The current revelation seemed to happen to someone else, and I was merely a witness to the shift in perception. I was dizzy. I needed water and to stand somewhere solid, and Doreen helped me out of the crowd. I followed the little halo of her plastic camellia through the vibrating mass of warm bodies to a far corner with two stools, holding her soft, sweaty hand. We laughed for a while when we made it there, because it had seemed, at times, that we never would.

"We crossed the sea; we parted the sea." Doreen was laughing, but despite my level of inebriation, I only wanted to know one thing.

"Do you have a boyfriend?" I touched her hand, the silver rings cold on her fingers.

"Yes," she said. "But it's complicated." On her face a worried expression, or a warning, I couldn't tell. What I knew, however, was that I was not invited to ask further questions. We sat on the stools and watched people walking in and out of the area, kissing. A man pulling another by a dog collar, his fingers curled in the metal ring. Three gaunt girls in pixie cuts and with matching septum piercings walked by, smiling helplessly, as if they had been initiated into some new ritual. "They look like Uma Thurman in that Tarantino movie, no?" Doreen said. "They look like me as a teenager." I tried to imagine her with the artificial box hair dye from the drugstore. A septum ring instead of the nose ring she had now; a harsher haircut. She told me about her childhood: a house in a village outside Hamburg; her mother's obsession with wolves and coyotes; her older sister, with whom she felt in competition. Her father was an electrician. It was the pseudo-profound talk you yearn for when high. After dancing for hours, dripping with sweat, you suddenly need to analyze, discuss, dump the memories rising to the surface of your mind: the colors of your childhood swing; who hurt you when you were in middle school; garden hyacinths. Everything glows with new importance, your teeth rickety and overactive. Eventually she began speaking of Marlowe. "My boyfriend sometimes punishes me with silence. It's one of those periods."

I weighed my responses, tried out different versions in my mind. At last, I asked her, "Why?"

"It's not about me. It's about him. He is unhappy with his life." She shrugged and looked away, slightly annoyed. I had asked the wrong question. "I love him," she said, smoothing out a crease in her blouse. "But I feel alone with him."

"You deserve someone better," I said, meaning it: Excitement and guilt mixed in me, and I sensed a perverse longing to right her wrongs. It wasn't totally unlike sympathy. We hugged and, in that moment, because of the ecstasy and the horse tranquilizer and the perfect little camellia in her hair, because of the hi-hat and the disco sample mixed into the techno track, and because Anna had left me, I loved her.

MY PHONE HAD died, but I recognized an odd twitch, like I should be looking for Anna. Once we had a plan to meet again downstairs: It was too late now. I told myself that if she really wanted to find me, she would. Eli invited me to Rico's house, and I joined the group, walking a few blocks through the icy sheet of day, seeing everyone's faces in the morning light. My heart jerked. As always, I felt small and scared when I saw the jumble of taxis out front, afraid to be seen by my uncle or a friend of my father's, but Doreen hooked her arm right through mine, and suddenly I hoped, the way children do with unabashed wishful thinking, that maybe Marlowe would meet us there. Though I couldn't say his name without arousing suspicion now, I listened attentively whenever he was mentioned. The light was perverse in its brightness, almost clinical. Little droplets of snow fell from the sky onto our hair.

RICO LIVED IN a shared apartment with thin walls, so the only room we could hang out in was the big kitchen. We lit taper candles dripping onto empty wine bottles and drank hot toddies, snorting lines and talking about nothing. Rico shut the blinds and sat down at the far end of the table, Doreen to the left of him, Tamara on the right. Eli and I were splayed on a hard red sofa pushed against a wall with peeling black-and-white art deco wallpaper. For a while we played tarot, Tamara reading Rico's fortune. For me she pulled the Tower, a dark card on which you saw a burning building.

"This is bad, right?" I asked her.

"It's basically 9/11," Eli said, making fun of me.

"No," Tamara said, her voice hoarse from all the smoking. "It means you're going through a transformation." The conversation petered out, but I couldn't stop feeling the weight of the card and noticing the day's serrulate edges: The magic of the prior night ran like sand through our hands. We couldn't contain it, but it was Sunday afternoon, and we were scared of being inside our own heads. Tamara cuddled me, touched my hand. At 7:00 P.M., Rico put a frozen pizza into the oven. Then he turned off the music and turned on the small tube TV on the counter, and instead of music or an ironic procedural, he put on the evening news, as if to signal to us idiots that reality still existed: A woman in a starched gray suit was talking about a shooting in Potsdam, the glaciers were still melting, and the Black president of the United States was shaking someone's hand and smiling. The news in the background agitated me, like the noise of an unpleasant memory. This habit of Rico's, I later learned, was compulsive and necessary for him. It was the cue for everyone to leave the house right away and for him to remember that he too had to leave this world and reenter society tomorrow, taking off his eccentric black swathes of clothing, swapping them for a button-up shirt and managing insurance sales.

"I'm surprisingly good at it," he said, snorting a last line and wiping his mouth. "I'm fucking smart."

———

OUTSIDE, TAMARA INVITED the rest of us to grab food together. The pizza place had a ramshackle interior, plastic furniture and screeching yellow signage for everything. The men working there wore hats like cartoon bakers and earnest expressions on their dark faces that elicited in me a vague desire to die. The smell of fried oil and baked bread hung thick in the air. Doreen wouldn't stop snickering and asked us several times if we wanted to drink more booze. In the end, we shared two pizzas and a few lemon beers, but Doreen had her own. We sat facing the windows. Bars and other restaurants lined the street with leafless trees. It had stopped snowing, but the light remained the same. Tamara was curious about where Eli and I knew each other from.

"It's too complicated," I said, swatting a fly from my face. Why were there flies in the winter?

"It's not all that complicated," Eli said. "Nila dated my friend Felix. And we hung out a lot when we were teens."

"Technically, you are still teens." Tamara smiled. Even with pizza grease lining the corners of her lips, she looked elegant.

"I'm twenty-five," Eli said. He told them he had dropped out of his architecture classes at Potsdam and was taking a break from college, although he still read a lot on city-mapping. I was waiting for Doreen to say that Marlowe was writing a book on architecture, but all night she had refused to mention his name, and when one of the others did, she made a mean remark about him.

"Even if I end up at a good firm, I will never be happy, because I will always have to betray what I truly believe in. And what I believe in is being anti-gentrification. Sounds corny, but it's true. The developers are the essence of gentrification."

"You can't really do anything against it, can you," Tamara said, with a curious grin. "People will have to move eventually."

His face tensed up. Doreen, who had been silent this entire time, started speaking now. She was laughing. "That's all you have to say? There's nothing we can do against it? That's basically the attitude that this country is so well-known for."

"We're talking about buildings, not killing people."

Doreen put down her slice of pizza and licked her lips, then put a palm on the table. "See? It's not semantics. It's people's lives. We aren't talking about buildings; we are talking about housing inequality, gentrification, and pushing people out. We are talking about the ghettoization of certain districts. It's not that different."

"Gropiusstadt is not a ghetto. . . ." Tamara was laughing now. "Can you hear yourself speak?" It hurt me to hear the mention of Gropiusstadt, but nobody noticed.

"Fascism has many faces," Doreen said. "It's in all of us. Just look into a mirror."

"The pizza is kind of amazing," I said. "Don't you think?" They all stared at me, unfazed by my attempt to change the subject. I found it fascinating that people our age and with our educational level would openly speak for gentrification. But then again, I would've probably considered the same thing if I were Tamara, if I had a Prenzlauer Berg apartment with floor-to-ceiling windows and had pushed a Vietnamese family out for it. But still, I thought, I would have never said it out loud.

"Anyway," Eli said. He and Doreen looked at each other for what seemed like forever. When I asked Tamara what she was doing for work, she said she was modeling or doing art or both but also "kind of not doing anything" at the moment, which meant that she subsisted on unemployment benefits or generational wealth. She was enrolled in school, but I suspected that she did what I did: used her matriculation to get the perks. She hadn't grown up in Berlin but in a place outside Potsdam, from a town with much more poverty. That made her comment more puzzling to me. Everyone who had grown up poor, I assumed, was against gentrification. It was the first real meal I'd had in two days, and a tiredness crashed over me like a truck.

ON THE WAY home, Eli and I took the same train, enveloped by the neon ugliness of the U1, and shared his earphones. Before he plugged them into the MP3 player, he took an anxiety-inducing eternity to untangle them. I stared at his cleanly cut fingernails, and my chipped red nail polish embarrassed me. He played a song by Thom Yorke and then one by Tom Waits.

"Elias." Saying his full name seemed appropriate. "You really love the Toms."

He smiled and fumbled with his phone. The next song he put on was a track by Radiohead. All those years ago, when we were at a party, we had gone out to smoke a skinny joint, and we stared at the sky. By the time we returned, the DJ was playing this song. Eli saw me smiling. I looked away and drifted through the old and familiar lake, our legs and shoulders touching. The train jolted, and for a moment he gripped my hand in his, a cold boat.

He got off at Kottbusser Tor. *Bye*, I waved, confused and nervous as a grass stalk in the rain. Eli was still on the platform in his black jacket, engaging his phone, as the train moved infinitely farther away from him. I looked at my hand. The train was above-ground now, new snow falling against the glass panes. When I closed my eyes, I briefly remembered the man in the club, the light refracting from the silver gleam of his incisors. And when I opened my eyes, I saw what I still see now when I remember those years: the snowy cityscape, my district, the streetlamps casting the buildings in a yellowish light.

# Seven

To an outsider, it might look like I come from a family of hitters. But it was our love language. Sometimes the only way we touched. My parents and my uncles and aunts didn't even roll up their sleeves. They liked to slap my cousins and me reflexively, with hands wet from dishwashing or greasy with face cream, and in return we broke plates and screamed. Then brushed our hair into strict braids, and put on our ragged clothes, and went to school, and smiled and got angry with one another, or with ourselves, pinching our skin under the table or skipping meals until that hollow darkness of hunger felt like a warm embrace. Our parents did to us what their parents had done to them, and their parents to them, ad infinitum. A satiny scar divided half of my father's arm. His brother, my uncle Rashid, had thrown him through a glass door in Afghanistan.

"We were children," my father said. "It was normal for us."

Violence stunted such neighborhoods with triviality. Chairs hurled from one room into the other, toddlers harangued as if they were adults: *Why would you spill the milk on the floor, are you an idiot?* In Kreuzberg, a Serbian man dropped his decapitated girl-friend's head out the window. "Her voice annoyed me," he said on TV as he was handcuffed. The Kurdish girl next door lurched through hallways with a black eye, fixing her sunglasses. A Lithu-anian neighbor hit her child repeatedly with her handbag, for all of us to see. My cousin Nadia pulled up her skirt and presented her thigh: Her mother had kicked her until a blue and purple and yel-low bouquet bruised her skin.

In contrast, my parents were soft. European, almost. They didn't leave marks. And never hit each other, not that I know of. Of course, the belt was something my father threatened me with, as in *My parents did that to me* or *I should get the belt out and hit some sense into you*, but I never made contact with that belt. I was afraid of him, and so I began to hate him, the way children are wont to do. But my father slapped me only when I misbehaved in an espe-cially ferocious way, and I can count the times on one hand. Once because I offended his father by dyeing my hair blue. Once the summer I stopped eating and cried in front of a Mars bar. And then that other time when he almost suffocated me to death because I wanted to wear a bikini.

More frequently, our mothers were the bedfellows of evil: They flagellated themselves with shawls in mosque, eager for the pain to prove their love for God. And even my rich aunt Sabrina, the thin and perfect bird, hurled belts and books and plates across the room, aiming at her husband in a hot, brilliant fury.

There were rules: I had to be home on time, do my homework, and be polite to my elders. Otherwise, my mother twisted the skin on my arms, or slapped me across the face, or screamed so loud I started kicking the furniture or hit my head against the wall until she stopped. My mother's viciousness, I knew, derived from her unsatisfied need for regularity, the convivial light of afternoon tea and dinner parties. And that peculiar ambition she snuffed out every evening like a candle, but which returned in the mornings, burning in her center.

She was openly humiliated that parent-teacher conferences could be held only in my presence. Her eyes turned a lighter color, her pupils small as needle heads. She stood with a straight carriage in the hallway, and when no one else was there, she looked not at me but at the wall behind me—colorful with science projects and children's drawings—and gave me a slap on my face, trivial and polite, as if she were handing me a plate of food. I'd withdraw within myself, cognizant that I had wounded her. But after a while it morphed into a game we played: If I was patient enough, if I didn't complain or cry, if I didn't acknowledge that she'd hurt me, then she'd return. Whispering apologies in the dark of my childhood bedroom: *sorry, sorry, sorry.* I ignored her, smiling into my pillow. But it meant I won the game.

"I love no one more than I love you," she said. And I loved no one more than her. She turned on the radio in the mornings, dancing when rock songs filled the kitchen with bygone delight. Recited poetry in an old, formal Persian—lines that I didn't understand but whose cadences imprinted themselves onto my brain—and took me to local libraries, where I was allowed to read as much as I wanted, the weight of the laminated library card like a luxurious treasure in my hand, my own name written in blue ink underneath: *Nilab Haddadi.* I loved the books on animal kingdoms, the *Sailor Moon* mangas. I was arrested by how mature the Sailor Senshis looked in comparison to those on the animated series I watched on TV—these girls were uncensored, long-legged, and often nude. Looking at their parted mouths, the sleepy eyes—I felt an elemental thrill contract between my legs, and I memorized the pictures for later, when I would rub myself against my teddy bear.

"Don't do that," my mother once reprimanded me when she caught me with the green bear between my legs. "That's disgusting. Good girls don't do such things." And I was ashamed, the way children are when caught—but also titillated. Aware that now I had a secret. That something had come between my mother and me, something that was only mine and that she, when she turned into that other woman who slapped me, could not reach.

When my mother took me to the library, she spent the time at the desk, her head bowed over a yellow legal pad.

"I'm writing letters," she said, though she never revealed the addressee of those Persian letters inscrutable to me. Only after her death did I realize those were never sent to anyone. She kept the notepads with three photographs of her own mother in an old shoebox, fastened by a pink ribbon. The orange sale sticker scratched off. Stashed under her clothes, which for a few years after her death retained her powdery scent. Sometimes I'd go and open the box, letting my finger wander over the words—they were diary entries, documenting her new and convoluted life, the ink as curled and black as my mother's hair.

On the way home, she stopped in front of the window of a closed antiques shop, mesmerized by the frosty lamp, the oblong golden mirror. The lamp irradiated my mother's face like those Orthodox icons hanging in Russian people's apartments. Her periwinkle coat, that round face with the full lips. Even with the hollows under her eyes, she was beautiful, in a haunted way that was close to death, and it frightened me. She wasn't looking at herself—she was looking at the lamp, or something behind that lamp, something in the future or the past, I couldn't tell. I knew I was not allowed to disturb her dream, or she'd get angry. So I stood at an angle where I couldn't see myself, just my mother's apparition, this woman with a secret inner life, adrift in our strange city. Later, when I took pictures of her, or of other people, I believe I was trying to create a carbon copy of this scene: a woman with an unknowable loss marking her eyes.

CULTURE FUND, SHE called the money for my extracurricular education, stacking a careful curl of bills amid her nylons in a drawer. I shared my music class with three other girls. And because we didn't have the money for a piano at home, I practiced at the piano of the spinster next door, Frau Storz, the German lady who had lived in our building since the seventies. She owned dark-wood furniture, and seven ferrets crawled around her floors.

"It's actually good to hit children," Frau Storz said when people from the Jugendamt beleaguered the Lithuanians' door for the third time that month. "The only form of discipline."

She sizzled with historical facts, snapshots about the city being rebuilt after the Second World War. Checkpoint Charlie, Berlin's heart cut into four. Per Frau Storz, you could diagnose an evil heart because it made the carrier's face resemble a "root vegetable." She brought out sweet potatoes and turnips to demonstrate her theory. Told us about her father hiding people on his farm, her sister sent to a camp for marrying a Polish Jew, and both my mother and Frau Storz started sobbing uncontrollably. I thought of Anne Frank's diary, the most striking book I had read in childhood. The Jewish Museum, colossus of sorrow in the soul of our city. Or the Holocaust memorial that tourists liked to pose in front of, holding Starbucks cups like idiots, and whose sight sent such an icy terror down my spine I could barely speak.

WHEN I WAS nine, my mother fell pregnant again, and Frau Storz brought out a yellow ceramic plate with a giant coffee cake that tasted of mold. Dimples appeared under my mother's eyes when she laughed, in a voice so real and rough she seldom used it at home. While my fingers wandered over the piano, I stole glances at her—the deep cherry red of her lipstick she used as blush, the tortoiseshell clip that she kept in her hair, the invisible fetus twitching in her, small as an eyelash of God.

One day, when it was spring and the air was full of pollen, I misbehaved solely because I could. I don't know why; children, like artists, just follow impulses and inspiration. So instead of walking home right after school, my friend Sasha and I sat under a bridge and looked at the canal. I knew I would get hit later, but I didn't care; I was so happy about my future brother and enticed by the water and insects of April.

When I came home, the apartment was dark, and a lurid odor lingered. The windows were thrown open, and two flies had made it inside, buzzing around the ceiling fans. I couldn't find my mother. The kitchen, which usually roared with clutter and mess, was deserted. Radio frequencies hovered in the air, some news anchor's soothing lull. I turned off the pot of beans simmering on the stove.

I looked for her in the bedroom, anticipating one of her crying fits again. But she wasn't in the bedroom either. I found her, delirious, in the pink-tiled bathroom, her body radiating heat. Hair matted on her forehead. Brought her water, towels. Stroked the limp, hot belly in which a creature was swimming, a creature that was my brother. I whispered prayers to her, and my mother begged me not to call an ambulance. Hours passed. She gagged, leaning against the bathtub with her legs splayed wide. She was bleeding out of the crotch in her pants, the towel twirled like an expressionist scarlet painting. She assured me that it was fine, that she just felt weak. *I'm okay,* she chanted, *I'm okay.* Her eyes were blank but still secretive, as if inscribed with a dark intelligence, and with some horror, I realized that I loved looking at her like that, as much as I loved looking at her in the shop mirror.

When my father came home, he kicked off his shoes and stared at us. Under the garish hallway light, he looked giant, sad. His face contorted with exhaustion and disgust. He hesitated but then tumbled into the living room to lie down. Rage flared—for myself, for my deranged impulse to think of my mother's beauty even now, and for my father, and his carelessness, which was my carelessness. Shouting, I ran after him.

"Let him sleep." My mother's voice was weak, a useless protest.

"She needs to go to the hospital," I said, shaking my father awake. My father, grunting, accepted. Blood trickled between my mother's slippers on the elevator floor. The lamp buzzed. We drove through a long, meaningless night. He laid towels out on the back seat, *to save the taxicab.* My mother's eyes fell shut. Her hand in mine a block of ice. She was drenched in sweat, but the car smelled of salt and pennies, an astringent sweetness mixed with leather. My father turned on the radio, and Dolly Parton's high-pitched voice warbled about jealousy.

"I love this song," my mother said when her eyes fluttered open.

She lost the baby that morning. At least she survived, everyone said. Upon her return after three weeks in the hospital, my mother's hair was curlier, the puffiness under her eyes lending her a youthful devastation. She looked happier than before, rosier.

"You wanted to die," I accused her, in retaliation for everything: forcing me to serve tea to my uncles or finishing my rice. "You wanted to leave me here alone."

"I did not want to die." My mother smiled. "I was sick, and you saved me, and now I am alive."

I pouted and played with my hair, convinced that a terrible darkness dwelt in my mother. I still yearned for her, but whenever she tried to be kind to me, I flinched. I had grown a protective, repellent membrane. In the following months, she spent hours in front of the television, hypnotized by the blue light of nature documentaries. Collected brochures about spirituality, books on philosophy and ethics, which she never read, books she stuffed under the sofa and bed when the shelves were full. For when? For when she'd learn the language, finally. She forgot to bring me to music lessons, and most of the time she refused to let me out. Dishes piled up in the living room, and a distinct mold grew in the corners of the bathroom, where for hours she lay in the tub. She didn't slap or pinch me, and we only touched when she called for me to help her scrub her back.

———

THEN, TWO YEARS later, at a Christmas market, I asked for a chocolate-covered strawberry, and there it was again, that old reflex: Her eyes glimmered, her smile contorted to a grimace, and I knew to offer my cheek to receive a slap.

"Don't hit your child. You're in Germany now," the lady behind the counter said. My mother regarded her with spite. *It was a slap*, I thought. *My mother didn't* hit *me*.

"This is my child, none of your ugly strawberry business." I stood there, debilitated in my loyalties, baffled by that woman with her inflamed, bulbous nose and sunken cheeks. She must've had a mean heart: Her face really did look like a root vegetable. Not at all like my beautiful mother.

"Do you need help?" the woman asked me with urgency. She must've seen in me what I saw in the deformed dog that the neo-Nazis kept, or the beggar with the amputated legs who carried a bottle of vodka around—I could barely look at them, unwilling to see what they reflected about me but suspecting that their souls were inscribed with some secret, ontological truth about mine. She pitied me, I understood, and in turn I felt degraded. I ran toward my mother with an aberrant joy.

"Good," my mother said, and winked. "Now let's find a different shop so we can get you strawberries."

# Eight

THE SKY TURNED a garish blue, and the entire city was busy shoveling snow and salting the streets. My nose hair froze on my way to work. I served twenty-nine beers and three dirty martinis, dropped a plate as I daydreamed of Marlowe, and my boss called me *the clumsiest waitress in all of Berlin*. Afterward, I met Eli at the Bunker. They had given me a guest-list pass, so I didn't even need to stand in line. "Alone tonight?" the Cyclops asked as I entered from the right side. "Yes," I said.

I practically ran upstairs to the lounge. It had been three weeks since I'd gone home with Marlowe, and like a dog, I intuited his presence. He was cocooned by a group of friends, but his posture changed momentarily when our eyes met. He waved at me as if I were an unwelcome acquaintance. I played cool, like it was all a game. I saw Doreen too and briefly considered my moral obligations to her, but there was too much to process: that tiny nasal bone, the glint of her teeth when she smiled. She wiped the back of her hand on Marlowe's upper arm, then turned toward me.

I didn't think I would still be attracted to him, now that I had hung out with Doreen several times, now that I knew her childhood nightmares and the name of her sister. She was happy to see me, she said. Her blond bob was sleekly combed to the side, revealing a shiny forehead with one dried-out pimple, caked over with powder. She wore dangling earrings and a low-cut dress, a cigarette tucked behind her ear; another in her hand, lit, the filter soggy and smeared with red lipstick.

"Hi," Marlowe said, but barely even smiled. My insides turned to ice. I made small talk with Eli and the others, then observed Marlowe with fastidiousness: The people around him formed an audience. He lapped up the devotion, made several jokes. I remembered Anna, the way she demanded people's attention, how she liked to touch everyone. I hadn't seen her since that night, and when she texted me that I was a bad friend, I didn't respond. He hugged men with dark circles under their eyes, high-fived leather queens. Told a tall woman with pink hair to take it slow today, and she turned around, chuckling, taking his face in her hands and kissing him on his cheek. We were caught in his orbit, like flies in the viscous silk of a spider. Marlowe quietly delivered a punch line, and everyone's bodies reacted, with a few seconds' delay, as if he were the conductor, orchestrating their movements. His effect on Doreen too was thick and urgent. She couldn't focus, giggling more than usual, pulling at his sleeve. I pictured them together in bed under cold lights. Her mouth wide and open for him, hair slicked with sweat. She was so petite next to him, much shorter than I was, and the idea titillated me.

Tamara and I vanished into a toilet booth, and we dipped MDMA out of a purple baggie. The pure crystals still a novelty back then, turning me mellow and elastic, as if I were an animal with a slobbering tongue. Huddled on some seats, with a cold layer of sweat on my face, we spoke about love. Rico joined and quizzed me about Nietzsche, and I felt elated by the challenge, this group of friends who took David Foster Wallace too seriously and deodorant not seriously enough. I chewed on gum; spat it out again. Tamara had a twitching eyelid and always demanded to dance. In later months I'd lose touch with her, and she'd turn into what one imagined an amphetamine junkie to be like—drawing window blinds, looking over her shoulder. Intent on discussing MK-Ultra and the reptilian brains of politicians. But right now she was still relatively sane and pretty.

ON THE DANCE floor, we staggered and twisted around one another. The tunes were lighter and overlain with disco tracks, Diana Ross trilling about a lost love, singing, *Love taught me who was the boss,* heads bouncing up and down. People threw their arms in the air, mouthing the lyrics, pointing at each other with their beers and cigarettes. The window blinds opened and closed to the rhythm, sunrise briefly flooding the scene. Sticky and aroused, I stumbled to the bar, asking for a glass of water. And there he was again: Marlowe smiling deviously at me in the silver light. As we hugged, he moved his hand up my back, brushing through my hair. He touched my neck. I had been right to wait this long.

"Nila," he said. "I missed you."

"You missed me," I repeated, laughing, aware of Doreen sitting right next to him on one of the yellow chairs, her fingers drumming against her thigh, her blue eyes darting from him to me. She smiled innocently. "Where were you all this time?" I asked. He clasped the bracelet around my wrist. I was shaking.

"I was working," he shouted over the music. "In Amsterdam. The architecture firm I'm writing the book with is going to be at the Venice Biennale next year."

"You're writing the book with a firm?"

"Yes, I'm covering their project. Shadowing them, helping them. There will be pictures, I guess." He lit two cigarettes and handed one to me, pressing down my bottom lip with his thumb. Ash fell onto my dress.

"What is the project about?"

"Social housing for the immigrant communities in Berlin, but with exciting lines, different shapes." He was speaking close to my ear, whispering more than shouting, and kept touching the part of my collar where the ash was, as if to rub off the stain. I was laughing loudly for no reason. He left his hand on my shoulder, and with the other one he presented an ecstasy pill. "Want to share this?" I was aware of Doreen watching us and the fact that my neurons were already overwhelmed with MDMA, but I was drunk on the idea that she might be jealous.

"Yes." I bit off a quarter of the blue pill—another Nike—and took a sip of his drink. Doreen shook herself abruptly and said she was going dancing, but something furtive passed from her eyes to his. Then she was bobbing away from us, past the drag queen blowing us an air kiss with red puckered lips. The track went like, *sunshine, sunshine, sunshine,* and her blond head merged with the crowd. Doreen didn't look back.

We talked about things I barely recall—the Bunker's architecture, the DJ who played an hour ago, whom Marlowe once saw perform at a festival.

"Sorry I didn't text," he sighed eventually.

"It's okay," I lied. We smiled at each other briefly. I felt a thin layer of sweat on my upper lip. My scalp burned. I craved to chew on wet soil, or suck someone's dick, or maybe dance too. Then I sensed his finger on my arm, drawing slow waves. And there it was again, that feeling of being nude and vulnerable and very cold. He grabbed my hand and pulled me into the hallway, into the cubicle of a bathroom. *It's happening,* I thought, my body a throbbing cell.

"YOU NEED TO be patient," Marlowe announced once we collapsed through his apartment door, and I nodded. Nothing happened in the bathroom, except for a hot finger he inserted through my tights.

"I want to show you something—is that okay?" He leapt up the white-painted ladder to his bedroom, and I followed. He turned on a small lamp, and I felt very high. The battered copy of Proust was still on his nightstand. The cap of the water jug was opened, and I could see the image clearly: Marlowe rupturing out of sleep to take a drink of water. He pulled out a big book from his closet.

"You remind me of her." He showed me a painting of a woman in an old Egon Schiele book. "That first day, you evoked the image. When I first saw you." The woman was painted in craggy, modernist lines, lying on a bed, wearing black stockings. Then he handed me the picture of myself he took that Sunday, in my tights, sitting on his bed. In a different pose, but I could see the similarity.

That unruly hair. Looking at the photograph aroused a staggering sensation in me, like the girl in the picture wasn't me at all.

"What are you, Robert Mapplethorpe? This is an amazing picture."

"Very funny," he said.

"I mean it. It's a very good picture." He showed me the photos I had taken, which were objectively worse, unfocused. Only one of them—the second one, in which he looks solemnly to the side—had turned out all right. On that photograph, I noticed a small picture of a butterfly above his desk. Embarrassed by the quality, I said nothing.

"You're going to get there. An SLR is a piece of technology. You need to learn it."

"I know," I said defensively. "I just don't know how to work with that $f/1.8$ lens." I thumbed through the book's pages. Bones protruding through gaunt women, men with convulsed facial expressions, skeletons everywhere.

"Schiele was a narcissist." He lit a cigarette. I stood up straighter and opened my mouth slightly, like I had practiced in the mirror. He ran his thumb over my lip, then along my neck and collarbone.

"Maybe I'm a narcissist," I said. "It's flattering to be compared to a painting." He laughed, but then we heard the ringing. Doreen's name blinking on his phone screen. I looked away, as if that would dissolve the situation.

"You can pick up."

"I don't want to." He turned off the phone, then threw it onto the mattress. "That was awkward."

"I don't care. I am aware what we're doing is secret."

He laughed and said, "You know it's complicated. We're not really in a relationship." I was aware that he expected me to ask another question, that he was waiting to be interrogated. But Doreen's spectral presence intimidated me into reticence. We sat down on the mattress, a few feet apart. I felt disappointed. Perhaps it wouldn't happen after all; perhaps he thought of me as some Jungian psychotherapist, some aunt or sister he could talk with. He played with his hands, massaging one with the other.

"Should I go?" I asked.

He looked at me with an amused expression. "You're always quite quick to leave, aren't you?"

"Well, I just get the feeling you don't want me around." I didn't really want to leave, of course. I wanted him to tell me to stay, which he didn't.

WE SNORTED SPEED to stunt the ecstasy, drank some wine to stunt the silence, then collapsed side by side on his couch and smoked about a thousand cigarettes. Snow drummed against the window. Iciness crept in, due to that bad prewar insulation. Freezing, I inched closer to him, but I was still not touching him. For a while we talked about books and movies. Dostoevsky was his favorite author, he said, and he loved the films of Akira Kurosawa the best. In addition to my stubborn attraction, I began to feel truly comfortable around him.

"Can I ask you something?" I said after a while.

"Sure."

"What did it feel like? To have completed a book."

He deposited his cigarette in the ashtray. "If I'm honest, it feels like it isn't mine anymore. Sometimes I hate it. It's almost hard to feel proud of it, because I don't really feel connected to the person I was when I wrote it."

"What do you mean?"

"I was so young then. I had that one job in life, and afterward a great silence set in. This silence was both frightening and relieving. Like I was freed from a contract with some higher power."

"A Faustian deal."

"Well, if you consider a fulfilled life the bargain at the end of that deal, perhaps yes."

"You think you are happier now?"

He looked up, as if to consult the ceiling. "I don't know."

I was thinking of how vulnerable I felt after reading his book. "But isn't making art more fulfilling than not making it?"

"Most artists, let me tell you, are bad at living. They're bad people, frankly: bad husbands, bad friends. Making art takes sacrifice. It's not about you. You're an apprentice to the craft, to something bigger than you. You are secondary. Magic happens, the gods speak to you. If you're lucky, language moves through you like something uttered from the dead, it's true. But to remain open to those impulses, you must hover at a constant remove from real life, at a remove from the people around you, and I just don't want that anymore."

I remembered my father telling me that you couldn't trust anyone except for books, that books couldn't leave you. "But people hurt you."

"Art can hurt you too," he said.

"Really? Like, making art? Or experiencing a work of art?"

"Having a gift can be a burden, naturally. But I mean experiencing art can injure you: Art can unbolt your soul and reshape the fundamentals of your life."

I told him a story I had heard in school: The mother of one of the girls had been given Tolstoy's *Anna Karenina* by a young co-worker, and she read it twice in a row. Entranced by the tragedy and destiny of the characters, she left her children and husband for her colleague. An addiction to morphine, a rental somewhere in Spain, a hurried look in her eyes.

"It happens more than you think," he said. "Real art inspires an effect of utmost violence. Velásquez, Mozart, Brecht . . . hell, even Salinger killed John Lennon. I wish my book could do that, change someone's life."

"I'm sorry your book has not killed a Beatle yet." Something in me strained from telling him how much it had moved me.

He laughed. "I was seventeen when I took ecstasy for the first time, some overdosed pink pill. I suffered a psychotic break, couldn't even breathe. Afterward, I had constant panic attacks. The colors in the sky changed, like there was a thin layer of graph paper laid over everything. I was so afraid of going out, or even tying my shoes. For years I was afraid. Then, one day, I listened to this song." He got up to rummage in his record bins. He hooked the needle onto vinyl and sat back down as techno bloomed from the speakers. Its harshness astonished me. "Nothing special, just this track by Jeff Mills. My fear disappeared, all at once, as if I had found the right frequency to survive. And I could write again and finally wrote the book. . . . I needed to face whatever had happened to me. I was healed, you know, but as things go, something had been taken from me."

"Something had been taken?"

"For a long time, I thought I was monstrous." He paused to light another cigarette. "Like I was incapable of true feeling, of love."

I started laughing at this, but he didn't chime in. When I looked at him, I understood he was serious.

"I'm just kidding." He smiled, widening his eyes. "I'm not a monster." I stared at a scar on his cheek and was grateful when he changed the music to something more melodic. "But here's a story. I've always been horrible at breakups. I left the love of my life on a beach in California and I . . . I walked off. Adrienne. It was a normal Sunday afternoon and we had just gone on a hike, and we sat there picnicking on the sand, and it was something about the color of this shingled roof—a buttery yellow—and the texture of her hair, and I could taste the salt in the air, and it reminded me of my mother, and I said, 'I'll be right back.' I took the car and drove off. Two weeks later I left for Europe."

So that was Adrienne: the person the book was dedicated to. When I asked him if they were still in touch, he said that she had to hitchhike back home and wouldn't speak to him.

"That's what I mean when I say artists are bad people," he said. "All I cared about was myself."

"Oh," I said.

"Of course I think about her, but there's never been a response, even after I sent her the book. She's married now and lives somewhere in L.A., doing media work. Her husband works at a bank, I think. It's not like I don't want that. Marriage and a house. But I don't think it's meant for someone like me." He showed me his sleeve of tattoos—fish and sparrows on one arm and, on the other, the snake cradling a golden egg—and said he got the tattoos so he would never betray himself and work at a bank. We laughed, clenching our jaws. *I don't want that either,* I thought, dumb in my juvenile brain and giddy with dreams of wilderness. "And now look at me—am I not lying next to a nineteen-year-old? Doesn't that make me immoral?"

I smiled at *nineteen.* He remembered my birthday. "It's not my fault I'm so awfully interesting."

"And there's another girl waiting somewhere in this city. I am awful." The words stung. I didn't want to talk about Doreen. He turned around to face me. "But it's true, you are the most interesting person I have met in a long time."

I started laughing in a mocking way.

"Now you know what you're getting yourself into." He kissed me with unexpected force. I pulled away, unable to reconcile him with the man who had touched me through my tights in the bathroom just an hour earlier. I was transmuted, suddenly still and very shy despite the earlier bravery. It was my stiffness that made him bold. He took off my dress and unrolled my tights, commenting on my cheap lace underwear, which everyone until then had ignored, kissing my skin very quickly and proceeding to enter me before I was even wet. He reiterated that it would be okay, and from the way his eyes darkened, I realized that he relished it, the idea of our age difference and my relative lack of experience, and so I played along, saying, yes, yes, when he asked if it hurt. He fucked me right there, pressed against the cold leather of the couch, and all the tension of the prior weeks dissolved within the first few minutes. *Finally,* I thought. *Thank God,* I thought. He pulled my hair, and I came within minutes, but he took a while and made me follow him upstairs, where he took another picture of me: naked, in the exact spot where he'd photographed me on the first night. When he wiped my face with a white towel afterward, my eyelashes sticky, his face was vacant.

"Sorry," he muttered. I didn't know what he was apologizing for; I thought this had been consensual. I felt terribly embarrassed and sore. Did I even know how to do anything? Something frail between us had been divided, and he too looked less confident, despite his large stature. "God, what are you doing to me? You confuse me. I wanted to protect you."

"I don't want to be protected," I sneered.

"Yes, I can see that; that's the confusing part."

For a while we just lay there on his mattress, dozing, and I thought I could feel the city's loneliness—the exhaust fumes and mulled wine and dirty snow—moving in my chest.

"Do you do this often?" I asked after we finished a bottle of red wine. "Luring girls into your house?" Already there pulsed a familiarity between us, a desire to hurt the other.

He rolled a cigarette and smoked half of it before he responded. "It's not too bad, is it?"

"I never said it was."

"I just can't leave her yet."

"I don't care," I said.

"You know that I'm ruining you, right? Even if I am trying not to."

"You're not ruining me."

"Yes, I am." He was laughing, but there was earnestness on his face, and then he entered me again, half-hard. This time my mind was elsewhere—his smell and the freckles on his shoulder couldn't distract me—and I was suddenly afraid. "Yes," he whispered, "that's good, that's very good." I stared at the ceiling, as if trying to look my fear in the eye and conquer it, and an image of my parents entered the room, then passed. Oh, how much power it had taken me to defy everything they wanted for my life.

# Nine

O F COURSE, I had tried to be good. But the women in my
family have always been misfits. My father's side—the
only one I knew and lived with, never having met my mother's
family—was strict in their following of traditional Afghan honor
law and the Shia denomination of Islam, which meant that we had
to bend before our elders, kiss their hands, and use the formal *you*
to address them. And still there was a riotous anger in the women
that I couldn't place. Aunt Sabrina, a trained oncologist in Afghanistan, came to Berlin and refused to get out of training and so,
bound by the bureaucracy of labor laws for refugees, just worked
as an intern for seven years without ever seeing a paycheck. Much
to the detriment of her daughter and her husband, she got up every
day and went to work anyway, even on Sundays. The day she finally received her work permit, she began studying for a new medical license, eventually becoming head of the oncology department
at the hospital.

"I never wanted a child," I heard her say in the kitchen as she took off her jewelry to wash the dishes. "Children make you weak." Her daughter was seven, I was six, and we could both hear her clearly. She became one of the most successful breast cancer specialists in Berlin, co-chaired a research institute, and bought a house with a heated pool in the basement in Charlottenburg.

But her daughter became mentally ill, and her quasi-battered husband tried to hang himself from the shower with the belt she had given him for his birthday. And maybe this unforeseen tragedy explained her sadness and recurrent visits back to Gropiusstadt. She was the eldest daughter of the family, tasked with being the backup mother, and ultimately that role of distanced parental control was better suited for her than real mother and wife. Despite her fancy house, she was rarely in Charlottenburg.

"She doesn't eat enough," the other aunts said. "She's too skinny. She never sleeps. She isn't healthy."

"Sabrina is the best daughter," my grandmother said. "But she should've been a son."

And then there was my cousin Nadia. She awed and confused my family with her beauty and confidence. She was very tall, the daughter of my father's younger sister, Fairuz, who had married a Russian man. She was three years older than me and painted purple liner around the large, feline, mischievous eyes that I also had, that all the women on my paternal side had—but unlike our brown ones, hers were mystic blue, with a crown of yellow freckles splashed around her pupils. Stopping at construction sites, she would pull up her black sweatshirt to reveal a metallic bikini. The workers gave her cigarettes, juice, calling her *Miss Universe*.

At age fifteen, she ran away with the thirty-eight-year-old neighbor, a Ukrainian electrician who abandoned a wife and a new baby. Nadia stole all the savings her parents had accrued to buy a house one day. And while my uncles threatened to kill her in the name of family honor, my aunts tried to plead with the men.

"We're not like those uncivilized Muslims, remember?"

"She is just a child."

Eventually, my aunts picked her up at a gas station by the Czech border. She'd used the payphone to call home and asked explicitly for her mother, my aunt Fairuz incoherent with worry. The August heat turned Nadia's hair into a sad frizz, and there she stood, barefoot and ashamed, a blue bruise on the side of her face and snot coming out of her nose. All that was left of the thirty thousand euros of her parents' money was a plastic bag with her bras, some leave-in conditioner, and her high-heeled tie-up stilettos. On the drive back, she hugged her knees. When Sabrina asked her if she could stop smoking in the car, the only thing she said was, "You are all making me sick." She went to a women's shelter, returned wearing a hijab (which my mother found laughable), took it off two weeks later, and moved in with my grandmother. She never spoke about what happened during her two weeks away with the neighbor, but when she put on my makeup for a wedding the following summer (I was rarely allowed to hang out with her now), she said that men were bad and made me promise not to sacrifice myself for love.

But a few minutes later, she rubbed the chromatic blue off my eyelids and said, "What am I saying? Love is worth everything."

I liked her, despite her preposterous soap-opera truisms—she had ruined the family honor. But now she was endowed with the glamour of tragedy, like starlets who died young. She had a story. We children born in this new country: We were untethered, without history. From neither here nor there. Nadia had left a mark. And I knew, from an early age, that I also had an iteration of her illness in me—for that is what my father and mother and uncles and aunts called it, it was an "illness" that she suffered from, an "illness" that sprouted her desire for liberty and sex and wildness and alcohol. My parents wanted women to wear their hair uncovered, to have political opinions and a taste in music, and to go to college, but we were still obliged to play by the rules, and the rules were patriarchal, strict, and most of all, they were permanent. You had to be a *dokhtare khub*, a good girl, in order not to turn into a *dokhtare kharab*, a broken, bad, ruined girl. No boyfriends, no foul language, no sybaritic lifestyle. These traditions were woven into the fabric of reality, and you couldn't get out without ostracizing yourself. If you wanted out, you were out for everyone—you had to build a new reality, find a new family, be shunned. And to be shunned, we all knew, was worse than to be dead.

There were other Afghans—more-modern ones—whose houses we sometimes went to after weddings or funerals, in cities like Wuppertal or Hamburg, and the girls spoke about having boyfriends in front of their fathers. I left those meetings confused and hurt by my circumstances, and my wounds were infected further and further, and out came a riotous feeling of anger.

WHEN I WAS younger, younger even than when Nadia had run away—an occurrence so sharp in my memory that it marked a clear before and after of my life—I used to revolt about these inequalities. I would scream at my mother, *Why can I not be free?* And more unoriginal things, like *I hate you. I hate this life. I hate this family, I hate all of you,* until either my mother or my father stunned me into silence. The problem was that I didn't accept their reality as true. I had a different reality. I wanted love and everything around it—I wanted what my male cousins had, which was the privilege to be unbounded by an ancient idea of honor and purity. Their purity and honor were innate and untouchable, while ours was subject to the ubiquitous threat of being besmirched, and thus our every movement had to be girdled.

My parents must've sensed the illness sprout in me, because they discouraged friendships but reinforced an infinite supply of books. But the real knowledge I wanted was the knowledge from the novels and films and pictures I studied in secret. I swore to myself that one day I'd live a life like the one outlined in Ginsberg and Burroughs. I loved Andy Warhol's pictures of Edie Sedgwick, and the Czech girls gorging on cakes in Vera Chytilova's *Daisies:* The political implications were too complex, but I understood the sense of rebellion. Or the faces in Diane Arbus's or Nan Goldin's pictures—grotesque, and sad, but very, very alive. It was the opposite of purity, though I suspected—no, in some deep part of my soul I knew—that this type of life was also a life of purity, a purity of experience rather than of honor and abstinence. *I want to live! I want to live!* every little cell in my body screamed. It didn't matter where they sent me or that there were no boys in school. I could find my way around any rule or limitation.

# Ten

I RETURNED HIS COAT, reluctantly. For a couple of weeks we met at parties, but also in private—as friends, walking through snowy streets. He told me about Berlin exploding in the roaring twenties. Friedrichshain breaking open at the seams. His eyes twinkled as he leaned against the kitchen counter and stirred ice into liquor and told me of DJs migrating from Detroit in the eighties. Plumped on the couch, I shared what I was reading for class: analytic philosophy, which went over my head, and aesthetic theory. Marlowe only laughed about Vasari's claim that painting and sculpture are the most sublime forms of art.

"Music is the most sublime," Marlowe said. "And then dance. Then painting, and then writing, and then perhaps sculpture."

"But Michelangelo's painting on the Sistine Chapel—"

"No. It's the choir and the organ, connecting you to death, and to the word of God."

———

HE GIFTED ME a seventies Nikkormat SLR. Helped me find the right positioning for the 50mm f/1.4 lens, his slender hand resting on my shoulder. Pulled at my sleeve, pressing a finger against my wrist. I took dozens of pictures of him in his bed, a triangle of light against his cheek. I knelt on the floor, trying to perfect the shaded background. When I told him that I wanted to take candid pictures that looked like no one had interrupted anything, he said that I needed a vision for my art—otherwise, "anyone could take pictures." That I needed to learn the virtuosity of manipulation. When he looked through the viewfinder of my Olympus, he raised his eyebrows.

"It's greasy; you need to clean it. Do you develop your own film?"

"Not really." I had done it once or twice in school, feeling clumsy and purblind in the darkrooms.

"You should develop your own film." The next time I saw him, he handed me a plastic tote with three rolls of black-and-white Neopan 400 Fujifilm, a reel, and developing tanks.

ON THURSDAYS, WHEN Doreen worked at a secondhand store in Mitte, he gave me ecstasy and took me to dinner at a ramshackle French café close to his apartment. They offered vegan options and a freezing bathroom that reeked of piss and patchouli. He told me about his vision for a free and socialist society, while I watched him pick apart plant-based food. He was very precise with his knife, and there was never any parsley stuck between his teeth, and he sat up with a straight back and commanded the waiters with a peerless confidence. While there was a shyness in him—a shyness

I hadn't noticed before—when the waiters spoke in a German dialect, which relayed the power to me, that power didn't last long. I didn't know that you put your napkin in your lap. Or that one had to tell the server how you want your steak: Well done? Rare? Medium rare? I had never heard of those things, and while I was humiliated, I was also drunk on curiosity: The limits of life had been stretched outward. If I couldn't leave Berlin, I wanted this Berlin, his Berlin. I told him about that Sylvia Plath book, *The Bell Jar*, the scene in which Esther goes to a restaurant and drinks the little bowl of flower water you are supposed to wash your hands in. He laughed and laughed and a darkness flickered across his eyes, and afterward he was a little warmer to me.

He called these dinners *reading time*. The MDMA would start kicking in after two drinks, during the main course, and I'd have to go to the bathroom and throw up. I always threw up when the nausea began—it was a reflex—but afterward a fuzzy clearheadedness set in. He had a particular way of holding the wineglass—not by the stem but by the bowl—that was erotically charged. He only occasionally excused himself to the bathroom, while I'd start sweating and biting my lip. The salty, brothy meat dissolving between my chattering teeth. He touched my thigh under the table and told me to be "patient."

One day he asked if I had considered becoming a vegetarian, to save my carbon footprint.

I scoffed, but then I stopped ordering steak. We stayed for dessert, and I watched him touch a silver spoon to the panna cotta, the white soy cream deliquescing into the red berry sauce, and then I watched him smoke a cigarette, the hollows of his eyes accentuated by the yellow lamp of the streetlight, until at last we walked to his place, and I could finally relax.

The moments when we entered his apartment and he took a few minutes to get ready were my favorite. I sat on the sofa, listening to my breath and the sounds of him engaging in private and mundane activities: opening cupboards, using the faucet, his slippers moving across the floor. At times he fell into a deep silence, and I couldn't understand what was going on in his mind at all. I recalled what Anna had said about him, that he was a creature of darkness. "We're just friends," he said. He said it when he made me touch myself in front of him, and he said it when he took my face in his hands and stuck his tongue down my throat. He tasted of ash and breath mints, and his skin was always cold. Sometimes he told me to shut up and pressed one hand against my mouth, the other lazily circling my nipple through my dress. And he always drew a line, even if I didn't understand where this line was. Suddenly he would get up and say, "Enough," like that first Sunday, when he wiped his hands on his trousers and there was this feeling like I had been slapped. Then, one day, he asked if he could wash me.

"Don't be so prudish," he said when I looked at him in disbelief, and I followed him into the bathroom, and he knelt in front of me under the stream of the calcified showerhead. With a bar of green soap, he stroked my legs until the scent of cheap verbena filled the air, pausing on the backs of my knees, the place where it tickled me the most. I shivered, a cold trickle running down my spine, as he looked up to me—but he stopped at my inner thigh, and my breath slowed. Outside, children shouting, someone was disposing of glass in the courtyard, there was the low hum of a neighbor's radio in the air, and I almost forgot my parents and the building in Gropiusstadt and my own sad life outside this shower, my guilt about not being allowed to be here, because all that existed in those moments were steam in all its glory and the tiles cold against my back. Then he retrieved the razor—a pink women's razor, which he sometimes used on his face too—and began his work, starting at my heel and scraping the blade against my skin, up my calves, all the way to where he could hurt me, where I wanted him to go further, but he didn't. Restraint, I learned, was something Marlowe was exceptionally good at.

Wilting in the stuffy air of the heaters, the oxygen thick between us, Marlowe and I laughed. He demanded I tell him the worst thing that had ever happened to me. But the worst thing that had happened to me was secret; it was our building, buried deep in the swampy forest of my childhood, the forest whose leaves glistened but were too far away to reach, and although the memories were the cause of pain, like a heavy stone leaching toxins into the soil, I couldn't bear to speak about them. Still, I indulged him. Let him trace my rib cage with his fingers and spoke of boarding school, the lonely winters, Romy's blue eyes.

"I never felt at home in the world," I told him once.

"You shouldn't be so scared," he said. "I can tell you're afraid."

I DIDN'T UNDERSTAND the rules. I didn't even fully comprehend it was a game—it seemed that we were waiting, and eventually I would be ushered through a threshold to a white room and see what was happening to me. Sometimes we didn't have sex at all. Talked all night, with the coffee table between us, snorting line after line. It unlatched me, his awful, vehement restraint—I was nervous under his watch, and I came very easily, high and covered in goosebumps. And after he deposited me in a bus back home, and

I returned to the darkness of my childhood bedroom, I masturbated. I was close to losing my mind, but I was constantly taking pictures, more than I'd ever done in my life, all in black-and-white. At home, I'd bring all the lamps into my bedroom, illuminating the pink wall. Wearing nothing but a long black glove on my right arm, I tried to imitate my favorite Man Ray photograph: *Meret Oppenheim at the Printing Wheel*. I fastened the Nikkormat to a tripod and posed in front of it, hiding half my face with my hand, a chair in front of my legs. I tried to look forlorn, as if I were both exposed and hardened by despair.

But perhaps the best picture of that time is of Marlowe: He's lying on his mattress, wearing nothing but a watch and his necklace, the white sheet covering his sex. His arm propped under his head, a cigarette resting in his right hand. The photo is surprisingly precise, showing all the veins and scars of his body, the faded tattoos. Light falls like abstract brushstrokes along his torso, as if he'd escaped a painting. There is a thin scratch on the film, in the shape of a crescent, blurring the light coming from the left of the frame. But his eyes look black and pure. And he stares up at the camera with an expression I rarely remember him with, an expression that surprises me every time I look at it, even so many years later: an admiration so intense it already contains a kind of grief.

Developing pictures too was an act of chemistry and patience and precision. The darkened window, the exact temperature of water and solution, the fixer—the seven minutes I'd agitate the film by turning the tank over and over like an hourglass. Washing the film, the watermarks when I forgot the wetting solution. You never knew what you'd see on the other side, if the image was ex-

pected or if it would change you. Hanging the negatives to dry in
the bathroom; my father complaining about the obstructed shower.
And the hours I'd spend scanning the negatives to inspect them—
the hairs and specks of dust, the granular breakage on the film—on
my laptop. Zooming in to the shadow of the tiny scar on his cheek,
the origin of which he kept secret. On my walks, my eyes were
sharper, hungrier—discerning the world as if for the very first
time. The way snow melted upon contact with my skin, the neighbor's black dog guarding the bus stop, and that burned-down balcony on Hermannstraße: I tried to photograph it all.

IT WAS IN this state of mind that one evening, electrified and still
coming down from amphetamines, I opened Melanie's email
again. Blue pixels. Highlighted the words, let my cursor hover
over the text. *You should apply to these schools.* . . . Closed the laptop, opened it again. And then, without telling anyone, I collected
my best photographs—several self-portraits, as well as one picture
of my mother and two portraits of Marlowe—into a portfolio and
applied to all four colleges in London.

# Part
## Two

# Eleven

THE QURBANI BAKERY in our neighborhood was owned by
two Afghan brothers, but they ran it more like a café: tables
and chairs, a glass vitrine with salads and lentil soup for the lunch
crowd. They made their own bread and biscuits as well as an array
of fruit and cheese Danishes, which glinted in the greasy display
case. There was a shelf filled with glossy baklava and Turkish
goods from a local confectionery. A cooler in the corner with
sodas, pomegranate juice, and the kind of chocolate milk my
mother bought me whenever we stopped by during the winter
weekends of childhood.

"Hello," I said over the jingling of the door chime while wiping my boots on the mat. I hadn't eaten all day and craved some
carbs before the party later. It smelled of burnt coffee and sugar,
and there was only an old couple at a window table, whispering
over tea. Ali, the younger brother, looked absurd in his black uniform, like someone in costume. Although he was well into his forties, he carried himself with the demeanor of a teenage boy, greedy

and uncomfortable with need. He was wiping a tray behind the counter, his eyes clinging to me as I looked through the shelf of teas and baklava.

On one of the stools, the shop cat, Jackie, lounged. She was a mouser in the kiosk down the street but had chosen the bakery as her preferred home. Orange tabby, rotund from treats. Agha Javed, the older brother, was stroking her head while staring at the muted TV on the wall, where a news channel reported on what I made out to be a frozen train. He was a corpulent man with a bad leg and receding hairline. He stood up and bowed his head, calling me *Bibi Haddadi*, as if I were my grandmother. His polite demeanor appalled me, the way his voice oozed with concern when he asked how my father was doing.

"Everyone's good," I said, touching a box of gingerbread cookies. A poster of a very young Elvis Presley was pinned to the wall, next to a picture of Ahmad Zahir, the Afghan rock star whom we dubbed *Afghan Elvis*, though his songs were so much more morose. Even as a child, I found this comparative display incredibly gaudy. I ordered a blueberry Danish, two cardamom cookies, and a coffee. The cat leapt from the chair and strutted toward me, butting her head against my shin. I knelt to pet her. She was purring and I loved her—I loved her as much as I disliked the bakery and its spartan immigrant aesthetic, the tiled floors and cold lights.

"Take some bread for your father," the younger Qurbani said with a fake smile. He had pale eyes and a wispy monobrow that gave him an otherworldly, almost handsome flair. "Or are you on your way out?"

He was trying to shame me, in the slant Afghan way: Only a bad daughter would leave her widowed father alone on New Year's

Eve. His civility was hypocritical. These were men who commented on my short dresses behind my back, men who were horribly bound to tradition. My grandmother loved them, because they loved their wives—*They're angels,* she said, meaning especially Agha Javed, who often brought her baskets of sweets. Occasionally I saw the younger brother carrying his baby daughter swaddled in a thick winter suit to the playground, and I tried to square his tenderness with the man who'd once told me, in the long hallway of a wedding after I returned from a secret cigarette, that I behaved like a whore.

"My father will appreciate your kindness," I said when he passed me the bag, but I barely even smiled. I petted the cat one more time, and then I was out.

"Happy New Year," I heard Agha Javed shout over the door jingle. It was only late afternoon, but the streets were already full of Chinese crackers and fireworks, boys throwing burning things after one another. Blistering with hatred, I walked past the corner store and then the shisha bar. Those frail glass panes, fogged up from the steam and coals inside, Oum Kulthum blasting over artificial watermelon smoke. The familiarity repulsed me: boys who looked like they could be my brothers, who were just as lost as me, and just as hungry for joy and violence.

I WOLFED DOWN the Danish and coffee and walked the length of two bus stops, then left the bread with a homeless man at the corner. He bowed and pushed his cart away; even he looked more at peace than I was. Smoking a cigarette while waiting for the train, I decided that my New Year's resolution was to discard the rule—

the rule being that a girl does not move out until she is married or moves to another city for college—and to get my own place. Out of Gropiusstadt, out of the orbit of people like the Qurbanis. But I didn't even have enough money for a deposit. Anything I earned over four hundred euros would be deducted from my father's unemployment benefits and void my student health insurance. And while my stint at the jazz café allowed me to occasionally take home a little more, I didn't earn enough to afford rent even in a shared apartment.

ONCE I GOT onto the U7, someone pinched my ass. When I turned around in shock, he grinned with discolored teeth and hazy eyes. He had a shaved head, was wearing a leather jacket and black combat boots.

"I want to shoot you in the face," he whispered in my ear. I was paralyzed by elemental fear—the garlic and alcohol on his breath, a pain throbbing in my temples. Whimpering, I passed a few people, but I could feel his eyes on me like an odor. When I stole a glance at him, he was talking to himself. He had Tourette's. Or his affliction was simpler: He hated people who looked like me. It had happened before.

ANNA AND ROMY had invited me to a raclette dinner, but I decided at the last minute that the more interesting conversations would probably be happening with the junkies. Marlowe had told me that the publisher and the architecture firm had rented a hotel ballroom to celebrate the Biennale and that everyone was going to Rico's afterward.

The doorman motioned for me to go to the right, and I walked down the parquet hallway to the Renaissance ballroom: Ivy crawled up to the ceiling, and exotic petals floated in water bowls. Quiches on lacquered platters. The gleam of silverware, light refracting from crystal. A lady in big Chanel glasses who looked like she could be broken in half like a twig grabbed my arm and told me that classical music is good for the plants. Everyone was wearing black, I realized, except me. I caught a glimpse of myself in one of the mirrors: too much eyeliner, the flashy emerald of my hand-me-down dress. There was a tear in my nylons, just above the knee, and my curls stuck out of my unruly ponytail.

I saw him across the room, next to the DJ table, and he immediately detached himself from the conversation and moved toward me. His hair slicked back, an oversized cable-knit sweater hanging from his shoulders. He smiled in a way that made me want to strip naked, right there. But he was all manners, trying to show me the architect who had commissioned him, the lady with the gray hair "over there." He pointed at a table with three women, all of them identically nondescript and gray-haired in such a consistently German and organic-produce-only way that it was impossible to discern Gabriela von Ascheberg, but I nodded.

"Wow," I said. "I feel like I'm in a commercial for a credit card."

"Commercial? This is more of a Fellini film, I would say."

"What I mean: It's gorgeous here. I can't believe how beautiful the interior architecture is." I had rehearsed what I wanted to say: *mention architecture.*

"Yes, isn't this a beautiful building? It was built in 1903." And then he said what I already knew: that on the opposite side of the street, the Nazis had burned books in 1933. He guided me to our table, and Doreen's face stiffened when she saw me. The pallid décolletage burst through the black chiffon of her dress. Her mascara was long and spindly, like in Man Ray's *Glass Tears*.

"You're going to sit here," Doreen said, patting the wood chair next to her. From the shriek of her declaration, I sensed something icy but frail: Her voice was like the surface of a thawing lake. "Funny, isn't it?"

"What?"

Doreen filled my glass with champagne when I sat down. "That you are always around now. You weren't here a while ago, and now you're always here."

"Yeah. I have a parasitic tendency."

She didn't laugh. Only raised her eyebrows and twirled a loose strand of her hair.

"Everyone," she said. "This is Nila. She's our new *friend*." I knew the others at the table; it was just Rico and Tamara.

"We already know each other," Tamara said, and rolled her eyes.

"Do you?" Doreen smiled without teeth, and Marlowe excused himself.

I tried to steer the topic away. "Who would've suspected that writers threw parties like these? Or even architects. I thought they'd be eating tapas, standing around in minimalist rooms."

"Gabriela is not just an architect." Doreen's voice regained a common pitch. "Hasn't Marlowe told you all about it? Gabriela's family owns this hotel; her brother is a publishing mogul. They took Marlowe in as a kind of mentee after meeting him at a reading. She is the reason his book was translated into German. He has charmed even her, Gabriela with the stoic face. . . ."

"He didn't even have a visa when they met," Tamara said.

"Anyway, Gabriela's family is blue blood. They own half of Munich. She's kind of a celebrity in Berlin too."

"Oh wow." My eyes darted toward Marlowe. My awareness of his body petrified me. I could barely focus on Doreen's words: My city was revealing itself to me; there was so much I didn't know. I was from here, I thought; I knew this place better than they did.

"Well, isn't your little boyfriend handsome." Tamara pointed in the direction of Marlowe.

I focused on the mushy strawberry floating in her glass and bit my lip to suppress the coal of anger, thinking of the Qurbani brother's glances. His suspicious gaze, the way he said, *Or are you on your way out?* I didn't belong to the people in that bakery, but I didn't belong to these people either. Everyone here probably revered Bauhaus and thought it was cool that Gabriela came from some inbred Habsburg heritage and knew things I didn't, like what *Műhely* meant in Hungarian or how long it took for Saturn to orbit the sun. I wondered if Marlowe enjoyed this kind of event. He looked entirely different than in the Bunker or at his own apartment, the sweater hiding most of his tattoos, his hair brushed back. He resembled the patrons at the jazz café.

The DJ stopped the music, and a young woman in a black jumpsuit took the mic and mentioned the great accomplishment for the firm and the publisher and Gabriela, who didn't clap for herself—or for anyone else, really—so I finally recognized her: green-rimmed glasses and orange-tinted lipstick, the handsome face of a woman who had been too smart to be regarded as truly beautiful even when she was young. Applause and murmuring preceded another lady who got up. She read an incomprehensible piece about shapes and cities, replete with metaphors about the meat counter in a supermarket. I chuckled and noticed a napkin fall out of Marlowe's hand, but he didn't pick it up. The exit sign glowed above a door behind the grand piano. Everywhere were these ashy German faces. Women with thin lips, conceptual necklaces. Bronze powder reflecting the light on the sagging skin around their necklines. Or younger women in asymmetrical cuts, petting their drinks. There was not a single immigrant in sight, not even the servers.

"This is pathetic," Rico said, grinning. He sat at the head of the table, an arm around Tamara. "Look at all these poor people in their ironed shirts. None of them know how to really live." I nodded, though I suspected I too did not know how to really live. It was a habit Marlowe engaged in too—pointing out that others, people who didn't engage in sybaritic excess, were lacking some foundational epiphany. Then, finally, my friend appeared.

"Eli!" I shouted a little too loudly, startling Tamara. I stood up and ran over to him, hugged him and his cold coat. When we sat back down, Doreen told me the story of how she and Eli had met at one of the parties Marlowe threw a year ago. It was when Eli moved to Berlin. At the time I was studying for finals, locked in the musk of my dorm room back in Rosenwald. When my life consisted of note cards and biology books, drawing little circles around mitochondria.

Doreen sucked at the oysters and piled the nacreous shells on her plate. Then she began talking about Yugoslavia and the communist wars, very loudly, often looking over to Eli, who smiled at her. I had no idea what they were talking about, throwing around words like *Shkodra* and *Tito*. She ignored my questions, absorbed by the import of her intellectual performance. I busied myself by drinking more and staring at Tamara, who was giving Rico a hand massage, entangled in their private murmur.

"Doreen, the Marxist," Eli said after a while.

"Marxist-Leninist, to be precise." She smiled, baring her perfect fangs, though there was a smudge of lipstick on one of her incisors. "It's always important to be precise."

When I excused myself to go to the bathroom to escape their conversation, Doreen said she would join me, her voice aflush with agitation. I wanted to be alone, but we picked our way to the women's powder room, decorated with blue tiles and swan wallpaper. She perched on the velvet ottoman, looking away as I peed, and this moment of intimacy—unasked for, yet stemming from feminine etiquette—endeared her to me.

When I got up to wash my hands, she walked to the sink. "Can I put some lipstick on you?"

I was puzzled.

"I would like to put some lipstick on you, I think it would really suit you."

"Okay," I relented. She stood very close to me, putting a hand on my shoulder.

"You're cute," she whispered. Her breath was warm, and she smelled of sourdough bread and rosewater. "I love your freckles."

She put a curl behind my ear and gently turned my head by my chin. Heat gushed through my body, augmenting my pulse, so I closed my eyes, and when she applied the cold unguent on my mouth, she either did not notice that I was trembling or she was too polite to say anything.

"Done," she said softly. When I opened my eyes and looked in the mirror, the Bordeaux mouth had altered everything. Older, harsher. I looked like my mother.

"You have a very classical look to you with a red lip. Almost French." I was a head taller than her. With her blond bob framing her smooth features, she looked very elegant. Defamiliarizing, to see another's face in the mirror for the first time.

She coughed and the softness dissipated, as if she had willed it to. She pulled a baggie of white powder out of her bra. I saw a flash of her rosy nipple, the blue veins under her papery skin. Of course, women like Doreen carried drugs in their bras.

"Marlowe has been really odd lately." She leaned against the sink. "Will you tell me if he comes on to you?"

I halted my breath, raised my eyebrows. She didn't know anything.

"Nothing has happened, right?"

"Nope." I didn't even flinch. She hugged me and I snorted a bit off her key.

"I knew we would be friends." But before I could open the bathroom door, she firmly placed her hand on the knob and said, "You know, I find it cute that you want to be a photographer. It's so . . . sincere."

It wasn't just the tone of condescension in her voice. It was the fact that she let me understand anew that she and Marlowe were talking about me. That they laughed about my pathetic dreams.

BACK IN THE ballroom, Marlowe and I stood by the bar. I couldn't think of anything smart to say, and the space between our bodies felt both too narrow and too wide. I dropped my napkin, my empty cup. I didn't know what to do with my hand. I had walked there to evade Doreen, to parse the conflicting whims of hurt and guilt, and he joined me a minute later. Maybe I was imagining it, but there was a hint of tension in him too—the fidgeting, the low register of his voice.

"Like lilies," he whispered in my ear.

"What is like lilies?"

"You're avoiding me." He touched my butt, only for a nanosecond—but he touched it.

"No, I'm not."

"You smell like lilies."

"Stop this, she will see." I swatted his hand away. The waiter served us two glasses of sparkling wine. Strawberries bobbed on the prickly surface.

"Like lilies and . . . garlic sauce. Did you eat a döner today?"

"Fuck off." Despite myself, I tried to smell my breath.

"I'm just kidding. Are you joining me for fresh air? I'm done now." There was a small crumb on his hand. Reflexively, I brushed it off.

"Finally," I said. "I'll just get my bag."

BUT WHEN I walked back to our table, Doreen was already calling my name, telling me to come with her: "Upstairs, just for a minute."

"What's upstairs?"

"The best view of the fireworks in the city."

"Should we tell the others?"

"Who cares about the others," she said. "I need only you."

I wasn't dumb, I knew that her *I need only you* announced a threat, the way my family's *I love you*s were manipulation strategies with only one goal in mind: to hurt me. Still, I followed her into the elevator, which was very clean, up to the twelfth floor. Then we walked through a heavy fire door and climbed up the stairs to a shaft, Doreen's short legs trotting in front of me, her voice circling the air, talking about Kosovo.

"Ta-da," she said once we arrived, and the wind spanked our faces. The rooftop bar was closed, of course, but she said she knew the entrance because she had been here before. The view was, there was no other way to say it, incredible. You could see the Fernsehturm, the T-Mobile building, the dazzling shopping malls, and I believed I detected the Kreuzberg–Friedrichshain bridges and even that tower that resembled a phallus. The city glittered in the distance, and through the fog everything seemed benevolent and beautiful; buildings with wrought-iron balconies, trains, and tiny dots of humans dashing around, everything covered with snow. I had never seen Berlin like this. Melancholy overcame me; I was from here, and not once had I stood on a rooftop of this caliber. Neither had my aunts or uncles or parents. My dead mother. I thought of the elevator, the twelve stories, the length it would take to run and go home. I thought about Marlowe waiting for me downstairs and the hand on my butt. It became very cold as Doreen spoke about Yugoslavia, my ears full of wind. And then the fireworks erupted at a quicker pace than before. Again and again they exploded, white dahlias and chrysanthemums, peonies and spiders, then spirals. The railing of the balcony reflected the lightest glimmer of green, then white, then red. Doreen's mouth was agape, a thread of saliva between her lips, the eyes blank—and for a moment she looked like a child, full of genuine wonder for the fireworks, and it made me feel terrible. In the black sphere of her iris, I could see the lit-up building behind me and a small, warped version of myself.

"Happy New Year," she shouted in my ear.

"Happy New Year," I said, and then, before I could stop myself, "I've been sleeping with Marlowe."

"Excuse me?"

"Yes, I'm sorry." The abrasive speed trickled down my throat.

"You are sorry."

"The whole thing is kind of an accident," I said.

"An accident? You slipped on the floor and fell on his dick? Repeatedly?"

"That's one way to put it."

"God, I knew it," Doreen laughed with theatrical timbre, as if she were trying to drown me in the well of her cackle. With boisterous determination, she darted to the door. Then she turned around. Inhaled expectantly. "Let me make this clear. I always thought you were weird. I bet you have no friends of your own, because why else would you always cling to us like a creepy leech? You're so pathetic, I can practically smell the loneliness on you."

The click of the heavy door lock falling into its frame wasn't a sound I had ever heard before, not like this.

# Twelve

THE SPRING AFTER I turned twelve, I jumped out of my grandmother's second-floor apartment and into a row of bushes because she reprimanded me about wearing a miniskirt that revealed my vanilla-colored underwear. She slapped me, and there was that half-eaten apple on the table and her chador draped on the arm of the sofa, and next thing I knew I leapt from the window. It was a melodramatic affair, resulting in three stitches to the forehead and a broken elbow set in a blue cast that my classmates wrote on with felt tip, but the doctors considered it a cry for help.

My parents took me to a children's psychologist who looked like someone had put a pair of glasses and a cable-knit sweater on cardboard—kind of cute but hard to respect. I stopped going once he suggested I read the news and consider Jesus's stigmata. Instead, I made friends with some beautiful Persian girls from our neighborhood, who smoked and wore crop tops, and whose mothers were Christian (*new converts*, my father called them), not Muslim, and most of the time they were encouraged to engage in activities I wasn't allowed to participate in. One morning, when I asked my father if I could go to the pool with them, he said no, indicating that boys would see us, that we were going there to flirt.

"So what," I said. "So what if I flirt and have a boyfriend, what are you going to do?"

I cried and hit my head against the wall, and my crying changed the air in the apartment. It made my father angry, and my mother begged me to stop; and my father, with every minute of my loud and hysterical sobbing, got more infuriated. I knew what I was doing, but I couldn't stop provoking him. A strange weather came over his face and he hit me, and because I continued screaming and shouting and saying all kinds of rude things, my father grabbed a pillow and started to smother my face, leaning over me in my bed and pressing the pillow hard into my mouth, and I don't know how long he did this—he would take the pillow away, check that I was breathing, and then put it back on my face, smother me again— begging me to shut up, to shut up, to come to my senses and stop wanting to be bad.

Later, he sat in the living room, disappointed in and afraid of himself, I could see—he wasn't proud of what he had done, but he was even more afraid of me, of what I would become, and I understood myself as separate from my parents, from everyone I had come from. My mother, who had been trying to drag him away from me, apologized on his behalf.

"But you're lucky," she said, the expected addendum a day later. "Look at how much you're allowed to do; you're allowed to do many more things than other Afghan girls." It was true: My parents were lenient, somewhere in the middle between Afghan tradition and Western emancipation.

"We love you," she said. I stared at the ceiling's watermark that looked like a dancer. A histrionic sting, typical for teenage girls, agitated me: imagining dead girls everywhere, their wispy hair tied with ribbons and velvet, smeared mascara.

"I wish he had killed me," I said. "I don't want to live like this."

THE PRINCIPAL FIGHT of my home ensued shortly thereafter. My mother snubbed my father for days, locked herself up. Shrieking, crying, vowels muttered in Farsi. My father banging against the door, shouting obscenities. Begging her to hang up the call. He pulled the cords out of the wall, and my mother threw the phone at the door, the black plastic scattered on the bedroom floor. Aunt Sabrina came over with my grandmother, carrying a new telecom set. My grandmother fanned out brochures of private schools on the coffee table. But there was no all-girls school in Berlin.

"You cannot take my daughter from me," my mother shouted. "Why aren't you sending your own daughter there?"

"Liana is already—she is already such a homebody, she . . ." I knew my cousin was not allowed to leave the house at all. Although she was rarely home, Sabrina was crazier than all of us, perpetually scared of vague but terrifying perils: rapists hiding in bushes, kidnappers who poured chloroform on napkins, atomic bombs that would erupt when Liana was alone on the bus. Neuroses decayed our mothers' minds. Every time a girl disappeared and turned up murdered, my aunts showed me newspaper articles: *See, this is the fate of those who misbehave.*

"What will happen to her here?" my father said, and I sat with my ear pressed against my bedroom door, attending. "She will be ruined."

"She's the only thing I have."

"It's not too late to—"

"The world breaks girls everywhere," my mother hissed. "It's too late."

LATER, AFTER DELIVERING a frantic litany of sorrows—*Sabrina's arrogance appalls me; she never even eats; has anyone seen her eat something besides those dumb walnuts; why isn't she taking care of her own ugly daughter rotting away in that house*—my mother invited her over again and they convened in the bedroom for hours, using such low whispers that I couldn't hear them. Sabrina left in her long black coat, and my mother arose, red-eyed and gritty. There was a pot of steaming tea on the table, into which my father cracked cardamom pods. Three vermilion saffron hairs rested at the bottom of my glass mug, the kind of mug somehow every Afghan family owns, no matter if they raise mujahideen in Helmand or reside on a flowering estate in Perth, Australia. My mother wore a bow-tie blouse and blue clip-on earrings that collected afternoon light. She spoke in assertive tones, her back straight, her lips curling into a thin smile. My father's voice sounded distant and tender, like that of a schoolteacher. Years later, he'd sing to the cat with the same inflection: something small and dumb. They would be sending me away.

"It's for your own good," my father said. "You are a bright child; you are the best student in your class—you don't want to get distracted in this terrible district. This dark city."

I clung to my mother, as I did in the days of early childhood—touching the cold flesh of her upper arms, inhaling her sweet fragrance. Talcum powder of her makeup bottles. Jasmine soap. I looked for protection, trying to manipulate her into conspiring with me. But she just brushed my hair with cold, resigned fingers and looked at me with cautious eyes, as if trying to communicate without words. I couldn't decipher what she was saying.

"Remember when you were in first grade and your teacher invited us over?"

"Frau Klein thought you had a German parent because your language skills were so good," my mother said.

"She told us you were special. She saw it even then. Just think about it. If you go to that school, you can do anything you want after. You can fulfill your potential, get out of here. You could move anywhere."

I PROTESTED AND cried, but to no avail—my parents applied on my behalf, and I received a full ride. A check from Sabrina for cafeteria cards. It wasn't enough to cover other expenses, such as school trips to Paris and Rome or the thick, exquisite Latin dictionaries designed by Hundertwasser. My parents decided to incur some debt—it was an investment in my education, after all. And so, with great hopes and even greater fears, that August I was driven to the bilingual Catholic all-girls school far away from everyone and everything I knew. It was a dark estate by a pond with reeds and weeping willows, in the foothills of Rosenwald, a village of four thousand inhabitants in the west of Germany. The region had been destroyed in the war but was rebuilt in the mid-century, old façades pinned to new roofs with metal rods. Gloomy churches rose against a backdrop of wet grassland. A canal and a slight band of a river ran through the municipalities, linking sprawling fields of corn and pastures green as jewels and villages with half-timber houses. The closest city was a college town with gothic architecture and an icy history of murdered Anabaptists. Cobblestoned streets led from one church to another, and women with fur-trim coats shopped at stores I had never heard of. Foreigners lived there too, but you rarely saw them outside the main shopping street; almost everyone was blond and riding bicycles, even in the depths of winter. Most people believed in God or pretended to because they believed in tradition. The region was right by the Dutch border, and I spent the next six years memorizing Latin grammar, conversing with priests, solving arithmetic, and learning English. The other students flocked in from all over the area, daughters of doctors and lawyers, girls with plaited hair and pearl earrings, and two or three locals with slumped shoulders, who, I could detect from a mile away, were also on scholarship.

BUT DESIRE CAN'T be girdled, especially not the lavish, life-altering, catastrophic kind that girls feel for wildness. And thus my life at Rosenwald became a time of intemperate experimentation. While I maintained good grades, I mastered my pathological habit of lying. I told people my parents were Italian, or Israeli, or Greek, or a mix of everything. Within me burgeoned the shame my parents had taught me, but I could be anyone I wanted there. I snuck out of school to take the bus to Münster or the train to Cologne, with its stygian cathedral and secret network of parties and gay clubs, and I kissed men by the canal or lost my underwear on the back seats of cars.

When friends from school or girls I'd met online in chat forums and developed intense virtual friendships with visited Berlin in the summers and wanted to see my "house" or meet my parents, I made up excuses. I never let anyone too close. Embarrassed by the district that smelled of excrement and wet dog. Did anyone suspect the truth? That the colossus of secrets I guarded was just a normal, two-bedroom apartment, was commonplace poverty? I am sure they were suspicious of my incessant lies, but as contradictions surged—my friends at school met my parents once, and sometimes I spoke Farsi in my sleep, but, most important, I had those terrible plastic suitcases they sold at Aldi, proof of my economic milieu—my friends stopped pressing for answers. It was easier to lie with Felix and people I met outside school, where my origins could be vague and malleable.

Summers, I returned with a straighter back. The train ride made me retch, the sight of the building always, always, broke my heart. I couldn't believe Berlin's ghetto was my *home*—and yet it was the only one I knew. The teachers told us we were extraordinary, and, believing them, I considered myself superior to my cow-faced cousins, proud the way I imagined my parents were proud in the old country. Watched art-house movies, listened to indie music, made friends with older kids. Read Kafka and Büchner, devoured a canon my parents had very little understanding of. Sure, they knew math—it was the same everywhere, the only truth, as they reiterated—and sure, I could ask them about membrane-bound organelles or mitochondria or the electric voyage of cristae. But what I really loved—literature and art— displaced me into a person incomprehensible to them: That thick blue book I read for my Abitur. Heinrich Heine's *Die Loreley*. Hugo von Hofmannsthal's letter about words crumbling in his mouth like rotten mushrooms. My parents and I recoiled from one another, month by month. I was home neither in Rosenwald nor in Gropiusstadt. And like so many children before me, I became my own exile.

AT SCHOOL, THE girls wore padded down jackets and boots I had seen only in equestrian ads. They knew how to ride horses and drank expensive water and used Dr. Hauschka products, which felt so expensive back then, I believed only millionaires could afford them. Longingly, I used a pump of their creams, inhaling that herbal scent. I dreamed of affording Evian one day and just smiled when they spoke of brands I didn't know—German designers their ancestors had trusted too. Some of the girls brought their own pianos to school, hired help carrying the Schimmels and Yamahas out of vans and into their dorm rooms, and with the bitterness of people much older than me, I thought of Frau Storz and her cranky, simple Bösendorfer at which I had practiced all those years ago.

Throughout the academic year, I lived in a room with a window looking out onto a Norway maple. I had written a quote from Goethe's *Die Leiden des Jungen Werther* in golden lettering on a paper taped to my door, the same quote I had painted on the wall at home: "I couldn't paint now, not a single stroke, yet I've never been a bigger painter than in this moment." Books were everywhere, splaying out of the bookshelf. YA I had grown out of: *Gossip Girl*, *Goosebumps*, sordid crime stories. The copy of *Die Verwandlung* that I had read a dozen times, paragraphs underlined, the pages stained with fingerprints and coffee spills, a dirty sateen band separating the pages. Several copies of Virginia Woolf books. I loved the story about her death, how she'd walked into the river with stones in the pockets of her coat. *Dearest, I feel certain that I am going mad again.* . . . My favorite book those years, *The Virgin Suicides,* both in German and in English. I watched the movie a hundred times, mesmerized by its blue light. It was nice, I thought, that I was not the only person who had a feverish desire to die. It happened in literature all the time.

We had a sundial and a large track field, a swimming pool, locker rooms that smelled of incense and uncured meat. We had a gothic church we had to go to once every two weeks for mass, saying, *Our Father, who art in heaven.* . . . Yet the hymns, the hosannas and hevenu shalom aleichem, the psalms, the lessons of Genesis and Revelation, they do not remain. What remains is the searing loneliness I felt, the nights I stayed awake by myself, reading *Wuthering Heights* and *Lolita,* underlining everything, trying to forget the fact I was one of the only girls at school who had black hair.

# Thirteen

I RAN OUT OF the party after the confrontation, embarrassed and high, and walked home for three hours through the snow, promising myself to change. To never take a drug again. In the following days, I ignored most of Marlowe's calls, the messages he sent me. I cleaned our apartment with great fervor, dusted the cables behind the TV, scrubbed the syrupy grime from the exhaust hood, said *yes* and *amen* to everything my father asked me. I read Barthes's *Camera Lucida*, impossibly moved by the inquiry to find the *genius of photography:* my elusive, commonplace medium that needs a *punctum* to become art. I wanted to take pictures, I thought, because exile made my parents' life a mystery to me. I wanted to archive *my* life, to have irrefutable testimony. With the Nikkormat's viewfinder pressed against my eyeball, I sat on the balcony while cold air struck my face, inhaling every dewdrop of January. I was learning to love it like the slow framework of a new language, as if trying on a dress that truly suited me, looking into the mirror and saying, *Yes, this is the one I take.* My father's voice was like a leash around my neck, always pulling too tight. Some days it was enough for him to speak and I'd feel the tug: the asphyxiating tug.

THE NEW SEMESTER started in the middle of January, and I was enrolled in only one class, which was cross-listed for both graduate and undergraduate levels. Kafka's Minor Literature met at 5:00 P.M. on a Thursday. The lecture hall was a small, sooty room on the third floor of the main building. The radiator was broken, and I felt the drop in temperature the second I entered the room. The room was mainly empty, the fluorescent bulbs painting everyone in an unforgiving light. I sat down in the third row from the front, where you still seemed interested but not too keen. A girl was chatting with the professor in the front, leaning over his desk. She chuckled. He had a big beer belly and round, frameless glasses. I never understood this eagerness to woo authority figures. Our professors were never the hot young people that students in movies had affairs with. Instead, they smelled of salami and old dust and possessed the aura of an orthopedic shoe—something that was undeniably good for you and served a purpose, but nothing you wanted to flirt with. As class began, I heard a cough and a distinct harrumphing from the hallway, and of course there she was, cracking open the door with a low *sorry*, and after a cursory glance of the room, she sat down next to me: Doreen in her faux leopard coat and hoop earrings, smelling like outside.

The professor dimmed the lights and began class with an excursion into Kafka's life. There was a photograph of Kafka projected onto the white screen, and he never changed the slide. He sat down on the chair against the wall, resting his hands on his belly, and began telling us of Kafka's biography. Doreen only wrote down one thing, and with her as my audience, I felt too self-conscious to take note of everything, which is what I usually did, my spiral notebooks a scroll of indecipherable scribble, as if the act of writing itself were somehow facilitating my listening faculties. Her handwriting was absurdly small and beautiful. She only jotted down, *Compare to Benjamin's Kafka.*

I didn't need to learn much about Kafka's biography: I was a fan. Knew Löwy was his mother's maiden name. The spots on the Charles Bridge he liked. Kafka's inner world, with its despair and suffocation, the dark tyranny of his family. He was like me, I some-times felt: an outsider in the German language, an outsider in his family, an outsider in his country. *He was a stranger in a strange land.* . . . On a molecular level, I believed, I comprehended what he wrote, even why he turned Gregor into a giant bug. Who would understand the perils of a man trapped in his childhood room in unhuman form more than an Afghan girl trying to live? My whole life was like that, the rotten apple lodged in my chest. Sometimes I could even feel it in my rib cage, the apple thrown by my own fa-ther. Perhaps this is why I was taking drugs: trying to forget its existence.

AFTER CLASS, WE walked to a café outside the university plaza, all dusky tiles and a plethora of plants hanging from the ceiling. I fol-lowed Doreen's gaze to the long art deco mirror behind the bar. She frowned and stared at me, with those searching eyes that didn't let you go. I imagined her in Marlowe's shower, him kneeling in front of her, soaping her legs.

"I didn't know you studied German literature," she said.

"I don't; I just love Kafka."

"Another man we both love." I had to give it to her, she was funny. She reached her bangle-rimmed arms across the table and touched my hand.

"And as it seems, we need to grow accustomed to sharing." I couldn't shake the suspicion that she had lifted the line from a movie. It was the first time I was sitting opposite her, truly sober, able to fully take her in. She knew I was studying her and took her time looking down into her cup. There was loose glitter on her eyelids, some of which had become dislodged on her cheek. She looked beautiful, with supple skin and a beauty mark below her right eye. A tiny ring accentuated her nose. The only fault I found was her wide mouth, her equine teeth.

"Do you love him?" she asked with a sigh.

"What do you mean? I basically just met him." I regretted having said this—I should've denied, denied, denied.

"That doesn't mean anything." She waited a minute, as if she was expecting me to speak. "You know . . . when I met Marlowe, he did the same thing to me. He was cheating on his last girlfriend with me. It's probably karma. Has he told you about her?"

"No."

"Well, her name is Hannah, and I was friends with her—I met her at a party, like we did. There was tension between Marlowe and me from the beginning. One time, when Hannah wasn't there, we had sex." She opened the brown-sugar packet and stirred the contents into her cup. Then another. "I felt so guilty. He told me not to tell Hannah anything." Clanking the metal spoon, she swirled and swirled and repeated *anything*.

"Yeah, wow, that sounds like a crazy situation."

"Sorry, how old are you again?"

"I'm turning twenty this year." That was my new strategy: telling people what age I would be next, to make myself sound older.

"He's such a fucking asshole."

"Why?"

She laughed at me, baring her teeth. I stared at my hands against the green tiles. "Anyway, we are all at this dinner party, sitting next to each other. Hannah and Marlowe have an open relationship too. But not really open—like with us. And he tells everyone, *I met this young girl and we had sex and I came instantly. . . .* Meanwhile, I am just sitting there next to him."

I twitched, as if she were swirling the coffee spoon in the depths of my throat. I was embarrassed, remembering the first night with Marlowe, how long it took him to come. Did he not like my body? Doreen trailed off, and I looked out the window. On the opposite street, the buildings were all from a period before the war. They had survived the century. They had survived Nazi Germany and the DDR. Buildings: a shelter for human activities; how little we think of them, these buildings, and yet they are so much more durable than we. Conversations of other people threaded in and out of my audible field as Doreen continued to tell me of their life together, how difficult it was to declare a relationship between them until Hannah moved to Cologne for work. That there were always other women involved, that the secrecy sickened her. That she was young back then and knew better now. It was patronizing for her to say she was older than me, when in reality there were only a few years between us. I wondered what it meant—if the long, slick hours Marlowe put her through were enough to excuse her behavior. I hated her, I was sure of it, yet I wanted her to like me.

"I'm telling you all this because I care about you. I don't want you to fail, like I did. And Marlowe and I will remain friends. I won't cut him out of my life now—we're interlocked. But the moment I met you, I knew we could be friends too."

I wanted to roll my eyes into the back of my head. "Me too. Totally. That's exactly what I thought."

"So, if you're in love with him, I don't mind."

"I'm not in love with him. In fact, I don't think I've ever really been in love," I said.

"You haven't?"

"I guess not." It didn't sound like a lie in my head, but of course I was thinking of the first real heartbreak I'd felt.

"Listen, everyone knows what love is. You will be swayed by it." She took out one of her hoop earrings and placed it on the table. Then she stretched her palm out to me. "I forgive you."

"Thank you," I said, somewhat baffled. But then I couldn't help myself and added, "But technically you weren't in a relationship, right?"

She laughed and leaned back, reaching for her tobacco pouch. She started rolling a cigarette. "Well, that's what he told you. It's not what I experienced. And, anyway, you must be aware it happens to women all the time."

"What?"

"Women are left for younger women all the time." She winked at me. It irked me that I found this funny. Then she began asking about my studies. Even before I could answer, she rattled off what I understood to be basic high school knowledge of the foundations of philosophy. But she did this with authority, in a voluble flow. I only nodded and said, *Yes, yes, that's true.*

"Good job," I said as we exited the café.

"Do you want to come for a drink?" We stood outside, our breaths perceptible. It was dark, and the cold felt sharp and pristine as the blade of a knife. She looked almost Slavic in the amber light from the lanterns. "I'm having people over in a bit."

"I will have to think about it." I paused. "Probably not."

"Okay. Marlowe is not invited, don't worry." She came for a quick, unemotional hug.

I walked to the left, and my ears hurt from the cold. A man ushered a woman with a purple hat into the back of his taxi—an older woman with skin so thin it was almost translucent. It alarmed me that the man's silhouette seemed so familiar. Slowly, the figure became clearer and clearer, and I realized he was my uncle. I tried to look away, but it was too late; his face altered in recognition, a gradual difference in the eyes, and I sensed a tide of revulsion passing between us, a general mistrust in the universe that we were related. I can't say why, but when he waved at me, it was as if I were exposed to something indecent, as if a naked person ran down the street or a building was set on fire. A tear in the fabric of reality occurred, seeing Rashid there with his bad back and his creepy, wrinkly face. I had no other choice. I pretended I had not seen him and turned around, running in the opposite direction.

"Doreen! Doreen, wait for me," I shouted, my boots cracking through the ice.

# Fourteen

OREEN AND I sat in silence on the train as we rode to the better part of Neukölln. For ten minutes we avoided looking directly at each other, but I could see our faces side by side in the black window, where our reflections seemed despondent, spectral, as if sketched in oil. Leinestraße is where we got off. She insisted that she didn't pay much rent. Prewar building, a side street off Hermannstraße. In her apartment, which she shared with a stoner who was locked up in his room most of the time, nothing was finished. Appliances were broken, pipes were visible. Seeing her apartment relieved me, because it was in even worse shape than what I lived in in Gropiusstadt, and in a fucked-up way that seemed like pretty good consolation for how much smarter she was than me.

"Intelligent storage," she giggled in the hallway, and pointed at the purple bicycle hanging from hooks in the wall. I recognized her bike from the Facebook picture and admired the wheels, the fuzzy handles. How many stickers she'd put on the frame. A Palestine flag hung on the wall, and in front of an old Ikea dresser stood a congregation of shoes and more shoes: boots and flats, knockoff Converse sneakers and H&M plastic pumps, kitten heels I was sure no one had worn since the seventies, and a begrudgingly huge number of Vans in black and red tones. I was surprised the apartment didn't smell of unwashed feet or of cat piss, even though it looked like it would—in the corner was a blue litter box surrounded by a moat of strewn clay litter, guarded by a Siamese cat. The cat, she said, was called Leon. For Leon Trotsky, of course.

Attached to her room was a balcony overlooking the street and adjacent buildings. The balcony, I imagined, elicited suicidal tendencies in Leon, because the railing was extended with a pet-safe net no feline could jump through. Towers of old books were stacked on the floor, there was a chair weighted with a mountain of clothes, and on a small desk stood a black Dell desktop with black headphones. The Dell desktop and headphones—relics from a different time—moved me. I liked that she didn't use Apple products, which everyone else had normalized as the standard of electronic status symbols. On her door and on her wardrobe were posters of Kafka, Marx, and random women I couldn't identify. The room was nothing like I had imagined it to be, not girly or put together, not pretentious or clean or orderly. This was the room of someone who was not even trying to be anything beyond a twenty-five-year-old.

She pointed at the poster on the wall and handed me a beer can. "I really wanted to become a Kafka scholar. But that's the last thing the world needs. Another German Kafka scholar." She stretched her shoulders. "By the way, sorry for the state of the room, but we got it for so cheap when I moved to Berlin, and I—

I never got around to actually changing the wallpaper or doing work on it. It's so ugly. I'm sorry you have to look at it."

"I like it," I said, because not saying so would've been awful. I sat next to her and wondered how often Marlowe had fucked her in this room. "The place, I mean. It has character."

"Your face has character." She chuckled.

"What's that supposed to mean?" I grinned, trying to be cool.

"Oh, you know. It has character. Not classically beautiful, but it's interesting to look at. Prominent nose. Like mine."

"Thanks," I said. "Your nose isn't really prominent, though."

She squinted at me. "Did I ever tell you that Eli helped me paint the kitchen last year?"

"Eli?" I coughed. I didn't realize they knew each other that well. "That's great."

"Yes. He's a good guy."


"CIGARETTE?" I ASKED Eli after he arrived and we walked out to the balcony. As we smoked, Leon Trotsky came to stare at us with his sad, mysterious eyes. People were still shooting fireworks into the air occasionally, and there was the odor of charred things in the wind.

"Why don't you want to be with him?" Eli asked after we debriefed about the New Year's Eve drama.

"He doesn't attract me, that's all."

"You're scared, I think."

"I'm not scared," I said. "I'm not in love with him."

"Well, that happens gradually. I think you should date him." I stared at the balconies of adjacent apartments, unable to parse Eli's tone. Sometimes he said outrageous things to see if they stuck. He said he was a nihilist but found God everywhere. Listened to music with acerbic precision, could evaluate every synth and chord. He said he hated literature but knew passages from most classics by heart. Once, back in Münster, he asked me if he could snort a line off my thigh. I let him. Then he asked if I would ever assist him in suicide. Back then he had an older girlfriend, a redhead indie chick who worked at a cinema and wore blue eyeliner.

"By the way," I said, "you never told me that you knew her that well. That you painted her kitchen."

Eli put one hand behind his head and gently shoved my shoulder with the other one. "We're not close."

"You went and helped her move into her apartment. I think that's pretty close."

"It's not important." He pulled his hood up and stared in the other direction, then leaned down to stroke the cat.

"If you say so." The neighborhood square bristled. Trees bent in the wind, and an older homeless man crouched at a bus stop, clutching a beer bottle. He was loudly singing to himself, and there, caught in the middle of that evening, I knew that he had been beaten with a belt his entire life. "I really hate this city," I said.

"You always say that and yet."

"And yet what?"

"You came back, and you don't seem to be going anywhere."

"Well, it's better than the Catholic boondocks." I remembered my college applications and blushed. Below, people cut through columns of light with their tiny dogs, their partners. Held hands. After a while, the sky quieted. And small crystalline drops fell from what seemed to be a cloud just above our heads, commencing their slow journey to the ground and cars and buildings. I took out my Olympus and shot a portrait of Eli, his mouth half open in the grainy sorrow of that evening. "Hmm," I said, and lit another cigarette. "Snow."

"It's always like this, isn't it?" He gestured around.

"What exactly?"

"This." From the side of his face, I could see him smile.

# Fifteen

THE SNOW WOULD not melt. It glowed on rooftops and trash cans and set in our hair, and I was sure that spring would never come. In Kabul, an avalanche toppled from a mountain onto a road and killed more than a hundred people, and although Uncle Rashid didn't come over for a week—to recover, I assume, from my extraordinary behavior—he arrived that day to gripe. Proclaimed how cursed our people were and then sat on the sofa, picking at pistachio shells, dumbstruck by the news. Flights across Europe were canceled; dozens of pensioners froze to death in a Ukrainian village. A Turkish flower seller had been shot inside his own shop in Frankfurt. The news anchor smiled with a concerned demeanor: This was the twelfth in a string of unexplained murders, which my father believed to be right-wing but the news called *the Kebab Mafia victims*.

"Can you believe these people?" my father asked. "They're doing it again."

But the tone in his voice depressed me, and I did not want to or

could not bring myself to think of these instances for too long—
the bombings in immigrant neighborhoods, the curly-haired men
stabbed in alleys. A stone in my throat, I went back to my room to
read. Between my books, I found a flyer from a party series in
Münster that Eli had told me about two years prior, titled *Das
Land, das nicht sein darf:* the country that must not be, and although they of course meant the land of excess and hedonism that
existed in an autonomous third space, I thought of actual lands; I
thought of Afghanistan, and I thought of Palestine, my heart; and
in a way, I also thought of Israel, not as the nation-state it was now,
with its iron dome and military executing children, but as a mythical space where Jews, who never had a country, could go, where
children of Abraham could live in peace, where everyone who did
not have a country, people like Sinti and Roma, and me, also could
live. And sure, it was an embarrassing consideration, but there
were days like today, when my feet were numb and the umbrellas
would break in the wind, when I experienced with new acuity that
I was pinned to a cold, dark universe, when I wanted it all to be
real—Bethlehem, and fountains with milk and honey, and peace.
But of course there could be no holy place on earth; our life here
was purgatorial and meaningless, and God had forgotten about us.

IT WAS ALREADY dark when I got out of class, the streets wet with
ice. I huddled in my long green coat and tried not to think of him.
Marlowe and I had been ignoring each other—we danced through
the cosmos of parties, but the moment he came too close to me, I
would move in the opposite direction.

I felt newly shy around him. He, wearing his leather jacket, leaning against a wall or his foot pressed on a chair, looked amused. In his gaze I felt totally seen and also invisible, which is not something that had happened before. Images of him smirking or touching another girl's hair returned to me. *I don't want him*, I kept saying to myself: *I don't want him*.

I was walking down Dorotheenstraße to the Spree, when suddenly a small poster in the lit window of a closed bookstore brought me out of my daydream: Sally Mann's *Self-Portrait, 1974*. She looks in the mirror, her hair short and black, clasping her white, unbuttoned blouse with her right hand to hide her breasts. With the other, she employs the 8x10 large-format camera on the tripod. Her mouth is half open, and you can see her nipples through her shirt. Open and young, she looks more seductive than ruined. She is a silvery sylph flickering in the background, operating the machine from the side. It is not the woman who is centered but the camera, this black eye recording the scene. *You're an apprentice to the craft*, I remembered Marlowe saying. *You are secondary.*

THE PROFESSOR ASSIGNED Kafka's *Brief an den Vater*, and I read it on the train home, eyes fused to thin pages. Kafka begins by listing his father's accusations against him, like his unwillingness to appreciate or to pay back what has been sacrificed, critiquing his misplaced love and generosity for his friends rather than for his family. His father called the people he loved *vermin* or *dogs*, and when I thought of my own tyrant, the giant father of my childhood, the one who didn't want me to have friends or get any grade below an A, I wept in the bath. Afterward, my hair dripping on the pillow, I reread the opening. In a moment of weakness, awakened after a feverish nap and yearning for *Das Land, das nicht sein darf*, I sent Marlowe the quote from Kafka's letter: *My writing was all about you; all I did there, after all, was to bemoan what I could not bemoan upon your breast*. . . . I included a scan of a photograph I had taken of him: He sits on his sofa with wide legs, winking at the lens. Two days later he responded with one line: *You're a little too melodramatic for my taste*. And then he called me.

"I'm disappointed," he said. "You're avoiding me. You're behaving like I have done something horrible to you."

"I'm not avoiding—"

His voice was stern and full of ice. "You are, and it's frankly pathetic. I expected this from someone weaker—like Doreen, maybe—but not you. I thought you were different."

"I'm sorry," I muttered. It was a suffocating February evening; the radiator shrilled. A pot of tea stood on my nightstand, and I was too lazy to pour a cup. That's how lethargic I felt, how assaulted by the odor of fried garlic and eggplant wafting through the apartment. The jarring highbrow Farsi of BBC Persia resounded from the living room—another meddled election, the Taliban beheading a journalist, a commercial for dental bleaching. In the pungent jail of my room, huddled under the weight of blankets, I pressed my ear against Marlowe's voice. The cat's paws cut through the thread of light that burned under the door.

"Come on a walk with me now," he said.

"Marlowe. It's nine P.M. on a Wednesday."

"I'll come pick you up. What's your address?"

"No, thanks." From the other room, I heard my father shouting my name, *Nilou!*

"Was that your father? He called you Nilou."

"No," I said.

"Really, I want to come over and meet him. When can I meet him?"

I sighed.

"Why—is he going to kill me? I thought you're Greek and not Turkish. He won't kill me, will he?" On the news that week, there were reports of an honor killing—a young, green-eyed Turkish girl had been stabbed by her brother and father because she had a white boyfriend.

"Hilarious," I said, inundated by the certainty that I couldn't trust anyone. At the same time, I wasn't certain whether my father would kill one of us, or both, if he ever found out. Stranger things had occurred.

"Nilou," he said.

"I hate you."

He laughed, but I really didn't like him saying my most private nickname, which on top of it all, he mispronounced. I decided not to correct him; the only person who'd ever pronounced it right was Eli, and that was a long time ago, when we were sitting by the harbor in that small town far in the West and had taken mushrooms. Marlowe coughed, and I imagined him on his sofa, smoking a cigarette, wearing the gray sweater from the photograph. "I was on a walk earlier today, and I had this sudden urge on a bridge. Sometimes I look down from a height and I want to drop everything I care about into the river. Once, Doreen showed me this tiny heart-shaped stone her sister had given her, and when she told me the story, I was fighting hard not to throw it out the window."

"Now who's the melodramatic one."

"I'm serious." The image of the heart-shaped stone vexed me, and I wondered if it was a real stone or if he had made it up for this allegory.

"Well, I think that's a natural impulse, like wanting to bite a baby, maybe."

"What I mean is, you can start things or you can leave them. You can let yourself fall into the river and see what happens. Maybe you scrape your knees. Or you learn how to swim. Maybe you already know how to swim." His voice was breaking, and there was the clutter of something—faucet, glass—in the background.

"Why would I want to throw myself into the river in the middle of winter?"

"No," he said. "You need to imagine it to be summer. It's warm, but you're afraid of drowning. Why don't you throw yourself into it?"

"Fear therapy is not the way I handle most things. I have enough fear in me."

He laughed, but I thought I heard genuine hurt in his voice. "Remember what I said about artworks changing your life?"

"I remember, yes."

"Well, now is the time. Sure, there might be darkness. And pain. And knives we will twist inside each other or whatever that emo Kafka was writing about. I am almost certain there will be. But it could be an extraordinary thing."

"But with Doreen—"

"It's not like with Doreen," he said. "It's different. I want you. You're the one who will change the rule."

I was quiet, and on the other line there was the clicking noise of a lighter, then the sharp exhale.

"Well, I'm not going to ask you again," he said with heightened agitation. "I just need to know if you're in or out. And be-sides, it's my birthday and I'm sitting here all alone thinking of you." My face assembled into an involuntary grin. I didn't really want to say yes. But on the seabed of my filthy heart glowed some-thing else, like pity, and love, and victory—I felt victorious that I could have hurt him. That he seemed to care enough.

"You're manipulating me, Marlowe," I said, and visualized a dog plunging into an icy loch. "But I guess it's your birthday."

"Good," he said. "And to reward you for your bravery, I will take you to Venice."

I started laughing.

"You can finally see the sea, you dirty city rat."

He hung up, but his words resounded in my ear, making my head spin. Watching the few glow-in-the-dark stickers on my ceil-ing move ever so slightly, I felt terribly young, and when I heard my father calling me from the other room, I felt even younger. *You are the one*, I thought. *You are the one who will change the rule.*

# Sixteen

T HE BUNKER WAS housed in a former heating plant. Gray concrete, with narrow rectangular windows that resembled slits. It stood surrounded by trees at the end of a long walkway, majestic and severe. From certain angles you could see high-rises on the horizon, but the area gave me the sensation of postapocalyptic desolation. As Marlowe and I walked through the industrial park that ran from Friedrichshain to the Bunker that spring, I recalled flea markets where, trailing behind my mother, I suspected hell behind every stranger's face. As if the fabric between this realm and the other could rupture at any moment and we'd comprehend we weren't real at all. Gravity would malfunction, and we'd lift into space, exposed to the frail and cold machinery of existence. Marlowe called this the sole purpose of techno music and its subculture.

"It's Deleuzian, really. We're small machines trapped in the big machine of capitalism, and techno can defamiliarize this existentially fraught condition."

But I was troubled by the fundamental uncertainty inherent in post-structuralist theories—there was nothing left to hold you. I longed to believe in some a priori truth. Goodness and God.

It was a Sunday morning before dawn, and we stood in a very short line. Maybe a dozen people in front of us. Eli had not provided us with guest-list passes; in fact, he had not been reachable at all for the last two days.

"Will Doreen be here?" I asked. The snowmelt unveiled networks of grass. The earliest buds of spring emerged. I still hadn't told him the truth, about the building or my mother or my father. But who cared? We took so much speed I slept only four nights a week. He told me he loved me, not only when we fucked and my hair was matted and he was hurting me, almost, or when we were naked in front of the mirror and he said, *Look how beautiful you are,* and I lurched back in repulsion at my own reflection, but also at the end of phone calls. In Facebook DMs. In text messages and sometimes walking down the road, holding hands, and eating candied almonds. Or here, in line for the Bunker, his tongue hot in my ear.

"To answer your question: I don't know if she will be here, but Rico and Tamara are here, and they said that that Dutch lady will be DJ'ing upstairs." I loved the DJ, who was celebrated for her playful style, tribal drums mixed into minimal techno. It wasn't like the music on the main dance floor, where any semblance of sentience was abolished and you were just a molecule among the leather gays. Marlowe spat on the ground and opened a small liquor bottle by hitting the cap against his teeth. "She's been distant recently. Doreen."

"Oh, it's not like her to keep you out of the loop, usually. She loves *you,* that's for sure." I raised my eyebrows. The line stalled—the bouncer had disappeared inside for a bathroom break and closed the door. A collective sigh rippled across the group, and

Marlowe downed the brown liquor as if it were a health shot, then opened another.

"Keeping away the cold." He winked at me. "You should look it up."


DOREEN AND I had become curiously close—we went to Kafka's Minor Literature together and stayed for the length of several cigarettes in the courtyard, hoarse with excitement. She had visited Prague once and spoke about Kafka's handwriting. Brought folded-up flyers of speed to me during my Saturday shifts at the jazz café. But as so often with my female friendships, our interactions were charged with the slow-burning rage of hostility. There were days I resented her. How close she was with Marlowe: At parties, they gravitated toward each other, spellbound by the private opacity of shared history. Doreen's eyeballs would glaze with tears, a forgotten cigarette clutched between her fingers, burned to a column of ash. They spoke about people from a period before I knew them. Patrick, a friend who was addicted to opioids after returning from Thailand. Tim, a doctor's son who had drawers full of amphetamine pills and had been committed to a psych ward. *It's not for everyone, this lifestyle,* Marlowe liked to say.

"Well, she's so emotional. I'm worried. She's not like you— she's weak. I hope she's doing okay and it's not one of her depressive phases."

"Surely she's just studying, Marlowe. Finals are fast approaching." I was envious of Doreen's academic devotion. I was late on all assignments. Could barely focus on school, often fell asleep. The drugs burned holes into my gray matter, and the consequence was the forfeiture of IQ points. Marlowe texted all the time: demanding to know where I was, what I was doing. *Don't go to class,* he said on Wednesdays. *Come to mine instead, I can teach you more.* And I relented, went over, and he made me vegan zucchini boats, sandwiches with cheese and bell pepper.

When it was our turn, the bouncer looked at us for a moment too long. It wasn't the guy with the face tattoos but another bullish creature. Thick lenses, hair gelled to the side.

I halted my breath. Watched Marlowe's neck tense up.

A WEEK AGO, as we had stood there on a Sunday afternoon in a much larger group, we were turned away. Marlowe jokingly suggested it was my fault—my sequined bag was too girly. Too silver. Feral, he threw a red bowl at me at home because I made fun of him. It broke into pieces on the wall behind me, and though I was not hurt, the calculation in his gaze—his pupils increasing in size—felt outrageously mundane. A soft voice in me said to leave. But he gazed through my mind and commanded me to stay.

"I'm sorry," he said later with tears in his eyes, and then, "But you weren't hurt, were you?"

My shoulders relaxed. And it's bizarre—his weeping repulsed me. When Marlowe told me about his anger and showed me the hole he had punched into his wall after his breakup with Hannah, hidden behind a poster, I was almost disappointed to remember the boy from *Ceremony*. He was still trapped in those pages.

MARLOWE SWAYED AND joked around, a relief in his exhale when the bouncer waved us through. We had made it.

Inside, Tamara was seated on a barstool, licking at a dark ice cone. Her hair was clasped into a high ponytail, and she had an indefinable black smudge on her forehead. From the way she sat, her legs splayed wide, I could see the white underwear. Pubic hair prickling the cotton. Rico stood next to her, imposing and thin, moving his head to the beat. He wore a floor-length black robe made of linen; underneath it, denim shorts and sneakers, nothing else. His fresh belly-button piercing glinted in the light, a crown of blood crusted on his skin. Sub-bass thumped from the walls.

"Welcome to church, children," Rico said, and pressed his thumb into a small copper etui. He marked the sign of the cross with black powder on Marlowe's forehead, then on mine. The unguent cool and greasy on my skin.

"Ash Wednesday?" I asked. "Ash Wednesday was, as you can infer from the name, on a Wednesday. Months ago."

His index finger on his lips, he said, "Shhh. Why don't you want to play? Don't be boring." Rico had been reading a book on Teresa of Ávila, Tamara said, and now he was hung up on tradition. I licked some of Tamara's ice, then we descended into the dark terrarium of the dance floor. Swam through the thick atmosphere of music, and the next time I opened my eyes, I understood that I had drifted to another corner of the room. Out of breath, sweat running down my temples, I combed through the mass for Marlowe, because I needed speed.

"Here you are." Marlowe pulled at my ponytail when I reached the bar. "Can you give me some cash? I spent mine on the entry fee." I was happy to be helpful and handed him my wallet. As I waited next to Rico, someone tapped my shoulder. I turned around and saw Eli and Doreen. Things fell into place with a second-long lag: They had come together. Their hands were intertwined. Both were laughing, absorbed in the remnants of a story. Doreen's face was aglow with what I can only identify as an innate cache of happiness.

"What," she said, her dimples carving deep shadows into her cheeks. She retrieved a paper fan from her tote and started fanning herself. "God, it's so hot in here."

Eli smiled and brought her hand up to his mouth and kissed it, leading Rico and Marlowe to make hooting sounds. Equipped with drinks, we made our way back to a seating area. My eyes were glued to their hands, which were interlocked like that Brancusi sculpture of the kiss. "Sorry we were off the grid."

"We hung out on Friday afternoon and then we . . ."

"You were fucking." Marlowe furrowed his brows. He touched my elbow and pulled me closer to him, embracing me. "They were fucking."

Doreen slapped Marlowe's forehead with her fan but cackled.

Eli shrugged. "I heard some people do that kind of thing." Muted light filtered through taped windows, and Rico retrieved his etui again, riveted by priestly duties. Eli was willing, closed his eyes as if really engaged in a holy ritual, his hands in a Buddhist prayer position. Doreen, however, pushed his hand away so that her cross looked more like a shadow. Or dirt. They both smiled, and their smiles were those of teenagers. Eli let go of Doreen and handed me a hand-rolled cigarette. He smelled good, like soap. When had he started to bathe?

"Are you jealous?" Marlowe rammed an elbow into my ribs, and I realized I hadn't said a single word yet.

Doreen beamed. "Do you want to steal Eli too?" A wave of laughter swelled the group, and I forced myself to grin.

"Touché," I said, hating her, hating them all. "But Eli was mine first."

The sudden need to pee allowed me an exit. In the bathroom, illogical fragments of language teetered through the booths. Someone mimicked an accent, another moaned loudly. I felt impossibly small and alone: a child in a shopping mall, lost among rows of clothing, touching the fabrics, looking for my mother. A coldness bloomed in my chest, as if remembering it for the first time. She was dead.

I took my time to squat, then checked my face in the oval mirror of my powder box. The cross was intact, lending me an alien flair. An almost involuntary laugh escaped me, and when I opened the door, Eli was standing in front of the stall, waiting. The writing on his shirt said *Amon Düül*. He pushed his way in and locked the door again. I held my hand in front of my eyes as he peed.

"You can watch," he said.

"I don't want to see your amphetamine dick, Elias."

Eli suggested we go outside for a minute, and I relented, following him through the drooping music, past the bouncers and short line. The breeze picked up dust from the gravel road. The midday sky and sudden paucity of techno disoriented. When the odor of fried meat wafted over from the food trucks, I tasted bile. Two men stumbled past us: They had the sunburned, cross-eyed faces of those on too much ecstasy. Drool dried at their chins. Like cattle, they stared at us.

"Mouth breathers," Eli said, and we walked to sit under a tree. I put on my sunglasses to hide from the industrial wasteland.

"Life is so crazy. Look how far we have come."

"All the way from that garage where you practiced music and thought you'd become Nirvana."

"And still, we are losers." Eli always held up a mirror to me.

His friends made jokes about his Kosovo-Albanian heritage, asked if his father was in the Mafia. And although he joined in, I sensed the brokenness at his center. He was mysterious, reticent about his parents. His family too had become refugees during the Kosovo war—and I harbored such affection for him, even if I never told him about Afghanistan. I knew his father had passed away and that he had a successful older brother, who earned a lot of money. But otherwise he never invited questions.

"What do you like about her? I mean, except for the fact that she looks like someone tried to draw Scarlett Johansson from memory."

"She does look like her." Eli started scratching circles into the dirt, then stood up to stretch. He leaned against the tree trunk, craned his neck. "She reads—everything, the news. And theory. And she does community work, and I—I don't know. I don't want all this Bunker crap forever, you know?"

"She is so smart, it's true. Annoying, actually." I lay down on my back, staring at the system of leaves comprising the crowns of trees. Someone shouted that the police were coming, but when I turned my head, it was just one of the drunkards from the food truck. He dragged a giant teddy bear after him. His jeans were drooping, revealing his butt crack.

"Do you think we look like that to other people?"

Eli lay down next to me. "Oh, all the time."

"What do you mean," I asked, watching the slow dance of leaves, "when you say you want more than this?"

Eli exhaled audibly. "I want what everyone wants. A town-house. A wife, two children, and a dog."

———

I WOULD OFTEN reminisce on this scene in the following years: how surprising it was, his blunt earnestness. Until that point, I believed all of us were committed to the parallel world we had constructed out of techno and drugs, the nocturnal underbelly of our city, precisely because we rejected those things. My hedonistic soul rebelled against a nine-to-five job, a townhouse, parents with a child. I did not want tradition. What my parents wanted and had not been able to achieve in this country. This life of the people we called *Normalos*, the strictures of those we called *Spießer*. They didn't know what it meant to live, after all, did they?

MELANCHOLIA PERMEATED THE air around us, enveloped the trees like a gas. Eli had gained a new, tragic dimension. *He didn't really want this.* I dug my nails into the dirt, as if clutching driftwood, so as not to glide away from him on the sea that opened between us. But my love for him stood fierce and absolute, like that for a brother.

"Eli," I said, trying to mask the pain in my voice. "You will have it."

"She's making me a better person, that's all. And she's funny."

"Do you think she's cuter than me?"

Eli poked me. "There is something inherently good about her. Even if that sounds inherently clichéd."

Eyes closed, I smiled.

"But listen," he said. "If we are both single when you turn thirty, then we are getting married. And we will have the hairiest children alive."

"Monkeys, basically. Deal?"

"Deal." There was the hard impact of hot liquid on my shoulder. A bird had shit on me.

BACK IN THE club's darkness, I rubbed the shit off in the bathroom, and Eli had to work the coat check for three hours. Although I was afraid of Marlowe's reaction to my absence with Eli, he only smiled. When I laughed, he reached out and scratched my canine tooth. It was my chain-smoking tooth, turned yellow with nicotine. *Charming*, he called it: like a character in a movie. He pushed me against the wall in the bathroom and kissed me. I laughed out loud, his tongue all over my face. *I love you*, he whispered in my ear. After snorting a line, we disappeared into a different booth with an old man in a cowboy hat and leather pants, who was sharing cans of nitrous oxide. Despite Marlowe's disapproval, I grabbed the silvery bullet out of that person's hand. Inhaled the bitter gas. An icy feeling numbed me, then it turned very hot, and it was difficult to remove the can from my lips. Clamorous ringing rushed through my head, like at the onset of a migraine. I had taken laughing gas before but always out of balloons. Now goosebumps covered my neck and back. Some static had been broken in my field of vision, and I laughed out loud. The lightness bewildered me, as if a vacuum cleaner had sucked up my entire consciousness into some astral plane of darkness—for a second, I understood that the veil between this realm and the other had been ruptured; but instead of the dark depression I anticipated, there was only happiness and light. Everything was going to be okay, and behind that bright light was the meaning of life—I had seen it—though when I tried to reach for it, I was back in the aluminum bathroom, my head leaning against the wall, and Marlowe was touching my hair.

"Wow." I kicked open the door and walked into the hallway.

"I just saw the meaning of life," I said to Tamara, and sat down next to her. She was chewing gum and looked at her fingernails.

"I want acid," she said. "Or heroin. Or whatever you just took."

I grinned foolishly and touched my knees.

"Marlowe, where did this little Amy Winehouse get acid from?" she asked when he approached.

"Oh," he said. "That was laughing gas. She inhaled it right out of the can. Look at her lip—freezer burn!"

"Who has that kind of epiphany on laughing gas?"

They were both cackling then, and there was an auditory lag to my perception, as if my ears were filled with chlorinated water. I cannot describe the feeling—it might've been the laughing gas, or the speed, or the blue Nike, or everything together—but it was an immaculate sensation of euphoria, the Platonic ideal of a high, the kind you experience only a few times in your life. And I wanted to crawl right back into it, a violent hunger scratching at my heart.

LATER, IN MARLOWE'S stuffy apartment, we were trying to wind down from the weekend and listened to groovy house, which Rico was playing, mute and fidgeting behind the record player. Out of nowhere, as always, like a war whose threat is in the air even when it cannot be seen, the topic of immigration came up. I cut a line, poured vodka into a tall glass of orange juice, and tried to slow my breathing. There had been a bombing in a train station in Denmark last week. There were no casualties, and the story was still developing, but the news had labeled it an Islamist terrorist attack.

"It's like that bombing in Bremen." Tamara took the cigarette out of my mouth and puffed on it. "Do you guys remember that? My mother was so scared." Of course I remembered it from childhood: the way my father had turned off the news and left the apartment in a sour mood. The widow's blue eyes on TV, speaking of bean soup. *At this time*, the criminal profiler had said, *we do not believe this to be a racially motivated attack. There is simply no evidence.* No one had been charged, even after all these years.

"That wasn't the same at all," Eli said, putting his hand on Doreen's knee. "That was . . . right-wing Germans, probably."

"No, it wasn't," said Tamara. "Or who knows. It could've been anything."

"You don't really believe that, do you? That they bombed themselves?" Doreen was alluding to the media theory that it had been an inside job for insurance fraud. "Europe has a *problem*."

"You guys have to calm down," Marlowe said. "Nothing bad is ever going to happen in Germany; this country has itself under control."

Doreen laughed and played with the resin button on her shirtsleeve.

"I'm serious," he said with a grin. "Gun laws, well-integrated immigrants, memory culture . . . and these bombings are warnings, mostly. Nobody even died in that bombing in Bremen."

"Somebody died," I said with a hazy voice, and suddenly thought of the flower seller who'd been shot in his shop a few months back, the police calling him part of the Kebab Mafia. "One man. The kiosk owner."

"Exactly," Doreen said.

"Well it was ten years ago," Marlowe said, and I watched his face change: It was the face of someone who had lived in a different world than me. "I'm sorry, how am I supposed to remember that someone died?"

As I poured myself another drink, Doreen brought up another topic: A German politician had recently published a book, *Germany Abolishes Itself*, which was critically celebrated as prescient, albeit polemic. The author diagnosed the degradation of German culture because of relaxed immigration policies and proposed stricter borders, especially for those who sank into parallel societies and did not want to assimilate. Doreen vehemently argued against his stance, warning again of bogus media theories, but Marlowe stood up, leaned against the wall next to his giant canvas, and started scribbling on it. He wrote down the words *Why not?* He was interested in the idea: that *certain* people like *them* could not understand how to live among *us*. I was still thinking of the man in Bremen, killed by the bomb, when Marlowe brought up *Platform* by Houellebecq.

"And it was prophetic, wasn't it?" Marlowe asked. "Because 9/11 did quite literally happen a few months later."

"Yes," I admitted, because I was getting bored of the conversation, or didn't want to participate in it anymore. "It was prophetic."

"Who has ever learned anything from Houellebecq except for hate?" Doreen asked.

"Well," I said, trying to be funny, "I probably learned how to use my vaginal muscles from reading Houellebecq."

I remembered the darkness that *Platform* had opened over my life. I loved the writing and had read it many years after it came out, when I was dating Felix. Lying in his bedroom on the eggplant-colored sheets his mother had bought him, both of us reading the book side by side with the windows open to birdsong. *Intellectually, I could feel a certain attraction to Muslim vaginas,* the narrator notes in one of the earliest chapters, regarding a young Arab woman. This is the representation I saw of myself in those books everyone lauded in my youth—a disgusting hairy cockroach of a being, uncultured and uncouth, barely good enough for sex. Later, when I turned to my lanky, sheltered boyfriend and tried to unbutton his pants, he stopped me with a disapproving look. "You are deranged. Who would want to have sex after reading something so disgusting?" And I laughed, embarrassed by my abject desires.

MARLOWE'S PROPHECY FOR me—of an Epicurean life fully lived—was coming true. We dropped acid in his apartment, and when we touched our hands together, tiny molecules traveled from the tips of his fingers to mine. A tear fell down his cheek as he talked about disability law: *Everything deserves to live,* he said as he showed me the tiny ladybug that had survived the winter on a cactus in his bathroom.

More ecstasy? More ecstasy. Dealers frequented the apartment. Marlowe bought drugs, replenished them. A big order of speed came from the Czech Republic, which he stashed in his freezer, gave out freely at first, then started selling in small transparent baggies. He bought a drug scale.

"What is going on?" I asked, helping him weigh the powder and spoon it into tiny baggies.

"Well, I might as well make some profit off it."

"That's not very Gatsby of you," Doreen said. For the first week or two, our friends paid, but then Marlowe started handing it out for free again. And with me he had some mysterious contract—he refused to take my money for drugs. *Just buy me some booze,* he said. Or: *I'll get to you when I need to.* Often, he invited all his friends back to his apartment. I saw who used the big canvas: Rico threw paint at it. When everyone left, we spent hours in the shower. Crushed pills to snort, and he said, *You will be spoiled; you will never be able to fuck like this again,* and I laughed, unconcerned with what I sounded or looked like. I wanted to say other things, like: *I'm sad.* Or: *I am thinking about those nights on which I lay awake, listening to my mother sob in the other room, the way my father's body collapsed on the couch after a long shift, the scent of fried oil on his shirt. A frenzy of black bugs in the corner of our every room.* Instead, I always said the same thing. I said, *Touch me.* It was its own language, and imprecise, holding in it the fullness of my world. Of two different worlds trying to do the impossible thing, ferrying closer to each other.

We came back to ourselves, sweaty, disgusting. I took the bus home, my body shivering, coming down. I never looked my father in the eye, his presence large and looming in the hallway.

"Where were you?" he asked.

"With Romy."

"Your hair smells bad," my father said.

"Romy's parents smoke," I said.

My father frowned and let out a theatrical sigh.

"What do you mean?" he said. "Do you think I'm an idiot? My own daughter thinks I'm an idiot, that I don't know what she's doing. People are seeing you everywhere, drinking, smoking. You have no shame, no honor, nothing. Aren't you sick of yourself?"

"Papa—" I stopped myself. "I was with Romy, you can call them. . . ."

"You make me sick," he said. "You want to kill me." And although he raised his hand, and I closed my eyes in anticipation of a slap, he just walked away. Violence hung between us, unfulfilled.

I lay in the bathtub, combed out the cigarette smoke and dirt from my hair, saw the faintest fractal shapes in the air, but mostly I stared at a point on the wall where the ceiling moved, and I started crying because the world was worthless and God made me a woman, because he wanted me to suffer. Or I sat crouched against the heater, or at the desk, and read. Studied the pictures of Ren Hang, that oneiric aura. The self-portraits of Cindy Sherman. The poems of Paul Celan. I took more shifts at the jazz café, counting money, counting a way to get out. Where did I even want to go? I barely went to classes, though when I did go, I returned with a new and triumphant motivation to read more about photography, to learn. Dreamed of shots with a vision, shots for which I talked to strangers on the street and photographed them. Some days, consciousness was not so easy to drown out. And so, after the bathtub, after my father was asleep and I was still shivering, and the music was drumming in my head and I couldn't read or edit my pictures, I remembered my bad thoughts. All the lies I had told. Not only to my friends about where my parents came from or to my father about where I went out. A mouthwash I had stolen. The lipstick I had touched to my own lips in my aunt's apartment. When I thought that my life would be easier if my father was also dead. Or how often I had cheated on Felix with random boys at parties. In those moments I remembered my favorite story from the Quran, as if it were etched into the tempered glass of my mind: When the prophet was a young boy, the archangel Gabriel cut his heart out of his chest and washed every sin—every speck of dirt, every black spore—from it with the snowy waters of Zamzam. This story of the washed heart appears in the Quran three times. Whenever I harbored guilt, I prayed to the angels and God to cut out my heart and wash it too. My heart sliced open, rinsed in snow. I knelt and saw my heart phosphoresce with God's love, white at the edges. *Please*, I would pray, *I want to be good*, though in the mornings, the yearning for God, like every true thing I had ever felt, embarrassed me, and I knew to whittle it down, until it paled in the back of my mind, like a pebble filed by the sea.

# Seventeen

BIRDS STUDDED THE canal, and groups of friends traipsed by my bike. That evening, I had drunk too much Aperol, and the alcohol softened my brain, making me yield and droop and smile at strangers. My arm hurt from where Marlowe had pressed down with his weight during sex a few days earlier, but I cherished the bruise with a misplaced gentleness.

Seated on the rug by his coffee table, we ate vegan sandwiches on sprouted rye and drank lemonade out of glass bottles. Then we snorted some speed, and as the bitter drugs kicked in, Marlowe started touching me—with a shy, feigned formality. We were playing a game: I'd be kittenish, like the girls I had seen in magazines. Twirling my hair, protesting first with playful agitation, then with a frightened look in my eyes. I had to kill all sense of self; otherwise it wouldn't work, making it impossible for me to climax. We climbed that white-painted ladder to his bed to fuck. If the amphetamines were too strong and he couldn't get it up, he brought out a blue vibrator he kept in his closet. I tried to think of nothing, and when I managed to wipe my mind's slate clean, it was bliss. He would not stop, not when I whimpered or tears were running down my cheeks, and only did so when he descended into minutes-long sleep—despite the drugs. I kissed his forehead, his chin. How attuned I'd grown, in the months we had been together, to the growth of stubble on his cheek, his sweat. Sometimes, a sleeve of my shirt would trap his smell, and I was overcome with a longing so exhausting it felt like pain. It was the first time I really loved another's scent, as if reduced to my most primitive instinct. His body was taut and muscular, especially his legs, but there was a strength to his arms too. I stroked the fold of his elbow, the bone where his clavicle met his shoulder, intoxicated by the drugs, yes, but also by the fact of our closeness. Sweat-drenched, the sheets regarded me. When I looked in the mirror next to the bed, I remembered the manga characters I loved as a child: long-legged, smeared makeup, and that vacant look in their eyes.

Sometimes even this was not enough, and I yearned for more— spit and welts, for the glitter of skin and bites to accumulate in violent domination, to achieve total obliteration of consciousness. The goal of sex was not just to lose all sense of self but to forget death. Push and pull of desire, the blood and awkwardness, the strange odors and liquids, the power, which was both mine and his, regardless of submission—all these mechanisms produced the illusion of having stopped time. When it was good in bed with Marlowe, I felt both like an animal and a god. But sometimes he just fell asleep or I started dissociating while he pushed my head down, and I'd try again, waiting for the moment we entered the other realm. Like a good high, the promised bliss was waiting just around the corner, I was sure of it.

This obsession was like a dance, I thought later that week, when we attended a matinee show of a ballet adaptation of *Antigone*. Rico had invited us; one of his lovers was playing Creon. The theater was on Tempelhofer Feld, the stage a black platform on the grass. Ismene wore a pink dress and Antigone white silk, almost sheer. I watched their chests rise and fall, their arms drawing circles through the air. The movement came from their feet, yes, but also from their necks, their wrists—it was everywhere. Even their eyebrows danced. Creon in his haggard suit stood still as a skeleton. This stillness was so concentrated, so radiant, it made the sisters fall again—bodies lunged, convulsed, and dithered around him. Antigone swooped to the floor, then, waveringly, tugged herself up by her own hair. The hand pulling her ponytail was both hers and not. And in the cold of the audience, I surprised myself by weeping.

We wandered through the meadow afterward, and sunset cracked the sky into a vehement orange. As Marlowe and Rico walked ahead, I stopped to light a cigarette, staring at the field. Everything glimmered with hard precision.

"Are you having a Sturm und Drang moment again?" Marlowe asked when he found me. I wiped a tear and laughed. It wasn't that—it wasn't raw emotion. Something tribal and ancient, but also utterly modern and post-linguistic, had occurred on that stage. The dance was political.

"The performance was like watching something sacred," I said.

"Because dance reminds us that we die."

"I want to take photos like that," I said. I handed him the cigarette and knelt down, tore a handful of grass, and closed my fist around it. When I got back up, Marlowe opened my hand.

"You need to search deeper." He took the grass, scattered it back onto the meadow. One by one, he closed the fingers of my palm again. I looked at him, fixed in that moment on the field. I felt the need to hide my face but only looked away. *I love him*, I thought, and the emotion was overwhelming and almost violent in its totality.

THE NIGHT GAVE way to a balmy morning, and we took blankets up to Rico's unfinished rooftop to watch the sun eat up the city. Some chairs, picnic blankets spread out on the tar. The cylindrical water towers were decorated with torn Chinese lanterns. A chimney that someone had sprayed graffiti on—two yellow palm trees, some stick figures. Dawn was like a pill broken and scattered across the horizon. Dirt lined my fingernails. Marlowe's voice trailing off, putting songs on a boombox. It was the kind of music we rarely heard those days, except sampled into a house track—Soft Cell, Cyndi Lauper.

Rico told us a story of his lover, the dancer who played Creon: He was in love with him, he said, but the dancer was still in love with Amelie, a woman I thought was pretty but whose dental hygiene was so poor, she resembled a drawing of a vampire. Rico's solution was to propose a threesome. They had slept together, awkwardly, and the woman with rotten teeth started crying. And then this Creon, who had been so still onstage, got so upset that he ate an entire tube of wasabi paste.

"As self-harm," Rico announced. "So it wouldn't leave any scars. Isn't that the most innovative thing you have ever heard? I loved him even more."

I sensed that somewhere in that story was an important lesson about romance or art or both—but I couldn't really wrap my mind around it yet. Was mostly stunned by Rico's ample capacity for feeling.

A few photographs of that day still exist, but the film turned out blurry. My hands were shaky from the drugs, and the old Lomo had a faulty shutter, miscalculating the light thrashing through its lens. A haze of black and blue, which could be Eli drawing circles upon circles in his speed notebook. A white ring of light around the girls' faces, cuddling on the red couch when they were meowing. *Pose like this,* I'd directed, trying to get Doreen and Tamara in perfect symmetry against the cityscape. One picture shows Marlowe's shoe in the corner—this was in Rico's kitchen, where I dropped the camera while we crouched in front of his oven, waiting for the ketamine bottle to change aggregate states, liquid to powder, watching the oven as if we were watching TV. I remember his roommate coming in, asking us when we would be done. How he pulled a bag of bread rolls from the freezer, scraping off the frost, rubbing his eyes. We all burst out laughing. I looked around, at overactive jaws, pupils dilated to spheres. And suddenly I felt sorry for us, Marlowe with his books, and Rico with his broken heart. We were like Dionysus, who kept dancing and drinking and fucking to forget who he really was: Hades by another name, trapped forever in the underworld.

AFTER RICO'S ROOMMATE kicked us out, Marlowe and I went home by bike. We tarried rather than cycled through the humid air on Geibelstraße, and perched high on that metal frame, I felt my heartbeat accelerate. The maple leaves glowed, hoary with anticipation. I thought of Creon in his loose suit, still as a column. Or Antigone's pale feet. Swirling in the grass in her white dress. She seemed light-years away. We cycled past a Turkish bakery on Prinzenstraße that had been broken into and vandalized, partially burned down. This district, I remembered reading in school, was bombed to scraps and ash by U.S. air forces, and now there were these dreadful modular apartment buildings, populated by people who looked like me. The sooty shop front had been secured by caution tape, which had been ripped off, the shuttered windows tagged with fresh graffiti. Only one window was intact. We got off our bikes, and when Marlowe went to buy some tobacco at the kiosk down the street, I took out my Olympus to photograph the scene. Later, when I developed the pictures, what would rupture me wasn't the smashed door, or the handwritten sign saying *Wir sind bald zurück,* but my own reflection in the glass of the one remaining window, a dark apparition, and behind it, two white bags on the counter, crumpled like gloves.

We were stunned into silence for the rest of the ride. At home, Marlowe quickly drifted into sleep. I observed him with the lull of perverse fascination, turning his words around in my mouth. *You need to search deeper.* I didn't dare to ask what he meant. *Destruction births the potential for the symbolic,* he told me when we discussed the architectural ghosts of Teufelsberg. He was racked by some enigmatic force, that much I knew. *There was a clear chasm in my life,* he said, *before my mother died, and after.* I was always trying to imagine the young Marlowe, on his mythical California ranch. The scent of his mother's hairspray still in the bathroom when he walked in. The musk of the horses his mother rode, the mother with a German name: Annette. Orange juice on the breakfast table, his parents fighting. The ease with which he said, *I am an anthropologist of real life.*

THE NEXT MORNING I felt unusually vulnerable, and Marlowe too was reticent. He brought me coffee in bed. Kissed my forehead, and we had sex. The window was open; the sounds of spring were coming in: a robin, children playing. He was affectionate, gently stroking my shoulders and neck. Afterward, he looked at me with a pained expression, his hand pressed against the spot between my shoulder blades.

"Sometimes," he said, and his voice sounded the way it had sounded on the phone call in February, when he asked me if I was all in, "when we have sex, I feel like I am traveling elsewhere. The trees—it's like I'm among the trees in my childhood."

I smiled.

"Do you know what I mean? We were not here, just now. . . ."

I nodded, though I didn't know what he meant. He pulled me closer and smelled the skin on my neck.

"Oh God," he said. "Nila, Nila, Nila."

It unsettled me when he held me like this, as if he was suddenly afraid to hurt me. He kept brushing my hair with his fingers and telling me of California. Sometimes I was sure that what flickered between us was real, that despite everything, I could reveal my true self to him, all my secrets, and still be loved. But underneath, a new suspicion smoldered, a fear that nothing he said was about me at all, and that when he touched me, it wasn't about me either. That his hands were grasping not for me but for something he had lost inside himself: morning light, the hyacinth gardens he had walked through with his mother, the small rivers where he washed his hands after a long day in the woods.

# Eighteen

B UT MARLOWE WASN'T the first person I loved. The first person was a girl I met the summer my mother would die, when I was back home from boarding school. I was sixteen, already taking amphetamines regularly. Low-grade speed bought from rockabillies in Münster, which turned green from the cheap metal in my small bullet-locket necklaces I'd copied from some silly movie. I was perpetually dressed in a vintage bridal gown from the 1930s, which I had bought for fifteen euros at a basement store. The hem cut off, so it looked like a minidress, the cotton and lace yellowed with age. My mind was cluttered with books and films I loved, and the Lisbon sisters in *The Virgin Suicides* were at the forefront. I wanted to look like Cecilia. Cheap, clunky jewelry weighted my wrists. The melodic clink surprised me when I applied lipstick in the mirror, and I lazed about, pouting at everything.

"Do you have to wear this all day?" My mother touched the frilly hem of my dress. I thought I looked romantic back then, but I probably resembled a street urchin begging for money. "Don't you want to wear a slightly more appealing dress?"

I could barely stand it, how her face betrayed her disapproval. "It's my body."

"Just something prettier. Your father will be ashamed if he sees you like this. You look like a gypsy."

"God," I said, raising my voice. "Why can't we be normal?"

"And normal is wearing some rags? This is normal?" My mother coughed, artificially, and walked back into the kitchen. "Give me the potatoes," she said, and pointed at the Aldi bag in the hallway.

A small iridescent spider crawled from underneath the apartment door to the hallway, and I shuddered as I carried the purple net bag of potatoes into the kitchen. My mother was hunched over the counter, swirling her hand through a bowl of rice. Her hand was already shaking constantly, some neurological damage corroding her spine. Without looking at me, she said, "If you love me, you will take off that dress."

Only years later I'd understand that my parents were confused. I was their only child, and they were growing up with me. They couldn't decide which rules to keep and which to discard. They didn't have the clean orders of God and religion, traditions written in a book, even though religion ordered most things. Their structure of behavior was dictated by a societal tradition in which reputation was the most important thing. As long as you had good standing in the community, you were honorable. But I envied the orderliness of religion—how easy it seemed to have a set of morals to adhere to, a set that connected you to the higher essence. Stupidly, I daydreamed about a version of reality in which we were God-fearing people and my heart would be pure. The only uncle I liked, Darius, was my father's eldest brother. He was a tall man with sculpted features and rimless glasses. He had been an engineer in the old country, but he had accepted his fate here with grace and gratitude; he prayed five times a day. He was soft-spoken, and often I wished that he were my father.

"If you believed in God, maybe we wouldn't live here anymore," I said to my mother once.

"Well, try praying harder," she said to me. "If that's the way it works."

The religious families seemed happier to me, calmer. Their homes were always clean. They looked like they didn't fight, had mothers who were content with their homemaker roles. Not as conflicted as mine, torn in two by a repressed need for liberty and the desire to be loved by her husband. She didn't leave my father, because unhappiness was not a reason for women to get divorced. Everyone was unhappy.

Occasionally, my mother's idiosyncrasy ruptured the fabric of our pretended customs. The summer I was fifteen, she saw me holding hands with a neighborhood boy. Instead of hitting or scolding me, she took me to the gynecologist and got me the contraceptive pill.

"You're not having sex," she said in the carpeted waiting room in Mitte. "But if you do, I want you to be safe. But you're not having it." Afterward, she didn't want to talk to me about it, engrossed by the display case of the bakery, studying the tarts and cherry cakes. When I wore very short skirts and my father was not at home, she didn't force me to wear something less revealing— instead, she gave me a long coat to wear on top, one that I could take off once I left the perimeters of our neighborhood. When I told her I would hang out with boys, she only told me to be careful, not that I wasn't allowed to go. And when I started partying, she quickly realized she could not stop me.

"I need you to be healthy," she said, pulling up my eyelids and scrutinizing my pupils under the lamp. I could see the disappointment in her face, the sadness of my entire childhood emanating from that dark glimmer in her eyes, the glimmer that used to move her to slap me. But she restrained herself.

And I could've cooperated; I could have been content with those limitations. I could've learned from Nadia's mistake and become like the other girls, the Kurdish and Arab girls who hid everything. Some of them even really did save their virginity. They were home by 8:00 P.M., prim and proper, pretending to have studied. Adhering to their parents' rules until they moved out for college, to different cities where they lived in freedom, storing small containers of their mothers' food in their freezers.

So why was I plagued by some strange splinter, why did I have to snort every drug and go to every party, always running farther than everyone else, toward the nucleus of darkness and ecstasy? What did I find there? I stayed away for two to three days in a row. We snuck out of boarding school, our teachers reprimanding us. I returned with ripped tights and smoke in my hair for my 8:00 A.M. classes, trying not to fall asleep next to girls named Elisabeth and Anna-Lena. I excelled only in philosophy, analyzing Kant's categorical imperative. I didn't pick up my phone when my mother called me; turned off, it lay at the bottom of my bag for days. Her worried tone irritated me: It reminded me of childhood, a time I so desperately wanted to shed from myself. There would come moments, after three days on speed, when a frenzy befell me and I called her—I'd be at some after-hours thing outside Rosenwald, with strangers. Three in the afternoon, sunlight everywhere. The conversations sluggish with the idiocy of the sleepless and drunk. People were playing Yahtzee, Anna draped across someone's lap. Romy half asleep in a corner, snoring. And I'd feel terribly guilty, thinking of my mother unhappy in that kitchen with the Aldi bread and the mandarins and the curlers in her hair. She loved that terrible radio. I locked myself in the bathroom and, searching the mirror for a semblance of grace, dialed her number.

"I love you," I said on the phone. "I love you, I'm sorry."

The audible inhale like a knife twisting in my chest. "Are you okay? I need you to be healthy."

"Yes," I said. "I'm okay, but I miss you." And I'd babble on, waiting for her to tell me that she loved me too. Empty promises of coffee dates, of movie dates when I'd return home. The lie I lied every time, that I would not turn off my phone again, that I would call her more. But those moments were rare. Sometimes, fragments of girls like me appeared in movies. Evan Rachel Wood in *Thirteen*, screaming at her mother. Or Sibel Kekilli in Fatih Akin's *Gegen die Wand*, slicing open her wrists, desperate to break out of her home: *I want to live, I want to dance, I want to fuck. And not just one guy.*

DESPITE THE SCHOLARSHIP and Sabrina's support and the credit cards, there was never anything left for pocket money. Every summer since my thirteenth birthday, I'd jobbed at the local gelateria, run by a Lebanese family pretending to be French, even though Italian would've made more sense. LOUIS'S GELATERIA, the sign said. The guy's real name was Labhan. He wore a black apron and waxed his mustache in a small compact mirror. He only employed pretty girls from the neighborhood, paid us cash under the table, and told me to brush my hair. That's where I saw her, at Louis's Gelateria, under the purple awning with a spray bottle in her hand. She smiled at me, dressed in the uniform ice-cream-parlor shirt, the black apron.

"Hey," she said. "Cute dress."

"You're new?"

"I'm here for the summer." A leggy, almost androgynously slim girl with raven-dark hair she wore in a French bob, with two strands falling into her eyes, a reddish lipstick. Otherwise, her face was bare. Her gait came from her hips—she had wide hips, even for a skinny girl, and moved with a cool confidence. Mystery flickered through her eyes when she smiled—wickedness, curiosity. My neck constricted with recognition: I could tell that she was Persian too, from where I was. She introduced herself as Setareh, pronounced it the Afghan way.

"I think our parents know each other," she said. "I think I saw you once, at a wedding. You're the Haddadi daughter." During the shift I dropped too many things, stuttered. Her hands, I noticed, were slender and delicate, the fingernails filed to almond shapes. They surprised me, those feminine hands, the way the silvery bracelet dangled from her wrist, since everything else about her was androgynous and severe.

NOW, THINKING OF Setareh, she is water in my hands: cooling, elusive. An oceanic feeling seeps through my mind, and she is always there, those murky waters where the dirt has settled into stagnancy and moves only with the indication of dreams. We lay in the meadows around Tempelhofer Feld and ate cherries. Light strained through the opalescent window in her bathroom. She used a blue ceramic bowl as an ashtray. "My friend made this," she said, and it seemed to be the coolest thing I had ever heard. I told her about the nights I'd sneak into the Bunker with a fake ID—it had opened only two years before. A different, wilder time. How safe I felt there, adrift in a sea of gay men, the smell of smoke and excrement sticking to my hair. She was from Hamburg. Had graduated high school a year early and was taking summer classes in sculpting, living in a shared house with artists in Mitte. She said she had never been liberated from her parents' gaze. That she loved them and loved her two younger sisters, her older brother.

"In a different life, my mother would be an artist," she said. I told her I didn't understand the way my mother lost it, and she said her mother never even had it. We never specified the *it*. I barely saw her roommates when I went over to her place—but their belongings told a story of their own. Wooden salad bowls, organic shampoo in the bathroom. Curious, I studied the cosmetics jars and white-toothed combs, wondering which one Setareh used. Which cream had touched her skin. I felt things for her I had never felt for a girl before. We slept together under her white sheets, and her arm drifted toward me. Setareh—the name means *star* in Farsi—with the black hair. I loved her, but I was careful enough not to say it to her.

ONE MONDAY, LABHAN seemed unhappy that he had booked too many waitresses and sent us away "because of rain." Setareh was in a particularly peculiar mood that day. Picking at the rosy skin of her cuticles. Stopping mid-sentence to laugh. A mischievous grin.

"Let's go to the lake. Krumme Lanke."

"I don't have a swimsuit," I said. "Or a towel."

"Who cares."

We took two trains to the lake, chatting about nothing. Once there, the sky had changed to a grayish color, as if dipped in paint.

"It's going to rain," I said. "Labhan was right."

"No, it isn't. He wanted to scare us." I knew better, but still I followed her enigmatic determination. We walked through the dense and lazy air, mosquitoes nibbling at the backs of our knees. She untied her black boots, slipped out of her long denim shorts. Her calves were strong, stronger than the rest of her body. She pulled off her white top, and when I saw the transparent black bra, I gasped. Tried to look away. She jumped into the water, moving with the unanticipated elegance of a great egret, and laughed. Her mouth full of water.

I was scared to get in. That rot of algae and small fish. The lake looked brown, stagnant. Eventually, step by obdurate step on the craggy stones under my feet, I descended into the icy wetness. Shielding my bare breasts with my hands.

"You're very pretty, you know." Setareh was swimming in a small circle, her face lit up with the excited glow of an athletic child. "You need to be more confident."

She swam away with assertive, quick strokes. That entire afternoon she drifted far from me, absorbed in her own azure planet, drawing circles in the middle of the lake. Diving for long periods, disappearing from my gaze. But before fear materialized, her head would pop up again, like the black dot underneath a question mark.

"It's going to rain," I shouted again.

"No, it's not." Setareh's voice was a stone skipping across the lake. I drifted around on my back. Amber clouds strolled through the sky with the viscosity of a Renaissance painting. A type of equanimity filled me: This too was Berlin. This lake begetting this afternoon. Then, expectedly, raindrops fell from the clouds, breaking the plain surface of my dream.

"Oops," Setareh said, and we swam out. She was once again quicker than me. The rain had gained traction. She stood by the shore, hiding her breasts with her arm. She had lost her bra. She didn't get dressed until I got to the clearing, and she helped me out of the water. Our clothes were wet, and we put them on anyway. Hand in hand, we ran toward the train station, where we bought powdery lemon tea and a Brötchen to share. The crumbs stuck to Setareh's chin. The train's air-conditioning was on—we were freezing. And yet all I could see, when I closed my eyes, was the mud crusted on her thighs.

We took the tram to her house. Absentmindedly, she stared out the window. Her eyes were a greenish brown, the color of clouds in the sky before it rained, or my father's eyes, and when I looked at them for too long, I was very certain I would dissolve. Her roommates weren't home. We showered, separately, and the steam cleansed and purified me. When I came out, Setareh was uncorking a bottle of wine. A pot of tea steamed on the coffee table, which was a slab of wood balanced on concrete. I was giddy with the fact that I was wearing her underwear, her pink sweat shorts. Laughing, we sat on the sofa, eating saltines and cookies straight out of the box, watching an incomprehensible Hungarian movie from the sixties on their projector.

All the energy in my mind gathered into a single, intense beam focused on her physical proximity. Her knee-high woolen socks had slipped down, revealing her ankle, and she pulled up her knee to scratch at her Achilles tendon, and I kept staring at it, the bone of her ankle. A primordial feeling pulling between my legs. Her slim fingers moving up and down her calf, the almonds of her fingernails. Even years later, with Marlowe, I would sometimes think of the veins and sinews, the perfect skin constructing the landscape of her ankles. I must've fallen asleep on her shoulder; I woke up with a parched mouth. *Water*, I wanted to say, but Setareh was already lifting a cup of cold tea toward me.

"Here," she said, her eyes hazy. The back of her hand touched mine, and my whole body trembled. I wanted to weep, that's how much I wanted her.

"Oh. What was that?" A smile, followed by that devious blitz in her gaze. She must've sensed something—a flicker—as well.

"I don't know," I said, placing the cup on the floor. Her bracelet gleamed. I lifted her hand to my face and kissed the bone of her wrist. Her breathing slowed down. Got heavier. She hesitated, but it was a timid hesitation, awash with curiosity. I let my lips move up her forearm, onto the blue vein pulsing under her inner elbow, her shoulder, her neck.

"What is going on?" She laughed, a choked laugh that divulged nothing. She withdrew her hand and got up, circled the slab of the coffee table.

"I'm trying to be more confident."

"Oh my God," Setareh said. "Oh my God." She pressed her palm to her forehead, as if nursing a fever. Looked down at me, biting her bottom lip. I was frozen into a pillar of longing. After seconds or minutes or years, she sat back down and let me kiss her.

We kissed for a long time, the taste of ash on her breath. Her tongue in my mouth spoke a newfangled language, tender and soft and simple, then dense with structure and depth. There was awkwardness, but when she put her hand between my legs and rubbed my crotch, I sighed. Now it was me who was feverish, shivery.

"Let's go to my room," she said. I followed her, stupefied, into the small room with the yellow satin curtains hanging from the window. The soothing scent of detergent, girlish conditioner. Clothes and books stacked on the wood floors; the Ikea frame pushed next to the heater. Her bedsheets were embroidered with small purple daisies. Distant streetlamps blanched the darkness of her room. And still we were Afghan girls: There was a formality to our movements as we undressed, even here. We touched each other timidly, her hand moving up my thigh. Then anguish followed insecurity, and I turned into a kind of animal, biting her neck. I didn't know who was supposed to dominate whom, but I wanted to be inside her, to taste her, to be her.

Later, I was drenched with sweat, and she had a hickey. She lit a cigarette. The glowing tip of ash moved seamlessly through the grayish light, as if it were transcribing secret words into the air. Tangled between the sheets, I couldn't tell my leg from hers. Between us gleamed an absolute, almost terrifying openness. I didn't even need to explain anything. Would I ever feel this kind of empathy with anyone again?

"No one can know." That hoarse voice of hers aroused me.

"I know." She had a boyfriend; we had our traditional families. Once, I had asked my mother what she would do if I fell in love with a girl, and on that winter morning her face changed with disgust, asking me why I would say such a horrible thing. I had kept mum since, my heart clenched into a taut bud. But now, even with the impossible pang radiating in my chest, I experienced the repose of being initiated into a new phase of life, in that bed with the high ceilings above us, the cold air of Berlin-Mitte.

MY MOTHER DIED a week later. "I feel very tired," she said in the morning, and by 7:31 P.M. she was pronounced dead. She had a blood clot in her brain, a type of thrombosis. My mother's death tore a black curtain out of my life, a grief so fundamental that even now I am still living in the shape of its loss. She left me when I was at an age where I was inaccessible to her, lost in my adolescent haze. An age when child and parent are strangers to each other, where daughters are appalled by the awareness of their makers, and she never saw me grow into an adult, into someone who would like to touch her hand and say, *I understand now.*

A few people flew in—my mother's sister from America, her husband. People I had never seen before. Their children had small, ski-slope noses they wrinkled up in pity at the sight of our desolate apartments. Their clothes emanated the comfort of posh people. Through them, I saw the version of the Anahita I had glimpsed in childhood: the glamorous, strong figurine she had been before she became my mother.

"You came too late," I said, unwilling to engage with them. Thinking: *Where were you when she was alone for so many years?* At her funeral, I was high, snorting the last of my speed, holding a tissue to my nostrils and smoking out back with some of my male cousins. They were like brothers to me in those days, passing vodka in a water bottle. Good boys who would grow into respectable men. Those days, our usual rules meant nothing—they treated me as one of them.

My mother was not burned; she was buried, wrapped in a white shawl, to be closer to the God she only sometimes believed in. For months the grave looked unmarked, a grassy rectangular patch buried with bouquets and families of ants, like those of political prisoners in war zones.

"Headstones are expensive," my father said, and walked back into the bedroom to sleep. In the end, Sabrina paid for a gravestone. She called me and, sitting on the acacia bench in the hallway of my dark northern boarding school, I snapped at her. The reddish leaves of the maple outside were so bright they looked like they were burning.

"Just choose whatever the fuck you want," I said. "She's dead, what does it matter?" I hung up, and then ten minutes later I called back, apologized.

"It's okay," Sabrina said. "I'll choose a simple stone. One that everyone will like."


FOR A WHILE, Setareh and I met in the desperate, sweat-drenched vigor of secrecy, breath sickly with cabernet. I remember her thighs, my lips closed around her mouth, the glossy strap of a sandal around her ankle. I felt twisted in my love for her. Anna had had a girlfriend once, but she was much more masculine, a bigger woman. With Setareh, I sometimes felt scared of breaking her—it confused me, the desire I felt for the frailness of her body. I kissed her wine-stained teeth, and remembered my dead mother, and sobbed. But it was too much, the colossus of my grief. She could not stand the outbursts or understand my need to lose myself in nightlife. For a while my father stopped caring about my whereabouts. He rarely left the apartment, sat frozen on the couch and stared at the wall.

At the end of that summer, Setareh broke up with her boyfriend but scoffed when I proposed to be together officially.

"What does that even mean to people like us? There's no such thing as official." She cracked jokes for an hour, and then we fought. She wore a white dress that day, ugly cowboy boots. I fell silent, and before I left the apartment, she kissed me with a bewildering gentleness, both of us crying. She gave me her favorite coffee mug and a book by Barthes. She didn't appear for her next three shifts, and eventually Labhan told me she had left for Barcelona. Hearing the news prompted me to walk out of the gelateria, and I never returned. I was furious and swollen with heartbreak— but I still have it, that green mug, and that battered German translation of *A Lover's Discourse*.

WHEN I RETURNED to boarding school, I fell through crying fits. I snorted more, logged into online chat rooms for students, and met Felix. He wrote, *Your erudition is turning me on,* which was pathetic but impressed my grieving, immature brain, and we met in town, where he gave me a copy of Hesse's *Siddhartha* and we split the bill for two Coca-Colas. Two weeks later he said he loved me, and I took the bus back to my dorm and vomited. I was afraid of having sex with a boy, but soon after, desire raged. I wanted to have sex all the time, with everyone. Everything else slipped from my mind. First I lost my mother, and then I lost Setareh, and with them my last cherished connections to my origins.

My father, in turn, was broken.

"My heart feels like those green-plumed lovebirds who fall to the bottom of their cages when their partner passes away," he said to me. I was moved by his sudden bursts of poetic expression. He lost weight. Gone was the athletic, brooding man who, despite the occasional cigarette, ran every day and drank homemade protein shakes. His cheekbones fell in, and I noticed him talking to the plants in the living room. The inscrutable parts of childhood disintegrated, and he shrank to something fine and transparent, two-dimensional in his needs. He began resembling my uncle Darius, the religious one, and I realized that what I had taken for peace in Darius was in fact profound anguish.

His eyebrows grew to long bushy curtains that covered his eyes. When I went home, I made him sit down on the couch, a napkin spread around his neck, and cut the eyebrows, watching gray hair fall onto his freckled cheeks. His neck, his lap. The brown, wrinkly neck, those moles—the earlobes I loved touching in childhood while falling asleep. He'd been going to her grave every Thursday, bringing tulips.

He called me at school when he found a dragonfly in the kitchen, when a pigeon looked particularly pretty in the sunlight, or when a butterfly soared through the cemetery. He stopped working. Lived on a widower stipend and unemployment benefits. One day he brought back a kitten he had found in a dumpster at the cemetery.

"It was meowing," he said when he called me that afternoon.

"That's what cats supposedly do. Meow."

"It has these blue eyes."

"Anything else, Dad? You should bring it to the shelter."

"No," he said. "It's so small. It's like—it has no parents."

"Well, it will find people."

"Where is it going to find people?"

"The shelter will find it people, Dad. That's what they do."

"Oh."

"Do you want me to look up some numbers?"

For a long time I heard nothing, except for my father's baby voice with the cat. Then he sighed. "You know apricot was her favorite fruit?"

"Oh, Papa."

"She loved those apricot Danishes from the Qurbani Bakery."

"Yes."

"She loved them, and they had two-for-one specials on Sundays. And I had to get them for her. She needed to have one with her sheer chai. It was very important; she would get so mad if I woke up too late and they had run out."

"Okay."

"I can't believe she's dead, Nila. She's dead. I can't believe she died before me."

"Yes, Papa. I can't believe it either."

"It's so small, Nila. I will send you a picture." That evening he emailed a pixelated rendering of the cat. I pictured Frau Storz next door, with the gramophone and piano, and the seven ferrets ambling around her heavy wooden furniture, and the hair and dander and dust and terrible musk, and the synchronized chirping I had heard growing up, and I started laughing.


I STOOD INSIDE the grassy expanse of Neukölln cemetery, by my mother's grave, and I thought of this, of Setareh, and of the many hours my father had been gone. I thought of my mother's loneliness and my own loneliness. I wanted to tell her of Marlowe, of photography. Of having applied to schools in other countries. Of Eli's ridiculous jokes. I was sad, and then I was angry. We never had a relationship like that, even when she was alive—but the thoughts made up the touch of my daily life, and sometimes, standing on the street and looking down at my shoes, I remembered sitting on her lap as a kid, how close she held me. The tuberose of her perfume. The yellow frame of the bicycle she taught me to ride. And a lump would form in my throat, and I had to stop myself, remind myself that I needed to breathe. It wasn't my fault that she died, and yet—and yet. She liked to brush her teeth for exactly three minutes; she liked to eat pastries with apricot filling. She cut cucumbers into thin, perfect moons. I touched the ground, and there were so many ants scurrying around the earth; I closed my eyes and let the sunshine warm my eyelids, the heat filling the red room of my mind, and when I opened my eyes, there were the bees and pigeons and sparrows, everything so mundane and alive, every cell in me raging, saying, *but I, but I, but I.*

# Nineteen

MARLOWE SHOWERED AND put on Scriabin. He ironed his shirt over the edge of the coffee table, which he had padded with blankets. This happened occasionally: a weathering of his mood, obvious as a gust of wind. It was just him and me. We'd gone to one of those basement stores for used designer wear and found a dress for me made of blue vintage silk, for which he paid with his credit card. We walked through Mitte with our shopping bags, smoking hand-rolled cigarettes, and Marlowe pointed at people, saying, *They don't know what life is.* But at home he told me to brush my hair. *Real event,* he said, laughing, shaving cream covering his jaw, *with real people.* What he meant was, no junkies. Intellectuals and their friends. People with real jobs. He needed to know that he could still blend in. The smell of aftershave on his skin, an herby cologne. The crispness of his linen shirt, the sleeves of which barely covered his tattooed skin. When I did my makeup, he told me I looked like Frank-N-Furter from *The Rocky Horror Picture Show,* and so I applied cold cream to my eyes to remove the eyeliner.

That humid evening, we were going to a fundraising dinner at the apartment of a girl with a delicate face. I had seen her at a party earlier. People always carried it with them—their upbringing, their mothers, their houses. They thought they didn't, but you could read it on their faces, elevated and stiffened, like braille, waiting to be touched. I couldn't read Marlowe's that well, but I read hers. Lina was skinny, waifish. She looked southern, with large eyes the color of hazelnuts. An air of tragedy in them—she was raised sheltered and had been protected her entire life but had experienced profound loneliness; I could tell. The pain I saw was the pain of vulnerability that had not yet been the target of anything; no one who had been hurt could look so open. Immediately, I was intrigued. I said to Marlowe, "I want to take her picture." I wanted to pierce it, the vulnerability in her. But more than anything, I wanted to know if she lived in a place like the one I imagined her in—something festive, full of tiny trinkets, an unusual house that was still classical.

"What is the fundraising for?" I asked on the train.

"The fuck do I know." Marlowe grinned, clutching the pole and studying himself in the dark U-Bahn window. "They're always raising money for something. Poor children in Guatemala. Turkish widows. I don't know, it's very vague."

WHEN WE ARRIVED at the apartment, I briefly forgot about the cause, as I was shocked by the interior architecture. It was one of those prewar buildings in Kreuzberg, with outrageously high ceilings, on the third floor of the front house—the kind of building I'd love to see on walks, peering through windows into the paraphernalia of a different life: stucco and light, tall shelves filled with books. This was an old ballet studio, with floor-to-ceiling mirrors affixed to one of the large living room walls, the barre reaching across the horizontal middle, its golden paint chipping off.

Giant, empty fireplaces with art deco tile. A molding that crawled up the sides of the walls and culminated around the ceiling lamps, like a floral bouquet of extravagant whites. A few of the windows were made of tinted glass, so that evening light painted those of us walking through the western part of the room in fractals of reds and blues. The walls had trapped the odors of cigarettes and dust, but generally the rooms had the aura of a church or cathedral; I felt the urge to kneel and pay my respects to God. People whispered and clinked glasses; laughter was muted. String music playing in the background. Lina, the hostess with the open face, walked around the room to distribute dishes with incense.

In one sweeping motion, Marlowe introduced me to a group of people as his friend, the aspiring photographer. They were wearing casual chic, and it was a type of wealth I had no access to and did not understand. Brandless, conveying an aura of exclusivity based merely on material and cuts that other rich people could decode, like the shoes the girls at boarding school wore—black leather, seamless and embossed with some German brand. I was useless; I, who studied brands and fashion through glass panes or the gloss of magazines.

As more people arrived, I skirted the corners, aware of the sweat under my arms. It was the most beautiful apartment I had ever been in. Apparently, for a short stint after the ballet school went bankrupt in the nineties, this apartment was used as an anarchist gallery space. Marlowe fondled the orange slice in his Negroni and told me of the golden Kreuzberg years in the late nineties:

the last hippie squatters living in squalor, barracks filled with tap-
estries and dirty children crawling around, everyone rolling their
cigarettes and talking about art. "It was the best time of my life,"
he said. I tried to imagine him: twenty-five years old, his hair
bleached from the California sun, smelling of leather and citrus
rind, still believing that he could get Adrienne back.

There was a silent auction, a concept that I had never heard of
before. I didn't engage with the sellable items, though I let my
hand wander along broadsides and heavy mugs. Wood-framed
paintings, a vintage carousel horse painted in porcelain gray. I kept
complimenting things as I got drunker and felt Marlowe's hands in
my neck, my hair.

"It's very special," Lina said, and smiled at me without teeth.
But I couldn't stop exclaiming how beautiful everything was, as I
feared I would lose myself in the crowd otherwise. But then Marlowe squeezed my shoulder and said, "That's enough." There it
was: the dread of shame, for my exuberance and what it betrayed.
I was envious of how easily Marlowe merged with the rest. A
memory emerged, a memory of Marlowe asking me to kneel on all
fours, his words husky and full of need. I suppressed a smile.
Though he was a chameleon, there was something off about him,
something I knew and could fixate on like a sparkle.

AFTER AN EXCRUCIATING twenty minutes in a corner, holding a
paper plate with cheese and crackers on it, I forced myself to mingle.
I went to speak with Lina and Gabriela von Ascheberg, Marlowe's
boss from the architecture firm, and her husband: an arbitrary man
who looked like an accountant or a lawyer, so bland and regular I

would have never recognized him on a street, but he introduced himself as the head of a vegan bakery chain. They stood next to a gay couple in gray suits who looked like a set of slightly chubby Ken dolls. One brunette, one blond.

"Oh, hello, Nila," said Gabriela, her green-rimmed glasses reflecting the chandeliers. She wore a strict red lip, and I could tell from the way her eyebrow twitched that she hated me.

"You like books, right? We need your opinion on this."

"I guess I like to read," I said.

"Well, we were discussing whether Baudelaire is more poetic than Nabokov. On a sentence level." The longer I looked at her, the more she looked like a caricature.

"I think Nabokov is more poetic," I said, without feeling the need to defend my choice. I had read only the most famous Baudelaire lines, but he seemed too romantic; Nabokov, on the other hand, was one of my favorite writers. He wrote with a lushness that embraced both beauty and irony. I always thought that the poetic intensity of his style stemmed from the fact that he was exiled in English; that he excavated the strangeness of English because he was a foreigner in it. He encompassed everything I loved, and I wondered why I was taking so many drugs when instead I could've been learning Russian.

"Lina said the same thing."

"Lina is always defending the Russians," said the blond gay, and gently patted his partner on the back. He intently observed Lina, who exuded fundamental ennui in her white dress. I tried to figure out what to say next.

"What are you all raising funds for?" I asked after a little while. They looked at me, and then at each other, in disbelief. Increasingly, I became suspicious that we were raising funds for nothing.

"Oh," said Gabriela, "Marlowe must have not told you. We are raising funds for Afghanistan. Lina's mother is a great business-woman; she organized all this for the charity she founded."

"Lovely. For the women of Afghanistan? That's wonderful," one of the gay guys said.

"No," said Gabriela. "It's not for the women, actually. It's like that project we built for the Spanish islands. We're raising funds for the animals. Mainly the stray dogs. They really have no infra-structure for the animals there."

"Lovely," the Ken doll said, smiling thinly.

"Well, I know the women are suffering in unimaginable ways—really—and my mother has done a lot for Afghan women in the past," said Lina. "There's this textile business in Herat she has been supporting for years. Anyway, almost all charities for third-world countries are focusing on people. We forget about every-thing else that's alive. And we got such good feedback from the Spanish island fundraiser, so many of those dogs were flown out and adopted here in Germany. Animals have rights too, you know."

"Amen." Gabriela's husband raised his glass. "That's what I'm always saying."

"And our next fundraiser will be for Kurdish liberation fighters—for the women," Lina said, and Gabriela murmured something inaudible.

"Poor Afghanistan," said the brunette Ken doll. "It has been bombed back into the stone age."

"And the refugees . . . It's tragic. And they have such a hard time assimilating," said his partner. "Though I guess we are call-ing it integration now, not assimilation."

I focused on their shoes, black lacquer and leather against par-quet. They all had very beautiful shoes.

"My mother always says it was a beautiful country," Lina said. "It's too bad what has happened there and in Iran. It's really too bad."

"Lina is Iranian. But like, royalty . . ."

I smiled to myself. Of course Lina was Iranian—the right Persian, not the barbarian breed from which I stemmed. Of course her mother would help. Their conversation continued, but one of the items up for auction caught my eye. Framed in black wood, it was a black-and-white photograph of a young woman with curly black hair, wearing nothing but briefs and an unbuttoned shirt, being embraced by an older man. He cups her breasts with his hands like two clamshells. A cigarette rests between the fingers of the woman's left hand, and her eyes are closed, as if shielding herself from the sun, yet the man looks away from the camera, to the left. They look like they stepped out of their kitchen for morning coffee and are about to return to the bedroom. The languid demeanor elucidated that they were artists: the way they used their bodies as both language and prop. When I looked at the tag underneath the painting, it identified them as Max Ernst and Leonora Carrington. It thrilled me that this photograph, despite being in black-and-white, was more charged than most other photographs I had ever seen. Desire rose from it like a lawful act—as if it were the most natural thing in the world. After a minute or so, I heard someone call my name and returned my attention to the group.

"Nila," said Gabriela's husband, and turned to me. "What is your background? You are quite Mediterranean-looking yourself." The heat of their gazes inflamed my face, my hands, my shoulders.

"Greece," I said. "My parents are Greek." The group started

cooing like a bunch of birds, and I was happy they wouldn't know my real heritage—they would've probably asked me to give a toast to these Afghan dogs.

I wanted to excuse myself, but then Marlowe and a couple in matching linen stepped into the group and Gabriela asked me to explain more about my studies at university. For a minute I said nothing. My ear was straining to listen to Lina: I'd overheard her telling someone about her parents meeting her new boyfriend in Paris, and I imagined her life—liberated from secrecy, from hiding, a normal European life like all the German girls lived, without complication or grand betrayals, and I hated her or myself, I wasn't sure.

"Well, Nila, how are classes going? Philosophy, right?"

"Anything to counteract the innate wish to die. Philosophy is famously well suited for that," I said. *Get out of this conversation*, I commanded myself. How could I explain to them that I didn't want to go to classes anymore? As I stood there, insulted by the sweetness of these soft-spoken, educated people, I tried to focus on my life. Pain throbbed behind my eyes, and I bit on the inside of my cheek to suppress the tears. These people, even if they did not really know me, were trying to look through me and into me, as if pressed against the bars of my cage, illuminating me with flashlights.

"OKAY," MARLOWE ASKED. "Who wants another drink?"

"I'll get some," I said.

"No," he said, and grabbed my wrist very tightly.

"Leave me alone." I pushed him away. Maybe it was the alcohol: I wanted to fight. I walked over to the kitchen and grabbed a bottle of wine, appreciating that Marlowe would sidestep me for the rest of the night. When I refilled my glass for the hundredth time, I dropped two plates in the kitchen, two white porcelain plates Lina called heirlooms. A manic hiss of a laugh escaped my throat; of course Lina possessed heirlooms. A mother, alive, who raised money for dogs in Afghanistan.

"What's the matter with you?"

"Why? What's the matter with you? You're drunk."

"Now, that's very rich. You're the one who's drunk." And then, looking across his shoulder to other people, he said, "I will take her home."

"I don't want to be at a fundraiser for Afghan dogs anyway. This is pathetic." I wanted to say more but stopped—already I had exposed too much of my real self. But he must've seen it in my eyes, the pure and concentrated resentment. There was a shocked expression on his face. He pulled me by my arm out the door, and in the reflection of the ballet mirror, I was gaunt and dark-eyed, my shoulders glowing above the strapless blue silk. I looked beautiful, I thought, elegant, even with the mascara smeared on my cheek. Giddy from the wine, I felt an unexpected desire for myself.

In the hallway, the stairs were moving under my feet, and I remembered my anger. "You're a pathetic old man. A pedophile drug addict," I said.

On the ground floor, he pushed me against the railing and then punched my shoulder. It wasn't impactful or calculated—it was more of a reflex—but I started laughing.

"How original," he said.

"You hit me," I said, and in his eyes I detected a strange flicker, not unlike the flicker I had seen during sex sometimes, a rush that enlarged his pupils to little black moons. I touched my shoulder instinctively and looked at my hand, as if for proof.

"I did not hit you." He kicked the row of rusted mailboxes with his shiny black shoe. Then again.

"You hit me."

"Shut up," he said, and walked over to the door. His fists finding the wooden frame. Little shouts erupted from him, more like the yowls of a dog than of a human. A grin on his face. Or perhaps not a grin but animalistic terror. "Just shut up. Nila, shut the fuck up."

It occurred to me that I should calm him down. It would have been the right thing to do. In one version of the night, I would have shut up, gone over to him, apologized, and played the expected role. But I couldn't do it.

"You hit me." My laughter had a crazed and hoarse tinge, unfamiliar to me.

"I didn't hit you." He balled his hand into a fist and bit it, as if trying to muzzle himself. I stared at the pit stains under his arms. Then the hallway light turned off, the planetary darkness turning the corridor into a stage of fleur-de-lis tile and brass details. The scent of mildew in the air. Marlowe heaved with theatrical force. And I? I wanted to see how far he would go.

"Oh, Marlowe," I said. "Show me you can."

"Show you what?" Marlowe whimpered, kicked the railing. I imagined the vein in his neck pulsing under the tattoo of the spider. "You're insane," he said.

"What," I said, still laughing. "Are you a coward?"

He walked toward the other end of the hallway. Streetlights

filtered through the opaque window above the doorframe. He kicked the railing anew, with less force, and walked back to me. Step for step. In one of the other apartments, someone screamed. The light buzzed on again. I blinked, adjusting to the newfound clarity: An entire unspoken life transpired between our eyes. Then he tilted my chin forward. The thump was sudden. A strain in my neck. My skull, my left eye. It took me a moment to understand that he hadn't hit me in the face with his fist. Instead, he'd clasped my jaw, twisted my head to the side, and thrust me into the wall. The impact was blunt, a throbbing that felt like a brick inside my head. But not as bad as I expected. His fingers lingered on my mouth for a second before we released. Against all odds, I was vibrating with an unyoked erotic rush that originated between my hips and moved up my back, like electricity. Pain, and a gushing of endorphins. For a moment we regarded each other like strangers, suspended in blissful shock. But then there was a quivering in his lips. I felt the words before he said them. *Everything is ruined.*

We stood in the middle of the street, where it was unseasonally warm and balmy, the air studded with foreign sounds. People glanced at us, or tried to look away, as we screamed obscenities at each other.

Eventually he pushed me into a cab and said, "Take her home."

I rolled down the window. "I don't have any money," I said, tears running down my cheeks, tears of anger.

"Tell it to someone who cares." He planted his hands firmly in his coat pockets. He looked handsome in his trench coat. I searched for that look in his eyes, from the bar and the first time he balanced himself on top of me. But that man was nowhere on that street. This was a different Marlowe, with a furrowed brow, refusing to turn around. It infuriated me—here I was, carnal, in love. I felt humiliated and confused by the impersonality of his violence: He'd rammed me against the wall like a doll.

The cab driver, a Russian man with an oily forehead and eyes the color of swimming pools, grunted. "What now?"

"Sorry." I got out of the cab and ran off into one of the side alleys, emerging on another busy street. He did not follow me, but it was Friday night in Kreuzberg—the smell of kebab shops, the Fernsehturm, which I so rarely noticed, puncturing the sky. Sirens ebbed and flowed at traffic's distant shores. A layer of wetness shone on the asphalt. I wandered the streets, my head burning from the wine and the pain. Nursing my bruise, I sat down next to a homeless person, who shared two Camel blues with me. I don't remember what we talked about, but we sat there for an hour or two. Oh, Berlin, my old Berlin: Sometimes the streets did welcome you into their arms, no matter how far you sank.

MY FATHER SAID nothing when I came home; he just stood in the hallway with the peeled wallpaper. Wearing his slippers, a big stain on his chest. There were dumbbells on the floor, the wheels of his Aldi bike spinning. Persian pop songs in the background. The cat purred at my feet. I could barely look at him, suppressing the sensation that I wanted to scream.

"What happened to your face?" he asked.

"I fell," I said. "Down the train-station stairs."

"You fell," he repeated. Then stumbled back into the living room.

"You have mail," he said. I still loved him, that sad beast. I followed him into the living room, retrieved the pile of letters next to the fruit bowl with two saggy pears, and turned off the music.

"You should take a bath, Papa. Stop exercising now. It's late. Good night." I kissed him on his stubbly, sunken cheek. In the bedroom, I looked in the mirror: My hair was disheveled. I saw the swelling above my eyebrow, the first instance of a bruise forming around my eye. The overhead light terrified me, elucidating the mess of my childhood room. A silverfish darted under the bed. I drew the curtains, turned off the light. I slipped out of the silk dress, and by the glow of my laptop screen, I opened my mail: Two health-insurance bills. One new U-Bahn pass. And then the three brown envelopes with foreign stamps. I tore them open with equal amounts of hope and apprehension, barely scanning the text. Acceptances to three colleges in London.

# Twenty

I T HAD BEEN a week since the incident at the gala, and Marlowe told me he needed a break. All week I had lain in bed, wallowing in the warm blanket of sentimentality, the way girls did in movies, sulking in the bathtub to "Bette Davis Eyes" and screaming into my pillow and pleading with God before I began crying again. To my abject humiliation, I even watched romantic comedies in bed. Scraped my spoon into old ice cream, ate pickles straight out of the jar on the floor of the kitchen. When my father asked what was going on, I said, "Nothing, I'm fine." My need for a reaction seemed pathological. I was possessed, I deduced, by *l'amour fou*. I read André Breton's *Nadja* and convinced myself that our love must be like that, that I was a frail person he had chosen only for her vicinity to the other realm. In reality, of course, I was much more extroverted and bubbly than Nadja, and Nadja was a schizophrenic who ended up institutionalized and homeless on the streets. But at the time it seemed there were only two options: You could be the wife who was cheated on, or you were the it-girl mistress who then ended up fishing her dinner out of dump-sters. There was no in-between.

I TOLD MARLOWE about London, but he didn't react, besides a neu-tral *congratulations*. I finished work early and walked over to Eli's, laughing about the bruise on my heart and the bruise on my face. I told him that I had fallen too. The story seemed so simple, I had begun to believe it myself. We were celebrating the acceptances, drinking cheap, syrupy wine out of the bottle on his front steps, but it was hard to focus. I shielded my eyes against the evening sun as Eli spoke of commodity fetishism and Marxism and *The Com-munist Manifesto*. He asked me if I recycled. "I recycle," I said. "Good," he said. At the bus stop on the opposite side of the street, a group of Arab teens congregated like a lump of bad luck. I looked away. At dusk, it began to rain heavily, the kind of slick and sticky rain that slaps the streets and rises back in humidity, activating the chalk and earthy roots of the city until everything feels glorious and alive again, so we took a moment to stand there, letting the rain touch us, and the Arab boys began laughing like children, and I was giggly and distracted and thought maybe it wasn't all too bad, maybe I didn't need Marlowe. But when I went back upstairs and sat on Eli's sofa, my hair dank against the fabric, goosebumps covered my skin, and I could feel it again. The little voice in me that said, *Marlowe, Marlowe, Marlowe*. We were watching a movie on Eli's laptop—a documentary on the aurora borealis—until he fell asleep with his mouth closed, his eyes moving under his lids. A half-smoked unlit cigarette in his hand. He was deep in a dream about lights dancing through an Icelandic sky and green hills and a better political system. I couldn't stop myself. I turned the lights off and went out the door.

I CYCLED IN the rain all the way from Eli's apartment by Ankerklause to Marlowe's house. I raced through Skalitzer Straße, all the world's water sticking to my face and soaking through my cheap shoes into my socks. It was as if his love depended on my labor, as if I had to suffer for this arrival. The city lights were melting in the puddles on the streets and I remembered my father, whose calls I had been ignoring, and the sensation of moving at such velocity against the rain felt as though my mind wasn't really mine at all but someone else's, the city's, disintegrating in the wind. When I arrived I was overjoyed with adrenaline, but Marlowe didn't open the door. He refused. I rang and rang. Then I rang the neighbor's. And the other neighbor's, until someone finally buzzed me in, a black cat in the hallway zipping past me and into the dark yard. Up the stairs I could hear music, a thin thread of light glowing under the door, faint voices. When I called, Marlowe didn't say anything. I shouted and banged against the door. I didn't really want to pound my fists on his door, but there was another part inside me, my selves splitting in mitosis, and the new girl I had become wanted to behave as dramatically as possible. Marlowe only texted, *I am not here. I am not home.* And then, after a few minutes: *You're scaring me. You're crazy. I don't want to see you.*

"I fucking hate you," I yelled, and other improbable things I do not like to recall anymore, but eventually embarrassment clarified my anger. Drained, like after long periods of starvation, I walked down the stairs, sat at the bottom, and began crying. No dignity. I couldn't ride back in the cold. I couldn't do it again—this joy, it had only a beginning. A mystifying thought appeared: Maybe none of these feelings had anything to do with him. Maybe all I needed was to chase the sensation of intensity. I shuddered, laughed, a crazy person relieved by newfound revelation, but the truth left as quickly as it appeared.

I waited until the rain lessened, and in the courtyard I saw the black cat again. It approached me when I called out for it this time. It came closer. It wouldn't touch me, but it didn't avoid me either. When I crouched down to be eye level with the cat, I saw behind it the purple wheels, the scrubby frame: It was Doreen's bike.

ROMY POURED COFFEE from the French press into those mint-green Ikea mugs I loved. Still manic from my heartbreak, I had come to stay with her and Anna in Prenzlauer Berg last night. She looked well-adjusted and healthy in the sunlight, like she was someone else's friend. Her reddish curls had a blond hue. She wore a terry-cloth romper and leg warmers that reminded me of a Jane Fonda fitness video.

"Have you been eating well?" I asked.

"Do I look fat?"

"No, you look healthy." Resignation had settled in me, now that I knew he had been with Doreen. Serenity. Even though I tried not to believe him after I confronted him over SMS. He said he didn't sleep with her, that she was there as a friend. Eli too told me that they had only been talking—that he trusted Doreen, even if Marlowe was "an asshole."

"So what is wrong with you?" Romy asked, pouring more coffee into our mugs. Anna had gone to buy groceries. They wanted to make pasta today and sushi tomorrow. I sat at the table in the kitchen, on the armchair I knew was her favorite spot, and scratched my fingernails into the wood. "For someone who's just gotten into a dream school, you don't seem too well."

"I'm in love," I said. "With the wrong person." There was also, of course, the problem with money. The problem with getting anywhere was money—I couldn't afford it. Even with a student finance loan for tuition, rent was more than double that of a room in Berlin, and you didn't get free transportation.

"Oh, you knew what you were getting yourself into." Romy was leaning against the counter. "You are doing this to yourself."

"I'm very unlucky."

Romy sighed. "We warned you. Didn't Doreen warn you too?"

"Nobody warned me. Doreen told me she was unhappy with him. But he said it would be different this time. And besides, it's not like she is avoiding him like the plague or anything."

Romy meant the fact that she and Anna had had older boyfriends themselves—eccentric men whom they met during the last year of school. Drug dealers who got us guest-list passes to dubious parties, who hung out in abandoned houses with unattractive, toothless people and made crass jokes. Anna's ex was manipulative, a liar who loved to tell everyone some sad story. Early on in the relationship with Marlowe, Anna had sat me down and said, *You can only do this for fun. Do not fall in love with him.*

"Well," Romy said. "He looks like an ashy carrot. And he looks like he doesn't shower. You deserve someone who uses shampoo."

I laughed, remembering Frau Storz and her theory of root vegetables.

"You know you have a problem, right? You're addicted to him. Anna had the same thing with Erik. Thinking he could fill some void in her heart. All you do is spin in circles and circles, and then it ends up being self-destructive. Do you remember how much she cried?"

I reconstructed it: Anna's sleepless nights in boarding school. Sneaking into our rooms, demanding to share the bed. Sheets moist with her tears. That pile of used tissues she wept into. The only thing she talked about, waiting by the phone, like expecting good news. In conversations she trailed off, biting her fingernails. She brushed her hair into a long braid at night, then undid it in the morning for the waves. Bought a new perfume. For days at a time she stayed away. She was suspended from school for two weeks because of absence. Then she emerged again, with anemic shadows under her eyes. Her tights ripped. The scent of alcohol even on her bag. For months after, she had a thousand-yard stare, as if she was looking far away into the past. *Earth to Anna,* we'd say, and she barely smiled. She was a wreck. He had kicked her out. "I remember."

"We love you, Nila. We want you to be safe."

"Sure." It irked me: It was what my mother used to say when I had started doing drugs and going to parties. *I want you to be safe. I need you to be safe.*

"And we invite you to things and you always flake on us."

"I am aware. I'm sorry." I looked at her, infinitely removed. What was this sharp, acute twitch in my throat? A tear ran down my cheek. "I'm the worst." I stared out the window—you could see a church, some trees, and a cobblestoned street. Vietnamese restaurants on the ground level of baroque apartment blocks. The distant sounds of cars. It was a different Berlin up here—a clean, sweet Berlin with a tram. Their ceilings were higher than Marlowe's, and because of their large, west-facing windows, the apartment was drenched in sunlight. Light floorboards, homemade lampshades. A feminine cleanliness, despite the dog hair from Anna's chihuahua. Romy cleaned the counters, then brought out a bag of flour. It had a hole in it and left a trail of white powder on the kitchen boards. "We have mice," Romy said. "And for some reason they're obsessed with spelt flour. Who would've thought?"

"They're real Prenzlauer Berg mice," I said.

Romy laughed and deposited the bag in a trash can she kept under her sink. I glimpsed the flurry of bottles and cleaning supplies underneath, all organic brands, stocked in a clear box. A toilet plunger. She shut the door with the back of her foot. "Men like Marlowe. . . . I have only met him a handful of times, but he likes to be in control. He likes it—I saw it with Anna and Erik, and now I'm seeing it with you. I don't support it. But I guess you love him . . . so what can we do?"

I shrugged and smiled. "I know you know."

"You got into college in London," said Romy. "This is your chance."

"You mean this is your chance to get rid of me? Wow, thanks again."

She sat down opposite me and poured some sugar into her coffee, soy-milk creamer. The morning sun haloed her hair with an angelic crown. Her fingernails painted eggplant, moles constellating on her pale skin like stars. Looking at the blond hairs on her forearm made me wistful. "What I mean is, you're smart. You should actually attend your classes. When you're in London—you should go get your degree and leave all this shit behind. Make something." Romy got up again and began sweeping the floor.

"I will never be able to afford that." I detected a coldness in her. I imagined her and Anna during weekday mornings, sharing coffee and talking about the classes of the day. Or ignoring each other. Inviting their parents over, having brunch with them. Romy told me that Anna even sometimes talked to Romy's grandmother. What did it feel like—a normal friendship, where you could let someone so close they knew everything about you, like family? Where you opened the skin to the blood and muscle and bone of your being and they did not run away in horror but came closer, embraced you?

ANNA RETURNED LATER with shopping bags overflowing with carrots, celery, organic apples. Her chihuahua, Taco, was dressed in a neon-orange handkerchief. The dog yelped, then jumped on my lap. Shivery, its heartbeat drumming under my hand. Anna made an elaborate vegetable sauce, and Romy chopped up a salad. I busied myself making them drinks—cocktails with elderflower syrup and cheap prosecco. Leaning out their small, street-facing balcony, we smoked real cigarettes and laughed.

"You know," Anna said, "it's not intellectually inferior or square to stop blasting your brain full of drugs and go to college."

"What is that supposed to mean?" I tapped the ash into the metal ashtray we had stolen from a restaurant last summer.

"It means you're going to be fine not chasing some bohemian

cliché of an artist's life. We all did it, we all grew up, there is a life after it. Parties? Techno? Drugs? It's fun, but it isn't real."

Looking back, I am stunned by Anna's maturity. Perhaps it was her relationship with Erik that woke her up—or her family, who loved her unconditionally, supported her. *I feel empty*, Anna said one day after coming home from another weekend with Erik. *I am doing all of this to feel something.* It was the opposite for me—I felt too much. I wanted to numb myself. I smiled at her. "Don't let some washed-up writer ruin your life. He stopped being relevant like ten years ago, okay?"

She put out her cigarette and scratched her cheek. Then she touched my hair. Romy opened the door to the balcony, holding her MacBook. Melanie was on Skype—she was sitting in her room in London, her pale skin and black eyes pixelated. She had a dimple in her nose, and I missed her. "To Nila," everyone said, and Melanie held her beer bottle to the screen with a ten-second lag. "To Nila and London."

After dinner we went on a long stroll through Prenzlauer Berg, all the way to the big park with the wooden slide. I stopped at a Späti to buy a Diet Coke and nervously checked my phone to see if Marlowe had written to me. No messages. Anna and Romy walked a few feet ahead of me, Taco sauntering like a little robot. Greening trees shed pollen, irritating my lungs and sinuses but in a pleasant, cleansing way. I was jealous of something undefinable— the quality of the air, the way Anna kissed the dog's small forehead and laughed at Romy. They knew each other, they really knew each other. No, I didn't want their life of newfound sobriety and raclette and vegan-dinner nights, those weeks filled with long evenings at the pier and Saturdays at the farmers market, but I was yearning for a taste of salt. My own apartment. A best friend to hold on to.

I TOOK PICTURES of them in their living room with a disposable camera I had bought at a drugstore. They are sitting side by side, smiling at the camera. Taco has the severe expression of a president's son. One picture of Romy walking on the street, her back turned to me. A picture of her with her mouth half open, sitting on a bench, eating ice cream. Anna looked at her with an open mouth, her shoulders slightly slumped, less composed than usual. "I hate this photo," she would later say, when I showed it to her. But I loved it. I really did love it. I thought I could forgive her: the way she carried herself sometimes with such meanness, the fact that she used plum-stone cream and smiled like a German person, which means that she smiled coldly without teeth, as if she were about to lower the sword of Damocles on you. They asked me to stay another night—so we could spend more time together tomorrow.

"Brunch tomorrow?" Anna asked when we got back to the apartment, cradling Taco in her arms.

"Yes," I said. "I promise. And I will cook."

"Hey," Romy said, touching my hand. "I'm really happy you're staying over. I am."

THAT NIGHT, ALONE, I pondered Anna's words. The way she said, *It isn't real.* Anna's corporate-lawyer parents. Romy's mother, who wore expensive suits and bleached her teeth. She had once traveled through India and played in a band, but now she was married to the CEO of one of Germany's biggest pharma companies. Did I resent their wealth, the pictures of their vacations in exotic landscapes? Of course I envied the ease of their lives. I remembered Anna's tears, her insistence that she couldn't feel a thing. And now? What had changed? But this was not about that. I lay awake on their couch, hearing Romy mumble, talking with someone on the phone. Some pollen still clung to my nose and my hair, and when I closed my eyes, images of their apartment swam through my mind: Anna's yoga mat, Romy's red hair in the brush in the shower. Deodorant, some grime at the bottom of the sink. Tomorrow morning everything would be fine: I'd toast bread for them. Make coffee with soy milk and put the butter out. I dozed and dreamed of the dark corridor at school, the terrariums with praying mantises, a picture of a young and smiling Kafka hanging over the door in a basement classroom. When I woke up, there was a text message from Marlowe, asking me to come over. Before they got up, before Anna could look me in the eyes with that face, before Romy could find a solution for my financial hurdles for college, I was gone. I took the first train back to Friedrichshain.

# Part
# Three

# Twenty-one

ON OUR TRIP to Venice, I brought my Olympus and the heavy Nikkormat, as well as fifty euros' worth of film—three rolls of black-and-white, five rolls of color with low exposure. A lot of these pictures would end up overexposed, as if even the film did not want to commit the real outlines to light.

From Milan, we had to take a train to Venice, coiled around each other on a four-seater. Mountains blurred past, workers in green hats dividing wheat. Dust speckled the windowpanes. Could anything feel more fulfilling than lying there like two children, at once sexless and innocent, the heat rising through the train compartment? Marlowe had not apologized, and I had not asked him to, but when I went back to his apartment, he traced the outline of the paling bruise on my cheek, my forehead. I had taken his portrait with the Nikkormat in the morning light: He sits on his black sofa, his shoulders rounded and relaxed, his face entirely in shadow.

I remembered, in some lurid dreamscape, Rome from the time

I had visited with my school last year: the Sistine Chapel. It was under construction at the time, the scaffolding obscuring the structure. Michelangelo's *Last Judgment* and that blue so intense I thought God was speaking directly to me. It wasn't the sinewy Christ, I thought, but Mary's skirt burning in the azure fulcrum of the scene. I had sunstroke later that day. As I lay in bed in the convent, the nuns brought out wet dish towels to put on my forehead, insects whirring in the grimy air.

We pushed our bags up bridges and down again, walking the length of the canal, and after unpacking and drinking limoncellos at a wooden bar with no air-conditioning, we went upstairs into our suite and we fucked unceremoniously, sweaty from the travels. There was no foreplay, but he got hard quickly, and he shut my mouth while I sat on top of him, and afterward I bled a little, the sheets ruined immediately. Without saying anything, I followed him into the bathroom, where he washed me again. Then we spoke about nothing, lying side by side as if in graves, or boats.

"Would we still be together if I go to London?" Over the last few days, I'd wondered briefly whether I should defer the offers, but then I felt that clicking sound in my heart. I wanted to get out, I thought, but I also wanted *him:* I wanted him so much more than a glamorous life in another European city. And how ridiculous and expensive and impossible it seemed to ever move there for someone like me.

Now Marlowe turned around to me, touched my face. "It feels as though something is ending, doesn't it?"

"What?" I wondered if he was breaking up with me.

"Time is funny, isn't it?"

"What do you mean?"

"Nothing."

"Marlowe?"

"It's nothing," he said.

"Marlowe, please." I felt a throbbing pain, as if a little hammer were hitting my temples.

"Come on, we should go explore the city."

I FOLLOWED HIM, but it was then as it is now: I was an uneasy tourist. I didn't know how to behave normally. The school trips to Paris or Rome were meticulously planned and left us little room for exploration. In groups, we walked from Louvre to Seine, from church to ancient ruin. And my parents had never taken me on vacation. When we left the house to travel, we did it to attend someone's wedding or funeral, or took long car rides to visit a sick aunt or an uncle, where we slept on mattresses or blankets on the floor and made elaborate Afghan meals in the morning. The farthest we'd been was a small city in the West, where we buried my grandfather's cousin and afterward sauntered through a district full of Somalis and Sri Lankans. We went from one refugee cocoon into another, and we didn't really see any city; we saw Afghans in another city.

Now I trailed behind Marlowe into the small shops and corridor-like streets. I touched bags with ear-shaped durum pasta, wind chimes blown out of colored glass. When we got cold sodas at a kiosk, he held my hand.

"I haven't held it like this in a while," he said.

Venice burst and flared. We ascended, sweating, up cobble-stoned streets, the Doge's Palace: It was hard not to be blinded by

the light the domes collected and refracted back to you, so heavy
with gold it was vulgar. Utterly devoid of that blue of the Sistine
Chapel, which I'd decided was God's color. All these little churches
that Marlowe wanted to go into. Yanking me in. Churches with
sepulchral heat. I left money in the votive boxes, made wishes, and
lit candles. Marlowe laughed at this, shook his head. As we walked
through the city, I noticed that he avoided me. Always, he ran
ahead, his head towering somewhere between the marble columns,
a smile on his lips as he looked up at the domes, then took note of
them in his phone.

THE SCREECH OF seagulls surveying the waves, the sky. At night
you saw the city reflected in water like light filtering through eyelets
of lace. Gondolas and small boats and water taxis, dogs barking,
the smell of seawater and sweat and old restaurants with under-
seasoned food. I was scared of the nothingness that resounded
everywhere, and though I felt it more in Berlin—that city that was
so ravaged and haunted with darkness—I could sense it here too,
the abyss that breathed under every building, and I suspected that
the Italian desire for excess and baroque art, for this opulence of
beauty, was a mask to conceal, or distract, to stuff down the nothingness that burned and burned through.

THE SUN GLARED hot and white on marble and stone; not a single
leaf or flower moved, there was no wind; and Marlowe kept a distance from me as we walked down to the exhibition center. We
were by the water, and there was no shade. Perhaps it was the heat
or the fact that I hadn't eaten, but his silence unsettled me.

"When you said something was ending, did you mean us?" I asked. He was walking a few steps in front of me.

He did not answer.

"Marlowe," I said, "do you still love me?" He looked back with a furrowed brow, and then he looked away again. He stopped by one of those gondola storage halls.

"This is where the exhibition is." He held the door open for me and looked the other way.

"Marlowe?" I was chagrined by the creak in my voice.

"You're a menace."

"Why don't you answer?"

"Why are you trying to ruin this trip for me?"

"I'm not ruining it," I said.

"Not everything is about you." He went in, and I, the loyal stray, followed him, then watched him recede into the air-conditioned dark.

I fumbled my way through the well-dressed mass. People mumbling in various languages, women with handheld fans. Japanese men in white suits. I walked through an installation with vintage spotlights coloring people's heads. Then, finally, I found the room with Marlowe's group. The studio he was writing about had collaborated with a Dutch firm to build the Dutch pavilion, which focused on preservation and debris. They titled it "Anti-Chronology," on the importance of architecture in the history of humanity, though it looked less like an architectural project and more like a museum exhibition, with pictures taped to felt pin boards and framed photographs hanging on a wall. Still, I congratulated the people I recognized from the New Year's Eve party.

Then it was time for Marlowe's reading. I stood with my back against the wall, buoyed by the anonymity of the crowd. He stood in the middle, his shoes glinting in the light. His hair looked un-washed, stringy. He fidgeted and tried to charm the crowd. But he didn't induce laughter at the right times; a woman yawned. Gabri-ela was late, entering loudly on high heels and standing in the back. She fanned herself with a program. A man in yellow pants, loyal, laughed and smiled at him. I noticed a group of young girls and boys leave through a side door, the wooden heels of their sandals punctuating his words. Coughing and small talk rippled through the group. He read from a stack of printed papers that I hadn't seen him carry around before. He read about capitalism and communism and spoke for a return of opulent, futuristic aesthetics. Chains of capitalist developers had ruined the artistic potential of architecture, he said. But he warned against romanticizing the So-viet Union and utilitarianism of brutalist architecture. Instead, he argued for playfulness, to move away from production. Aesthetics for everyone, Hinrich Baller, and so on. He smiled, waited for the applause. Gabriela left immediately, slipping through the back door, not even looking at him.

After the reading, I dawdled in the corner. Observed him standing by the lectern. He was waiting for something, or some-one, to come up to him, staring in the general direction of the door. A minute passed, then two, and no one came. People regarded each other, moved on. I repressed the sensation of embarrassment for him. How absurd to see this side of Marlowe—bathed in the light of mediocrity. So unlike the confidence with which he soared through the Bunker, where everyone knew him—that parallel life where he was a rich and bighearted prince in a tower. Marlowe flashed his teeth and performed happiness. He ordered two wines at the bar and walked around carrying both. He touched a wom-an's elbow, offered her one of the glasses. And the entire time, I calculated his body language, predicted when he would run a hand through his hair, when he would scratch his nose or crack a joke.

"Good reading," I said to him later.

"Thanks."

I smiled at him. "I liked the parts about the aesthetics of collusion."

"You didn't."

"Yes, I did."

"Yeah, what exactly?"

"I liked what you said about accessibility. . . ."

"Oh, I don't care."

I looked to the floor.

"You look pretty," he said. It was his way of apologizing. In other moments a sort of pain washed over him, especially when he looked at the other, more-accomplished members of the firm. I wondered if he considered himself a failure. The defunct website, his interviews from years ago. And yet, access to such a place. This pain splashed over his face only fleetingly, like an unexpected draft of cold.

I SAW HIM again in the afternoon, to drink a beer with Leon and Pauline, his friends from the firm. They hadn't come to the reading, but everyone cheered for him. Marlowe was voluble but slurred his words. He was inebriated. We locked ourselves in the bathroom of a restaurant and snorted a bit of cocaine he got from Leon. I wiped my nose on his shirtsleeve and he started laughing. Still, I was afraid to ask the question again, afraid to make him mad.

"I'm sorry," I said. "For asking."

"What."

"If you still loved me."

"Good," he said. "Because that's beside the point."

I nodded, though I didn't know what he meant. A sting in my chest.

"Don't worry," he said, softly shoving me against the wall. Anger vibrated under his smile. He twisted the skin on my upper arm until I shrieked. "Let's not talk about that right now."

I stayed in the bathroom to wash my hands and took my time before I returned. I gulped. Tried to interpret the silence in his enigmatic words: *That's beside the point.* And the twisting of my arm, which made me want to hit my head against the wall. This negligible gesture of hurt. Not really hitting. More like swallowing glass.

Marlowe was gone when I came out; he had to go back to the exhibition. I made a show of not caring. Leon asked if I wanted to share a tab of acid, and I agreed. Pauline, he, and I meandered through the veiny streets, encroached upon by terra-cotta houses. Our bodies threaded in and out of exhibitions, where we stared at each other, laughing. Under the lifelines of my hands, the world breathed. I wanted beauty. I didn't care who provided it, but I decided I wanted to dedicate my life to it. A feverishly red sunset suffused the sky: the most magnificent sky I had ever seen.

Later in the evening, the heat of the city pulled through the windows of the hotel, and the light shone green, like a film of dust settling over walls. I lay in bed, breathing, watching fractals in the ceiling. When Marlowe came in, he smelled of alcohol. A great love washed through the room, as if catapulted from the canal and water outside. I had forgiven his violence. When he slipped out of his clothes and lay down next to me under the thin sheet, the fears of the prior hours retroceded. "Your body is good," I said. When he started touching me, I seemed to feel nothing, but I let him. He slipped off my bra. His hand on my breast. Tracing my collarbone. Clutching my thighs. It was as if I was him, I was me but inside him, fucking me. I came as he came, tiny wires of light radiating from his skin.

"You are so beautiful," I said, and Marlowe laughed. *Ich liebe Venedig*, I thought; I thought it in German. After he fell asleep, the room stirred in me. The glaring shapes sprouted darker colors. A kind of acerbic light leached from the seams of the room, changing the system of my interiority. I still consisted of love, but now a melancholy matured inside my bones as well. I shut my eyes and thought of Mary's skirt on the ceiling of the Sistine Chapel, that reverential, celestial blue of the sky caught inside the fabric, the white glare of sun. Pigments of lapis lazuli ground up and committed to the sky up there. Looking at Marlowe, I shuddered, momentarily estranged from this man with graying hair. Crumbs of cocaine stuck to his nostrils. And the revelation that was filled with hilarity transformed back into the old fear, the strain at the center of my life, this lack—this black square of nothingness—ridiculing me until the morning hours.

# Twenty-two

MARLOWE SHIELDED HIS face and lit a cigarette. Then he loaded all the luggage into the trunk of the green cab. Leon and Pauline were already cuddling in the back, and so I climbed into the passenger seat. We were invited to an after-party that the architects and publishing house were holding in another coastal town, near Trieste, in the old and infamous Castello di Duino, where many artists and writers had stayed in the twentieth century.

The driver, a thin, dark-skinned man in a khaki three-piece suit, smiled at us. During the ride, he explained that he was Tigray and then related the political history of Ethiopia and Eritrea and Egypt to me. He spoke of the Blue Nile, studding his speech with words such as *And then, finally, but then,* interjecting with dramatic pauses and exaggerated sighs. When I looked back at the others, Leon and Pauline were asleep, and Marlowe was staring dreamily out the window.

The car spun over the Italian highway, and the driver described his country, which was mountainous, he said, and very dry, so he believed it to be cursed. Listening to him, I was reminded of my father's years as a taxi driver, of him and my uncles, who probably divulged similar stories of Afghanistan. I wondered why all uncles were obsessed with watching the news; was it because they too needed to understand their fate, needed to comprehend why they were here now, enclosed by the walls of a new and scrupulous place?

The sight out the window seduced me. The seashore disclosed a sudden rift of landscape: Dark, ruinous villas whizzed past us, cliffy mountains and rugged contours growing out of the earth.

"The Italians colonized us, you know? They're responsible for the founding of Eritrea."

"Oh," I said. "I did not know this." His broken English turned into a singsongy lull, and the more he spoke, the more I was inclined to think that the vivacious story of the Tigray guerrilla fighters resembled ours, the myriad stories of Afghanistan and its freedom fighters. I cracked open the window, let in the air. Ocean salt. Warm sage, pine. Exhaust fumes. Somewhere, the yawp of forest birds. He told me about his children and his sisters, who were everywhere in the world; he told me he was alone in Venice, that he had no one; he told me too that he had been in prison in Eritrea. I knew, deep down, that he needed to tell the story because he needed someone to speak to; I knew I was a vessel against which his reality, far from here, became more real. My *yes, oh wow, that's horrible*, meant nothing, contained nothing, and didn't really change anything, and yet, for the first time in a long time, I felt as though I wanted to touch someone's hand, tell him that I understood him. That I was Afghan.

We got off the highway. There was more greenery here, and the wind was colder and wilder. Red doors and garden sculptures shaped out of painted clay. People with wrinkly, leathery skin playing cards on plastic patio furniture. We drove through a village with winding, hilly roads. A cliffy stone and pebble beach lined the horizon. By a row of white and yellow houses, the cab driver let us out. Leon and Pauline were staying farther in town. After Marlowe paid, I noticed he had not given the driver a tip, and so I searched in my bag for a few euros. It felt good to be more generous than he was.

The man regarded the shiny coins on his palm, and then he looked up at me and said, "They killed my brother," and looked away again. "Ten months ago now. I'm basically here so I don't get killed."

"I'm very sorry," I said, with hesitation, hoping that my words sounded sincere. "I'm truly very sorry."

"Don't worry," he said. "God is good, and God gives us only the battles we can bear to fight."

"Fuck," Marlowe said when the taxi drove away. He carried both bags and looked into the distance. I told him I didn't mind the talking, that he was nice. Marlowe scoffed. "Cab drivers are always so damn depressing," he said, and I felt terribly sad and alone, altogether much closer to the cab driver than I was to Marlowe. We stayed at a small guesthouse with a red roof, where even the kitchen smelled of synthetic lavender. The pillows had seashell and seahorse prints on them, and there was this colored sand in glass bottles.

Marlowe touched one of the seahorse pillows and asked, "How many people have wanted to commit suicide after seeing this design?" His raspy laugh colored the room. My shoulders softened. Our bags sat off to the side like two small creatures that didn't belong there. He asked if I wanted a line, but I declined and instead took half a Valium. "They don't check for it on European flights, bunny." He emptied the white powder on the nightstand, cut it with a credit card, and snorted it through a cut-up straw, those purple straws he loved using.

We had lemonades and gelato at the local gelateria, and when the check came, they said they didn't accept credit cards. Marlowe shrugged and asked me to pay because he had run out of cash. I thought of the bundle of euros I had seen in his wallet but didn't press further—I hadn't really been paying for anything, ever, anyway. Then we made our way to a church in the city center.

The church wasn't finished; the funds had run out sometime in the eighteenth century. But the ruins revealed an elegant structure, sandy pink stones. A figure of the Virgin in her powder-blue dress watched over us solemnly, her downturned, glorious eyes primeval and quiet as a forest. Grime sheathed the banisters. I tried to be still, but I was vibrating: I was yearning for the absolute.

It tugged at me, this yearning, in every house of worship, even though I couldn't admit this to most people. I sensed its pulse in me, in the taxi driver, in Doreen's feminine hands, or in the priest, whom I imagined drunk and asleep in his chambers, trying to escape the heat, a wasp whirring at his feet, a cat maybe, or a dog. The pastries in the fridge. Window curtains drawn, shutters closed, to keep summer out. And there, behind Marlowe's blue eyes, the optic nerve. Everything, even the pupil, distorts, like the camera obscura. Nothing is not upside down. I tilted my head, watched Marlowe appear and disappear in the viewfinder of my camera, the little crosshairs of my target. *We photograph things in order to drive them out of our minds,* Barthes quotes Kafka. *My stories are a way of shutting my eyes.*

"One of the first things I noticed about Europe," Marlowe said after he sat down next to me, "is that God is really dead here."

"Why are you trying to be polemic?"

"I am not trying to be polemic."

"Then what do you mean?"

He laughed. "What do you think I mean? I mean this, the sincerity of this church. There's no savagery here—I guess the gothic can be savage. But I am thinking of the baroque and Renaissance God as a god of clemency, of practicality. Here, God is present. Amid the gothic savagery, however—we are preparing for the nothingness." He whispered, and his voice echoed through the church. There were only two other people here, also tourists, I assumed, seated farther toward the front. "Germany is a godless place, though, isn't it?"

"Maybe it is, but it isn't more godless than America."

"Are you joking? America was built because we love God so much. It is the country of puritans and evangelicals. People flocked to America precisely because Europe abandoned any semblance of God."

"But the God of America seems so . . . literal and apocalyptic."

Marlowe got up and held his hand out to me. "I for one am happy that in Germany, God is dead as roadkill." From the way he smirked, it dawned on me: We were arguing about something else. Every conversation with Marlowe was a triathlon in subtext. What was it that he was telling me? Not about God or churches at all but about ourselves, and what we couldn't combine, and would never be able to combine.

AFTER THE CHURCH, we hiked up a narrow stone path through shrubbery so exotic and fragrant it filled my nostrils with the smell of limes and dark fir. The hedges throbbed with cicadas and cricket screams. Sweat collected on my temples, and my scalp felt itchy and oily. It was hard to blink. My eyes grew tired. I rubbed grime from my thigh. My body was alive with a dark essence: a rodent wading through dirt.

"I love Italy," I said.

"You love a lot of things," Marlowe said. "You need to learn to employ your critical-thinking faculties. Not everything is lovable."

"You're so boring," I said. Once we got up to the ruins of the old stone castle, you could see the jewel-green sea shimmering with heat on the horizon, and waves burst with vehemence against dark cliffs. I took several pictures of the sight: Croatia on one side, Slovenia on the other. Marlowe gave me a hit of a joint, and we sat by the cliff and listened to the frenzied insect music. Stared, stupefied, out at the sea.

"So," he said, "what do you know about this place?"

"Rilke sat here."

"Not exactly here. This castle was already ruined—he sat over there, on one of the balconies." To be with him, alone, inside a day, in a different country, holding hands, completely shielded from my cousins and aunts and uncles, to be liberated and peaceful and true—wasn't this everything I wanted? Fleeing who I am? I couldn't possibly express it out loud to him, but I knew that for a moment I was happy. For a long time, we said nothing.

And then he voiced it, quickly: "Those who lie about the past are chained to it."

"What?"

"I was just thinking of that."

"Of that sentence?" I was afraid I had exposed myself. That I was thinking out loud.

"Yes." Marlowe took another drag of the joint.

"Why?"

"What do you mean, why?"

"It sounds like you were trying to . . . maybe hint at something."

"I'm not hinting at anything, Nila."

"Well, I just think . . . It sounded accusatory."

"No. Unless there is something you are lying about." On his face, a hint of cruelty and joy, and his lips quivered ever so slightly when he smiled. "Women lie about a lot of things, as the Bible says. This Bible you love so much."

"Why are you trying to hurt me?"

"I'm not trying to hurt you. Don't you love the Bible? Don't you constantly want to give money to the church?"

I didn't say anything. Tried to imagine his flaccid cock inside his pants, to absolve myself from any power it held over me. It pained me to accept his sadism, which had morphed, it seemed, out of nothing. Marlowe was a stranger, I understood at that moment, and he would always remain a stranger to me. I was scared to look at him, so I looked at the sea, which despite its danger was overwhelmingly pure. Gulls circled the sky over our heads. A single crow picked at a napkin. I wanted to approach it. My hands looked small in my lap, though the fear of being found out radiated in me, hard and certain as a diamond. I couldn't move. When I tried to get closer to the crow, it got smaller rather than larger, but then I understood that I was not moving at all—I was still exactly where I had been, but the crow was moving.

WE FUCKED IN the shower, and we fucked again on the starched sheets with the scent of shampoo and sweat and sand rising around me, and Marlowe kept my mouth open and spat in it, laughing, and I, well, I wanted it. I don't remember if I asked him to hit me, but he did slap me across my thighs, and then my face, lightly, leaving no bruise. It was the thought of degradation more than the physical manifestation that turned me on. The pain was secondary and to be endured, but at least in the bedroom, the violence made sense to me. My thighs were shaking afterward; I was sore. When he watched me comb my wet hair in front of the vanity, he wore a smile that was cold, distant. He was disgusted with me, I thought— or disgusted with himself. I chose to ignore it, and we made it to Castello di Duino, walking up the long driveway to the crenellated wall.

Marlowe floated through the estate, leonine and determined. The gray in his hair collected the last rays of sunshine, and when we stood in the garden with the koi pond, he turned to me and retrieved a small baggie with pills from his pocket. For some reason, I swallowed a whole blue Nike and washed it down with an absinthe cocktail. Marlowe touched my butt, and then we dispersed. The indie music confused me. So did the party guests wearing old Venetian masks, which exuded a tacky quality. It occurred to me that none of this—neither the guesthouse, nor the Biennale, nor the Duino Castle, nor the sea—would have happened without Marlowe. That he had been my ticket into everything, every building I had seen, and the possibility of shedding my own building from me. Yet it was difficult to feel gratitude.

ON THE TERRACE, I found Gabriela, blue sunglasses shielding her eyes. A black pearl attached to a leather band sat between her collarbones. Behind her, the sun had started to set, and the wind carried the scent of salt water and lemon oil, rosemary. She swatted away a mosquito, smiled, and moved the toothpick around her martini glass.

"Isn't he wonderful, your boyfriend?" she asked, and I hated her. "Always so nice to bring you everywhere. How did you enjoy the Biennale? It is the one time every two years when architects can pretend that they still have any social relevance among artists. But you wouldn't know, would you?"

Of course she wanted to humiliate me, the way old people love to injure the young. But I also saw in her condescension a version of myself; I understood, albeit only momentarily, that she repulsed me because a part of me wanted to be her. Tall, gleaming, successful. Untethered from the powers of a man. I was envious of her sinewy body with her thin nose and her freckled skin—a body that I imagined no one touched anymore but that glowed with generations of money. She was judging me, I knew, and I presumed she'd never understand why I was judging her. But Gabriela surprised me.

"I envy you too, you know. I am sure there is something about life that I have forgotten and you are aware of. Don't waste it— you are still at the very beginning of your youth."

I didn't know it then. Too naïve to recognize her wisdom. She saw right through me into my own ignorance. That I was lucky to be unjaded, to still want to follow the abyss of my desire. *Here you are*, her gaze said, *you milky infant.* And perhaps it was a warning too: *Don't go too far. Don't touch the flame, or you will burn.* But before I could answer, Gabriela ambled away, and Marlowe called.


HE WANTED ME to get a good picture of him, and so we went on a mission to find the appropriate background. Not too portentous, and not too basic. We walked into the courtyard, where the actual party took place. People in satiny gowns swayed their hips slightly, but most were engrossed in small talk. Waiters spinning around trays of green liqueur and serving platters of bite-sized baguettes layered with translucent salmon.

"Eat one," a waiter with red hair said, winking at me, and so I did. The smoky taste was foreign in my mouth. I remembered our ecstasy dinners, the snow on my hair, and my mouth swelled with the sharp, dizzying recognition of nausea. I sailed behind Marlowe, bobbed along behind women with carefully made hair, in their boring architectural dresses. Brushed the silk and linen, inhaled their *fleur d'oranger* perfumes. Some women's eyelids fluttered, as if ashamed of the whole scenario, scared of opulence and what it suggested. They talked of buildings and book deals. Professional banter. I smiled and was greeted with white teeth. Almost painful, how clichéd it was: One could spot the Italian women from miles away—their perfumes were stronger, sweeter, layered with cinnamon; they were tan, wore tight backless dresses that revealed their glowing bronzed shoulders. Their décolletages. Their laughter roared; their voices catapulted through the air. The Germans paled in comparison: chalky and pillar-like, no makeup.

A man in a tux and Venetian mask shouted, hooted, and Marlowe ran toward him. Their tall, lanky bodies embraced. I followed, envying the spark of energy. The man sounded like a chain-smoker. He shook my hand and laughed, then turned to Marlowe and said, "How is the work coming along?"

"Good, good," Marlowe said, and whispered in his ear, and we dispersed.

We studied the bedrooms. The castle was much smaller than I'd imagined, the rooms sectioned off with red rope. And still, they displayed all the original furniture.

"Princesses lived here." We walked through the dining room, the parquet glossy under our shoes, fumbled through groups buzzing with laughter. Into a room with a piano.

"Liszt's piano," Marlowe announced. "Isn't it so incredible to see this piano right now?" I stared at the piano and nodded. It didn't stir anything in me. What did feel incredible to me was that anyone had ever lived like this. That people had walked through here, kings and queens. Helping hands. Even when entertaining the past, I couldn't imagine myself at the center of this castle— I saw myself in the fringes. Not even as an artist but in the kitchen. The powder room, lacing up my lady's corset tight, breathing in her solid perfume. And even here, what pulled me the most— though I couldn't tell him this without sounding like a bore—was the bunker from the Second World War, which the Germans had built during the occupation. It stood underground, beneath the garden, cold air wafting through its opening: low ceilings, like a prison. I was afraid to go in, afraid of what it would do to me. The bunker and the ruins of the old castle, which could not speak. Which had only silence and history and stone, no ornaments.

We settled on the small spiral staircase, which Marlowe labeled a masterpiece of Italian architecture, and which gave the impression of the Fibonacci spiral when you stared down from the top. I took a picture of him in his suit pants and sneakers, his blue shirt, the first two buttons open. His head tilted down, looking up at the camera. His brow in a perpetual furrow. A cigarette in his hand. In the picture, the flash is off, and his face is featureless, smooth. No lines, just a light tan.

Years later, when I developed the pictures, it wasn't the one of him that struck me. It was mine. I sit there on the stairs, not entirely centered, in my pink sateen dress. My dark curls look almost smooth, pulled to one side. One of the straps has slid over my shoulder. It struck me that there was no eroticism in this picture— I look like a child, bereft, with an uncanny tragedy in the black discs of her eyes, unaware of what is happening to her.

AS WE WALKED back to the courtyard, I realized that taking ecstasy had been a bad idea. The fear that had overshadowed this trip hardened. The DJ accelerated the music. Replaced one vinyl with another, and the repetitious smack and basso of minimal techno formed an event horizon on which my worries grew. The trees shivered in the wind. People danced. Light pulsed the glass of green cocktails. My heart was sprinting so fast I could hear its thwack against my ears. When I wiped my nose, the back of my hand was bloody. I went to the bathroom what seemed like a hundred times, checking if I had peed my pants, then standing in front of the mirror, nursing my nosebleed, holding bunched-up napkins to my face. "Are you okay?" someone asked. I flitted to the dance floor, body pulsating in the dark. I sat back down. Constant oscillator. Waves collided against primitive cliffs. The cicadas were alert, screechy. The back of Marlowe's graying head nodded in the crowds. Dark-blue blazer. His hands through his hair. Put an arm around Gabriela, and she leaned over with her hawkish face, whispered in his ear. A thump of envy flicked in me. To distract myself, I scrambled away from the dance floor, orange flower and sweat, and walked onto a balcony. There I got enmeshed in a conversation with a man in a striped shirt. Pink tie. He was the guy who had hugged Marlowe earlier. The Venetian mask hung around his neck, fastened by vermilion ribbon, revealing his pockmarked, aged skin.

"Are you one of the architects or one of the literature people?" he asked.

"I'm nothing. A guest."

He laughed. "One with ambitions, I hope?"

"Ambitions for what?"

"I mean, are you smart enough to use this as a networking event?" The man asked me to help him tie his Venetian mask back on.

"Well, I want to be an artist." The rasp of my voice perturbed me. We stood facing the sea, looking out like two wives waiting for their husbands to return.

"What kind of artist?"

When I held the bloody napkin to my nose, I noticed that my hand was trembling. "A photographer. But I don't know. I haven't really taken any professional photographs." My heart, that deceptive mare, was throwing itself against my rib cage. I tried to slow my breathing.

"You must be extraordinarily happy in this castle." He pointed out the good angles. The historic backgrounds. That Rilke and Hugo von Hofmannsthal had written there, and that many visual artists and intellectuals had taken refuge there. He mentioned the extensive library, filled with signed Freud editions, which were burned when the Nazis seized the building.

I was silent; my eyes fixed on the sea. It was black-blue, the color of ink. A tarp swaying in a gale. Moonlight coruscated on the surf; some waves refocused in the spotlight. Its chthonic music originated from somewhere remote, from somewhere alive yet deep in the past.

"The sea is too big," I said, out of breath, my head throbbing.

"Are you okay? Do you need a glass of water?"

"Why is everyone always asking me if I'm okay?" I threw the napkin to the floor and searched my bag for a cigarette. "Yes, I'm fine."

"Your nose is literally bleeding, miss," the man said.

"The sea," I said or didn't say, "has an evil force pulsing in it." I feared it. I feared it so much, and as I looked down at the cliff, the murky water corroding the crags, the shrubbery fragrant in the cold—a vision of myself appeared, jumping down. The heavy impact of skull opening against stone, my bones sinking into the icy mouth of the ocean.

"Honey, are you okay?" the man asked me again, this time with more urgency.

I looked at the silhouette of the old ruins, lit up now by artificial yellow lamps, and suddenly everything came rushing up my throat, the pill and the churches in Venice and the tiny translucent salmon and the cab driver saying, *They killed my brother,* and, pressing my hand like a muzzle against the bile in my mouth, I walked quickly off the balcony and into the courtyard and onto a different balcony, and I remembered God, who won't forgive anything. I tried to see the cliff on which I stood but saw only seafoam. The perverse, fundamental blue of the ocean filled my heart and replaced everything I ever was and had ever known. It came into my cells and imbued them with water until I was drowning underneath. But it is just a sea. . . . *Es kann dir nicht wehtun.* I stared at my dirty hands and my hair streaked with vomit, and snippets of poetry came back to me, pleading with me, snippets of other people's poems. Everything on the balcony was blistering with a stark and mysterious purpose. *The objects are in on it,* I inferred, *the taxi driver is in on it, Marlowe is in on it, and Gabriela. They all know!* And, paralyzed by this dread of a titanic yet vague conspiracy against me, I closed my eyes. Darkness rushed in, and it became black and very cold, and I couldn't see or think or speak.

LIFE FLUSHES THROUGH me, and in return my soul is anguished to translate that movement. To make part of it real. It had little to do with me. I did not see a cliff the way Doreen saw it, or Marlowe. Or even Elias, who contemplated, who experienced it fully. My entire life I danced on the outside, looking in. I saw a cliff and I became the cliff. A part of me was gone. Usually, when I lost myself like this—and it had happened before, it had happened in childhood—I went home, trying to figure out where that part of me went, how to recuperate the loss. And art, I thought, once I'd figured out how to find the right image, the right composition, once I'd turned the loss into an object, would bring a piece of me back. Not the one that I lost. Something else. It would bring me closer to God. But this was my life's quest. This was, I understood, what drove me.


WHEN I WOKE up, a heaviness pressed down on my chest, and there was a sour taste in my mouth. Marlowe's face hovered above me. He helped me up, kneaded my shoulder.

"Why are you crying?" He hoisted me up onto a bench. "Why are you crying now? Isn't this what you wanted? Seeing the sea?"

"But it's not even really there," I tried to explain. "It's not here."

"My God, why are you upset?"

In the bathtub at the guesthouse, he combed my hair, brought me lemon tea. I sat there shivering like a child and couldn't speak; the only words that I could procure were *sorry, sorry, sorry.* My sateen dress was crumpled, my underwear lay on the floor, stained, and the sight of it embarrassed me. He was talking, but I do not remember the words, as it so often is. All I remember is the feeling that he was straining to soothe me, that there was wickedness in his face. He lathered my shoulder with soap. Foam on his cheek. I had never seen him like this, with such concern and horror lining his face, a horror that was mixed with wonder: How could I have done this to him again?


LATER, WHEN WE lay in bed, he turned to me, shook me.

"What is wrong? Will you tell me what is going on? I don't understand what's wrong." And then I saw that, underneath bombast and sadism, there hid the fear that it all had to do with him. That it began with him.

"What is it?" he said, his voice papery and dark. I thought of the cliff, the inky water corroding the stone.

I opened my mouth. Then I shut it again. Took minutes just to breathe. And then I muttered, as if awakened from a subterranean and chilling sleep: *I lied. I am Afghan.*

# Twenty-three

AFTER 9/11, EVERYTHING burned. Not only did the towers go, the thousands of lives lost in those towers, office people and cleaners and waiters and children who remain unburied to this day, the metal and ash and plastic melting into rubble and bone dust. All matter around the event decomposed too. Like the eye of a hurricane charging everything into its slow and ruinous orbit. On that day I saw my home country mentioned on television for the first time. I had come home, alone, with a faded dark-blue Digimon key chain hanging around my neck. I made myself a Nutella bread. Ate it at the foot of my parents' bed, legs dangling from the frame. Turned on the cranky eighties TV my father had hauled in from the street. You changed the channels by operating the knobs on the panel to the right side of the screen. Even on MTV, the towers were ablaze in New York's skyline, and I remember a certain kind of silence, a shock, or a halting of breath, ossifying the neighborhood. My sticky hands, the chocolate melting on toasted white bread. A single fly buzzed through the room.

Later, theories sprouted in my father's mind. He showed me documentaries, swore me to secrecy. He closed the curtains before presenting the videos, which always struck me as odd, because I couldn't imagine it: the fear he must've felt, being observed through the windows of the seventh story of an apartment block. "It was an inside job," he said. "It was planned. As if it isn't bad enough that we are Afghans. . . ."

In the weeks following the attack, one of the buildings that housed asylum seekers on the outskirts of a Belgian town was burned down. The perpetrators weren't even skinheads, just neighborhood kids: a young blond son of a city-council officer and his schoolboy friends. In court, the kid, with his combed-back curls and ruddy cheeks, looked at his lap, said, *I'm sorry; I didn't know our people lived there; I assumed it was only foreigners.* Two children died. On the news, they showed the image of a tiny blue coat and a scarf outside the burned-down husk of the building for weeks. "They're vultures," my mother said. "Why are they insisting on this picture?" In Berlin, women in headscarves were attacked; people changed seats in the U-Bahn if you had a beard. Mosques were vandalized. Shut down and inspected for "terrorist activity." Meanwhile, in another town out east, a Syrian bakery was burned. A Turkish girl was stabbed on her way to work, the perpetrator running through the streets, screeching, *Scheiss Ausländer.* . . . My parents stopped going to the mosque in Lichtenberg, and what now remains in my memory of that building are fragments. Fabric embroidered with burgundy paisley, which my grandmother used as a blanket. Earthy, cold taste of the praying stone I sometimes put to my tongue. And musk, and shit, rising from the horse barn close by. Horse snouts to which I reached my hands, their velvety eyelashes. Eyes so large and black and kind they seemed to betray a transcendental truth. Visualizing how big their hearts were, pumping blood through all that meat. Pressing fistfuls of hay into my cousins' pockets, or one of them throwing snow down my neck. The call of prayer. The imam, his acrid, sing-songy voice broadcast through speakers on our side of the mosque, the side of women, partitioned by a giant white curtain. Holding my ears shut, while my mother laughed. My aunts cooing and whispering like fat, exotic birds that the devil has possessed. Wondering what my father did, gilded, on the other side. In winter you could see the scorched fields, when a thin layer of snow sheathed the soil. Flower buds underneath, coiling inward. Children in old hand-me-down anoraks played there, shouted, chewed on bark, dug up sticks and old bones. Walked home with dirty clothes, holding hands. Occasionally, for funerals, we went to my uncle's makeshift community center in a district so similar to ours, like Gropiusstadt, but more historic: In Rixdorf, at the beginning of another century, they had corralled all the Bohemian-Austrian exiles to save them from persecution. There, the ghosts of the other refugees still raged. When we walked through the streets, the mist gnawed at elm and maple. A sharp frost coating the grapes of our lungs.

But during the actual attack, my father was in California. We didn't have papers yet, and for a month we didn't hear from him, and my mother began shouting in her sleep. I didn't understand her fear, hadn't heard of disappearances. Six months later he walked through the door carrying two black hard-shell suitcases, replete with stickers, and collapsed on the rug. His old trench coat smelled foreign, like dust and lavender.

"I can't live like this," he said, and slept for a week.

———

SWASTIKAS TAGGED TO our doors, the skinheads down the hall greeting us with predictable slurs. Their pink-gummed dogs on chains growled at us, techno blaring out of their apartment. Frau Storz, obsessed with her ferrets, called us Oriental, oblivious to the current trend in politics. Her disposition was a relief. A charm from a different century. Not friendlier, per se, but more inclined toward an aesthetic worldview. The satires and comedies that made use of words like *Lampukistan*, used hairy monkeys under blue burqas. Teachers probing me about my father's involvement in al-Qaeda. *How often do you pray? What is the name of your god?* Every day we were afraid to read the news, afraid of another Afghan man committing an act of terrorism in the name of religion. The hard tilt in my mother's gaze when confronted with her own identity. One day I stood next to her at the pharmacy, and when the pharmacist asked her where she was from, she said France. "Oh," the man said with a thin smile, handing her the plastic bag with cough drops, hand cream. "How wonderful. For a moment there . . . Well, you know how those other foreigners are." The lies buttered us up. Allowed us entrance into a world of inclusion, where we looked down on the kind we really belonged to. Where we learned to resent ourselves with precision. Elen, an Iraqi girl from my neighborhood, told people she was from Colombia. She lied in front of me, rammed an elbow into my rib. Later, she would say, "Some people can't deal with the truth. I don't need to answer their fucking questions." And there it was in front of me: the acknowledged shame of our origins. That it was safer, in those years, not to divulge the truth.

———

EVERY DAY AT school, an interrogation. I can still recall it, like a metallic, medical jolt—the first time I lied. A scene in the dim boarding school hallway, spring, the first green buds piercing the snow. A girl with red pigtails asked where I was from, and I said: Italy. Hundreds of miles away from home, I could be anyone I wanted. I was from Spain. I was from Colombia. I never told anyone my whole name. Nilab Haddadi. The consonants rang harsh and wrong, betraying the other side of the world. The weak girl who was spat at and grew out of Gropiusstadt. When people found out and quizzed me about my name, I said I was Christian Egyptian. Or that I was Israeli. Anything, anything but Muslim.

During the school year I was cocooned, quickened by the filmy illusion I had started to believe in: of a family that was more intact, more worldly than my own. A family who accepted my desires, my wishes to wear miniskirts, to kiss boys and maybe even girls. Parents in a high-ceilinged apartment in Berlin, doctor parents who read Western books and had intellectual discussions I too could participate in. I told lavish fabrications about my family life, enticing the girls at school. In the summers and winters, I returned home reluctantly. Almost stupefied to find out, again and again, where I was really from. The universe must've been wrong. I couldn't really be from here.

And then, when I was fifteen, my grandfather died, and instead of going to his funeral, I went to a rave. My body throbbing in a forest, the trees decorated with mirror shards and trash. Glitter in my pockets for weeks. A sunburn on the right side of my face. My mother screamed at my indecency and I laughed at her. A year later, it was she whom we buried. You could forget it, during sex or on drugs, or when I developed pictures. But otherwise it caulked the marrow of your bones. That thump toward gravity. The way Setareh had told me, *I am waiting for my parents to die before I can be out with a girl.*

My mother, who was as lonely as I was during those years when I still lived at home, circled the apartment at night, sitting by the phone, which never rang. Those were the hours when no one else was awake. Me and my mother, with her long black hair. I listened to her pace around, my breath imitating hers, my sobs synchronized to hers as she sat crying. Howling for things I didn't understand, both of us sleepless and hemmed in the gauze our days had become, weak against the workings of our minds. I barely existed then, and I couldn't hear my own thoughts, because I focused so intently on hers.

When she called my father, nobody picked up. The last week of the month, we ate flatbread with strawberry jam and drank water out of the tap. Heated it in the kettle, reused the same teabags three or four times. She was too proud to ask Sabrina for help. My mother and I stood in the cold, in the rain, in summer's slick heat in front of the church, picking up the boxes at the food bank. What did I feel when I saw her in the afternoon sun setting over the gray cityscape? Love, yes, love. And then, sure as a clock: I felt shame.

THE NEXT MORNING, a soft rain rippled the sky. I don't know how much I had really revealed to Marlowe about my life. All day, I couldn't speak. Our connection was frayed, porous to the wind. We walked through the city center of Trieste, where a local band was playing an Italian bossa nova cover of Britney Spears's

"Oops! . . . I Did It Again." And it winked at me again, the universe and its silly sense of humor. A swift rainstorm wetted the streets. And the rotten pain of my childhood washed over the boughs.

I dried everything against the small heater in the guesthouse. And then the journey back to Berlin, a bus, a train, my shoulders painful under the straps of the backpack. I lost a shoe, walked back. A dog barking at me. The shiny colossus of Milan Malpensa airport. Blip of sky, polyester seats. Marlowe ignoring me throughout the flight. A baby screaming. Descending again over my gray, terrible city. When we landed in Berlin, even more rain poured from the heavens. The storm had made it over. Oh, godforsaken airport.

"I need coffee," Marlowe said after we retrieved our suitcases. I walked to the kiosk and got him breakfast. We stood under the awning, Marlowe sipping his drink, awfully quiet. He smoked a cigarette, and I watched the rain pool on the ground.

"Let's get a taxi," he said, but the first one drove away. Then another. The line in front of us consisted of four people under black umbrellas. One by one, they disappeared into the vanilla-colored cabs.

Then, finally, our turn. I avoided looking at the driver. The trunk opened and I got into the car. Scent of pine cones, the furry sweater hanging over the seat. Persian music played on the stereo, which worried me but not enough. I closed my eyes, pretending not to notice what was unfolding in front of me. Marlowe put both suitcases in the back and I saw the black trench coat, his silhouette, moving closer, coming in. Musky with the scent of rain, he shook himself like a dog.

"To Friedrichshain," Marlowe said.

"Okay," the driver said. "Which street?" And as if by instinct, I opened my eyes. Looked up, shot through by the familiarity of the voice. The thick, almost French-sounding accent. Now, I knew, there was no going back. There he was, as if I had been waiting for him my entire life. My uncle Rashid's eyes looking at me in the rearview mirror.

# Twenty-four

AND YE SHALL *know the truth, and the truth shall make you free.* This is what the Bible says, what the priest once whispered at service, what hung in stitched lettering in the dark hallway of the children's psychologist I had been sent to. And yet? Was I freed? I was relieved, that's all I can say. Hushed and punctured, I sat in my room, texted all my friends: *I lied. I am Afghan.* Theatrically, I punched my pillow. Calmed myself down. And waited, like a child king at the end of his reign. To be denuded. Paraded. To be seen, at last, for everything I was.

RASHID HAD TOLD me to stay in the car. "Who is this man?" Marlowe asked, then stared out the window, shaking his head, lips upturned into a light grin. I couldn't answer him. Instead, curious, I studied Marlowe, whom I saw the way my uncle must've seen him. The way others saw him. The vision from the end of my acid trip in Venice: gray streaks in his hair; lines marbling the depth of his forehead. He was handsome but also spent—like someone who had lived a little too much, had lain out in the sun without sunscreen one afternoon too many. Fury and something pathetic lighting his eyes. Suddenly, without real force or reason, images came to me—his mother's emerald earrings he had described in the novel, or Setareh's chin covered with crumbs. Who was I? It destabilized me, sitting there, next to these sudden strangers. *I am not yours*, I thought, of both men. I watched Marlowe's face get smaller in the distance after he got out. And stayed in the back of the car, as instructed. The song "Jaane Maryam" playing on the stereo, the same song that had filled my grandmother's carpeted apartment after my mother's funeral, when I sat slumped in a corner and inhaled the dregs of July. Did Rashid remember the froth of that day? I didn't say anything, but the strings undid me. I remembered my mother's soft skin. I remembered young girls dancing the Attan, the dance of warriors, at a wedding. Had my mother been here, I would not have unraveled—that was the logic of my family. But hadn't they seen that the bad seed had always been there, even in childhood? My uncle muttered under his breath. Then he turned on Quran recitations.

"*Besharm hasti*," he said, loudly and with confidence. *You have no shame.* How ironic, I wanted to respond; I do have shame, I am ashamed to be your niece. The rain lessened, the sky the color of soot and antique silver. Those buildings, the sight of which made me feel sick, as if I were being punched in the chest. Jackie, the bakery shop cat, lounging on the street. The Palestinian boy I'd once had a crush on, smoking and nodding his head to some beat. Then the long ride up the elevator, standing next to Rashid, who did not look at me. A fly buzzed against the broken bulb. I stared up, into that fluorescent wound of light, and remembered being four years old, standing there with my parents. The same swastika coated the right wall. We walked down the hallway, past the door of the neo-Nazis, whose dogs yowled over the acid techno track. And then the solemn signs of life escaping from under the door of Frau Storz, who was playing Mozart's Requiem and cooking with too much garlic. Another Monday in Gropiusstadt, hallelujah. My father, dressed in linen pants, stood expectantly in the doorway. He looked jowly and shaved. At first, relief washed over his face when he saw me with his brother.

"Hello, kid." Neither Rashid nor I said a word.

"What's wrong?" he asked. I couldn't meet his gaze. Instead, I slipped past him into my room. The cat jumped onto my bed and meowed, showing its belly.

"You slut," I whispered as I stroked its white tummy. My father's and Rashid's voices in the hallway sounded foreign, like I didn't know them at all. As a child, I'd always hoped that I was adopted—that somewhere my real family was waiting for me, with a large, quiet house and a kitchen island and dappled sunlight and liberal rules. I almost laughed when I studied the artifacts of my childhood bedroom. My floral sheets. The Goethe quote painted on my wall. Who was this girl, this girl who had wanted to live and feel as intensely as the poets of Sturm und Drang? Who was ever that young and so impossibly naïve?

Mesmerized, I stood in front of the oval mirror, studying my reflection like a photograph. My hair was longer, straighter. My cheekbones sharper. I had lost my baby fat. Shadows under my eyes. But the static picture moved—my father appeared in the corner. I turned around only when his body was so close I could smell the embers of anger sizzling under his skin, but even then I didn't dare to look at him. Instead, I focused on his green slippers.

"I'm sorry," I croaked. I don't remember what he replied, only the impact of the heel of his hand when he slapped me on the right side of my cheek. I flinched, as if rehearsed. Tears formed in my eyes, involuntary tears.

"I'm sorry, Papa," I repeated.

"I don't understand . . . I never understood this. Why are you trying to kill me?" As my father left, closing the door after him, the cat leapt from the bed toward the frame and began meowing with a terrifying, solemn despair. Little fool, thinking she could get out of here.

He did not speak to me for four days. For the first two, he confiscated my phone and laptop. I was a child: I was grounded. Most of the day, I stayed under the sweaty, petulant sheets. I read books and sometimes snorted a small line from the baggie I kept in my wallet, the speed numbing my heart. I let the London offers expire, smiling at the other life I'd once imagined there. The cat made biscuits on my chest, scratched my hand. "You cannot judge me," I said, suddenly amazed by the loving ignorance of the animal world—no sense of ethics or delusion. No shame. My grandmother's eyes shimmered in the sun. Blue mascara coated her lashes, her gray irises swimming like planets in the milky dough of her face. I wondered if I was still a little bit high. She dragged me closer by my collar, hissed at me.

"Don't you have any regard for your family? Do we mean nothing to you?"

They didn't do to me what they did to Nadia. There was no intervention. No threat of an honor killing, no real beating. Only my aunts came over, shaking their heads. They shelled pistachios and cooked for my father, as if after a funeral. Filled the rooms with a vivacity I had forgotten was possible. Stood in the doorway, gossiped about Sabrina's expensive new BMW. Saturated my days with oud-heavy perfumes. Told me I had shamed the family. That I was killing my father. Had I learned nothing at that fancy school? What I did was not only disrespectful to my dead mother, may she rest in peace in heaven, and my father and uncles and aunts, but also to all Afghan people on earth. I almost laughed in response: How bad could it be, my having an older American boyfriend? Like electric eels, they undulated in the rooms around me, emitting shocks of insults and wisdom and light.

Only Sabrina dared to really speak to me. Came over and sat by the foot of my bed and sighed. Brushed her fingers through my hair. She smelled of disinfectant and dried figs.

"I know you miss your mother," she said, and tears came up my throat, and into my eyes, and ran down my cheeks and onto my neck. *Fuck off*, I thought. And the sobbing exasperated her, but she robotically stroked my forehead. This was my aunt. This was my blood.

"What would she have done?" I asked her, my voice tinny from the snot. "She was weak."

"Don't say that." Sabrina sounded cold but composed. I wondered if she was annoyed with me. "Your mother was a complicated woman. But she was strong-willed, often to her detriment. And you got that sense of justice and rebellion from her."

"She never even ended up working as a doctor again." I grabbed a tissue and blew my nose.

Sabrina paused for a moment, then withdrew her hand, touching her wristwatch as if to check the time. She exhaled, but this time it was a different sound, like the air had been waiting for years to be released.

"There are things about her life—all our lives—you can't really understand, so don't make these grand pronouncements about strength and weakness. Did you live through war? Did you see your home being torn to pieces? Your parents stayed in Kabul very long—maybe too long. We came to Germany seven years before them, and I don't know what their lives were like in those seven years. Your mother was an intelligent woman, I remember, but she was sensitive. And exile is like fate. You can't choose what happens to you. . . . In the end, your parents never managed to feel at home here. By the time they arrived in Berlin, I was already getting a new license. I knew the language better, had my degree papers. Your parents didn't have theirs. Mostly that's what it was." I listened to Sabrina's breathing. And considered it: an entire livelihood placed in the absurdity of bureaucracy. Kafka was right. The parable of "Before the Law": infinite obstacles leading to an invisible and terrifying superstructure made only for the man from the country. And though I knew the complexity of our fate couldn't be reduced to a single sheet of paper, she nonetheless had a point: Evil expressed itself through administrative language. *Language.* That's all it was, wasn't it? Between one body and another: touch and sound and words.

An astonishing image came to me, an image I had always taken for granted: the foreign books stacked in my parents' living room, with their black and terra-cotta covers. A translation of Umberto Eco's *The Name of the Rose.* Leather spines embossed with golden letters, dictionaries with pages thin as flower petals. My mother's handwriting on those legal pads. I thought of her in her sunny kitchen in Kabul, pouring milk into her coffee before going to work, the sun shimmering in her hair. Even in my imagination, I couldn't see her face, her back always turned to me. My parents were, I was only beginning to realize, intellectuals in a language I couldn't read. Farsi, that elegiac, simple speech. The only one they could really speak.

I needed to understand, Sabrina said, that these people, *my people*, didn't know better. They came from a country where girls are the caretakers of a family's honor. Back in Kabul, many students had been political prisoners, among them my mother. *She was in prison*, I repeated to myself. For a brief period, when she was my age. And it dawned on me that there were years and periods of her youth I would never know, things she never told me, which would hang in the ungraspable darkness of her shouts and sobs at night. My mother had a full life before she became my mother; convictions, friends, streets through which she jogged. Brushing grasses out of her hair, washing her makeup off with a bowl of cold water. I remembered, from my early childhood, some women's meetings she went to. Political events. Why had she stopped? There was a jolt in Sabrina's voice when she said that she hoped the next generation of our family would have it easier. I thought of Nadia, who had dropped out of school and had four blond children and no job. Liana, whom I hadn't seen in years—skinny and dying in the Charlottenburg villa.

"Your mother was very reluctant to send you away, but even she knew it wasn't good or safe or quiet enough for you here. We wanted you to succeed, to have the best opportunities possible. You were always so perceptive, so impulsive, and angry. You were not an easy child. On some level, I thought you might feel happier there."

"I would feel *happier* there?"

"Or freer at least—out of everyone's sight." I thought of Werther shooting himself in the head at his desk, *Emilia Galotti* spread out in front of him. All those dumb books, my only friends. I started hiccupping from the tears. A small laugh fled my throat, thinking of my stern mother with her clip-on earrings, telling me I would be going to Rosenwald.

"Who is he?" she asked me when I stopped crying. "Is he a decent man at least?"

I shrugged. "He's a writer."

"I hope he treats you well," she said. "I hope he is a good person."

WHEN MY FATHER left the apartment, he took that dangling chain of keys and locked the door from the outside like a janitor. Not once did I hear him say anything about Marlowe, or men in general. When he did speak to me, hunched over his cold cup of tea in front of the TV, it was with cracked resignation. I felt sorry for him, this widower, so bonded to the green slippers I had given him when I was only a child. The dark footprint on the inner soles. My father had sent me to a bilingual school with hopes I would one day make it and move to America, the country of his dreams. When I saw him in the hallway with that weary look in his eyes, I thought of Kafka writing of his father, that the difference between them was one of temperament, as if their rift was irresoluble, no one's fault. And at last, I broke the trench between us. Climbed through the singed shrubbery of my girlhood and hugged him. My tall, skinny father with silver streaks in his hair, the eyebrows that I brushed and trimmed for him.

He didn't let me speak—but for a minute we stood there, two figures in the dark hallway. Father and daughter, touching without violence.

# Part
Four

# Twenty-five

I N JUNE MY father lifted my house arrest so I could go to work again, but because I had not appeared for a month, I was fired from my job. My boss handed me the letter, my last tips stuffed in an envelope. I traced the shape of coins through the frail bluish paper. I had thirty-two euros in cash in that envelope, a couple hundred euros in my bank account. A pouch of Pueblo tobacco in my tote bag, a few lighters. And now I had been fired from one of the few jobs in the city that allowed me to work under the table.

DOREEN ONCE SAID, *There are two things that necessitate violence: overthrowing capitalism, and love.* She'd laughed, but from the way her eyes lit up, I knew she was serious. I experimented with the idea. Marlowe did not believe in the throwing of Molotov cocktails or the assassination of politicians. Doreen, Eli, and I, on the other hand, craved revenge.

"Your imagination needs to be bigger than that," he said. Earlier that year, Marlowe had insisted we all go to this festival—the anarcho-communist autonomous zone he'd once told me about— so I could see, at last, that it was possible to create utopia without violence. Without executive forces or a government. Without police. Through some communist form of lottery, he procured tickets for himself, Eli, Doreen, and me.

IN THE MONTH since returning from Venice, I had written Marlowe an email, apologizing. He responded with an essay about what truth and selfhood mean, ending with, *We can never know another person. The only thing we can hope for is to know ourselves.* Otherwise, we had not spoken, except when discussing logistics about this festival in late July.

But now, when I read about the RAF or other far-left terrorists, I flickered. I thought about Meena Keshwar Kamal—I brought out the portrait that was in our photo album and wept stupid and sentimental tears for my mother, that mysterious figure who once, in youth, knew a revolutionary. Carefully, I slid the picture of Meena out of the album sleeve and pinned it to the wall above my desk. Then I lined my eyes with kajal, puckered my lips as I applied gloss. I put on a hoodie to hide my tight dress and kissed the fat Persian cat on the forehead. I told my father I was going to see Romy and that I'd be back that night. He knew I was lying, I assume, something devastated and conclusive crushing his voice as he called his goodbye from the kitchen.

ELI'S STUDIO APARTMENT smelled of cigarette smoke and dust. Boxes and bags cluttered the hallway. He was putting a handful of books into a green peach crate when I entered, then disappeared into his kitchenette. Minimal techno boomed, mixed with the exhilarating cacophony from the street. The bed was made, and neatly folded piles of clothes were arranged on the duvet. From the kitchen, he asked what had happened to me, and I only responded with laughter, asking if he was moving.

Eli carried two beer bottles on his way in. "You're deflecting my question." We were both excellent at the play of avoidance. I sank into his battered gray couch. Slouching, he collapsed on the other end, handing me one of the bottles. He was wearing what he always wore those days: skinny jeans and a black sweater.

"So how is work going?"

He sighed. Took a gulp of his beer and lit a cigarette. He shook another one out of the pack and offered it to me, the long NIL lying flat in my palm. "I'm sick of it; I want to get out. It's too much—all this partying. I'm just sick of it. How about you, hottie from the jazz club?"

"I got fired."

"Oh."

"And, well, I'm Afghan, so there's that." I took my time to let down my hair and redo my ponytail. When I'd texted him, he only wrote back that it was okay and he cared about me, that he wanted to see me. "But, more important, should we snort speed?"

Eli hesitated before handing me a scratched Pink Floyd CD case, and I emptied the little bit of drugs I had left onto it, cutting it up. Fearful of meeting his gaze, of saying something unkind, I studied his walls: a poster of Radiohead's *Kid A* cover peeling in the corner. A shelf with a dying cactus.

"Marlowe told us the story with the cab. He's an idiot. But you're aware."

"Yep." I snorted a line and tried to laugh. "Here I am. Little Miss Liar."

He joked about Kosovo, discussing whether the Balkan countries counted as European.

"Any other secrets you want to inform me about, now that we're at it?" Eli tapped his cigarette against the mouth of a beer can on the floor, then leaned back and crossed his arms.

"I don't think so. Well, my mother's dead, for starters."

"I already knew that. I have a dead father, in case you forgot. I can play this game."

"We really are the dead-parents club, aren't we?" I walked toward the record player and looked at the vinyl spinning on the deck, the needle scratching the dark landscape of the plastic. Turned up the volume on the motherboard.

"Everyone needs at least one dead parent." The initial laughter dissipated into an awkward well of silence. Unsure what to do with my body, I went back to the couch, sat down next to him. Thought of Kreuzberg in the eighties, all those freaks making music with drum machines and Einstürzende Neubauten playing at SO36.

"Nila." He touched my cheek with the back of his hand, and the kindness unlatched a door in me. I rubbed my eyes with my sleeve.

"I can't believe I'm fucking crying." There were still many defenses when someone confronted me with the truth of my origins. I felt embarrassed. After my grand confessions, Romy texted that she didn't care where my parents came from, that she loved me anyway. On the phone later, she said, *We always assumed you . . . I don't know. That you wanted to sound more special than you were. I swear once you said you were from Italy. It didn't always add up, but whatever. We thought you must have a really big, mixed family. Or something.* I cringed, knowing I had let shame make a fool of me. "I feel pathetic."

Eli put an arm around my shoulder. "The only pathetic part is that you pretended to be Greek. You could've chosen anything— Greek?"

I wondered if he had always suspected my real heritage wasn't Greek but was scared to ask. I remembered my mother saying, *I'm not crying,* while tears streamed down her cheeks. Like her, I wanted to move on as if nothing had ever happened, as if I had always told people that I was Afghan. Over long emails, Doreen mentioned how common identity crises were for girls of *my background.* But before generalizing, she suggested I read a book on it and sent me elaborate paragraphs on Frantz Fanon and the self-hating Black, or the self-hating Jew, who either ignored what he was until he reached amnesia or mentioned it over and over again, before anyone else could draw attention to the fundamental lack of his being—his otherness. The self-hating Afghan, the self-hating Muslim. I considered it a symptom of the twenty-first century.

"I am moving out, by the way." Eli's doorbell rang, and he disappeared into the hallway before he admitted the obvious. "I'm moving in with Doreen."

"I'm happy for you," I said dryly. I was jealous—of the normalcy of their relationship, of Eli slipping through my fingers. Rico stumbled in, his pupils dilated. Out the window, dusk broke the sky into mauve streaks, and we could hear skaters down on Skalitzer Straße shouting. Rico placed a dry, stubbly smooch on my forehead, then scooted down next to me.

"So," he said, after the usual small talk stalled and jokes had been made. I swallowed, still fearful.

"What's new with you? Are you okay?"

"Yes," I said. "I don't want to talk about it, really."

"Give me one of those." I handed him a cigarette. "Did anyone hurt you? Are you safe at home?"

"Yes, oh my God," I said defensively. "I'm safe."

"So you're Afghan. Like Osama bin Laden." When he said the name, Rico appropriated an accent that I assumed he thought to be Arab—but it sounded Dutch or Nordic, too much labor in his throat. Like Oedipus, I yearned to poke my eyeballs with one of the needles of my earrings.

I felt sick of the perpetual confession and disappointed by Rico's idiocy, by how long it took before Eli said, "Osama was Arab, you imbecile."

Rico insisted it was just a silly joke and spoke of Tamara, whose political views had turned conservative, propelled by a paranoid bent. I hadn't heard from her in weeks and wouldn't see her again for a long time: She'd slid into a different friend group, had quit her job. Eli lit another cigarette and walked over to his swivel chair.

"By the way, I always found that Persian girls have beautiful eyebrows," Rico said, and pulled a bag of vinegar chips out of his backpack, ate a few, then discarded the bag again. "And the fact that you do so well on drugs makes more sense if you're from that corner of the world."

We were all laughing then, though I could still feel the sting.

"Well, Europeans aren't very good at it."

"Freud! All the Nazis?" Eli asked, spinning in a slow circle. "And don't worry, Nila. Don't worry, because Rico thinks you have gorgeous eyebrows."

Rico felt galvanized to speak about opium dens in Iran and fields gleaming with poppies in Afghanistan, and my neck felt very hot. I had the sensation that I wasn't in my body at all—or that I had been born just a week ago. "It's friendship," Rico said. "We are here for each other. You shouldn't be scared. But friendship also means that you must be able to take a joke without pitying yourself."

I laughed, but my voice was still wobbly. I looked to the floor, remembering my father's suspicions. Anna and Romy cuddling with such unabashed openness under the Prenzlauer Berg trees. Perhaps you could trust people as much as you could trust books. But I couldn't let go yet. I imagined something—the page of a book, or the camera's lens, those liars—shielding my heart.

IN THE MORNING hours, consciousness greased with 2C-B and two entire rounds of listening to "Bohemian Rhapsody," we left Eli's apartment. Walked past bars closing their doors, past bakeries that had just opened theirs. Senegalese dealers smiling at us in Görlitzer Park, with coffees in their hands. Invincible, we moved toward the right side of people waiting in line, the guest-list line. Gone was the anxiety of my youth, of whether I'd get in. Now the face-tattooed Cyclops with beautiful sunglasses scanned the paper in his hand and waved us through. *Elias Zeneli and friends.* And we wound around the sweat-drenched masses, up and down, exchanging money for beer, exchanging a jacket for a number.

"There she is." Doreen was laughing loudly in the upstairs hallway. She said she missed me. A large run in her tights exposed her pale, knobby knee. Some blood crusted on it. She gave me a kiss on the cheek. Her eyes couldn't focus on me directly, and there was a distinct disorder about her presence. Her strap had fallen off her shoulder, lipstick smeared at her chin. She was chewing on Hubba Bubba and offered me a strip of the powdery wheel. Like a Proustian madeleine, that plastic packaging catapulted me into the depths of my childhood with my cousins. Beverage stores in dark, large warehouses, where it smelled of rat poison and wet concrete. Sickly-sweet jawbreakers, impossible to chew on. The jolt of "center shock" chewing gums, with that liquid, aromatic nucleus. And the peculiar loneliness of summer afternoons, when Nadia and the older kids disappeared and I was left behind in the shade of a tree on the playground, looking up at the sky and experiencing anew the vastness, the nothingness, to which it led.

"Here we meet again," Marlowe said when he saw me. "In the underworld."

"Yes, in the underworld."

He was wearing an inappropriate white button-down shirt, transparent with sweat. The shirt was half unbuttoned, revealing the tattoos on his chest, and I noticed that his gold coin was missing. His eyes looked glassy and stoned. He handed me the joint, the filter soggy and smeared with two different lipstick colors. He touched my hair, my cheek. "Doreen kissed you. She kissed my bunny."

"Don't you dare bunny me."

He grinned, and the sight of his dimples made the hairs on my neck stand up. There it was again, the desire that felt like a slap.

"Really? I can bunny you all I want." Marlowe reached out to touch my earring, a cheap, enamel-plated pinkish flower. "A peony."

He stroked my earlobe, and a part of my soul dislodged, and I experienced the room from above: color drained from the scene, everything turned gray scale. Marlowe and I, illuminated by the bare-bones lighting, the low synth melting whatever it was we called the space-time continuum. Behind him, on the leather couches, our friends coiled around one another like fabrics. Their black clothes accentuated by dots of curious white. Then Marlowe released my earring, his finger tracing the stain Doreen had left with her lipstick. I saw his little scar, his expression assembling into a wild smile. The music picked up, over-layered with spacey effects, and Rico jumped up from the couch, as if rising from the dead. Everything tinged in a medieval hue, even now, when things were motile again. He sauntered toward us, and when he touched my shoulder, I grinned from ear to ear. My lips chapped, as if I had chewed on sandpaper.

"Bathroom break," Marlowe commanded, and we followed him through the slipstream of warm bodies, like molecules in an electric circuit. Opened an unlocked booth where, under the ruddy light, a man was setting himself a shot. His head leaned against the wall like Hippolyte Bayard's *Self-Portrait as a Drowned Man,* the end of his belt clenched between his teeth.

Rico, Marlowe, Doreen, Eli, and I were oily sardines packed into the metallic box of the bathroom. Rico had draped his arm around my shoulder, and he kept kissing me on the part of my hair. In the other booths, voices discussed something in passionate continental Spanish.

"We are not Spanish," a girl shouted back after Rico complained about the sounds of their language. "We are Catalan."

"Oh my God, I'm so sorry," Doreen said. Everyone laughed, and Doreen giggled like a child, guarding her mouth. "You can't make fun of other European countries. We are the worst European country there is." She fell backward into Eli's embrace and whispered in his ear.

"Hey, Doreen," Marlowe said. "I really like your dress."

"You do?" Her spine uncurled, as if summoned by a teacher. She let go of Eli's hand and turned toward her bracelet, trying to disentangle a knot, then looked up at Marlowe. Beaming, she placed a foot on the toilet, worrying the hole in her tights. "My mother made it for me."

Eli raised an eyebrow. "Could we get the refreshments now?"

Marlowe wiggled his index finger. "Everyone be patient." Doreen kept relating an anecdote about her mother, and Marlowe listened, as if it was the most important thing in the world. He stroked Doreen's blood-crusted knee with tender circles, and she pushed his hand away, giggling.

"Speed, please," I said.

"Greedy little child," Marlowe said to me with a mysterious grin. "I have seen the monster in you."

"What is that supposed to mean?"

He pulled me closer to him, out of Rico's grip, and his breath was warm in my ear when he whispered, "You know exactly what I mean."


MORE THAN TWENTY-FOUR hours stretched and burst between the walls of the Bunker, time like the frail skin of a soap bubble. Ghouls rioted and licked, chests lifting to music, perversions proliferated, strangers touched each other's body parts, a man knelt to drink someone's pee, and Marlowe insisted we stay as long as possible, a hackneyed determination on his face. It was a test, and I accepted the challenge. Dashing through sodium light, stumbling over acquaintances, dancing until I couldn't feel my knees. Queued for the bathroom with a rapt look in my eyes as a random woman wept on my shoulder. We shared a line, and she left a wet kiss on my arm, then ebbed back into the dark. Doreen left at some point, and eventually the fluorescent overhead lamps were turned on, and the music stopped with an abrupt thump, a shrill tinnitus tearing through our ear canals. In the floodlit factory hall, a war had ended: The bouncers strutted in like soldiers and shooed us out. With brooms and sticks they directed us into the terrifying fangs of the day outside.

"Time to go home, freaks," they shouted.

We were cattle; we had to be shepherded. I felt vulnerable and exposed, as if a burning lesion studied under a microscope. There was nowhere to hide—all our secrets, magnified for one another to see: plastic cups, tiny baggies, straws and coins and syringes and rolled-up flyers, cigarette butts, someone's socks. A blue patent-leather shoe. Used condoms. Glitter, and some indefinable substance smeared on the walls. My senses adjusted to the sudden visibility, and I could smell everything I saw. The DJ in the little balcony screeched, shielding his eyes with his hands. The iconic gay Vietnamese twins in fetish gear twisted and tousled, then stumbled out. In the hallway, the man with the safari hat and toothbrush was wiping a chair. I put on my sunglasses and lit a cigarette. I had never stayed at the Bunker that long, and I didn't want to ever again.

# Twenty-six

IN THE DUSKY light of that Monday evening in June, Marlowe came out in a frenzy, dragging with him a girl—I had not noticed her before—dressed in a meshy shirt, with nipple piercings and a buzz cut. Everyone was slurring their words, and I felt too tired to entertain the venom of jealousy. We walked through the grassy expanse of the industrial park, and the streetlights turned on all at once, helixes of insects flurrying in orange beams. I slapped my arms to deter mosquitoes and felt, cold as a hand on my forehead, my father's worry. Two days, and I had not turned my phone on at all. And as so often when I was high, strangers talking on benches and laughing on picnic blankets resembled the visages of people I knew, their voices like voices of aunts and cousins and uncles. Tired of working, of staying awake for more than thirty hours, my neurons sought solace in the old and familiar but produced only a destabilizing, bizarre mirage—nothing looked quite right, as if everyone was watching me.

"Are you okay?" Eli asked, and offered me a hand-rolled cigarette.

"Sure." But my hand trembled when I tried to use the lighter. Concrete, grass, trash cans overflowing with juice cartons, aluminum foil, half-eaten sandwiches. Broken bottles of liquor. Items of unbounded consumption. A woman with a stroller walked past us, and it felt illegal to be in the proximity of a pink, innocent baby. The tabula rasa of its pure, untainted consciousness. "I don't want to be in public. All these normal people make me feel insane."

"It's paranoia time, I know," Eli said. Marlowe was a few steps behind us, arm in arm with Rico and the girl with the buzz cut, discussing the closing set.

"Can we hurry up and go to yours already?" I asked Marlowe.

"I don't want to go home yet. Let's stay here. Everyone, this is Lexi, and she will get us some booze, right?" A violent expression opened on his face. Recklessness. The insistence on staying in the Bunker until it closed, and now the desire to stay in the park, susceptible to the outside world.

"Yes, I will." Her voice was guttural but pleasant. She searched in her bag for money, and Marlowe said, "Nila, don't you have some? Or Eli? Give the girl some money."

I had about fifteen euros left in cash, but Marlowe's rabid, myopic mood infected the air, compelling me to spend it all.

"I'll go to the store with you," I said.

Giggling like idiots, we walked through the discount supermarket. The black plastic of my sunglasses tinted the scene with a surreal hue. Lexi was an art student at UDK, she told me. She was from Cologne and loved hyperrealism. Touched every fruit and box of cereal, as if trying to divine information from its material quality. Settled on a basket of kiwis, the cheapest vodka, and a carton of peach iced tea. I got tobacco, rolling papers, filters, and plastic cups. We must've looked insane to the cashier, in our sweat-drenched clothes, emanating the fetid odor of cold ash and latex and feces. But we laughed, and I had the sensation that I was part of something bigger than myself. I smiled as we walked back to the park, cured of my paranoia, almost excited for the evening in the grass.

WHEN WE RETURNED to the bench where we had left Marlowe and Eli and Rico, they were gone. Lexi obviously did not have Marlowe's number, and I feared turning on my phone. For a few minutes, we searched for them.

"Men have once again proved their worthlessness," Lexi said. Annoyed but entertained by the complications, we ambled through the backstreets to Marlowe's apartment, stopping to roll cigarettes. Trying our luck, I rang the doorbell. When Marlowe operated the intercom, music blared in the background, and I started laughing. By the time we reached his fifth-level apartment, I was covered in a layer of cold sweat. My knees wobbled, and my head was swimming. I ran to the bathroom and retched, then splashed my face with cold water. Only when I returned to the living area did I notice that the party had grown. Rico worked the DJ set, playing inoffensive minimal techno. Eli sat in the corner of the room with his hood pulled over his eyes, tapping his feet and humming like a tortured circus elephant. Lexi crouched over a cutting board on the coffee table, peeling the kiwi. But there were two other people present: two burly creatures in combat boots, making the hairs on my neck stand up.

One of them, seated on a folding chair I did not remember Marlowe owning, was a middle-aged man with a stubbly shaved head, exposing a skull shaped like an American football. Dark shadows under his eyes. He wore a bomber jacket with silvery lapels. Next to Marlowe on the couch sat a younger guy with thick eyebrows and dyed-black hair shaved to an undercut and skin so pale it was almost pellucid. Blue veins pulsing in his temples. He wore an acid-wash denim jacket and a thin white scarf that looked inappropriate for this weather.

"I'm Frederick," he said, grinning. He had a rather pouty mouth and surprisingly flawless teeth. He reminded me of young Elvis Presley, of the poster that was hanging in the Qurbani Bakery.

"And who are you?" American Football was looking straight at me. His pupils were like black planets ringed by a skinny band of green. There was a craze in his eyes, a total lack of fear. He was on cocaine.

"This is Nila, my very special Nila." Marlowe, garbling his words, circled a stick of incense around the room, trying to mask the odor of decay.

"Hi, everyone," I said timidly. The constellation of people, the sudden subjugation of feminine energy—even our boys were soft, after all—made me bite the inside of my cheek. I sat down next to Eli, on the floor, and closed my eyes. Thinking about how long it would take, and where I would sleep tonight.

"So, who lives here?" American Football asked as Lexi handed out saccharine drinks. Vodka with peach tea, kiwi bobbing on the surface.

"That would be me." Marlowe barely managed to smile. His demeanor reminded me of foxes you saw at night, rummaging for food. A gauntness, and embarrassing despair. His shirt hung across his torso too loosely. "The best apartment I have ever lived in."

"Crazy place," Young Elvis said, and crossed his legs. "So, what about the drugs now?"

"Nila, go get the drugs out of the freezer," Marlowe said. I grimaced but was grateful for something to do.

Before I got up, Eli turned to me and whispered, "Don't ask me who they are. Marlowe picked them up in the park like bulk trash."

I walked into the kitchen and knelt in front of the small fridge. The drugs in the freezer had multiplied. A giant rock of solidified speed. And a plastic bag with dozens of pink and orange pills. Questions ran through my head, but I pushed them down. Got out the blue tile with the Dutch maids, taking my time to warm up and crumble the amphetamines. I snorted a line in private and took a drink from the whiskey in the fridge. From the other room, I heard someone say, "Marlowe's a writer," and one of the strangers made an approving sound.

By the time I returned, Rico had changed the music to goa, which lent the atmosphere a psychedelic twinge. It was dark outside, and the banker's lamp on the table imbued the scene with a cold hue.

"Okay," Lexi said. "Let's cut to the chase. I don't know anyone here. What's everyone's biggest fear?"

American Football and Young Elvis grinned.

"That's such a gay question," American Football said. He was holding a giant bottle of beer, taking gulps that foamed at his lips. "Do you miss sucking your mother's tiny tits?"

"Oh my God, what are you, twelve?" Lexi said. "And that is a very normal question to ask. It's human."

American Football laughed. "Normal? We're not in some community center for love, peace, and harmony, or are we?"

"What's your problem?" Lexi picked a kiwi slice out of her cup and bit into the green circle.

Marlowe stood still like a marble column by the bins of records, staring at the wall with slight distress.

Young Elvis yawned. Cracked his knuckles, then punched the arm of the couch repeatedly. "My God," he said, and cackled. "I thought you were all intellectuals here. You must understand some humor."

Lexi rolled her eyes and fished for another kiwi, and I wondered how much they had established in the few minutes I was gone. "You should calm down, dude. Anyway, I think my biggest fear is to die without ever having found my artistic voice. And nuclear war, of course."

"Well, if that happens, we're all dead within a second." Eli took off his hood. I leaned my head on his lap, and he stroked my hair. I wanted Marlowe to be jealous, yes, but I also wanted to be comforted.

"Oh, my biggest fear is the pollution of our country by—you know—*Kanaken*," American Football said. *Kanaken*. I hadn't heard the word in a while, though everyone used it. The racial slur for people of a "southern look" with "an immigration background." It could be used for anyone: Italians as well as Sri Lankans. Sometimes Eli and I said it to each other, because even when masquerading as Greek, I was an evident foreigner in this country. American Football took the blue tile and dipped a finger into the powder. I swallowed.

Rico yanked off his headphones, turning the music louder. "Are you trying to be polemic? That won't work here. You're being extremely pathetic and racist."

"Polemic. Oh God. You want to hear something polemic?" American Football handed the tile to his young friend, looking in the direction of Eli and me, then sucked at his giant, foaming beer.

As if on cue, Young Elvis straightened his back and began speaking. The beautiful mouth spitting as he rattled on about darkness and light, the Middle Ages and social Darwinism. He even mentioned Nietzsche. "The Orient had its golden period in the medieval age; now it's our turn. It's natural progress. It's—what did you say, Lexi—it's *human*."

American Football nodded and grinned after snorting a line, evidently impressed. "How are you supposed to argue with that?"

I was laughing incredulously, puzzled both by their racism and their odd dynamic. Marlowe looked at his hands with a bizarre grin.

"Employing Nietzsche for racism—very original," he said in a low voice.

Rico just shook his head and said, "That's fucking disgusting. Next thing you'll say is that the Holocaust wasn't real." He turned the music louder, forcing people to shout rather than speak. The goa music morphed into a hallucinogenic soliloquy.

American Football got up and moved with quick and arrhythmic legwork, his jaw muscle pulsing like a food processor, wiping a thick layer of sweat from his forehead.

"Let's be civilized, everyone," Marlowe said.

Young Elvis hopped up from the couch and started pacing. "We're all civilized here, debating ideas and fears, aren't we? We could have guns on us. I could just shoot you right here and call it an act of fear or conviction. Muslims do it every day, don't they? We can retaliate."

"Okay, calm down," Eli said. "First of all—no. Second of all, this country already had this problem once and learned its lesson accordingly."

"Changed its constitution accordingly." Lexi put a finger in the air, head nodding to the awful beat. I detested them all, I thought, and suddenly I missed Doreen.

"Maybe you guys should go," Rico shouted, and threw his arms in the air, leaping to the beat like a star in front of a giant crowd. Marlowe asked him to turn down the music, and American Football yelled to turn it louder. Young Elvis walked over to Lexi and crouched down next to her, putting a hand on her back. Disgusted, she pushed him away.

"There's this amazing gun, vintage, with a silencer," he said with a loud voice. "They sell them right down the block from here, actually. You could just shoot everyone in here and no one would hear. Back in the countryside—you city kids wouldn't know—we all learned to shoot. We shot birds, rabbits, deer, pigs, elk. But deer were my favorite: Their large eyes look so terrified when they're dying. They look human." With something like wonder in his face, he put his hand over Lexi's head and repeated the word *human*.

"Fuck off." She pushed him in disgust, and he walked away calmly. He pretended to hold a rifle, concentrating at a target outside the window.

"I used to be the best in my rifling club. The best. That guy over there taught me how to shoot. I have perfect aim." His foot tapping in one spot, he grinned and pretended to aim at Marlowe's head, one eye pressed shut. "And the Holocaust wasn't real. Not the way they say in history books."

Rico shrieked over the music in disbelief.

"Hey, hey, hey. It's all okay," Marlowe said, a shrillness in his voice as he disappeared into the kitchen.

"What the fuck is happening?" I pulled at Eli's trousers.

"Should we take acid?" American Football asked, smiling like a schoolchild. He collapsed on the sofa, legs spread wide. Even his trousers had sweat stains on them. He took off his bomber jacket, revealing sleeves of tattoos on both arms.

Marlowe returned, holding a turquoise bowl with neon-green pills. When I picked one, I saw it was stamped in the shape of a Pokémon. The Pikachu pills came from a lab in the Czech Republic and had 120 milligrams of MDMA. Like the blue Nikes, they were overdosed and should be taken with caution. "I think we all need some MDMA here. To soften the mood, maybe? Does anyone want some MDMA?"

Rico muttered a recital of *fuck*s, then put the headphones back on. Finally, he turned down the music.

"This plethora of drugs," Young Elvis said as he took a pill and swallowed it whole. "They're from where?"

"A village in Poland," Marlowe lied.

"And these curtains"—American Football yanked at the blue sheet and imitated Marlowe's accent in an exaggerated way—"are they from a village in Poland too? Pretty cute. Did you choose them, Herr Marlowe?"

Marlowe fished a pill out of the bowl and inspected it. He broke it in half, offering the other to Eli, but he declined. The music was too extraterrestrial, and these men stank.

Lexi chortled, but in an offended way. "You guys are pretty fucked up," she said, tapping the cut-up straw on the tile. American Football broke a glass, spilling his drink on the floor and leaving a dark patch on the white wood. It occurred to me that no one with a normal life or a job would be hanging out at Marlowe's Friedrichshain apartment, ingesting amphetamines, on a Monday at 7:00 P.M. "Everything you have been saying is objectionable."

"Don't be so fragile, Lexi," Young Elvis said with his Colgate smile. "We're all friends here, aren't we?"

"Yes," Marlowe said. "We are friends. Rico, change the record!"

Shaking her head, Lexi pulled a sweater over her shirt. The abysmal bpm increased, accelerating my pulse. Marlowe walked with hurried steps toward Rico and started sorting through the vinyl, his hands like rats crawling across the sleeves.

"What about some acid?" American Football asked again, and I wanted to punch him.

Young Elvis aimed his invisible gun at me now. "You, over there. Curly Girl. You have very beautiful hair. Are you using special shampoo for all that hair? Like Indian shampoo?"

He threw a cigarette at me. Unaware of what to do or say, I lit it.

"What the fuck, man," Eli said. "Don't you have something else to talk about?"

"It's kind of a long, unique nose, isn't it? Your nose? *Judennase.*"

A deranged cackle escaped me. I shook my head. The same comment that had haunted me at school and even in Gropiusstadt. Jew Nose. As if the last one hundred years had not happened. I remembered the anti-Semitic drawings we studied in history class, the caricatures of greedy, shady people who conspired behind

Aryan backs. And I felt an unexpected tribal rage. *How original!* I wanted to shout, but I was paralyzed. Reflexively, I averted my gaze, looked at the shelf with the cameras and the animal skull. Marlowe's copies of *Ceremony*. When I looked at him, his face had a melancholic or apologetic expression.

"Oh, it's not a Jew nose," American Football teased Young Elvis. "It's a Muslim nose."

"What's up here, Herr Marlowe?" Young Elvis placed a firm boot on the ladder's middle rung. He was speaking with a faux American accent, a pale hand on his hip.

"Oh, nothing, nothing, just my bed," Marlowe said. He was smiling, but there was real fear in his eyes, which made me afraid too. I wanted everyone to leave.

"Deranged assholes," Eli muttered under his breath.

"What did you just say?" American Football frowned. "We're just joking, you know that, right?"

Eli jerked to a stand, as if a pail of water had been thrown at him. "You're assholes, and I'd feel sorry for you if I weren't so disgusted."

"I think it's time to finish the evening," Marlowe said quietly. Looking at him, I felt a sympathy so intense it was as if I became him, seeing the room through his eyes. This is what had happened to him. The once-glowing writer from America, after so many years in Berlin, this city where everyone's dreams came to die. He was trying to sell drugs. He too was a foreigner, and he must have felt this with a painful intensity. Something changed in his eyes.

"This is unbearable to watch; you guys are insane. I am leaving. Nila, do you want to come with me?" It wasn't until Lexi got up that I began to understand the extent of what had just transpired. I looked at her athletic figure in the doorframe. An *inherent goodness* flowed through her, like through Doreen. Confident, with her pierced nipples somewhere underneath that sweater. Yearningly, I studied Marlowe. *Do something*, I ached. *Tell me to stay.* But he didn't even notice. Instead, he pushed past us into the bathroom and locked the door, the water running. I sighed and grabbed my bag.

"Oh no, you don't have to go. We're going to go, all right? We're going to leave." American Football got up. He threw a pack of Marlboros in the direction of Eli and me, and it fell to the floor.

"For our new friends," Young Elvis said with a wink. I was paralyzed on the rug, and only when he and American Football walked past me, fishing several pills out of the bowl, did I see that their boots were embossed with a familiar sign: the white German *Reichsadler*.

# Twenty-seven

WITH THREE FEET between us, Marlowe and I walked down Warschauer Straße, over Grünberger Straße, through the fizz of a summer storm. We huddled under an awning, sharing a bag of candied almonds from the Turkish confectionery. Under a clear umbrella, we hovered between elongated bank buildings, awkward with each other. I was still shaken from the night before, but he was trying for intimacy. He wasn't severe or cold with me; he touched my cheek and apologized for the neo-Nazis, whom he insisted on calling *skinheads*. Lexi had stayed for half an hour, and Rico and Eli chastised Marlowe, calling his drug dealing imbecilic and dangerous, unsustainable. But he was drunk and high and fell asleep on the rug while Rico was still talking to him. Now he coughed, ruffling my hair.

"Hey," he said. "So will you tell me why you lied?"

A torrential dread came over me and I yearned to go to sleep. "I already explained this to you."

"I want to hear it again, like this, sober."

"On the street?" I thought of the breakdown in Duino, the email. *The only thing we can hope for is to know ourselves.*

He nodded with an earnest look that betrayed more insecurity than cruelty. A tram ambled through the road, splashing water, projecting blurry light on the buildings. My knees were shaking, and absentmindedly I deconstructed a tissue in my pocket. I was at a loss for words.

"Because I'm dumb," I said as I stepped around a puddle. "Because I am ashamed of who I am. And I have always been ashamed. I want to be someone else."

"We all want to be someone else." Marlowe chewed on his lip.

"Not you, though."

"Yes, I definitely want to be someone else," he said, and put his cigarette out. But the minute he did this, he took out another one. "I need a drink."

We settled on an empty bar on Warschauer Straße and sat down at a table facing the street. Eighties pop murmured from the speakers, and a young man with long hair tended the bar. Marlowe briefly held small talk with the bartender and returned with two pints of India pale ale. He wiped the fogged-up glass. Gulping the bitter, yeasty beer, I prepared to speak.

"I grew up sad. And poor. There is something about poverty that—"

"You don't need to explain poverty to me," he said. "I know what it's like."

I shut my mouth. He didn't understand what *my* poverty was like—he was someone who came from a ranch, who inherited money, not debt.

"Tell me one true memory, for once."

"Okay," I said, but I was hurt. I gathered myself, my memories, into a tidy pile and arbitrarily fished for truths. Boarding school, the dark dome of the cafeteria, chocolate croissants I rationed money for. Buses driving through streets that hadn't ever been touched by the Soviet empire, air so clean and unlike Berlin's. The first ghost roll I shot. Pictures I took of Setareh on a Yashica T4—trying to impress her, early in our courtship, before anything happened. When I got to the end of that roll, I realized the film had not been spooled on correctly. Sprockets broken. None of the scenes outside the gelateria or under the maple trees existed. It felt eerie, almost perverse, to think of the cellulose roll inside the machine, imprinted with nothing, just ghosts of images I made of her. A grand betrayal of the medium. It wasn't like losing an undeveloped roll of film or a notebook with your writing—those images and words survived somewhere, even in the bottom of a trash bag: They were real. This felt like a dream—everything was lost, yet the film had been right there. I tried to explain my grief to him: I was haunted by a voice telling me to render the people, and this world that I loved and feared, into something memorable. I wanted something to last, for it to get out of me. For a long while he stared out at the street, which was almost empty, except for a homeless man under the red awning of a shuttered jewelry store, his body contorted inside a shopping cart. The beer softened my insides.

"It's the artist's itch," he said. He blew a few strands of hair out of his eyes and took my hand into his, fingers intertwined. "What you're feeling, it's what compels artists to work. You just have to listen to it. You have it in you to make real art. One day." His concept of *one day* seemed very remote, and his voice sounded soft, almost sorrowful.

———

BACK AT HIS place, we sat on the rug. I placed my finger into a burn hole and imagined the cigarette responsible for it falling from someone's hand. It was like the early days—the coffee table between us, White Russians in glass mugs. The Velvet Underground was playing on the tinny laptop speaker, and Marlowe was twitchy. He snorted a small line of speed and wiped his nose with his palm. He moved closer to me, pushing up my skirt, a hand between my thighs. We hadn't had sex since Italy, and I felt sheepish around him.

"You know you can't be near me, right?" he said, tilting my chin toward his. We fucked on the couch and afterward lay side by side on the rug.

"Remember when you thought I changed you?" I asked.

"You did change me," he said, burying his face in my hair. For a while we dozed there. Then he got up and pulled his robe from the ladder. "I need to tell you something."

"Oh?"

"Gabriela didn't take the project." He stood with his back against the wall, arms crossed around his torso, and looked dreamily to the side.

I didn't believe him at first.

"Basically, Gabriela canceled the project. She didn't just push it back. I was . . ." He paused. I filled in the blank, even though he did not say it: embarrassed. He said she'd pulled the funding after reading the manuscript and that she turned cold and severe as a stone.

"I never liked her, you know," I said, thinking of her pearl necklace in Duino.

Marlowe nodded and breathed heavily. He went into the kitchen and returned with a drink of vodka, taking a sip before setting it down on the coffee table. "And I have to pay back my advance."

I was flabbergasted and out of my element. The inappropriate, gleaming look in his eyes suddenly made me think of my mother standing in front of the antiques store, studying the mirrors and Tiffany lamps. Searching for solutions, I suggested he talk to the publisher again, to ask for extensions, for help.

"Didn't you hear what I said?" He walked over to the window. "She got the editors and the publisher to fire me. They scrapped the book and my entire fucked-up career. There is no way in hell I will crawl back and beg for another project. I have my dignity."

"Okay," I said. I sat back up, leaning against the couch, and took a drink of his vodka. "There are other jobs."

Marlowe paced up and down the room, gesticulating wildly, saying he was relieved, that it might all be a blessing. "Maybe I will finally return to my other writing. Or DJ'ing. DJ'ing—the art form closest to life."

I tried to keep a straight face, but we both started laughing. *Sure,* I thought, *another DJ is exactly what Berlin needs.* He walked over to the laptop and shut the music abruptly, as if its mere existence offended his vision. Then he played around with the faulty speaker cable that had stopped working last night. He twisted at the cord, then threw it against the wall, making a grunting sound.

"Everything is fucking broken." He pulled at his sleeve and brushed his hands through his hair. The image of the thin man whom I had just photographed disturbed me now. His whole behavior of the last few days—the agitation and meanness, the reckless feeling toward time—fell into light. "What am I going to do about the money? It's the worst possible time."

The last few months replayed in my mind. Intervals of deep work, rare occasions when he'd lock himself in his apartment all weekend to sit by the green light of the banker's lamp and write.

"You know what she said? She said I should go to rehab. That I have a problem. I don't have a problem."

"You don't have a problem," I repeated.

He sat on the floor, placed his right hand on the coffee table, as if to study it for a possible solution. Then snorted another line. I observed his nicotine-yellowed fingers, steady on the straw, and the way his hair fell into his eyes.

"I'm sorry, Marlowe," I said, muttering useless things. "I wish I could do something."

"How on earth will I afford rent here? I don't know what to do about this place. And to pay her back. God."

"Pay rent? I thought you owned this place."

"I never said that."

I was taken aback, certain he had told me this on the first night, but I relented. "Roommates—you should get roommates."

He scoffed. "Who is going to accept a room with no door? And their roommate in the living room? This isn't an apartment for roommates."

I felt cold and looked at my knees, studying the fine dark hair on my thighs. I wish I had been able to document this scene from above: the naked nineteen-year-old girl on one side of the white coffee table, the man in the black robe on the other, his fingers circling the glass. She looks at the floor, and he looks at her, reaching across the table to touch her breast. *He needs me*, she thinks, knowing that she is done for. *He literally, materially needs me.* He gets up and walks around the table, sits down next to her, and slides a hand between her thighs. *And I would die for him,* she thinks, the thought moving through her like water. He whispers something in her ear, but the words take years to reach her. She knows what is expected of her: They don't need to discuss it for long. Moving in with him is the only obvious solution. Even if he had not suggested it, she probably would have brought it up herself.

# Twenty-eight

DOREEN PICKED US up in her red Toyota, Eli asleep in the passenger seat, his hoodie pulled over his head. The car was full of candy wrappers and half-filled water bottles and rolled-up yoga mats and random shoes, so that before we could get into the back seat, we had to brush everything to the floor. Doreen put on a Johnny Cash CD and I wanted to ask why, but it was too early for deep talk. Marlowe kept on opening the window to smoke, his cigarette secure in the crack, while the loud wind crashed into the car, carrying the penetrant smell of manures. Still, I drifted into a dreamless sleep, my head resting on Marlowe's lap, and when I woke up, my mouth was parched, though my chin was wet with drool. We took the exit off the highway. We followed a long chain of other cars that were evidently going to the same destination, through a village so small and flat and low to the ground, it looked like a diorama. Doreen rolled down her window and greeted the locals, who were gathered in their front yards and glared at us as if we were a circus troupe.

———

A MONTH HAD passed since I moved in with Marlowe. Instead of paying 430 euros for matriculation for the fall semester, I decided to contribute money for drugs and rent. He asked me for two hundred euros for rent, which was much less than most rooms in shared apartments. So overnight I became a college dropout and rode the train without my free U-Bahn pass. How easy it was to suddenly not be a student—it was mostly just a piece of paper. For one blissful week we played house—fucked and cooked, scrubbed the dishes with soapy water as his old Prince record spun on the Technica. On my mother's death day, he cooked an elaborate meal, and we sat for hours by the canal. He taught me how to season a cast-iron pan, placing it upside down in the oven. How to make soy cutlets, hydrating the hard pellets with broth, massaging them with rosemary twigs and oil. He was happy I knew how to make a good salad but was irate that I didn't clean the toilets properly.

My father left me constant voicemails, begging me to come back, and I could barely stand to listen to them. *You don't need to move out,* he said. *Don't you already do everything you want anyway?* For the first two weeks I worked at an ice cream parlor and took shifts through a temp agency as a receptionist in Steglitz; then I found employment at the American Apparel in Kudamm four days a week, but they often sent me to the Mitte branch to fill in when others were sick. And Marlowe started work at a call center for a bank, fielding customer-service questions all day long.

"I can't believe I'm working for a fucking bank," he said. "I'm doing what I promised myself not to do."

"Maybe Adrienne will finally marry you now," I said, and he

threw the glass ashtray at me. I collected bruises: on my arm, my thigh. A split lip he left when I talked back. I provoked him; he apologized and sometimes let me bite his arm as revenge. Every weekend he got lost in the Bunker for large swaths of time, trying and failing to sell drugs, while I stayed home and took self-portrait after self-portrait in the bathroom, all in black-and-white. I dressed up in his clothes or wore nothing but a hat, pouting into the camera. I grew obsessed with the new gauntness of my body, the hollows under my eyes. On Sundays, he stumbled home and fell asleep next to me, talking in non sequiturs about other women. On Monday mornings, he was gone before I woke up, leaving a Post-it with a heart on it next to a cup of coffee.

WE DROVE FOR what seemed another hour through a forested area. Doreen said the trees were a special type of oak; they grew only here, because of some glacial movement thousands of years ago. Everything looked flat and very green when we arrived at the festival grounds. The first thing I noticed was that there were no advertisements, no billboards, no brands, no one trying to sell you a thing, except for a makeshift sign that said, DON'T FORGET TO CALL YOUR MOM.

Music boomed from various campsites, the competing soundwaves not canceling one another out but creating a disgusting tapestry that nestled in your eardrums like gauze, and Marlowe let out an ecstatic shriek, saying, "Welcome home." After a bit of quarreling, we settled on a camping spot farther from the stages than I wanted. Next to our car, a man in red cotton pants was doing a handstand. The legs of his trousers bunched at the knees, gravity pulling his shirt up and revealing his skin, which resembled blotchy, aged ham. I wanted to ask why, but I intuitively knew that the answer wouldn't satisfy me. Girls in rain boots and greasy ponytails danced in circles, arms hooked together. In the distance, the infamous hangars from the military base arched upward, overgrown with wild grass. The festival name was written in large Cyrillic letters on a banner above the hangars, which had been turned into a stage, and on top of the green hill there was a red flag—for communism, I supposed—and a large silver rocket to symbolically launch us into this utopian space, even if we would never lift off.

Doreen took out a tube of glitter and, without looking in a mirror, applied some generously to her eyelids. "Tomorrow we all have to go to one of those workshops, so Eli and Nila understand how to become comrades."

"I am not here to go to a workshop." Marlowe lit his seventh cigarette in a row.

"I was a comrade when I was born," Eli said. "And besides, that's not how revolution works. It doesn't happen at a festival with junkies, last time I checked."

THE MAN IN red pants was still doing a handstand, only now he was also doing the splits. Marlowe pretended to be a tour guide, introducing each part of the campsite. The streets were named after revolutionaries, like Karl Marx Allee and Friedrich Engels Allee and Olga Benário Straße. Marlowe told me that the festival organizers had bought this plot of land, that it was "free of fascism," whatever that meant. He looked beautiful when he was smiling, all dimples and curls and white T-shirt. He seemed taller and happier

here. Then he pointed at a blond girl in an H&M dress and balle-
rina flats.

"Isn't she cute?" he asked, looking at us for approval. This was
a new habit of his: He'd started singling out beautiful women and
mentioning them to me. Of course, the girl didn't only start chatting with him; she also continued walking with us.

Her name was Nikita, and she was from Munich and kind of
chubby. She was wearing these hideous rhinestone-studded sunglasses, a pimple shining on her forehead. I tried to be cool with his
flirtation, but in my heart there was a splinter, the form of which
was becoming more and more indecipherable to me. Nikita and
Marlowe whispered and touched each other and looked over at me,
engaging me in some humiliation ritual. I despised the heat of Doreen's pitying glance, but when we arrived at the actual festival
ground, I muttered to myself in soft disbelief, stunned by the am-
bience, my shoes sinking into the moist grass. And yet it was impossible not to compare our body language—the way Doreen and
Eli held hands, as if they had never done anything else in their
lives. As if they were the ball people from Plato's *Symposium*, cut
in half and returned to each other.

We got beers and strolled westward, and I had the strange sensation that the festival was trapped under a bell jar: Mothers cra-
dled their barefoot children, stretched out on Persian rugs in the
grass, and made tipis of sheets tied to sticks; the sweet murmur of
wind chimes and xylophones threaded in and out of techno, and
everywhere silver tinsel hung from trees; then, of course, there
were these goa hippies, all harem pants and appropriated dread-
locks; and at last, the lake, rife with lithe-limbed girls in ponchos,
girls who could've been copy-and-pasted from fashion editorials;

and in the middle of the Venn diagram of hardcore hippies and techno nerds, there were we, neither rich nor part of a cult, just here for the hi-hat and a bit of dancing. And drugs, of course.

"I am this close to confessing my love to all of you," Marlowe said, and Nikita giggled, and I imagined slicing her neck with a knife. Guiltily, I forced myself to smile. Marlowe stretched out his hand, presenting MDMA crystals, and everyone took turns dipping into the powder.

"You too, grinch." He approached me with an uninterpretable grin. I licked the cloudy, bitter crumbs straight from his palm, tracing his lifeline with my tongue. Before Nikita left, she and Marlowe exchanged phone numbers, and I decided to repress any memory of her existence.

DOREEN KEPT TALKING about how wonderful it was that there were no police allowed on-site because it was private property, and I was skeptical, though in fact the whole setup was quite incredible. Everywhere, copper sculptures and art made of recyclables, robot dogs and burnt cars out of which grew plants, hollowed-out machines that had given in to the ruthlessness of flora. I couldn't shake the feeling that it was making a point, nature and technology coalescing and breaking apart and recalescing over and over again. It was part Disneyland on crack, part Hades's underworld, part eco-futuristic paradise. Clowns in all-white gear cycled on minibikes around a firepit, and some sort of serpentine creature with Medusa hair unleashed the biggest soap bubbles I had ever seen. Night crept up in slow motion as we walked back to our campsite, where Marlowe and I tried to have sex in the tent, which smelled of human excrement and hand sanitizer, but he was on too much ecstasy to come, and while soft laughter traveled over from Eli and Doreen's tent, he said, "I want to have a threesome."

Of course, I was shocked. I tried to keep my composure as I groped for my panties amid the mass of sleeping bags and un-identifiable fabrics. The darkness of the tent was totalizing, though there was laughter and bug-song in the distance, the sounds giving shape to the lack of light.

"With whom?" I pulled up my underwear, trying not to acci-dentally punch him with my elbow. Suddenly it was very cold, so cold my teeth were chattering.

"I don't know. Anyone. Any girl." I recalled his hand on the small of Nikita's back as he whispered something into her ear.

"With Nikita? Am I not enough?" I tried to make it sound like a joke, but there was nothing funny about the way my voice trem-bled, the question hard like the splinter in my chest.

"It's not about being enough," he said. "No one is ever enough for anyone else."

"I thought she was ugly." I zipped up my sleeping bag and wished I was in Berlin. I thought of my mother's pale hands on my father's body and dreamed of a hole deep in the earth, where I could lie down and sleep in peace.

"I've always wanted to have a threesome here. It's been my dream. . . . It was something I had planned with Hannah. And don't you like girls too? It will be fun for you, I swear. It's a once-in-a-lifetime opportunity. It might be good for us."

"I don't like *girls*," I said, thinking of the one or two other women I'd found attractive since Setareh—they were all smaller than me and confoundingly unapproachable. A lost cause. "I liked one girl. Once. A long time ago."

"What happens here stays here—haven't I told you this?"

"It's not a question about taking it outside." I sighed and decided that I needed to move out.

Marlowe laughed, and I turned away from him, trying to focus on the sound of the cicadas and footsteps rather than Doreen's giggling in rhythm with Eli's voice. The mat and sleeping bag were too thin. Sticks pierced my back.

"I hate camping," I announced.

"Hey." Marlowe put his hand on my neck. But I was made of stone, so he gathered the skin between two fingers and pinched it slowly, and when I still didn't react, he twisted the skin and let it loose, then twisted it again. The pain was both familiar and unbearable. I tried to maintain control, but I squealed. He moaned loudly, theatrically—a groan that would travel over to the other tent. Then he giggled with infantile glee. There was nothing surprising about this, though I did feel a thrill in my chest. His hand wandered over my eyes, feeling for tears.

"Don't cry," he said. "You can choose the girl." I was debased not by the fact that I was crying but because he had felt the tears. He pushed his thumb into my mouth, the rest of his fingers spread across my face like a muzzle. With the other hand, he unzipped my sleeping bag. His hand was everywhere, under my shirt, on my hip, until it settled between my legs and his fingers started circling the cotton of my underwear. Marlowe whispered into my hair, and the entire time, there was this hot snot coming out of my nose.

# Twenty-nine

OVERNIGHT, THE TENT turned into a sweltering, suffocating container. Sweat pooled under the polyester sleeping bag. The light was a shock of purple, and there was a numb feeling radiating from my head and chest. Marlowe was gone. I unzipped the tent, a waft of warm oxygen diluting the murky concentration of carbon dioxide inside. When I stepped out to stretch myself, my body seemed to be made of wood. The idea of camping for another two nights infuriated me. I wanted plumbing, a bed.

Eli said that he'd barely slept. He was preparing coffee on the percolator over the blue flame of a camping cooker. I sat down on the butterfly chair and used my makeup mirror to inspect the blue-and-red contusion blooming on my neck, too large to be a hickey, but Eli didn't ask me about it, and I didn't try to cover it up. Beyond the circle of my mirror, I stared for a moment too long at him, the way he sat cross-legged in the grass, tending to the coffee. But he returned my gaze, and lingered there.

_____

AFTER BREAKFAST, DOREEN and I walked to the open-air shower stalls, where people lined up with towels under their arms to climb into adjacent curtainless booths. I was envious of the ease with which they paraded their nudity, especially Doreen, who nonchalantly pulled off her yellow polka-dot dress and threw it on the grass. Her flesh was white and blinding in the calcified sun, her nipples large and baby pink. Looking at her, I was reminded of a basket of apples, a glass of milk on a picnic table, a field of wheat glowing in a sunlit afternoon. When it was my turn, I tried my best at the impossible project of hiding myself as I undressed, because despite everything, despite the MDMA and the lying and the reckless partying, inside me was still an Afghan girl who was ashamed of the fact of her body, how real it became when it was perceived. Under the merciless ice-cold water, it remained impossible to rub the dirt off me, and I was already covered in another layer of musk by the time we arrived at the little stage outside the theater hangar. Someone in neon glasses and a huge mushroom-shaped hat gave out lines of cocaine as if they were supermarket samples, and I happily accepted one. Marlowe forced us to sit through an entire session of marionettes enacting some bizarre medieval narrative, the political dimensions of which he was discussing with Doreen and Eli. But because I had no idea about the history of the Medici, I only nodded and said, *Oh wow, that's crazy,* and scanned the crowd for girls Marlowe might find more attractive than me, which frankly was everyone.

ALL WEEKEND I had not seen a single skinhead. Still, there was darkness in the air; I could sense it in people's eyes when I stared for too long. There was the Louise Bourgeois–esque spider sculpture, aptly titled *Mother*, and the Ferris wheel with its endless revolutions of skeletons. And then those trees. The meadow and the wet earth under my feet, roots of trees that were older than all of us. This was a military airfield, after all, the Third Reich's main Luftwaffe testing ground, and later it belonged to the Russians. Many decades ago, the aerodrome had housed executioners, massacres were planned, drones engineered. Cold steel of military machines planned to kill imprecisely. Even here, the earth continually whispered of the secrets of the dead, regardless of the volume of the music or how much we danced.

"Let's go to yoga," Doreen said later when we were sitting under a tree, her shoulders erect and the timetable in her hand. "Communist yoga—it will be good for us."

*Communist yoga*, I thought, *who invents such scams?* But everyone seemed convinced that it was a good idea, so I kept quiet. After all, what could I even have said: *No, I don't want to go to yoga; I heard the dead speak to me?* That sounded even more ludicrous than the concept of socialist gymnastics.

"I'm going to the mosh pit," Eli said after we passed the footbridge to the forested area.

"Please come with me?" Doreen asked. But Eli shrugged and walked away. I felt the urge to follow him, but the idea of going into a mosh pit seemed more depressing than communist yoga.

The instructor crouched on a white platform and didn't really move. She had a French accent and bleached hair. Marlowe picked a spot near the wall on the left, framed by other yogis, so that I couldn't lie down next to him, and Doreen went all the way up to the front. I was not surprised by either of their choices, and I was sure they weren't surprised by mine either, for I lay down at the very back, close to the exit, next to a sweating, heavily breathing bearish man. I went into the sun salutation sequence and took a long, unembarrassed moment to stare at the instructor, who was skinny and white and beautiful and wore almost no clothing. We were forced into various positions through a repetitive vinyasa, until eventually she conducted a fire-breathing exercise and every-one, including my sweating bear of a neighbor, started crying. I couldn't see Marlowe's face, and suddenly it bothered me that he had gone to a spot so far away from me. Why had he asked me to come to this festival if he didn't want me to be here? *I am going to count to three*, I told myself, *and if he looks back, he loves me. If he looks back, I will stay.* But he didn't look back, of course. I wanted to cry now too, but my neighbor smelled of turmeric root and was making these seal-like noises. So I stood up and left, and just in time, the instructor opened one of her kohl-lined eyes and said, "Do not be afraid of letting go," but it was too late. I was already out under the freedom of the sun, where it smelled less like tur-meric sweat and more like the chemical toilets fermenting at ninety degrees Fahrenheit.

I WANDERED UNTIL it got dark, but I liked getting lost: A punk show, where everyone seemed to be having the time of their lives and moshed like it was 1982 and where I suspected Eli to be. An LSD tent, where psytrance hippies were stepping into another dimension, with an orchestra dressed like a family from an Eliza-bethan play—full of frills and regalia—and techno, of course, ev-erywhere. I walked by another post-punk show, where the band shouted, *ALERTA ALERTA,* and the audience returned the call with *ANTIFASCISTA, alerta alerta, antifascista,* over and over, and the scent of burning things again, and everywhere I saw the infantile, visionary art of psychedelic flowers growing out of some fairy's eyes. It was pitch-black now, and I had forgotten the way back. So I sat down on a log by the crossing to the campsite in hopes of serendipitously finding one of the others, but instead of any of my friends, a young man in a blue shirt approached and hugged me out of nowhere.

"You don't need to be sad," he said, as if I were made of glass. "It will all be okay." And although I wanted to *let go* and sensed the salt water rising to my tear ducts, I couldn't cry. I couldn't even speak, icy and embarrassed in my muteness next to this nice stranger. I felt small and imbecilic and terrified of something vague. He bought me tea and held my hand for a long time, bearing witness to my impossible silence, and eventually he faded into the night. I wanted to hate him, but he had only been kind. After I finished the tea, I felt renewed energy to try to find our tents and walked on with an exhausted smile on my lips, but at the next crossing I saw it, like a mysterious sign sprouting out of the earth: a street named after Meena Keshwar Kamal.

"Sorry," I said to the anonymous crowds. "Sorry." My words leapt, and I needed to make sure I wasn't hallucinating, but people were having too much fun to even see me—girls in unicorn costumes passed, and every time someone with a flashlight walked by, mosquitoes and moths were aquiver in cylinders of bright. Then from far away I recognized Eli's husky voice, though I couldn't make out what he was saying.

"Why are you wearing a unicorn horn on your head?"

I took his hand. "Can you please tell me what that street name is?"

"Meena Street. Why? You don't look too good; do you want to sit down?" What I needed was not to sit down but to be sick on the wet grass. Eli awkwardly held my hair. After I was done, tranquility arrived. There I crouched, still and cold and afloat in the water of some obscure force. I felt as though a fog had been lifted. Thinking of Meena Keshwar Kamal, the young revolutionary, and of my mother, and of her life before she had me, and of all the other idealists—people like Doreen and Lexi and even Eli—reminded me of the unabashed earnestness it took to change something: a country, a city, a culture, or even just your own life. I thought of a minor scene in a book we had read in school: The Czech president gets kidnapped by Soviet services and is tortured until he agrees with their vision for Prague. The protagonists watch him from their living room, their good and honest politician, battered and humiliated, with tears in his eyes, betraying his country on public television. How moved I was, back then, to read about this man choking up on national TV. Moved by the politician's love for his people but also by the protagonists' belief in his goodness: To really believe in a country was futile. It was like love, or a vocation— betrayal was part of the pact.

I had gone to such lengths to separate myself from everyone and everything I came from, and still here it was, even in the middle of a festival full of techno and drugs: my heritage. Meena, my mother, all the women who had come before me—holding up a mirror to my face. It wasn't an epiphany as much as it was the universe winking at me. I was not alone on earth.

"I love you, you know?" I said, looking up to Eli.

"You're very high, that's what I know," he said, and pulled me back up. But I just had to let it out.

BY THE TIME it started to pour, we'd returned to the campsite, where the others had promised to wait with pizzas, but when we finally found the red Toyota, neither Doreen nor Marlowe was there. Because we didn't have the keys to open the car and it was raining too much, we went back to the festival. Walked to the wooden stage, everything bracketed by primordial, illuminated trees. Danced for a while, the ecstasy of the crowd buoying us. Everything, even the leaves and grasses, vibrated with aliveness, while overhead the rain gained more traction, accentuated occasionally by thunder and lighting, and a woman in rubber boots, who was aggressively dancing in a puddle, started shouting, "Is this everything you have to offer, Nature?"

But we had only one umbrella, and when the music changed from experimental house to hard techno, we slid our way through the aggregation of the night, through white-haired circus clowns and people on stilts (how many people came here with stilts?), then tumbled through the magical forest, which provided half a shelter from the rain. Hammocks hung between the trees, and in the middle of a clearing towered a twenty-foot sculpture installation made of intricate gold-sprayed metal plates and luminescent string, which in their totality displayed a ruptured, upended rocket. Inside the rocket were four or five little tables, around which stood tree stumps, as if to host a tea party. We sat down on two stumps under an awning inside the rocket, the table littered with half-filled glass bottles and, for some reason, a single red shoe. Finally, our cigarettes did not wilt as soon as we extracted them from the pack. When Eli touched my hand to give me a light, there was an electric shock, and we both laughed.

"I'm grateful that we lost the others," I said. "Is that making me a bad person?"

Eli smiled. "It doesn't make you a bad person, don't worry. Besides, Marlowe isn't on his best behavior." He squeezed my shoulder, and then we did bumps of speed to keep awake.

"I would . . ." I started, then collected myself. I needed to take a step back; I needed to be careful with what I said. "Sometimes I want to say an impossible thing. Like right now I want to say something, but . . . it's hard. It's hard to articulate it."

"Aren't you obsessed with books? And aren't you dating a writer? Shouldn't it be easier to find the right words?"

"Maybe that's precisely why it's so difficult for me. Or let me rephrase it: Maybe that's why I am so drawn to books. Because my own thoughts are not in words, and every time I try to express what I think or feel, I fail."

"So you've chosen photography to complete this impossible task."

"It seems that way. Besides, photography is visual, temporary. In photography, death reigns, don't you think? And a single picture—it can . . . contain everything. It's magic, really. There are no verbs. Nothing moves, everything is."

Eli was distracted by the forest, and I stared at his hands, his trimmed, oval-shaped nails. His hands were long and pale, and his forearms were slender and white, marked by green veins. I had to force myself to look away. But even with my head turned, I could take in all the smells of him. Rain, laundry detergent. The ash on his breath. He had a mole on his cheek, a light beauty mark where his beard stubble began.

"Sometimes I would like to go the other way and turn things around," I said.

"What do you mean?"

"I think I regret the situation I'm in, and I'm sure there's a way out, but sometimes you walk in the same direction for so long it seems impossible to return, though of course I want to, I want to go back and change it all."

"You know how people always say they do not regret situations," Eli asked, "that *je ne regrette rien* bullshit?"

"I think that's wellness propaganda. If we didn't regret our decisions, where would we be?"

"Most aphorisms rely entirely on the condition that you like the person you are. As in, I do not regret what I did because I like who I have become. What if you hate who you have become? I think we have to reassess our relationship with regret."

"That would be a great campaign slogan. More regret for everyone."

Warm wind emerged; the rain slackened. The forest blinked red and gold. People stumbled into the forested area and out again. I had the weird hunch that Marlowe was looking for me, that he was trying to communicate with me through some supernatural channel, but I refused to acknowledge it.

"Do you believe in fate?" I asked.

"It would be almost masochistic of me to believe in fate." Eli took a drag from the cigarette and then scratched at his wrist. "Because it'd mean that I would have to accept everything that happened to me as some divine plan—and not as the fault of others. It would absolve them, I think. My father hitting my mother, my father leaving us—all of that, it can't possibly be fate. War is supposed to be fate?"

"I guess there is the fate of your private life and then the big public forces that alter it."

"If I were to believe in fate, I would have to think it's all fate, the macroscopic and the microscopic. There is no free will in a predeterminate universe. I cannot believe in God. You know, we are from Kosovo, we were born into communism, and we were born without religion. The state was God. And the state was horrible; we had to leave. There was no benevolent God or godlike state in my life. Everything was so entirely godless, and then here it was horrible—we didn't speak the language, I didn't know what the word for *door* was, so I started crying in kindergarten. I hated kindergarten. My mother had to pick me up and bring me home, and for three days I couldn't go, because all I thought was that I didn't know the word for *door*. I dropped out of school. You don't understand. . . ."

He hesitated, and his silence opened in front of me like a hallway. I was overcome with the desire to explain it all to him. All I had done was send him a text, telling him I was Afghan, and then that brief conversation at his place. In more clarity than ever before, I wanted to tell him: *I am like you, I understand you.* But instead I said, "Marlowe hits me."

"Pardon me?"

"Yes, he hits me, and sometimes I hit him back."

"Nila, what the fuck?"

"I mean, it's not that bad. It's only happened like twice, but I don't actually want to be with him anymore. I don't know why I moved in with him—it was kind of thoughtless."

"Well, you shouldn't live with him."

"So you don't believe in fate?"

The beginning of a chuckle died in his mouth, his eyes turning bleak. "I knew it was a toxic situation. I'm so sorry."

A single tear ran down my cheek.

"You're too young," Eli said, "to experience such things."

"You're not much older than me."

"This tear is the saddest thing I have seen in my whole life," he said, wiping it away, and it took a lot of restraint for me not to rupture. He said that Marlowe had been violent with Doreen too, that he had left her alone during panic attacks, had thrown a chair in her direction. Threatened to throw her down the stairs. But he had never actually hit her. "He never went that far with her."

"Oh," I said, not knowing what it meant. *He never went that far with her.* If it really meant that I was the first person he'd hit, if I was the first person who'd stayed, if I was the first person who had, because of some secret desire, wanted it. In the hallway after the fundraiser: Had I initiated it? Not this way, though, I thought. Not this way. I wanted it to be part of a game, of erotics. *Not this way.*

"I think you should stay with us for a while, and we'll figure it out. I can't believe you didn't tell me before."

"I'm sorry."

"You told me now. Let's get out of here."

"Wait," I said to Eli.

"What?"

I drew him close to me, and I kissed him, a soft long kiss, which for a while he returned. Then he abruptly let go of me, shaking his head.

"No, Nila."

"Oh, I'm sorry," I said, embarrassed.

"No, it's fine, it's just . . ." He reached out to touch my cheek but then stopped himself.

"Forget it," I said.

"Don't be sorry," Eli said with a shrill pitch, looking at the ground. "But let's go now."

ON THE RIDE back, Marlowe drove, and I sat shotgun. Eli was asleep in the back seat with his hood pulled over his head. Doreen chitchatted about this and that, the way she always did, saying, *wind, cow, moo moo,* behaving like a child one minute, then serious and charged like an academic the next. Marlowe was evidently drunk, sipping on beer, a cigarette clutched between his lips. His driving was surprisingly smooth, cruising through the middle section of the highway like a skilled bird. When we arrived in Friedrichshain, the sky was grim, the grime of the festival still on our skin. We all climbed out of the car. Eli stretched, looked at me for a long minute. I stared at the pavement by his feet.

Doreen leaned against the driver's door. "Are you ready?"

Eli finally said, "Nila is going to stay with us for a bit."

All day he hadn't spoken to me, and now this.

"What?" Marlowe sighed. "That's ridiculous."

Doreen shot Eli a strange look.

"Don't be weird," Marlowe said. I looked at him with a combination of valences—disgust, desire, affection, annoyance. A stupid smile came over my face, remembering the brief kiss with Eli. The way he had said, *He never went that far with her.*

"Actually, it's fine," I said to Eli. "Don't worry."

———

MARLOWE BOUGHT TWO Club-Mates and a vodka from the kiosk downstairs. As we trudged up the stairs with backpacks and sleeping bags, a sharp scent hit our noses on the fifth floor. The door to his apartment was hanging open. Fearing what we would find, I let Marlowe go in first. After a few seconds of silence, he started screaming with the decibels of a wounded dog, and when I finally followed, I saw that almost everything, even the rug, was gone. The apartment had been robbed blank.

# Thirty

THE FREEZER DOOR hung open, and the drugs were gone, and Marlowe said he couldn't imagine who on earth could have burglarized the apartment, but there was a small swastika on the bathroom tile, and I suspected that it had something to do with me. That it was one of the two skinheads he had dragged to after-hours. He couldn't look me in the eye as we sat on the floor, taking alternating swigs of vodka and Club-Mate, his knees pressed against mine. That first night after the festival we slept on the mattress, one of the only things that was left behind. We shared a throw and one pillow, because even the blankets had been taken. And no matter how often I tried to drape his arm around me, he withdrew it.

THE DRUGS MADE me weepy, and I failed to reach that addictive bliss of euphoria, that nascent feeling when the speed hit your system. At the few parties I did go to, I grew increasingly catatonic and sat in the corner like a bundle of nerves. I clocked into work and sorted through the neon nylon and the thick polyester, pulling a neat finger-width between the clothes hangers, and counted the hours with my perfectly normal co-workers with their perfectly normal lives. There were days when my hands were tingling so hard they turned numb and I dropped the clothes. Could barely hold a camera. Sometimes I looked at Melanie's Facebook profile, her life in England with friends in colorful clothing. Her pretty, blurry face. I offered feedback to customers and joined calls from the California office during closing hours.

A new co-worker, a Somali girl with glossy eyes, endured rotten jokes at work, and a dreadful love for her broke open in me. If I had it bad here, then what was this country doing to her? My boss took a liking to our new hire from Barcelona, an aspiring poet. Unable to speak German, she worked the backstock. It was a different time—a year or two before it became acceptable, even in Berlin, for front of house to speak only English.

"Inventory! Count the scrunchies," they said, and I did. Twenty-three scrunchies. I folded shirts, rang up customers, smiled at them. I counted the hours and how much I would take home—€8.74, €17.48, €26.22. I stashed away money, kept it in my pockets, in envelopes I hid under my books. I was saving for a new analog camera, for film, for my escape. Evenings I stood in the wet, dark courtyard and smoked a cigarette, inhaling the scent of Berlin-Mitte, which was that particular odor of warm magazines and piss drifting up from subway grates. I bought a pretzel at the bakery inside the station, chatted briefly with the Syrian baker under the fluorescent light, then took the train home, the Fernsehturm a ridiculous and glossy scepter in the night. I crossed the streets at red lights, a small part of me yearning to be run over by a car—just to see what would happen—and, at last, when I arrived at our apartment, I ate the pretzel while sitting in the dark of the stairway, counting the minutes before going in. When I finally opened the door to the apartment with greasy hands, Marlowe and I ignored each other, though sometimes he forced me to communicate with him and sit on the sofa and listen to his opinions about writers or music. I didn't want to listen to what he spoke about; I didn't want to learn why vinyl was special, or why the needle was an elemental part of how music functioned, but he continued to keep me hostage to his realizations, and when he was done, I climbed back to the upper floor. A whole shoebox filled with undeveloped film. And books strewn everywhere, even though I could not focus on anything for longer than a page.

# Thirty-one

SEPTEMBER WOBBLED; OCTOBER flitted by. By November, the news was all we talked about. It was too hot and windy, the sky too close to the ground and fading into a dark purple by dusk, and the dried-up soil from the sewers and cornfields bracketing Berlin traveled with the wind and thickened the air, so that most of the time we shut the windows and touched each other to forget about the news. And when we had to walk to work or meet a friend somewhere or go to a protest, we were not just sweating under our jackets, we were also coughing and wiping the grime from our eyes. Of course, the news simply confirmed some knowledge I had already felt, though the nervousness was palpable, and it seemed that everywhere in the country, both in the small college towns and in the big cities and on the farms, the dust in our lungs became proof that nature, too, knew something monumental was being revealed.

———

SUNDAY MORNING, AFTER another lonely weekend, I turned on my phone to a plethora of messages and missed calls. Most were from my father, who said, *Look at the news.* I climbed down the ladder and opened the laptop to google. There had been a fire at a shisha bar somewhere in Neukölln. The reports didn't identify the name or where exactly, but when I finally saw the photo on a news website, I recognized the trees on our street and the Qurbani Bakery's neon sign. *It wasn't a shisha bar,* I wanted to say. *It was a bakery.* At least two people had died. Allegedly, there was a shooting beforehand. *We don't have any more details at the time,* a report said. *It's a developing story.* I tried to dial my father's number, but my hands trembled, and I dropped the phone twice before I got it right.

"Nila. It's okay. It's okay." He sounded very young on the other end.

"What happened?"

"They shot three people," he said.

"Who?"

"They came to the bakery at closing time. I looked out the window and there was smoke everywhere. They also killed the shop cat—the kiosk cat."

"Who, though?"

"They killed the cat. Jackie. The cat. Can you believe it?"

I thought of the last time I'd seen Jackie. "Papa, who killed them?"

"Are you coming home?"

"But who killed them?"

"They don't know yet, Nila. Don't make that noise. I'm okay; it's the Qurbani brothers who were shot, but—"

"Are you home?"

"Of course I'm home. Where else would I be? Are you coming home?"

I paused and took in the room around me: the sun dappling the walls, the window with the courtyard view. Marlowe was at the Bunker or some other club. "Yes," I said. I packed my bag and took the train, and then the bus, pulling at my cotton skirt. Our street was cordoned off with plastic tape. Police swarmed and dithered, their uniforms glinting like scarab beetles in summer. The bakery was barricaded and locked, the glass broken, an auburn wind carrying ash. My fingers curled tight around the straps of my backpack.

"Do you live here?" a police officer asked. I stared at him, his large nose, his navy uniform. His bulletproof vest. "*Sprechen sie Deutsch?*"

What could I have said? I walked away. I didn't have it in me to go inside our building, to see that small apartment with the silver floral wallpaper and the balcony filled with empty flowerpots and plastic bags. Or the orange couch my father sometimes slept on. Instead, I wandered the streets until I got cold, passing between the old buildings and parks, and by the time I got back home, Marlowe was already asleep.

THE NEWS REPORTS said the shooter was a man in his thirties, *European-looking*. He loaded up one Astra P3 600 and a Walther M2, rode his black bicycle to Neukölln in the evening, sat down at a café. After three cups of tea, he shot into his surroundings but didn't hit anyone. Then he got scared and fled the scene, but his anger picked up again after a few hours. Once he got to Gropiusstadt, he used his silenced Astra to shoot two Afghans—the Qurbani brothers—just as they were about to lock their bakery. He then shot a Syrian woman on her way home, carrying a bag of bread and a glass jar of marmalade. The bakery door hung open to the tiled interior, the clean display case, the boxes of baklava and tea. In a frenzy, the perpetrator decided to tamper with the scene of his own terror: He dragged all three bodies back inside, their blood mixing, their limbs draped around one another. And then he set the bakery on fire, trying to burn everything, including all the flour and sugar and eggs in the kitchen. The cooler with the chocolate milk, the posters of Elvis and Ahmad Zahir. He shot Jackie, the orange cat, on the street outside, then ran into the dry evening and escaped via a side alley. He must've had at least one person to help him get away, but the details remained unclear. How jarring it was to see these Afghan brothers, these men I knew, pronounced dead on the news. At first, the rumors went wild: A tabloid speculated about a domestic dispute, a hazy affair, or an honor killing, even though it was clear that the Syrian woman did not know the Qurbanis.

On Tuesday afternoon, Mirko H., a thirty-two-year-old unemployed accountant with wild, prematurely gray curls, green eyes, and a history of depression, sat down at a bus stop in Potsdam and wrote a cryptic letter of confession about the shooting, calling out to the Aryan race to defend the German nation. He walked around the block and shot himself in the temple in front of a flower shop, blood splattering buckets of yellow amaryllis. Cleaners mopped up the blood from the street, between petals of protea and eucalyptus. Perverse impulse in me, I yearned to have seen it—or taken photographs.

———

TEN DAYS LATER, suspicious packages with a video arrived at newspaper offices, media stations, mosques, and Islamic and Turkish cultural centers across the country.

In the lunchroom at work, with the windows open to the arid November air, I listened to the news on the small, antiquated radio. The host sounded robotic as she described the video's contents: a fifteen-minute montage of scenes from the animated *Pink Panther* TV series, cut and edited to include images of shop owners gunned down in their stores, small businesses bombed, family members grieving at the gory crime scenes. The Kebab Mafia murders had puzzled authorities for the last decade, and now someone was using the Pink Panther, with his whimsical top hat and rebellious schemes, to confess to the dozen murders. The radio report played the cartoon theme song, the famous jazz tune meant to underline the Panther's cool and elusive manners.

A few days later I was passing a newsstand near Rosenthaler Platz when I saw it on the front page of *Bild:* the Pink Panther smirking and pointing a stick at the passport photo of a dead man who looked like he could've been related to me. The headline read: WHO KILLED THE KEBAB MAFIA VICTIMS? For a few minutes I stood there, transfixed by that ludicrous image. An older lady in a tattered trench coat rammed into me, and I moved to leave.

The video must have been more than a year old—it did not include the Qurbani victims, nor did it include the flower seller who was shot in Frankfurt earlier that year, though it announced Berlin and Frankfurt as upcoming targets. The full video was never released, but from what I learned in the months and years afterward, it was meant to function as propaganda for the deed: The Panther, dressed as a news reporter, yawns, sits on the couch, crosses his legs, and wonders when the German public will understand that the group called National Socialist Underground was responsible. *Stand with your country*, the Pink Panther commands. *Continue the fight of cleansing Germany.*

TWO WEEKS LATER, a bank robbery went wrong outside Frankfurt, and they found the offenders—two men who also escaped on bicycles. They turned out to be connected to the Qurbani murderer and to the Pink Panther video: These were the people of the National Socialist Underground. Mirko H. was not a loner, as people speculated, after all. Before police got to the two men, the trailer in which they had lived off the grid for years was set ablaze. The pair died inside it by murder-suicide. Red and yellow flames licking the metal and plastic parked in a field of dying rye. And amid the cauterized interior of the trailer, the SWAT team found stolen weapons, an excessive amount of ammunition, a Česká, USB sticks full of incriminating material, and the silencer.

On the same day, an apartment in a neighboring town exploded in flames. At the scene, police found more weapons and a computer containing the Pink Panther video, neo-Nazi flyers, and an array of books on race science. After a week of traveling through the country by train and foot, a woman with eyes the color of the Adriatic called the Frankfurt police station and turned herself in. IS THIS WOMAN THE MASTERMIND? one news headline said. She was their co-conspirator, the fourth main member. On TV, I saw her back, her long blond curls. Lawyers escorting her, their arms resting on her Zara blazer. She had lived in that apartment and set it on fire after sending off the Pink Panther DVDs, probably with help from other Underground members. She'd hidden in the apartment, cooked meals, made their beds, opened the door for them when the others came. It was the most ordinary thing: *This woman must have loved them*, I thought.

MUCH WAS MADE of their radicalization. Mirko H., the Neukölln shooter, was a late addition, their "dim-witted" cousin. They had grown up in the same 45,000-inhabitant town in the East of Germany, during the right-wing terrorist attacks against the refugee wave that my parents belonged to, when asylum districts and businesses were burned down. Back then, the targets were primarily Vietnamese refugees. While the Taliban burned people's libraries across the cities of Afghanistan, and satellites discovered water on Jupiter's moon Europa, and I was sent to play with a blue plush elephant in Neukölln, this group of friends met at a youth club in a district of town that, to my surprise, looked exactly like Gropiusstadt. They drafted a manifesto delineating the cleansing of Germany. Between 1995 and 1998, they received assistance from a double agent who worked in parliament and helped set up the Thuringia underground. In 1996 they went to the Buchenwald concentration camp wearing bootleg SS uniforms, laughing at the guards until they were kicked out.

That shooting spree in Gropiusstadt was only the escalation of Mirko H.'s long career. Frustrated by the lack of recognition, he wanted to go out with a bang, the news said. The others were quieter, more methodical. Once they'd grown out of teenage rebellion, they looked like normal people—wearing button-downs and jeans, sneakers. No fancy tattoos, no alternative gear, no imposing brawniness, no combat boots embossed with Nazi symbols. Instead, they lived with their hatred stowed away in a dangerous, secret ideology, their *propaganda of the deed*.

The trial for the woman took years. But her police confession corroborated the Pink Panther video: She claimed the group was responsible for all of the Kebab Mafia murders and bombings and robberies going back to the nineties. All of the victims—most of them of Turkish background—were killed in different towns; most of them were killed with the same type of weapon—a silenced Česká CZ-35. *The gunmen had to be in a group of at least two and intimate with their victims*, police argued back then, since the victims had been held down before they were shot. They had looked their killers in the eyes. The underground was responsible for dozens of bank robberies and three bombings, one of them that kiosk bomb in Bremen—the kiosk owner's blue-eyed widow speaking of bean soup, and my father leaving the apartment without his coat. *At this time, we do not believe this to be a racially motivated attack.* Or Marlowe saying, *How am I supposed to remember that someone died?* And that Greek restaurateur, who died so close to my school, dragged through the news for weeks, whose mother and brother had moved back to Greece—they had killed him too. *He's olive-skinned, isn't he? It's always easy to confuse those people*, my teacher said. Another victim was a locksmith driving a van through the town square. A young boy who had taken over a shift for his father in a kiosk after school and was doing math homework on the counter, pencil in hand. Another shot inside his ice cream truck—he had no family, but on his body they found a notebook in which he'd documented his life, his dreams, with a purple fountain pen. *He who has no home,* said Adorno, *will find it in writing.* And there were more, all of them men with dark hair, men who kept notebooks, or liked to go home to cook bean soup, or sold flowers. Five euros for a dozen tulips, five euros for a dozen. They had all looked them in the eye, had looked their unmasked shooters in the eye. Months and years separated the attacks, and I saw all this unfold on the news, all these other victims I hadn't cared about, had never paid attention to, although their deaths ran in seams underneath my own life, like the waterways underneath a city. *The Kebab Mafia is at it again.* These men, whose faces resembled the faces of men around whom I grew up, men like my father and my uncles, men who I too had hated, men whose faces were so easy to hate.

# Thirty-two

SOMETHING BIG HAPPENS. Something bigger than you. My mother marches at a student protest in 1984, wearing suede boots, the sun rising over the mountain. Or, seventy years earlier, Kafka wakes up and learns that Franz Ferdinand was assassinated. Sunlight moves through the water glass on the nightstand. God comes down to Moses and tells him to refuse the golden calf, to take his children out of Egypt. My great-great-grandfather leaves his tribe on the Iranian border and settles in Afghanistan and says the Shahada. A whistleblower sits in a courtroom, his gaze turned toward a blue book that contains the sentence that will define his fate. Trials are held. The world spins. We send rockets into space, robots that take pictures of planets we have never been to. We write down the law, we amend it, and we define who is good, who bad. Documents are classified, hidden for years. Exile. War. Terrorism. A girl brushes her hair and plants a bomb in a café in Algeria. *I felt no regrets. I did it for my people,* she will say from her prison cell. *Apokalypsis,* which means *revelation:* the bride removing the veil, turning her face in the direction of the grainy wind. Sand fluttering in her eyes. You watch the news; everything you feared is true: They hate us. You belong, you understand, to the others. You think of Celan's "Todesfuge," the image of graves in the sky. You think of Palestine. And then, as always, there is loneliness. A loneliness as old as your childhood.

These thoughts passed through me as I stared for ten minutes at a photograph of my father; he is with his cousins, presumably, though these other men could have been anyone. The picture, taken from the frog's perspective, is backlit, eliciting an aura of darkness. The men are crouched on a hill toward the right. Gray, minimal shrubbery dots the landscape. Only my father looks into the camera. They wear cotton pants and keffiyehs and dismaal shawls on their shoulders, one of them holding what I at first glance mistook for a rifle but is just a camcorder. I kept staring at it, wondering who they were or where it was taken. Then I put the picture back in the notebook where I'd found it, where years ago I must have left it: either as a note to myself or to hide it.

DOREEN HAD INVITED me to a protest for justice for the victims' families. "The German intelligence is in on it," she said as she painted signs, her hair pulled into a tight bun, a glassy look in her eyes.

The protest was small, maybe only two hundred people gathered. At the few protests I had gone to before—most of them for environmental justice, attended by thousands of students—I spent time with Romy and Anna and Melanie, getting drunk. Back then I would analyze the slogans or be too embarrassed to shout them.

But now I was too tired for sarcasm. I surrendered to the feeling of being present: A child was playing a beat on a traditional drum. The police stood in a different corner, glimmering in their idiotic uniforms. Doreen was speaking about a neo-Nazi protest elsewhere, in a town two hours farther east, which was being thwarted. On the stage, one of the leaders of the Central Council of Jews, a man in a corduroy suit with very dark eyes—a kind of look that reminded me of my parents in the early years—coughed. He put on a pair of reading glasses, and then he started speaking in solidarity.

By the time we started marching, the sun was beating down on us, the wind carrying dirt. People peeled off their jackets and scarves. Walking there among them, one step after the other, in that clarifying heat, I felt a slow dissolution of self. I kept looking for Doreen in the crowd, her blond head a few feet ahead of me. It wasn't totally unlike dancing: I remembered Antigone in her white dress on Tempelhofer Feld, her body lunging against Creon's. It was intoxicating to be a body among other bodies, even when we were mourning for something. I kept thinking of the shooting: the small rifle in the hand of that pale, curly man. Training it precisely on the brothers. The Syrian woman. First the young one, then the other. Then Jackie, the cat. *They also killed the shop cat,* my father had said. *Can you believe it?*

MOSQUES WERE VANDALIZED, death threats sent to synagogues, carefully typed up on the back side of postcards with Botticelli prints. A package of feces was sent to a Turkish community center in Dortmund. *You're next,* read the graffiti tagged on a bakery in

Kreuzberg after it was set ablaze overnight. But then the news died down. *We have it under control*, police said. *Everyone is dead or in custody.* And yet I saw the faces of neo-Nazis everywhere. Shrieked when I felt a hand on my shoulder in the supermarket, only to turn around and find a grandmother asking to reach for the milk. The fear wasn't unlike grief: like in the months after my mother's passing, when every woman wore her face. I imagined guns in handbags, behind counters. Dreamed of my father being pushed into traffic, someone putting a bullet through Rashid's head from the back seat of his taxi. Walking past newspaper stands or clicking through headlines, I feverishly anticipated finding the neo-Nazis who had robbed the apartment: American Football and Young Elvis. The way he'd quoted Nietzsche, repeated the word *human*. His Colgate teeth. I was sure they were affiliated with the Underground and was waiting for the great reveal, to learn that they had gone to high school with Mirko H. But they never appeared anywhere. And I didn't know whom I feared more—the ones with shaved heads and combat boots, who wore their logos proudly on their bodies, or the lanky IT guys in H&M jeans, who looked like you and me, who smiled, either coy or sweet, when passing you on the street. What we loved, what they hated—it all touched. And lingered in the dark, like a fine blue gas enveloping the forests, and rising slowly into the city, and settling in our lungs.

I WAS EXHAUSTED by the time we were done with the march. Back at Alexanderplatz, trash filled the train station, fluorescent light bathing the commuters in yellow. Like an insect, I fell into place among the stream of people. On the platform, I saw a few groups with signs, people I recognized from the protest earlier: Smiles passed between us, and I believed for a moment that there was a secret knowledge surrounding us.

I took my time while walking up the five stories to Marlowe's. I couldn't hear any music—but when I opened the door, the light danced, as if in a Renaissance painting. Tea lights were lined up on the windowsill. Marlowe was sitting on the rug, crouched in front of the coffee table, his head lowered over a notebook. A tumbler with something—vodka, I guessed—stood next to him on the table.

"I'm writing again," he said, without raising his head.

"Oh, that's great." I sounded flatter than I intended. I stood still in my jacket, frozen in that moment, staring at him in the flickering candlelight. He put his hand flat on the page and then looked up at me.

"How was it? Do you feel better?"

"A little." I slipped out of my boots and went into the small kitchen, then put on the kettle. I felt infinitely far away from him and annoyed by that notebook, the way he'd put the pen behind his ear.

Leaning against the counter with my eyes closed, I tried not to listen to the blabber from the other room. He was talking about something he'd read in an essay by John Berger. That night, on the mattress, Marlowe hugged me tight, his hand curled around my neck.

"You need to breathe," he said.

"I am breathing," I said, knowing that nothing would ever be the same again.

I woke up with my hands balled into fists, feeling a hatred that wasn't mine exactly but a hatred inherited from other worlds and peoples moving through me. Walking back from work through the empty November streets, I understood the man in the park, standing on a stool in his windbreaker and reading from the Bible; I understood Doreen with her political-theory books, that furious, righteous look on her face; and I understood, which was incredible, my father and his constant alienation, the way his voice broke over the phone with the darkness that for years I had despised hearing and that now I thought of as the strange darkness of that photograph on the hill, saying: *I was right about this country, wasn't I? I was right all along.*

# Thirty-three

THE CAFÉ, LOCATED on a busy street in Kreuzberg, had a glass front and was infamous for its vegan patisserie and the C-list celebrities who liked to frequent it. Marlowe had woken me up in the afternoon with an uncharacteristic sweetness and said that we should go for coffee and cake.

"Let's pretend it's your birthday." It was weeks after my actual birthday, but I played along. He couldn't take my anger: He was trying to cheer me up, he said. We smoked a joint on the way, and when we went inside, I glanced in the mirror behind the bar and noticed that my eyes were swollen. The waiter steamed the espresso machine. He had a green tattoo of a tiger on his forearm, and I remembered seeing him half naked, weaving through the masses on the Bunker dance floor. Smiling to himself, he used a pink dishrag to ward off the flies pestering the pastries in the fogged-up display case. I told Marlowe that I wanted the cheapest item on the menu, but he insisted on getting the avocado crème tart, a strawberry profiterole cake, and some mango chai sherbet.

"I want the cheesecake," I said.

"No. It will make you fat." He laughed, and so I laughed a little too.

I walked away and sat down at a table by the windows. I knew he needed my money to pay, since he spent his salary on music equipment and drugs, but I wanted to make him beg for it. He took an unusually long time to dawdle around the café and bathroom before he mustered up the will to come to me, and instead of asking me for the exact change, he demanded my wallet. I retrieved my brown leather wallet and gave him twenty euros and turned around again, staring at the table closest to us. I could look directly at them: two girls sitting with two older men. The girls were my age, and when they noticed my staring, one of them looked back at me with probing eyes, and a pulse of recognition troubled me. She wore a yellow velvet dress with a generous neckline that revealed her lace bra. To her right sat the man I assumed she was with—he was at least ten, if not twenty, years older, and very handsome and tanned. He wore transition lenses, and his black hair was slicked back, graying in parts. His clothes were clean and crisp and mono-chrome. I could make out that they spoke Spanish and English. I heard their voices more clearly than the music and glass chatter around me, and repeatedly, the girl and I looked at each other with curiosity. But something about them was different. I grew hyper-aware of my old, thrifted dress, of my chipped black nail polish. They drank champagne and clinked their glasses. Their skin was beautiful and refined, lacking a rawness, and everything about them had the sheen of wealth and taste. The man asked the girls what they wanted, then stood up to go to the bar. And I was sur-prised to see that he was short. He returned almost instantaneously with a second bottle of champagne. They all laughed in a way I never laughed, their voices reverberating with some malicious liberty. I was sure that they had not cared about the Qurbani shooting, that they thought it had nothing to do with them. The girl in the yellow dress looked at her nails, her phone, and when she thought I wasn't looking, she glanced in my direction.

When Marlowe returned with the cake and coffee, I barely listened to him. I was arrested by the conversation at the other table. From what I gathered, they were speaking about parties too. About the Bunker, even.

"What are you staring at?" Marlowe asked.

"Nothing." For a moment I studied the other young girl and the other older man, but they didn't seem to be in a relationship. The girl must've brought her friend along, and the man hoped to get it on with this young chick in low-rise jeans, but he seemed like a bootleg version of the man in transition lenses. His clothes looked unmatched, loose. The other girl was not interested in him; she was clever, though, giggling about all that free champagne.

"They're idiots." Marlowe noticed the subject of my intense study. "They think that's what life is about. Going shopping. Look at that Rolex. Sitting here and drinking champagne. Wearing those boots. Do you think any of them know about Deleuze?" Who cared about Deleuze? Her boyfriend hadn't broken her; she was still happy. Couldn't he see it?

"Right." Their table cheered about the weekend getaway to Ibiza. Marlowe barely touched his avocado crème tart and instead started rattling on about a record he'd listened to recently.

"I am going to leave you," I said.

"Not yet." He grabbed my hand, and for a moment I recoiled.

But it was a tender touch; with his index finger he traced the shape of a heart on the inside of my wrist, then smiled at me. "Not yet."

"Why?" I sighed, and when he smiled at me, I couldn't help but smile back.

"Because we're still playing," he said. "Happy birthday."

"Happy birthday," I repeated, and then looked back at the girl in the yellow dress, wondering if she felt repulsed by me.

# Thirty-four

THE PLAN FOR that Sunday was for Romy to pick me up in the afternoon: Anna had left to study abroad in Madrid for a semester, and I would sublet her room for a while, for 375 euros. By the time Romy finally arrived, my right arm was swollen, and my phone was irreparable, but we walked out of Marlowe's apartment with three plastic bags of clothes, three cameras. My little bonsai. Toilet paper wrapped around the toothbrush in my purse. The little gray lighter which Marlowe had given me on our first night together in my pocket. When we entered Romy's dark-blue SUV, there was no whiff of epiphany, nothing spectacular, just piss and döner shops and bridges and Stolpersteine and brutalist apartment blocks jutting out between parks and picturesque prewar buildings, this ugly and merciless blur of Berlin, and the great solitude of my life awaiting me.

"We need to eat," Romy said, and fiddled with the radio, and Leonard Cohen was singing of getting head in the Chelsea Hotel, and we both started laughing. We used to listen to this song when we were even younger than now. At the McDonald's drive-through, she rolled down the windows, icy air making us squint, and then we pulled into the car park. Sipped our Diet Cokes. Shared a bag of fries. Then smoked in silence. She cranked the seat back and lay down. I hugged my knees. The hot air of the heater made me sneeze. Romy reached out to hold my hand, and strange visions passed through the car: how Anna and she had lain in the same bathtub as teenagers, washing their hair. And I, scared, watched them from the sink. I would always stand there, at arm's length from the people who loved me, not letting anyone close. And still I'd come back, propelled by my slinky heart: Sleeping in beds with them. Pinching my friends' noses so they'd stop snoring. I would get married early, hurriedly, shaking cherry blossoms out of my shoes on the steps of a town hall, desperate to make someone stay. I would get divorced before I was thirty. Romy and Anna would be there, chirping, *We told you so*, maybe even Doreen, always making me sign petitions for some political cause. Eli would die young, I suddenly was sure of it, as if I were touching the ants crawling over the mound of his grave, the second great loss torn into my life. My father would grow very old and very cranky. And I would meet Setareh again, many years from now, in a dim room in a different country, sipping wine-dark stories from our glasses.

We drove to Ikea and purchased the cheapest of everything: a clothing rack, a nightstand, some bedsheets, and a lamp. It took only a few nights and the warmth of the globe lamp to feel at home in Anna's spartan, high-ceilinged room. I went to work wearing long sleeves and, with my new Polaroid camera, I documented the progress of the biggest and most interesting bruise to date. Bought an expensive picture scanner, a used MacBook, and a flip phone on an installment plan. Was promoted to keyholder and started work at the Mitte branch. I filled in when managers were sick, and after opening hours, I stood in the rainy courtyard and chain-smoked and sipped on cold coffee and tried to imagine all the other shops that had stood in this exact same spot, all the other shopgirls who had leaned against this wall, cigarette in hand, and tried their best not to lie down on the next available train tracks.

ONE DAY, AS I was walking back to our Prenzlauer Berg apartment, I caught my reflection in a large mirror someone had left on the street. That girl with long black hair and black tights and a bag filled with books was me. Instinctively, I brought out my Olympus and shot a self-portrait. The flash was turned on, I believed, so the picture would end up overexposed, my portrait just a burst of light and legs. But when I received the scans, the black-and-white photograph was eerily precise: my sunken face, the cigarette in my hand, the black box of a camera just before my heart. A scratch in the damaged film, a grain of sand caught in the lens. What pricks me in this image is not the mirror, shattered in the right-hand corner, but the camera itself—how it sits, with its quiet intelligence, between my breasts.

"You have a very good eye," the Asian grandfather at the photo studio said to me when I picked up the negatives and asked for a print. "Like that woman Sally Mann."

THAT NIGHT, I stayed awake and developed two Fuji rolls in the darkness of our broom closet. One roll from a year when my mother was still alive, and another imprinted with Marlowe in Duino. Seeing these faces come to light on the screen of my laptop was defamiliarizing. Setareh with the blue bowl, the memory so vivid I could sense the color even in gray scale; or Marlowe asleep between white bedsheets; Marlowe holding an ice cream cone, a flower tucked behind his ear. My mother sitting on the sofa with curlers in her hair, the framed photograph of the Hindu Kush on the wall above her lending her the aura of a crown. I studied them, scanning their lights in the dark. Thought again of *View from the Window at Le Gras,* the pewter sheet inside the camera obscura, touched by an image of light: roofs and trees. He washed it with lavender water. *Heliography* is what he thought photography was, the man who took the first photograph on earth: *sun writing.*

All the pictures that had been taken since: Gerda Taro's photographs, her shot of a high-heeled woman training for the militia, one knee on the ground, a gun trained at a target. Gerda, who fled Germany for France and was run over during the Battle of Brunete. The digital picture of the hooded man in Abu Ghraib. Or the first photograph of earth from outer space—this picture that now has become so integral to our consciousness, our subjectivity, that we can conceive of the small blue planet in black space and comprehend it as our home. *Earthrise.* Millions of years of evolution, darkness and brilliance, stars and oxygen, and then water, then trees, monads and multicellular organisms, then a bony fish crawling onto land, fields of jade-hard poppies opening in the sun, and then this, one man shooting another for his origin, his God, his dark eyebrows.

As dawn poured its blue light upon my room, one of Kafka's

diary entries returned to me like a childhood prayer. I brought out a piece of paper and wrote it down, then pinned it on my wall:

"The tremendous world I have in my head. But how to free myself and free it without being torn to pieces. And a thousand times better to be torn to pieces than to retain or bury it in me. That's why I'm here, after all, that's completely clear to me."

# Thirty-five

IN MARCH, ON a surprisingly sunny yet icy weekend, I met Eli at
the Landwehrkanal, and after a long walk we climbed over the
bridge by the Admiralbrücke and sat down opposite the brutalist
structure of the hospital where I was born. Wearing scarves and
gloves, we drank warm vodka mixed with lemon juice out of a
thermos. "Like true Stalinists," Eli said, and we laughed. Both our
families forever entangled with the failed Russian dream, and now
we were adrift in a city haunted by that same dream. Eli had quit
work at the Bunker and was figuring out what to do next. Social
work, perhaps. Or sound engineering—he had, after all, perfect
pitch. He and Doreen still lived in that unfinished apartment on
Leinestraße. Sometimes I saw them holding hands, leaving early to
go home. Licking at Popsicles. They were happy or seemed to be.
How young we were on that bright, cold afternoon. I remembered
walking through brunch restaurants with him during my Rosenwald years, high off our tits, hiding behind sunglasses over a shared
burger.

"I'm sorry," I said, meaning all my mistakes: the night I tried to kiss him, and the eros that drew strings between us, sometimes so taut they produced a sweet and secret sound. But the friction was frail—it was never meant to make real music, just to suggest its existence, like a violin encased in glass at a museum, so old and brittle it would fall apart if you tried to play it. And then, of course, there was the fact that I refused his help when I needed it the most.

"I don't want you to be sorry. That's not what this is about." A duck with an iridescent splotch of purple plumage around its neck moved on the water. Leaves twirled in its wake, and a branch attached to a plastic bag floated on the black surface.

It felt urgent to tell him now. "When we were together there in that forest in the rain, there was something I tried to tell you. . . . I get that thing with your father. I understand it. My parents were violent too. And when my grandfather got sick, my father said that it was all my fault, because I behaved like a whore, because my mother didn't raise me right. You know the drill."

Eli sighed, as if exhaling a lifetime of sorrows, and took off his red glove, placing it between our bodies.

"And when he died, I didn't go to his funeral. I went to take ecstasy instead, at a rave with friends, and got so high that I didn't come home for three days. I just turned off my phone, and eventually my mother called Romy and told her I needed to take the train to Berlin at once. She was hysterical. When I got there, my mother couldn't even look me in the eye. She was wearing this blue housedress, and all I could think was that she looked beautiful, that she looked so beautiful in that dress."

"I'm sorry, Nila."

I lit a cigarette and tried to remember what the bizarre yoga teacher at the festival had told me. That I shouldn't be afraid of letting go. "I sometimes think if I hadn't been in my family, no-body would've ever felt any type of shame. And my mother in her dress, she thought it too. I saw it in her face, and she didn't want to conceal it. Every family has a curse, and I am my family's curse."

"That's not true, you know that, right?" He pulled me closer to him, awkward and bulky through all that padded fabric.

"I was just so ashamed all these years, I don't know why I was so ashamed of being Afghan. Being . . . Muslim. I still am, most days."

"I get it," he said. "Technically, I believe I'm supposed to be Muslim too. Or my ancestors were, in the past. I am not sure if I ever told you that."

"Wait—you are?"

"Yes, Kosovo-Albanian, it's a whole thing. Anyway, I don't care that you're a wreck. I lied too in school."

I considered this. "What?"

"I was ashamed sometimes too. It's not the worst thing in the world." Eli fell silent, and in that silence was compassion. That intimate, terrifying openness I thought I would never feel again. At that moment a woman approached the water, pulling a small black dog on a purple leash. The dog was eyeing the cold, dark water. Studying the duck.

"You can jump in," she told the dog. "Jump into the water!" The beautiful animal wagged its tail, yelped at her feet, looked at the water. Then back at her, expectantly. I loved the dog. "He's three years old, and he's still too scared to jump in! Every day he is eyeing the water. He's even afraid to bark at the duck. It's just a duck," the woman told us, beaming, then walked away, laughing at her pet.

"That's me," I said to Eli. "The dog is me."

Eli just shook his head.

"I'm too timid to actually be myself, to live life. To jump in. The water is life, it's real life."

Eli handed me the thermos, laughing. "What do you think all this is? This is life too."

WE TOOK THE U-Bahn to his and Doreen's place, where we sat at the kitchen table he had brought over from his old apartment, that table I had sat at dozens of times, and Eli made us chamomile tea. When I saw him now I felt tenderness, like for a sibling, his old familiar face. I hadn't understood how rare it was. When he sipped his tea, a sensation wandered from my skull to my legs, his hands like small boats on the river of my body. All those parties we left to sit in silence by the canal in Münster, never touching, just watching the water. The pelmeni we made. His body lit by the anemic light of the fridge. He rolled his cigarette, then stared out the window before lighting it, hesitant again. When we were together, there was a return to childhood, something no one else understood. A country, a lost land from which his and my family fled, the villages and the houses that were left behind, the ancient scriptures of our other languages. When we were together, what was lost started glimmering again.

He opened his mouth to say something and then stopped himself.

"What?" I said. "Say it."

"It doesn't matter."

"No, come on. Say it." But then the doorbell rang.

"Oh, Doreen must have forgotten her keys," Eli said, and

walked to the buzzer and sat back down. And through the heavy white door came Doreen, carrying a net bag with mandarins. She smelled cold, like the wind, and her voice carried the wisps of the outside world, and her presence changed the texture of the air. It was alive again, when before it had been a painting, static, alone. I excused myself, and from the way Eli looked out the window, his reflection in the glass, his eyes suspended into nowhere, I knew I wouldn't see him again, not like this. But maybe it was enough: I had been seen, once, in this life. Someone across the room had said my name and pronounced it the way my mother pronounced it.

"Goodbye, Elias," I said.

# Thirty-six

IN APRIL, I emailed the admissions offices at all three universities from the prior year and asked if, by some stroke of luck, my earlier application could be considered again. For weeks I didn't hear anything. Then two of the schools—one on the outskirts, and the other one my top choice—said no. I walked by the canal at Maybachufer, smoking and drinking by myself. Looking out onto the water, I remembered one of my walks with Marlowe last spring, the pop song playing from a small boat. *Music rarely makes me happy. It makes me sad,* I had told him. *Especially happy music.* He'd looked at me with a wistful face, a face of both curiosity and pity, and said, *Music is the greatest force there is.* Now I was alone, walking past teenagers playing secret games with each other, uncomfortable in their bodies, women pushing strollers, mattresses on the street, a man sleeping in his car. I walked underneath balconies that had been abandoned, buildings defaced and graffitied, others rising, new glass and metal structures. Ten days later, on a Thursday evening, an email appeared from another

London address, an art college in the south of the city: If I paid the application fee again, they would reinstate my admission offer. I tried out the sentence in my mind: *I am moving to London.* It was a step out, closer toward the life I'd once imagined. I had saved enough money for a few months' rent in the dorms and completed the forms to take out loans for tuition. With Romy's help, I applied for scholarships in Germany, for student loans, for every grant I could find. I would need to get a job, probably several, to make it work. But I was already accustomed to the struggle. I paid the fee again and formally accepted their new offer. Then I handed in my notice at work, telling them that I would move in August. I was ready, I believed, to leave Berlin.

A FEW WEEKS later, I went to the grave site of the Qurbanis and put down a bouquet of violet hydrangeas. The brothers were buried in a large international cemetery I had never been to before. I couldn't find a grave vase, so I stuck them on top, aware that they would rot and wither within the next day. I hoped that someone would come and see them, to affirm my performance of grief. There was such quiet in the cemetery, and when I walked through the park, I saw the long and ornate gravestones, families from ages ago: Jewish and Turkish and Muslim names, German names, all next to one another. One day I would be buried in one of these cemeteries too, my body taken by maggots. I came to the grave not to absolve myself of survivor's guilt or because I missed them but because it was the appropriate thing to do. And because I knew I had to pay my respects before I went home, and I knew I had to go home eventually. For an hour I lay on the grass, watching the sky turn purple and blue, and when I got up, I shook the dirt from my coat and took the U7 and then the bus back home.


IN THE LIVING room, my father sat on the orange sofa, peeling mandarins. The cat slept next to him, on the arm of the couch. A wave of tenderness filled me, for the cat, my father, this scene. I photographed him, his body thin and blurry through the Olympus's viewfinder. Three shots, his gaze turned toward the coffee table, the mandarin a small planet in his hand. In the last photograph, he looks up at me. There is no smile: A severity emanates from him, a confidence in his eyes. In that picture, I see myself in my father's face, as if he had inherited my genes, not the other way around. The same prominent nose. The dimpled chin and cheeks, the almond-shaped eyes. I sat down next to him and tried to make small talk. He wouldn't apologize, that much I knew. And I didn't really expect him to. But warmth flooded his voice. He was relieved that his daughter had come back home.

"Are you going to stay?" he asked.

"I am actually moving to London, Papa," I explained, and he nodded. After the initial disappointment that I wasn't studying medicine or law or engineering, he relented and smiled.

"Wow. London. Your bilingual education will be good for that. Maybe you will move to America one day."

"Yes," I said, smiling, seeing the image of myself in that mythical city again, in the black coat walking across the New York street. "One day."

"You know, I knew you'd come back to us. Your grandmother said, 'She's lost, she will never come back again.' But I knew you would. You should stay longer."

"I don't think I can," I said. And he sighed and turned the TV down and stared into space for a few minutes, the way my grandfather used to do. "I'm just here to get my books. I miss my books."

"Did we ever tell you why we called you Nilab?" my father asked eventually.

I couldn't sense where he wanted to go with this question, and I yawned.

"We named you Nilab because the river in Kabul empties into the Indus—you know, the big river in India that has many different names. . . . Afghans call it Nilab. Your mother loved that river. You know she had to fake her profession, take a fake passport with her onto the plane? She pretended not to have a job. They didn't want to let the doctors go. So she got on that plane with me, and from that small plane window, she saw the river in the city . . . not knowing when she would see her mother again. And she didn't. She never saw her again. Her sisters, she didn't see them again. I mean, one came to the funeral, but—do you even know what that means? She thought of the river and she knew she would call her daughter that—wherever that river led, it would be the future."

"She never saw them again."

"Not alive. You are this name."

Impossible to speak, to say anything to him. At this point, everything inside me cinched up. Absurd, the image of her on that plane.

"I'm sorry."

"It's okay, Nilou. But you cannot—you cannot forget where you come from. It's not a death sentence."

"Why are you always so dramatic?"

"It's not dramatic. I just want you to remember."

Of course, I couldn't tell him that I hadn't forgotten where I was from. That everything in my life had occurred exactly in this way because I couldn't forget it. My Afghan blood, this district, this neighborhood, these prefab buildings in which we lived, the streets full of grayness, the icy black wind in the winters, the beetles lining our drawers in the summers, silverfish hurriedly crawling out of the drains, the bus stop where the skinheads hung out, the aisles of the discount supermarket: It was rioting inside me, and it made me who I was. It was all I could ever think about.


AFTER MY FATHER fell asleep, I walked into the quiet of my room, shadows playing on my window. I thought of the history of this building, all the other girls who had lived between these walls, whose dreams were billowing then falling in the clammy, strange hours of the night. The burned bakeries of the city. The walls scratched with soot, the hours we spent between the shadows of houses, in alleyways, groping one another in the dark, hiding from our parents. The ghosts of those who came before us. All our dead rumbling in the blood. My mother's hands, her curls lit by the library lamp. In our other countries, buildings fell, hollowed out with smoke. The years I spent cycling through these streets, my legs pushing the rusted chain of memory, saying, *This is earth*. The strain of rubber hot against concrete. Years of want and friction, pulling against everything that was possible, the first night with Marlowe, Meena's name at the festival. All the after-hours we spent searching for each other's eyes, the balconies on which Doreen and I had stood. The first morning of January, the city stretched out before us in silence. I walked toward the column of light that spilled on the floor in front of my bookshelf. I pulled out the books that made me, searched all night for a word that might reflect myself, my story, back to me. I ran my fingers across the pages, and nowhere was a name like mine: *Nilab*. *Nil*, like indigo, like Nile, and *ab*, like water. Water of the Nile. My name, a strange percussion on my tongue. Not so special after all. The *b* I had been ashamed of all my life. A secret consonant to lean on, the hardness of a letter. But this, I knew, was the music inside me all along— a song waiting to be named. To name again, with care and purpose: each word a stone I take from the hem of my dress and lay out by the sea. Nowhere to go but here, where the water begins. Once, I was a girl. I wanted to be free.

# Acknowledgments

Let me express gratitude to the following people and institutions:

To Bill Clegg, the genius, an angel of an agent, my first reader—this book would not exist without you. To David Ebershoff, the editor of my dreams, for your brilliant, intuitive mind and suggestions, and for understanding my vision. You two saw what this book could be and improved it countless times, and ultimately changed my life.

To Marion Duvert, for seeing me; to the teams at the Clegg Agency and Hogarth/Random House, for your support, for your patience, for making this book possible.

To the following institutions: the Wallace Stegner Fellowship at Stanford University; the Wisconsin Institute of Creative Writing; the NYU Creative Writing program; the English Literature PhD department at the University of Southern California; the Hawthornden Foundation and Casa Ecco and that pink villa in Griante with Morgan Parker and Megan Fernandes.

To my brilliant friends, whose words and encouragements kept my writing alive and aflame: Asiya Gaildon, Fatima Farheen Mirza, Maggie Millner, Mary Terrier, Kate Wisel, Margaret Ross, Natalie Dunn, Solmaz Sharif, Sally Wen Mao, Natasha Oladokun, Kabel Mishka Ligot, and Derrick Austin.

To Nora, Isabel, Ilona, Lisa, and all three Julias.

To the makers of the Fusion festival, to the workers and bouncers and DJs and dancers at Berghain and KaterHolzig, for allowing me to experience freedom and utopia and abyss. To the Haverkamp in Münster for my first parties, to everyone I knew those years: Thanks for welcoming me into your arms and apartments and raves, for giving me a home when I needed it.

To Noah, who made me believe in love again. Thank you for my new lease on life.

To my parents and sister, Sima, Farid, and Nadine, for the relentless, infinite support and love. I would be no one without you.

## About the Author

ARIA ABER was born and raised in Germany and now lives in the United States. Her debut poetry collection, *Hard Damage*, won the Prairie Schooner Book Prize and the Whiting Award. She is a former Wallace Stegner Fellow at Stanford and graduate student at USC, and her writing has appeared in *The New Yorker, The New Republic, The Yale Review, Granta*, and elsewhere. Raised speaking Farsi and German, she writes in her third language, English. She recently joined the faculty of the University of Vermont as an assistant professor of creative writing and divides her time between Vermont and Brooklyn.

## About the Type

This book was set in Fournier, a typeface named for Pierre-Simon Fournier (1712–68), the youngest son of a French printing family. He started out engraving woodblocks and large capitals, then moved on to fonts of type. In 1736 he began his own foundry and made several important contributions in the field of type design; he is said to have cut 147 alphabets of his own creation. Fournier is probably best remembered as the designer of St. Augustine Ordinaire, a face that served as the model for the Monotype Corporation's Fournier, which was released in 1925.